ENTER THE ENCHANTING W...

Praise for her previous novels:

"Bright, cheerful, and charming, hotly spiced with magic and intrigue." —Simon R. Green, bestselling author of *Robin Hood: Prince of Thieves*

"A fun mix of magic, culture-clash, and fast-paced adventure that pushes all the right buttons." —*Locus*

"Highly recommended. Playfulness and pathos blend to form an entertaining and thought-provoking story." —*Starlog*

"Entertaining . . . plenty of magic, demons, and other dangers." —*Science Fiction Chronicle*

"Rollicking good adventure." —*Science Fiction Review*

ANNE LOGSTON

has been steadily building a body of work that has earned a unique place in fantasy fiction. With the novel *SHADOW*, she created a fascinating medieval world filled with magic, humor, grit, and a feisty, unforgettable heroine—an elvan thief who returned in the novels *SHADOW HUNT* and *SHADOW DANCE*. The adventures of Shadow's niece, Jaellyn—born of human and elvan blood—are vividly portrayed in the thrilling novels *DAGGER'S EDGE* and *DAGGER'S POINT*. She is also the author of the powerful fantasy epics *Greendaughter, Wild Blood,* and *Guardian's Key*.

FIREWALK

Anne Logston

ACE BOOKS, NEW YORK

This book is an Ace original edition,
and has never been previously published.

FIREWALK

An Ace Book / published by arrangement with
the author

PRINTING HISTORY
Ace edition / March 1997

The Putnam Berkley World Wide Web site address is
http://www.berkley.com/berkley

ISBN: 0-441-00427-X

ACE®
Ace Books are published by The Berkley Publishing Group,
200 Madison Avenue, New York, New York 10016.
ACE and the "A" design are trademarks
belonging to Charter Communications, Inc.

PRINTED IN THE UNITED STATES OF AMERICA

10 9 8 7 6 5 4 3 2 1

To Mary, Mark and Michael,
who Aunted me

FIREWALK

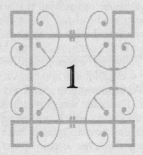

1

KAYLI INTONED THE EIGHTH-LEVEL MEDITATION chant as the assistant carefully untied the sash of Kayli's robe, slowly sliding the coarse fabric down over her shoulders. The first seven chants, progressively deepening her concentration, had taken all morning as she'd knelt on the stone floor of the forge while the younger novices had readied the fire—very quietly, so as not to disturb her. She'd prepared for this ritual for days—a sparse but carefully balanced diet, meticulous cleansing of her body, careful examinations by her teachers to be certain no cut or scratch, no cough or itch or aching muscle might distract her at the critical moment. One day, after Kayli's Initiation, a firewalk would be a simple matter, not requiring elaborate ritual and careful concentration. But in the meantime all her training culminated in this moment, the final test of her Dedication and her discipline, and despite the importance of this ritual, neither fear nor doubt troubled her mind. Her training had been exhaustive, her preparation thorough. The Order of Inner Flame rarely lost a novice in the first firewalk; danger usually came later, when ease and success made Initiates careless. Fatally careless.

As she finished the eighth-level chant, Kayli slid her *thari* from its sheath on the stone before her. The most important step in her preparations for this moment had been the creation of the ceremonial dagger to be consecrated in her first firewalk. Kayli had forged dozens of blades before she'd completed one that suited her, folding and hammering the metal the prescribed ninety-nine times, quenching the hot steel in her collected tears, in her mouth, in her blood. She had carved the hilt from black horn inlaid with the symbols of the Flame and her Order in red-gold firestone. As yet the blade had no edge; when her *thari* was properly consecrated in her first firewalk, High Priestess Brisi would judge and bless it, and upon Kayli's Initiation she would be allowed to sharpen it upon the temple's blessed whetstone. The blade was perfectly forged and without flaw in its preparation—as was Kayli herself.

She stood, and the novices glided back from the forge, kneeling well back from the firepit. Once Kayli began the ninth-level chant, they were utterly forbidden to move, lest some twitch or sound break her concentration.

Kayli stepped to the edge of the forge, her *thari* held point up between her hands. The heat embraced her, rippling over her skin like water. The flames had mostly subsided, leaving only the hot coals, a few blue and orange tongues occasionally reaching upward. It seemed that they reached for her, hungry for her flesh.

Kayli resolutely banished that thought. Her mentors believed her ready for this step; far more important, *she* believed she was ready. She'd proved it to herself a thousand times in simpler tests, holding the hot coals in her hands and mouth or laying them on her eyelids, holding her arms outstretched through the forge flames. This was her last test as a novice of the Order; if she succeeded, she would be judged ready for her Initiation, and Kayli knew to the depths of her heart that she would succeed.

Kayli stared at the flames, knowing them her friend, and stepped forward—

—only to be seized from behind by gentle hands and pulled back. Her concentration collapsed, and with it her training and control; she could not stifle a single sob of frustration—so much preparation, all destroyed! By the time she turned, however, she had calmed herself. Vayavara's own face was expressionless as always—*the Second Circle Priestess*, Kayli thought to herself, *had the most perfect control of her emotions that could ever be achieved*—but there was sympathy in the priestess's eyes.

"Your father has come," Vayavara told Kayli. "He would wait not a moment longer. I dared not risk that he might interrupt the ritual."

Now Kayli had mastered herself, suppressing the surge of irrational anger Vayavara's words had provoked. She'd been at the Order for most of her life, and her father had never set foot in the temple, although her home lay only a few hours' ride away. Of all times for High Lord Elaasar to visit the Order, why, why the day when she was to take her first firewalk?

She said none of this; she knew the cool Vayavara would have no sympathy for Kayli's bout of self-pity. Respect and duty to the family were as firm precepts in the Order as they were anywhere else in Bregondish society. If her father had come here, at this time or any other, he had good reason.

Silently Kayli retrieved her robe and the sheath for her *thari* and followed Vayavara from the forge.

The High Lord of Bregond seemed out of place in the comparative austerity of the Order's simple waiting room. He rose as Kayli entered, but his smile was distracted.

"Daughter," he said, taking her hands. His voice was heavy with relief. "I'm relieved to see you're well. They stalled me so long I'd begun to worry."

"I am well." Kayli accepted a tray holding a pot of *cai* from one of the novices and poured two cups, offering one to her father. "I was preparing for my first firewalk. Priestess Vayavara was reluctant to disturb the ritual, but she said your business was urgent."

"Indeed it is." Momentarily Elaasar looked even more uncomfortable, if that was possible. "You must ready yourself to leave the Order immediately, daughter."

A ripple troubled the surface of the *cai* in her cup, but Kayli remained impassive otherwise.

"Is there trouble at home?" she asked softly. "I heard nothing. Is Mother well? My sisters?"

"They're all well. Fidaya's preparing for her wedding with great joy." Elaasar cleared his throat. "As I hope you will."

Kayli was silent for a long moment. A thousand questions,

a hundred thousand protests wrenched her mind momentarily into confusion. She was only the fifth-oldest daughter, and one of only two who had shown the gift of magic. Any important marriage of alliance would have been made with one of her older sisters yet unpromised. Lesser alliance marriages could surely wait for one of her younger sisters to come of marriageable age; in the meantime surely a betrothal would suffice.

Kayli had been admitted as a novice to the Order of the Inner Flame in her fourth summer, when she'd been tested for the affinity to fire and shown great promise. She had trained at the Order for the past thirteen years, dividing her time between the discipline and ritual of the temple and the elaborate dance of etiquette at court as befitted the daughter of a High Lord. Only last year had Brisi, the High Priestess of the temple, agreed that the strength of Kayli's gift and her mastery of what she had been taught warranted sacrificing her rank at court in favor of Dedication to the Order. Her mother and father had agreed immediately, with the same pride Kayli had felt when her sister Kairi had been Dedicated to the Order of the Deep Waters four years earlier and later Initiated. At Kayli's Dedication, her father had formally relinquished her to the temple, releasing her from her obligations at court.

All her years of preparation, the encouragement of her teachers, her ambitions within the Order—*why* could he possibly ask her to sacrifice what had become her whole life, and what possible marriage could require it?

But in the end, family was family, and duty was duty, and the answers to those questions did not really matter. At last she set her cup down quietly.

"Is there no alternative?" she asked evenly.

"I have thought of none." Elaasar sipped his *cai,* shrugging. "When you asked to enter the Order, your mother and I had no reason to deny you. We had eight daughters, after all, and two of your older sisters were already betrothed to bring us good alliances. Jaenira's marriage to Lord Alkap has doubled our *ikada* wool trade. Fidaya's marriage to Lord Dannar will open new trade routes to the west. But there remains the north. And the east."

Sarkond and Agrond. Once the Three Kingdoms had been one great country instead of three small, until eastern mercantile families had sent mercenary armies to drive the proud Bregondish plainsmen out of what was now Agrond to the east, until Sarkondish raiders had swept down from the northern steppes to carve their own territory out of the rocky hills to the north. In the generations since, Bregond had fought fiercely to hold the arid plains that were its only remaining territory. Agrond had made no further military push—it became too expensive to hire mercenaries to meet Bregondish troops when the stories spread that the invaders had lost three soldiers to each Bregondish warrior who fell—but Sarkondish raiders still swept down from the north, attacking not in force but in stealth, avoiding Bregondish patrols like ghosts, ravaging villages and departing as silently as they'd come.

"High Lord Terendal has two sons," Kayli said slowly. "But the eldest is wed already, is he not?"

"Terralt is five years wed, with two sons and a daughter, and another child in the making," Elaasar said, nodding. "But it's Terendal's younger son, Randon, who has been named Heir."

Kayli sipped quietly at the *cai,* saying nothing. Whatever she'd heard about Agrond's politics had been long forgotten in the intensity of her studies. For the year since her Dedication, the outside world had ceased to exist for her.

"It's a complicated matter," Elaasar said slowly. "Terralt is an acknowledged bastard, but Terendal always favored him and so have most of the lords of Agrond. He's been the High Lord's right hand for ten years now. Everyone expected him to be named Heir. Randon's a rogue of sorts, charming enough, but found more often in taverns and brothels or in the saddle than in court. But a few months ago Terendal sent envoys to me, the first delegates to cross our borders in decades. He wanted peace and trade between Agrond and Bregond and offered military support against Sarkond—I've long believed that while our patrols watch the Sarkondish borders, the raiders pass through the northwestern portion of Agrond and attack from there—if I'd agree to a marriage between one of my daughters and Randon, whom he'd name as Heir. After long negotiations I agreed."

Kayli nodded. Her father would have been foolish to do otherwise. There was no greater alliance he could hope for, unless it was with Sarkond itself, and that would never be. Besides the much-needed military support, peace with Agrond would mean the opening of valued trade routes to the east, a great influx of new goods, plus access to the merchant caravans, which would in turn carry Bregond's goods to new markets. Why, the great trade river itself, the Dezarin, ran through the southeast part of Agrond not far from Tarkesh, the capital.

"While we were negotiating the terms of the marriage," Elaasar continued, "Terendal fell ill. He continued to fail despite the attentions of his mage, who I'm told is a fair healer. He signed and sealed the final agreement on his very deathbed, his councillors witnessing while he proclaimed Randon Heir. Now Agrond's in an uproar, factions splitting off. Randon's got some support, mostly among the guilds—as I said, he's a charmer—but Terralt's got a far larger following among the nobility. He's formally challenging Terendal's choice of Heir."

"I rejoice at the good fortune of our country in securing such an alliance," Kayli said quietly. "But still I do not understand—"

"Why I chose you?" Elaasar sighed. "Your mother and I felt you alone were suitable for such a marriage. Jaenira's wed and Fidaya promised. Laalen is frail and her lungs labor even in our good dry air. She'd sicken in the wetlands of Agrond, maybe die there. Danine, Melia, and Kirsa aren't of childbearing age yet, nor are they old and wise enough for such an important match."

"Surely Kairi is the best choice," Kayli murmured, "being water-Dedicated and three years older than myself."

"Kairi," Elaasar corrected, "would be wholly unsuitable, as you should know, daughter."

Kayli stared blankly for a moment until she realized what her father meant. Kairi was an Initiate; she'd already undergone the great and solemn ritual in which a chosen priest had Awakened her body and her gift. Doubtless there had been other lovers since that time, too; the currents of magic and desire ran closely together. More, Kairi would have been long taking the powerful temple potions which inhibited conception; she would not be able to bear the needed heir for some time, if ever. And with the throne of Agrond in dispute, there was little doubt that Randon's bride must be virgin in order to present Randon with an heir of unquestionable legitimacy.

Kayli closed her eyes. Legally, she had the right to refuse. Her father had formally relinquished her to the temple; he had no legal claim on her now. If she refused, the Order would stand publicly behind her decision. But by placing her own wishes above the welfare of her country, Kayli would betray the precepts at the very foundation of the Orders. Her father was right; there was no other choice. No use to protest. No use to bewail the death of her dreams.

"I will prepare to leave immediately," Kayli said quietly. "I have few belongings to gather. May I have a little time to take leave of my mentors?"

Elaasar laid his hand over his daughter's on the table, squeezing her fingers.

"Take what time you need," he said kindly. "I'll ride ahead with half the guards and begin the preparations at home. As long as you leave by midday, you should arrive home safely by dark, but wait no longer than that, or delay your departure until tomorrow. The decision to make peace with Agrond is not popular among all our people, and I'd see you safe within walls before dark. With luck, the escort from Agrond will arrive within a sevenday or so."

A sevenday. So little time to take leave of everything she had ever known. Or perhaps too much time—time enough for regrets.

Kayli stood, bowing formally to her father.

"I will be ready to leave by midday," she agreed. That was a lie in one sense at least, and they both knew it, but what else was there to say? "I look forward to seeing my family again, if only briefly." That, at least, was true.

Elaasar gave her a short bow in return, respecting her need for temple formality at this moment. He left quickly, kindly giving Kayli the empty waiting room and the time to compose herself before she must face others. When Kayli opened the door, however, she found Vayavara waiting for her.

"Novices are packing your belongings," the priestess said impassively. "Come. The High Priestess wishes to speak with you immediately."

Kayli stifled a sigh. She was still barefoot, dressed only in her plain robe, her skin sticky with sweat and grimed with smoke from the forge, and ashes in her hair. It was hardly respectful to appear before the High Priestess in such a manner. But the High Priestess must know already what had transpired.

Although High Priestess Brisi had personally taken Kayli's teaching in hand since her Dedication, Kayli had entered her private chambers only twice: once when she was accepted into the temple, and once when the High Priestess had summoned her to announce that she had been selected for Dedication to the Order. Those had been the greatest moments of her life.

Now she was returning to these rooms only to give up all she had gained.

Brisi was waiting, *cai* already poured. The High Priestess smiled when Kayli bowed, then motioned her to sit beside her. Kayli sat, involutary pride and regret warring in her mind. She'd always sat at Brisi's feet as a novice.

"I spoke with your father when he arrived," the High Priestess said without preamble. "It pains me to lose you as a novice of the Order. Your gift is strong, very strong, but more importantly, your determination and your hunger to learn are great. It is rare to find both strengths to such a degree in our novices. You would have risen far within the temple. I had it in my mind to train you as my successor."

A fierce pain stabbed at Kayli's heart. High Priestess Brisi was not given to praise of her novices, but the mere fact that she'd personally taken Kayli as a student had been a great honor. Kayli wanted to weep.

"Nonetheless the marriage that your father has arranged is crucial to Bregond," Brisi said calmly, "and service to our country is the only purpose of this Order and all within it. I have been asked to release you from your vows to the Order."

Kayli slid the temple ring from the middle finger of her left hand and held it out silently.

Brisi smiled and took Kayli's hand, folding her fingers back around the ring.

"I have refused," she said.

Kayli was shocked to inner stillness. Her duty—but if the temple would not release her—she must—but—

"Novice Kayli, discipline your thoughts," Brisi said sternly. "You discredit your teachings."

Kayli took a deep breath and cleared her mind.

"Forgive me, High Priestess," she murmured. A slow, cautious hope began to glow in her heart.

"You must leave us," Brisi said plainly, crushing the frail hope. "You must marry the Heir to Agrond as your father has said. But most of our priests and priestesses leave the temple in time to serve Bregond as mages, and the Order does not release them. Therefore, Novice Kayli, I do not release you. In serving Bregond, you remain in service to the Order. You will continue your studies on your own, and I do not doubt you will be a credit to us as you are to your family and your country."

Once again, Kayli was shocked to silence. Novices never left the temple for any appreciable length of time unless they renounced their vows or were, as Kayli had expected to be, released from those vows. Even Initiates remained at the temple until their training was complete and they ascended to the rank of priest or priestess. How could she continue on her own without a teacher? How could she continue at all, un-Awakened?

"Your eyes are scrolls written in a child's simple words," Brisi said gently. "Come with me." She rose and led Kayli to a nearby table, where a large chest lay open.

"Your novice journals have been wrapped for the journey," Brisi told her. "After your Initiation, as you learned the greater rituals, you would have copied them from your teacher's grimoire—mine—into a grimoire of your own, as I copied from my mentor before me. My grimoire is in this chest for you to copy as you learn. I trust you to gauge your own progress carefully and not too ambitiously. When you have completed your own training, return my grimoire to me. In the meantime I have the use of the temple originals."

Such a monumental gesture of trust awed Kayli.

"I pray I will do justice to this honor," Kayli said softly. "But my Awakening—"

Brisi nodded.

"I am loath to see you Initiated without passing your first firewalk," she said, "but have no doubt that you would have succeeded. Kayli, do you know why we allow a novice to select the priest or priestess for his or her Awakening, even a new Initiate?''

"No, High Priestess," Kayli said, confused. Vayavara had told her that the fire magic in her own heart would seek and find the proper priest, but it was rumored among the novices that that was only dogma, that it was the Flame Itself and not the priest, who was merely Its vessel, who Awakened the Initiate. Bowing her head, Kayli repeated what she'd been told.

"Both are right, and neither," Brisi said gently. "The truth is that it is the Flame within *you* that Awakens you. Close contact with the mage-gift of another Awakens your own, together with the kindling of your sexual energies, as a spark from a fire may light a new flame. This is why all Dedicates to the temple drink the morning tea that calms and suppresses those energies, that they may not be Awakened before they have learned the techniques to harness their magic. High Lady Ianora of Agrond was a mage, and it is likely that her son bears at least a spark of the mage-gift; and by rumor he is at least a *practiced* lover," Brisi added wryly. "It is likely that he can Awaken you."

Awakened by a stranger not of her choosing—somehow it seemed worse than marrying that same stranger and taking him to her bed. But even so, to continue her training!

"You know the required preparations for Initiation," Brisi continued. "I have packed the necessary herbs, potions, and ointments. Your father is sending with you your family's midwife, Endra, who trained in one of the healing Orders herself, and a Bregondish priest as well, that whatever outlandish wedding ritual Agrond requires, you may also be properly bloodbound. If you begin your purification when you leave for Agrond, you should be ready for Awakening on your wedding night. If your Awakening takes several days, be patient. As Agrond will require an heir promptly, I doubt," Brisi added wryly, "that your new husband will be less than attentive."

Kayli bowed her head.

"I will remember what you have told me, High Priestess."

"Of that I have no doubt." Brisi took two pouches from the chest. "This potion will increase fertility. Drink one sip morning and evening until you conceive, and mind you miss not a single dose, young one!''

"Yes, High Priestess," Kayli said obediently. She'd begin taking the potion that very night. The sooner she conceived, the fewer demands would be made on her. Perhaps if she conceived quickly, the lord would leave her to her studies until his heir was born. Jaenira had once confided to Kayli that her husband, Lord Alkap, hardly passed a word with her for weeks at a time.

"The potion I give you, as is my duty to our people," Brisi said quietly. "This I give as teacher to novice. It is a speaking crystal."

Kayli's fingers shook as she drew the small, irregular crystal from the pouch. Speaking crystals were rare, created only by the most powerful magic. More than the value of the gift, however, the gesture of faith in her ability warmed Kayli's heart. Speaking crystals could be used only by those whose gift had been Awakened.

"You will require guidance long before you master fire-scrying, so use the crystal when you need my advice," Brisi told her. "The ritual is detailed in my grimoire." Her face softened just a little. "Perhaps you will feel less alone in a strange place."

Kayli tucked both pouches back into the chest. At last she raised her eyes daringly.

"High Priestess," she began slowly, "how have you done so much in the short time since my father arrived? Was this somehow known to you before?"

" 'This'?" Brisi said gently. "The Flame has called you to a great destiny, young Kayli. Such a calling, in one form or another, was not unexpected. Do you think that because we live within walls that we close our eyes and ears as well? One does not learn, my student, by barring doors, but by opening them. Now, give me your *thari*."

Kayli obeyed. The High Priestess held the dagger up to the lamp, examining blade and hilt minutely. At last she nodded and stepped back to Kayli, holding the hilt of the *thari* in both hands, blade outward. Kayli clasped the blade of the dagger between her palms, her eyes joined with Brisi's. The blade grew warm, then hot between her palms, but she had held the unquenched steel in her hands when it glowed white-hot from the forge, and she did not wince now.

"I judge this blade well forged," the High Priestess intoned. "I gift this blade with the heart of fire and consecrate it to the Inner Flame. May it burn true and serve our people well and honorably. May the power of the Flame never fail to answer its call."

"I accept this *thari* in the service of the Temple of Inner Flame," Kayli responded. "May we burn as one in truth with the Flame. May I prove a worthy blade, well forged and strong in the service of the Flame and my people."

Brisi turned the dagger, handing it to Kayli hilt first.

"You will need an edge on that blade," the High Priestess said. She drew a small rectangle of stone from her pocket and handed it to Kayli. "Every mage who leaves this temple is given a whetstone cut from the blessed stone at the center of the temple. It is a bit premature to give you one, of course"— Brisi smiled—"but there you are. You will, of course, require a sharpened *thari* for your bloodbonding, as your Agrondish lordling will have none."

"Thank you, High Priestess," Kayli whispered, slipping the stone into her pocket. She'd make a special pouch for it and prepare a small vial of blessed oil this very night.

"Now go to your family, young one," Brisi said firmly, "and do not rage so against the path the Flame has burned for you. It is a great calling."

Kayli bowed.

"Thank you, High Priestess," she whispered.

Brisi smoothed one hand over Kayli's hair.

"Fare well, my student," she said. "Call me when you have mastered the speaking stone, and remember that the Order is not a set of walls you may enter or leave; the Order is a temple to the Flame within yourself. As long as you feed that flame and keep it sacred, you will never leave us, or we you." She touched Kayli's cheek. "This blade, too, is well forged."

"I will remember," Kayli said steadily. "Fare well, High Priestess."

When she walked from High Priestess Brisi's quarters, she did not look back.

* * *

"There. That's the last of it." Endra smoothed the wedding dress before she shut the lid of the chest and locked it securely. "It *is* a beautiful gown."

It was. Kayli had been surprised at the rich, wine-red fabric, so thick and soft, when the seamstresses had begun fitting the gown. She'd never seen anything like it. The seamstresses had told her that Lord Randon had sent it as part of his bride-gift not long after his father had died, along with his reassurances that he intended to honor his father's wishes in every way. To Kayli's surprise, one of the gifts was a handsome hunting hawk and ornately carved ebony saddle perch. Lord Randon could hardly have known that before her Dedication, riding and hunting had been her favorite pastimes.

Kayli was reassured by the hawk. So little was known about life in Agrond; Kayli had feared that it was one of the countries where women were kept like slaves and cosseted like sickly children.

More surprising still was the message which had arrived with the bride-gift. Lord Randon had not known which of Elaasar's daughters he was to marry, but he had addressed the message to his future bride and, judging by the atrocious Bregondish, clumsy script, and childish misspellings, penned it himself—apparently High Lord Terendal had not thought to pay merchants to teach his children the neighboring countries' languages, as Elaasar had, in hope of future negotiations.

With the greatest of respect and eagerness I await our meeting, he wrote. *In concern for your safety while traveling, I am dispatching three handpicked companies of my personal guard and my brother, Terralt, to escort you from your home. I pray that you will not be dismayed by the abruptness of this marriage nor by my brother's manner. I have never much prepared myself to be a husband or a High Lord, but please believe that I will do the best I can on both accounts. That you should not feel dishonored in any way, I have given up all intimate associations and promise that my future conduct will in no way cause you embarrassment. I beg that you forgive my plain speech, but I cannot count scribery among my skills . . .*

Kayli would have laughed at the clumsy missive were it not for the confusion and upheaval in her life of late. It sounded like something a small boy might write, not a message from such a courtly charmer as Randon was rumored to be. Still, it was kind of Lord Randon to write to her directly. The letter and the hawk warmed Kayli's heart; it told her that she was being seen as more than simply the means to an alliance.

It occurred to her that Lord Randon had been as little prepared for this marriage as she had herself. Likely he, too, had been certain Terralt would be named Heir. Likely he, too, had made plans of his own for his future. Like Kayli herself, he had no choice but to accept the path which had been laid for him and make the best of it. In that respect at least, they understood each other.

Kayli had insisted on choosing gifts for her husband-to-be herself as well. From the stable she had selected a string of the Bregondish horses so coveted by outland merchants, and she was carving a longbow for Lord Randon. Whether he would have any use for it she could not know—likely he used the Agrondish horizontally mounted bows that shot small bolts instead of arrows—but Bregondish longbows brought good prices in trade to the south, and the very act of the meticulous carving comforted Kayli.

Otherwise her time had been consumed by preparations for her departure, her parents' instructions in the proper conduct of a High Lady, and the endless fittings of new clothing, as Kayli had discarded most of her secular clothing at her Dedication. High Lady Nerina had fretted that Bregondish garb might be deemed unsuitable in Agrond, but nothing was known of what Agrondish women wore, and the seamstresses were hard-pressed enough to finish sufficient garments of familiar design in the short time before Kayli must leave.

Although Randon's message encouraged her to bring whatever servants she liked, Kayli had thought to take only Endra. She'd grown unaccustomed to servants at the temple, where novices, Dedicates, and Initiates alike shared in every chore, and in the short time she'd been home, the fussing of the maids already annoyed her. Endra, who had tended Kayli and her sisters since birth, pronounced herself quite capable of taking care of her lady with no help needed, thank you very much, and Kayli had relievedly agreed.

Her mother, however, had not.

"One maid?" High Lady Nerina had scoffed gently. "Kayli, Endra is a treasure, but she is no trained lady's maid, and as High Lady of Agrond, you'll require a proper retinue. Lord Randon would simply bring in maids for you, and who knows what sort of girls you'd get then? Household spies, more than likely. I'll put together a suitable retinue of sensible girls who can keep their heads in a new land. I'd have a groom ready, too, if I'd known you were taking the horses. I pray that your lord has a sensible groom who can keep his fingers from being bitten off until we can send someone."

High Lady Nerina glanced over at Kayli, who was staring blankly out the window.

"Have you met Lord Terralt?" High Lady Nerina asked.

Kayli shook her head absently. Terralt and his guards had arrived late last night in a great clamor of voices and hoof-beats, and Kayli had fled to her rooms, as if by locking out the envoys, she could lock out her fate.

"I wondered why Lord Randon sent his brother, when Terralt so opposes the match," High Lady Nerina mused. "Perhaps it's only intended to absent Terralt from the capital for a time. But perhaps your lord is deeper in thought than we realize. You should have met Terralt when he arrived. It was impolite to shut yourself away up here, and unwise, too, to miss a chance to meet your enemy on your own ground, when he's dirty and road-weary, too. Well, it's too late now. They're all waiting for you downstairs. You have just enough time for a last good-bye with Kairi before you go, if you hurry."

Kayli dropped the last of her jewelry in her satchel and closed it, suddenly terrified. She almost bolted down the hall to Kairi's room, pounding hard on the wood. Before Kairi could answer, she pulled the door open only to see Kairi herself standing there, one hand up as if to grasp the latch, an inquiring expression on her face.

As always, Kairi was so completely everything Kayli wished to be—utterly calm, her dark brown eyes serene, her black hair neatly coiled at the nape of her neck with not one straggling strand out of place, not one wrinkle in her simple gray temple robe. Those dark brown eyes which had always seen through Kayli so clearly saw through her now. Warm fingers closed over her own, Kairi drawing her gently into the room, folding strong arms around her sister while Kayli wept in terror on her shoulder. She clutched Kairi hard, remembering that day four years ago when Kairi had told her that she had been chosen to become a Dedicate of the Order of Deep Waters.

"You will soon be a Dedicate yourself," Kairi had said kindly. "And you and I will plan our visits home together, just as we have always done. You will hardly see less of me than you do now." And it had been true. But there was no such comfort to be had now.

Kairi let her weep for a moment, then gently pushed her away, clasping Kayli's forearms and shaking her gently.

"Kayli," Kairi said firmly. "You shame yourself and your teachings. You are the mistress of your emotions as you are of your magic, or you are the victim of them. Do you understand?"

Kayli gulped in a deep breath and nodded, impatiently dashing tears from her eyes. Tears were useless, and fear worse than useless. She took another deep breath and forced her hands to stop trembling.

"Why are you so frightened?" Kairi asked gently. "Are you afraid to leave your home? You left it for the temple. Do you fear your marriage, you who chose to walk in the heart of the fire?"

"I fear," Kayli said slowly, "that I am losing myself. I was born the fifth daughter of the High Lord and Lady of Bregond and I gave that up for life in the Order. I became a Dedicate of the Temple of Inner Flame. That was what I was, who I was. When that is gone, too, who am I?"

"You are the Dedicate, and the High Lord and Lady's fifth daughter," Kairi said gently, "and one other who is both, and neither. I wish you had been longer at the temple, Kayli. What you would have learned is that no matter what others teach you, all that you will ever learn was already inside you from the beginning. When you learn to see that, there is no more fear, for whatever is outside yourself is so small compared to what is already inside. Within yourself, all things are possible. Can you understand?"

Kayli sighed. What Kairi said sounded much like High Priestess Brisi's last words.

"No," she said. "I pray that one day I will. You mean that you are whole no matter where you are, whether you are far from your family or your temple?"

Kairi nodded.

"Yes, Kayli," she said gently. "All we need, we carry within us. Take that comfort with you. Nothing has ended, nothing is gone, any more than if you left behind your life as a novice to become an Initiate; only a new journey is begun."

Kayli understood not a word, but she gave Kairi one final embrace before she turned, rather stiffly, and forced herself back out through the door. She felt calm now, almost numb, as she walked slowly down the stairs, looping the satchel's strap over her shoulder. At the landing she paused, peering around the corner.

The main hall was thronged with strange-looking men—no women, Kayli noted uncomfortably. Perhaps in Agrond, women were not permitted to become warriors. By the Flame, they were so pale, these Agrondish men, their skins barely gilded by the sun. Some were as familiarly black-haired as any Bregond, but others had lighter brown or even yellowish hair. All had shorn their hair off at shoulder length like a child, and some lacked even a proper mustache, but most, as if to atone for the lack of a proper tail of hair on their heads, had let it grow on their chins. Their matching clothes were apparently uniforms, but the green-colored cloth seemed more suited to festivals than to hard riding on the plains. No Bregond would wear mere cloth leggings for riding through the tall plains grass, nor those silly low, soft boots that seemed mere slippers.

Elaasar stood in one corner, Brother Santee, the family priest, beside him, talking to what must be Terralt, a handsome, tall fellow wearing a surcoat. Suddenly the stranger glanced over at her as if feeling her gaze. Kayli took a deep breath and stepped out onto the landing.

The Agrondish guards fell silent, and Kayli saw the strange lord's eyebrows raise mockingly, fanning a small spark of anger in her heart. She knew she was not as beautiful as Fidaya, but by Bregondish standards she was lovely, even with her black braids coiled back and hidden under a riding scarf. Her skin, she knew, would be dark gold against the dust-pale cloth of her scarf, strange to their eyes, and her plain, sturdy buff riding jerkin and trousers, her high boots and sturdy leather jaffs covering her legs must look drab to the Agrondish lord.

Kayli felt her back stiffening, her shoulders drawing back. She was a noblewoman of Bregond and Dedicated of the Order of Inner Flame, beautiful enough, and gifted with magic and skilled in the thirty-nine arts of a Bregondish lady. She needed no finery or jewels to make her seem more than she was. If these outland louts wished to stare rudely, let them. Kayli descended the stairs slowly and glided through the crowd of guards as if they were grass to bend aside at her step, giving Terralt and Brother Santee a brief bow before turning to her father.

"I apologize for any delay my slowness may have caused," she said calmly.

"No matter." Elaasar smiled. "Brother Santee and I were explaining to Terralt the custom of bloodbonding. Terralt, allow me to make known to you my daughter Kayli. Kayli, I make known to you Terralt of Agrond."

Kayli turned and gave Terralt the full bow accorded to an equal; until she became High Lady of Agrond, Terralt's rank was the same as hers. He was even paler than most of the guards, his hair the color of dead grass, but his deep brown-green eyes, sparkling now with amusement, were mesmerizing.

"Terralt, I am honored to make your acquaintance, and I thank you for your trouble in making this journey personally to escort me to your brother," she said in Agrondish.

Terralt raised one eyebrow, and the faintest hint of an admiring grin twitched the corner of his mouth. To Kayli's amazement, he took her hand, kissing the back lightly.

"My lady Kayli," he said smoothly in heavily accented Bregondish, not relinquishing her hand, "if I had thought the journey an irksome chore, the moment of our meeting would have proven me wrong."

Heat rushed to Kayli's cheeks. He might have learned her language, but apparently he'd not troubled himself to learn Bregondish custom, or perhaps he had and simply chose to flout it. To address an unmarried woman as "his" lady was a claim to intimacy, and to take her hand in public, to speak to her in so familiar a manner, was unthinkable. It took every bit of Kayli's hard-earned self-discipline not to wrench her hand from his grasp.

"Terralt," she said serenely, "your respect for our language and customs is admirable. It is truly said that the measure of a man is his courtesy."

Terralt appeared pleased by the retort, rather than offended, and released her hand, bowing once again.

"Why, thank you, my lady," he said. "I believe that's the last of your boxes going out the door. I beg your pardon that we can offer you no carriage for your comfort, but as there are no proper roads between Agrond and Bregond, we were hard put to find wagons equal to the journey, much less a carriage. I have, however, had a wagon outfitted for our comfort as we travel."

Kayli chuckled, diplomatically ignoring "our comfort."

"I thank you for your concern, Terralt," she said. "But this is my first opportunity to ride in some time, and I will not be deprived of the chance to fly the hawk Lord Randon so kindly sent me."

Terralt looked momentarily annoyed, and Kayli wondered if he'd ridden in the wagon like an invalid all the way from Agrond. Surely he would not have expected to ride in a wagon with his brother's bride-to-be.

Kayli had turned to take her father's arm, but she found that Terralt had taken her hand again, tucking it firmly into the crook of his arm so that Kayli was forced to walk beside him. This was almost too much to bear, and she saw her father scowl, but Kayli understood Terralt's game now, and it was a game she'd played before.

From her first day at the temple so long ago, when the haughty High Lord's young daughter had been assigned to muck out the goat pen, to the day before her firewalk, when Vayavara had unexpectedly spat full in her face, her teaching had been interspersed with tests of her self-discipline. The Dedicates practiced amongst themselves as well, exchanging insults and pranks, endlessly worrying at each other's sore points, and anyone who became provoked was sentenced to the chores of the one who provoked her. Whatever insult Terralt could offer could not possibly match the combined efforts of all her teachers and fellow Dedicates. Kayli almost laughed.

"Whatever you find so amusing," Terralt said, glancing sideways at her, "I'm glad of it. I was half-afraid of nurse-maiding a frightened child torn weeping from the arms of her family, like my wife." He had lapsed back into Agrondish, which Kayli found a considerable relief after his terrible mangling of Bregondish.

"I am sure few are glad to leave family and home forever to wed a stranger," Kayli said levelly. "But I assure you that you need not act as my nursemaid. Doubtless I find the prospect of my marriage less dismaying than your wife did."

That was a telling blow, and Kayli was rewarded by silence from the lord at her side. The guards scattered to their mounts at a glance from Terralt. One of the grooms had already saddled Maja and led her from the stables, and held the restless mare now with some difficulty.

"That's your mount?" Terralt said amusedly. "A fiery beast." He glanced at her daringly. "Like her mistress, I suppose."

Ignoring the suggestive remark, Kayli freed her hand from his arm, and turning away from Terralt as if he no longer existed, she stepped over to where her family was waiting to say last good-byes.

Danine wept quietly as she buried her face in Kayli's vest. Melia and Kirsa were too young to understand what all the fuss was about, but they cried, too, because Danine was crying. Kairi's serenity was a welcome contrast, a warm strength against which Kayli could lean. Kairi bent close and kissed Kayli on the cheek.

"When you learn to use the speaking crystal," she murmured quietly, "I will be waiting for your call."

Laalen's eyes held a hint of guilt as she embraced her sister. Were it not for her sickliness, she knew, she herself would be making this journey and Kayli would be back at the Order. Fidaya's embrace was brief and absentminded. She was more concerned with her own wedding, eager for the present chaos to subside so preparations could resume.

And Jaenira, of course, was gone. Likely Kayli would never see her oldest sister again. If, indeed, she ever saw any of her family again.

Her mother's kiss was cool and formal and Kayli took no comfort from it. From Nerina's standpoint, Kayli was making an advantageous marriage into a wealthy country where she'd have comfort and power; what more could she want?

Elaasar's embrace was strong, but the warmth in his eyes was tinged with shame. He knew what he was doing—tearing Kayli's dreams away, bartering her to the ruler of a hostile country in exchange for peace. But he met her eyes squarely; he regretted none of it, and Kayli expected no less of him. She returned his embrace and turned away, saying nothing.

There was nothing more, after all, to be said.

Kayli saw that one of the guards had hastily saddled a horse for Terralt—one of the spare horses they'd brought, not one of Kayli's string. It might have been amusing to see if Terralt was capable of riding one of the spirited Bregondish mares. Kayli gave Maja's tack a brief inspection, breathed lightly into the mare's nostrils to calm her, and swung lightly into the saddle.

It was good to sit in a saddle again, to feel Maja's strength against her thighs. The ebony perch affixed to the already high pommel of the Bregondish saddle was inconvenient; any higher and she'd have difficulty mounting, and her shooting might be impaired as well. But there was nothing to be done for it right now. She accepted the hawk from its handler and transferred it to its perch.

By the time she had finished these preparations, Terralt had mounted his sleek brown gelding, far handsomer than the buff or pale gray thick-coated horses of Kayli's string. Kayli frowned at the gelding. Its sleek, short hair was no more a match for Bregond's razor-edged plains grasses than Agrondish low boots and soft trousers. But Terralt looked annoyed enough to be riding at all; he would not welcome any criticism.

Terralt waved his hand impatiently and the guards started forward, the wagons turning in a wide circle to follow. Kayli looked back one last time at her family standing quietly, as she had stood with them when Kairi rode off to her Order, grief tempered by their pride in their kinswoman. Brisi had been right. By marriage or by Dedication to the Order, Kayli's first duty was service to her country. Nothing had changed, after all, but the form of that service. She had passed every test the Order had presented; she would prove equal to this challenge, too.

Kayli raised one hand in a last salute, then turned and rode toward her future.

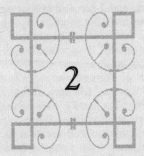

2

B Y THE END OF THE FIRST DAY'S RIDE, KAYLI'S sense of pride had changed, first to a sort of heady freedom—how wonderful it was to be riding again in the fresh sweet wind of the plains—and then to grim amusement as it became apparent just how unprepared Terralt and his men had been for their ride through Bregond. The wagon axles had been built high—probably to get the wagons through mud and swampy earth in the wetlands—and that height served them well in the tall grass, but thin cloth leggings and the horses' short coats were poor protection against the sharp-edged swordgrass and the toothed sawgrass that grew almost to the height of a man, or the barbed hookthorn thickets scattered thickly across the plains.

Perhaps Terralt had ridden in the wagon like a sick child on the journey to Bregond and had somehow ignored the cursing of his men as first their trousers, then their legs, were slashed and torn. Now, however, as his own curses joined the rest, he was obviously too proud to retreat to the wagon while Kayli rode.

"Pride and foolishness sleep in the same bed," Brisi had told her many times. "See that you do not sleep with them."

Kayli touched Maja's sides with her heels, urging the mare ahead to ride by Terralt's side.

"Endra and the other maids doubtless brought their jaffs," Kayli said, indicating the sturdy leather flaps she wore over the outside of her own trousers. "Riding in the wagon, they do not need them, and I have spares as well. There are not enough for all your men, but some can ride behind the wagons where the grass is trampled." She glanced at Terralt, saw his jaw clench. Pride again. "I suppose the grasses are very different in the wetlands."

"You speak as if Agrond were a swamp," Terralt said wryly. "It's not. But yes, it's very different. There are more roads, for one thing. The land's more settled."

"You mean permanent villages, farms to grow food." Kayli nodded. "The wetlands are well suited to such settlement. Our clans follow their herds from watering hole to watering hole, to new grazing. Our roads circle Bregond instead of crossing it. But a great river crosses Agrond, does it not?"

"The Dezarin, yes," Terralt said, nodding. "It links a dozen trade cities. Perhaps my brother will take you one day to see it." He glanced at her mockingly. "Or I will."

"Tell me about your brother," Kayli said, refusing to acknowledge the innuendo. "So few merchants trade with both Agrond and Bregond that my father had heard little of him."

"I'd have thought otherwise, judging from your gift." Terralt gestured at the string of horses tied behind the wagons. "Randon will be beside himself. I'm sure he'll insist on founding a whole new stable on them."

"Then he enjoys riding and hunting?" Kayli prompted. "I thought as much from the gift of the hawk."

"I can't think what he loves more, unless it's sport of a more amorous nature, if your ladyship knows what I mean," Terralt said smoothly. "But then, being a maiden, you probably don't."

"You speak as if you believe your brother frivolous," Kayli said calmly.

"Frivolous? No." Terralt shrugged. "But too full of foolish dreams. When he was younger he wanted to become a mage. Stevann, our palace mage, sadly encouraged him, but Father put a stop to it, said he'd not have a robed fop for a son, and he was right. Randon would never have made a mage in any wise. He shares Father's affliction."

"Affliction?" Kayli said slowly. "No mention was made of any—"

"Oh, it's no disease like whore's rot or shaking fits," Terralt said carelessly. "Father could barely read and write. He sees letters or words as if they were backward. I always had to read documents to him. Randon shares that affliction, or so Stevann says. Father spoiled him, released him from most studies, although the boy was bright enough. So he's done much as he liked since childhood, and that's been nothing of any worth. He's spent too much of his time mucking around among the peasants. None of the lords will take him seriously now."

"Perhaps he would fare better with the support of his own kin," Kayli said serenely.

"Support?" Terralt glanced at her again, then laughed bitterly. "Lady, I've spent years at my father's side, High Lord in all but name for the last months, while Randon played with his horses and his peasants and his women. Now he's been made Heir to ruin all I've worked for, and I'm set aside, my years of labor forgotten. You have no idea how it galls me." Kayli said nothing. She could sympathize with his frustration, but if she had whined so in the temple, she'd have been set to scrubbing out chamber pots.

Terralt swore and reached down to free the hookthorn branch snared in his boot, then swore again as the barbed thorns pierced his unprotected fingers instead. He straightened and shrugged apologetically at Kayli.

"Forgive the language, my lady."

"No apology is necessary, although my father would be scandalized," Kayli said, stifling a chuckle. "You further my knowledge of Agrondish. The merchants neglected to teach us such colorful phrases."

"I believe I heard your ladyship had been brought back from service at a temple or some such?" Terralt asked, sucking his bleeding fingers.

"The Order of Inner Flame," Kayli said, nodding. "I was a Dedicate at the temple."

"Bregond must be a sorry country when out of a High Lord's family of eight daughters, they have to drag priestesses from their temple to find a virgin," Terralt said sourly.

"I was not a priestess," Kayli said smoothly. "I was a Dedicate, as many others, there to study magic. When we have progressed sufficiently in our studies, most of the Initiates leave to become mages in the great houses or among the clans, wherever we are most needed. I might never have become a priestess within the temple." But Brisi had thought otherwise.

"Such a lovely, virtuous maiden, and a mage, too," Terralt said mockingly. "Randon will be beside himself at his good fortune. You, I fear, are getting somewhat less of a bargain."

Terralt glanced at the sinking sun and turned back to the rest of the guards, signaling a halt. The wagons formed a circle and stopped. Some of the guards continued outward to patrol the area and hunt; others dismounted to tend the horses and ready the camp. Kayli slid down from Maja's back and stifled a groan of pain. In the year since her Dedication she'd grown unaccustomed to long riding, and her legs and bottom ached wretchedly, but the Flame would burn her to ash before she'd give Terralt excuse to call her weak and whining.

Endra took Maja's rein, materializing by Kayli's side as if by magic.

"Some of the girls are raising your tent, lady," the midwife said cheerfully. "Take your ease and let us tend to this pretty girl and the rest of your string. It's a mercy to stretch our legs after sitting in that wagon all day."

"I thank you, Endra, but Maja and I are only just becoming friends again." Kayli laughed. "She's borne me patiently all day; now the least I can do is tend her myself." In truth it *was* pleasant to stretch her legs as she walked the mare, and the tasks of wiping dry the tack and brushing the horse were a sweet reminder of her chores at the temple. Working with her hands under the setting sun, in the sweet-smelling, clean breeze of the plains gave her a sense of place in the order of things, and with a lighter heart Kayli joined Endra at the fire the midwife had built in front of her tent.

The aroma of roasting meat drifted over from the main fire, and Kayli sighed. She'd begun her fast the night before, less than a sevenday after she'd just finished the modified fast for her first firewalk. Already her stomach was achingly empty after her day's ride. Endra had put a piece of the plains deer to boil over their fire with herbs; the pot liquor was all Kayli could eat until her Awakening—if, indeed, she reminded herself, her Awakening ever took place.

That thought alone was enough to kill her appetite, and Kayli, ignoring Endra and the maids, slid quietly into her hide tent. Kayli untied her jaffs and laid them aside, then unbuckled the straps tightening the tops of her high boots to hold in the bottoms of her trousers, and laid her boots and stockings aside as well, sighing with relief as she pulled off her scarf and shook her braids free. Now she could stop pretending to be Kayli the noble lady, and simply be Kayli the Dedicate again.

But was she? The temple lay far behind her and there was no promise now that an Awakening awaited her. Now the noble lady was as real, at least, as the Dedicate. Who was it standing here in her bare feet and riding clothes, freed of all masks? Was it either, or both, or some other Kayli who had not existed for the thirteen years since she'd first set foot in the Temple of Inner Flame?

"My lady?" Terralt called from just outside her tent flap. "I would speak with you. May I come in?"

Once more Kayli swallowed her irritation. Come in indeed, as if any honorable maiden of noble birth would entertain a man in her tent alone!

"You may *not*," she said sternly. "I will come out." She strode out just as she was, barefoot and with her thirty-nine thin black braids hanging over her shoulders and back.

Terralt raised one eyebrow and nodded with mocking admiration as his eyes swept insolently over Kayli. He held a platter containing a steaming leg of meat.

"Your pardon, my lady." He grinned. "I see that I've disturbed you. But the guards are complaining endlessly of their cut legs and I remembered my lady's kind offer earlier today. Also my guards' fire is no place for your gentle ladies, so I thought I'd bring some of the meat here."

"A kindly gesture, and one for which we are most grateful," Kayli said politely, averting her eyes from the food. One of the maids hurriedly took the platter and whisked it away. "Endra, Terralt's guards need jaffs for the remainder of our journey through Bregond. As you and the maids are riding in the wagons, I offered to share ours. Will you gather what we have and see if the ties can be lengthened?"

"Aye, lady," Endra said, nodding. "I'll make a salve, too, else swordgrass cuts will fester." She started to turn away, then hesitated, glancing at Terralt. "If there's nothing more, lady—"

"No, thank you, Endra," Kayli said, nodding reassuringly. To her discomfort, Terralt followed her to the fire; the maids hastily retired, laying out cushions for Kayli and Terralt to sit on. Anida alone remained, settling down a discreet distance away.

Terralt speared a piece of meat on his dagger, raising his black eyebrows again as Kayli filled a cup with broth and sat down on one of the cushions.

"Thin soup?" He chuckled. "Are you fasting, or merely afraid that I've poisoned your meat?"

"If I thought that, I would scarcely let my maids eat of it," Kayli said practically. "But I am indeed fasting, until my wedding day."

"But that's five days' ride at the best speed the wagons can make," Terralt said, surprised, for once without mockery. "You'll be gaunt as a stick. Whatever I think of my brother, I'd not have Randon say I've abused his bride."

"Then you can tell him you are no master of mine, and that I refused the food you offered," Kayli said serenely. "I am well accustomed to fasting on occasion, sometimes for longer than this. I will not starve in five days, and even if I did," she added mockingly, "would that not only further your own cause?"

"Indeed it wouldn't," Terralt snapped. "What support would any lord in Agrond give a man with no better honor than to starve a woman in his charge?"

Kayli was silent. She had made the remark to provoke a reaction, but it was not the one she had expected. Now she wondered again why Lord Randon had sent his brother on this journey. Was it to test Terralt's loyalty? Or was it, perhaps, a test of Kayli herself? Whose game was being played here?

"So you said you had studied magic," Terralt said presently. "What magic have you learned?"

Kayli heard the challenge in his voice and set down her cup. She closed her eyes and completed the brief meditation to clear her thoughts, then reached forward into the fire. She withdrew her hand, opening it to show Terralt the red coal on her palm, then tossed the lump back into the flames.

"Impressive," Terralt admitted. "But what purpose does it serve?"

"No purpose," Kayli said, shrugging. "It is but a test of sorts. Anyone could learn as much with the proper teaching, mage or not. But what must I prove?"

"I didn't ask for idle curiosity," Terralt said impatiently. "Soon we'll be crossing border lands where Sarkondish raiders often strike, both in Agrond and Bregond. If any spies noted the messengers passing back and forth, or saw me and my guards on our way to Bregond, raiding parties may be preparing an ambush. A mage could be useful in a fight."

"I am not a mage," Kayli admitted. "Not yet. I left the temple before I had progressed so far in my training. Endra knows a few simple healing magics, though. She trained as a midwife in one of the healing orders, although her gift of magic was not sufficient for her Dedication."

Terralt shrugged dismissively.

"Can you at least use that dagger at your hip?"

Kayli touched the sheath.

"This is a *thari,* a ceremonial dagger, not meant for battle," she said. "My training at the temple left no time for schooling in the warrior's art. But I am practiced with my bow, and my maids can fight with bow or sword if there is need."

The words came hard; how disgraceful, to hide behind the swords of her maids when the Order had stressed self-reliance above all else. That was, of course, why only the truly gifted were Dedicated to the temple; the pace of study left no time for learning the equally demanding art of swordplay, or of mastering any other trade by which they might support themselves. Only Kayli's aptitude for hunting and the Order's need for game to supplement their small herd had allowed Kayli to maintain her skill with horse and bow.

Terralt only shook his head, as if disappointed.

"Your father offered troops to escort us to the border." He sighed. "I should have accepted. But we would have been delayed while he mustered the men, supplies, and wagons, and a larger caravan would be all the more noticeable. I thought haste more important."

Kayli shrugged and sipped her broth.

"As a precaution, I will have the horses I brought saddled," she said. "All of my maids can ride, and if necessary we could abandon the wagons and make good speed."

"Abandon the—" Terralt choked, coughed, and spat out his mouthful of meat. "Abandon the wagons! Your entire dowry and eight wagons of gifts and trade goods, abandon them!"

Kayli suppressed a flare of irritation. Let Terralt die defending gifts and trade goods if he liked. She and her maids would show better sense.

Terralt was still shaking his head.

"Likely there's no real danger," he said, but Kayli thought he said it more to convince himself than her. "Even if Sarkondish patrols noticed the activity at the border, there's been no time for them to put together troops for a strike against so large a caravan. As long as we continue to make a good pace we should be safe enough."

Kayli frowned, but kept her thoughts to herself. If Sarkondish patrols had noted the messengers riding back and forth between Agrond and Bregond over the last months, they would have *plenty* of time to mass troops near the borders in case the messengers heralded a military alliance. The days since Terralt and his caravan had crossed the border would be an ample interval to ready those troops for an ambush. And if Sarkond could take the High Lord of Bregond's daughter captive—Kayli touched her *thari*. No. That, at least, they would never do.

A sudden thought chilled Kayli. Did Terralt covet the throne of Agrond desperately enough to strike a bargain with Sarkond, to coordinate an "ambush" which would eliminate the bride who would solidify Lord Randon's claim, while still leaving his own hands apparently clean?

Or, a more insidious thought, could Randon himself be trusted? Why *had* he sent Terralt on this mission? Might he not have dealt with Sarkond himself? An ambush might rid him of his rival for the throne and, at the same time, the bride that his father's bargain had bound him to. Freed of an alliance unpopular to the people of Agrond, he might gain additional support among the lords of his country, especially with the obstacle of his half brother removed.

Kayli must have shivered, for Terralt leaned toward her, draping his cloak around her shoulders.

"My lady, you seem to be growing chilled," he said with mock solicitousness. "Shall we move closer to the fire?"

"Thank you for your concern, but no," Kayli said. "I am only tired. I trust you will pardon me if I retire now."

"But of course." Terralt took her hand and kissed it, his eyes mockingly warm. "Dream sweetly, my lady."

This time Kayli was too preoccupied for annoyance; she bowed briefly in acknowledgment and hurried back into her tent. She drew her *thari* and contemplated the sparkling blade soberly. Since she'd left the Order she'd whetted it to an edge that could cut a breath in two. It was a sacred tool, consecrated to the Flame. Could she bring herself to use it to kill?

Endra poked her head in through the tent flap.

"Lady, Anida said the lord had gone," she said. "Is there anything you need of me?"

Kayli nodded.

"Endra, I want you and each of the maids to prepare packs of the most important of our belongings, together with bows and daggers and swords if they have them, and food and water. Keep those packs at hand every moment, day and night." She told Endra of her discussion with Terralt. "If there should be any danger, you and the maids must take horses and ride for home, or the border of Agrond, whichever is safer. They mustn't hesitate; I will be fleeing as quickly as they, and I will need them by my side if we find ourselves without troops to protect us."

"I'll see to each pack myself, lady," Endra promised. "But I say plainly, I'll not ride one step unless it's at your side, and I doubt the maids could say different without lying."

Kayli sighed, but she had expected no different, not really. When Endra had gone, Kayli packed her own satchel, adding as an afterthought her jewelry and her purse. If she found herself far from home, those valuables would purchase food and protection.

When she'd made her preparations, Kayli lay down on her pallet. Despite her anxiety, she found herself drowsy—no wonder, with all the excitement of the last few days! The pallet on the firm ground, too, was comfortingly like her pallet at the Order, to which she was far more accustomed than she'd been to the soft bed at home. Even her hunger was no barrier; the Flame knew she'd fasted often enough at the Order.

Kayli was asleep so quickly, she barely noticed Endra entering the tent and laying her own pallet protectively across the opening.

3

KAYLI SIGHED, RUBBING HER EYES. OTHER PARTS of her body ached more, but she would not rub those in front of Terralt.

For three days now Terralt had set as hard a pace as the draft horses pulling the wagons could endure. Kayli was tired from the continual riding, weak from hunger and the purgative potions, and weary of the need for constant vigilance against Sarkondish raiders, against treachery by Terralt. Now they were passing out of Bregondish lands into Agrond, and homesickness clutched at Kayli's heart.

The tall, wholesome gold plains grasses slowly gave way to shorter, greener growth, the shrubs and brambles to bushes and occasional trees. Streams crossed their path repeatedly, forcing detours to find fords for the wagons. No rain had fallen yet, but clouds had been gathering all afternoon, and Kayli was wretchedly certain that a good drenching could not be far away.

Terralt had made it his practice to send some of the guards ahead as scouts to be sure no Sarkondish troops were lying in ambush. Where there was heavier growth—thick clumps of bushes and trees lining the streams, for example—the entire caravan had to halt while scouts combed the brush before Terralt would move on. Kayli was too tired to fret at the delays.

"Had enough, my lady?" Terralt grinned, pulling his horse to a stop beside her. "I think we all have. It's a little early, but I'll call a halt."

Kayli could not manage to muster any embarrassment that Terralt had witnessed her weakness; she only slid from her horse and let Anida take Maja's reins. Tonight she must play the pampered lady; her weariness left her no choice.

When the maids had erected her tent, Kayli collapsed onto her pallet, sighing with relief. She had fasted many times before, sometimes for far longer, but never so soon after another fast, never with so many cleansing potions, and never when she had to exert herself so strenuously. Hunger made her weak; the potions made her dizzy and nauseous, and the exertion left her unbearably tired. She had begun to wonder whether she might not be wise to ride in the wagon after all. Terralt would undoubtedly gloat, but did it really matter?

Endra pushed open the tent flap and entered carrying two cups.

"Here's some hot broth and your potion, my lady," she said kindly. "Drink up and go on to sleep. If the lord comes by to annoy you again, I'll tell him you're not to be troubled."

Kayli drank, grimacing at the bitterness of the potion, but the rich broth was just what she craved.

"Thank you, Endra," she said. When Endra was gone, she paused only long enough to pull off her boots before she wearily pulled the covers over her and closed her eyes.

It seemed only a moment before she was shaken awake again, and she sleepily murmured, "Endra?", dismayed to think the whole night had already passed.

"No." The sound of Terralt's voice shocked Kayli abruptly awake, and she sat up, clutching her blanket tightly to her. The tent was still dark. "Put your boots on."

It was such an odd request that Kayli hesitated. Terralt cursed and picked up her boots, flinging them at her.

"Put them on or leave them," he said impatiently. "We're under attack. I've got to get you out of here."

"Attack?" Now Kayli moved quickly, pulling on the boots and lacing them haphazardly, snatching the pack and bow case laid ready beside her pallet. "Sarkondish raiders?" She could hear noise now, the sound of fighting, shouts and screams.

"Who else?" Terralt drew his dagger, slit open the back of the tent, and pulled Kayli through the opening. It was raining, a slow drizzle. "Hurry. Our horses are ready."

Kayli let him push her into the saddle before she protested. "My maids—Endra—"

"My guards will get them out." Terralt seized the reins of her horse and spurred his own; both horses bolted. Kayli couldn't be sure in which direction they were fleeing.

Terralt did not relinquish Maja's reins, so Kayli simply clung to her belongings and rode through the rain. Her cloak was still in the tent, and she was quickly soaked, but there was nothing to be done.

Maja fared better than her rider. The plains horses had been bred for speed and endurance, and could maintain a hard pace for a long time; in fact, Kayli was certain that Terralt's leggy but narrow-chested gelding would tire far sooner. She was right. It seemed only a moments before Terralt slowed and dropped back, speaking loudly over the now hard rain.

"Are you all right?"

"Yes." Kayli brushed sodden hair out of her face. "Are we safely away from the raiders, do you think?"

"I see none following." Terralt glanced behind him, but shrugged; with the heavy clouds and rain, there was no telling. "My guards were instructed in case of an attack to draw the raiders off from your tent, to give me enough time to get you away. What will your maids do?"

"Scatter and ride whichever way seems safest, back into Bregond or forward along our trail," Kayli told him. "I only hope none were so stubborn as to wait and look for me."

"They'll likely have ridden back into Bregond, then," Terralt told her. "I think the raiders came from the northeast. I rode somewhat south so we wouldn't cross their trail. How's your horse faring?"

"Maja is barely winded," Kayli told him. "Did we cross back into Bregond, or are we continuing into Agrond?"

"I think we can make Tarkesh, possibly near dawn, with hard riding," Terralt said. He squinted at Kayli through the darkness. "Are you fit for it?"

"Yes." In truth Kayli wondered. She was weak from her

fast, and so very tired. But there was no alternative. "I can ride as far and as fast as I must."

"Then take this." Terralt threw his own cloak around her shoulders. "Raise the hood and keep yourself well wrapped. I'll continue to lead your horse."

Kayli wanted to protest, but she kept her silence. Maja was unaccustomed to these wetlands and so was she. If she became separated from Terralt, she would soon be lost in this place.

The cloak was a kind thought, but she was already drenched and chilled through. She shook violently as she rode, occasionally wiping the rain out of her eyes. Obviously the wetlands were determined to earn their name immediately!

They had barely started again, however, when a dark form hurtled silently out of the storm, only the reflection of lightning from bright steel giving warning as the curved sword raised to strike. Terralt's sword flashed upward almost as quickly, but it was Kayli's quick reflexes that saved her life; instinctively she threw herself sideways out of the way, her knee hooking around the high pommel so that she rode almost on Maja's side, then pulled herself back upright almost immediately. Well-trained Maja recognized the maneuver and never faltered, only turning slightly to present a clear field for Kayli's return stroke, which, unarmed, Kayli could not accomplish.

Kayli scrabbled for her bow case, but by the time she drew her bow and strung it, Terralt had turned his gelding and run it solidly into the Sarkond's mount, leaping from his saddle to bear the raider down to the ground with him. The two fought with swords, but so closely that in the confusion of dark and rain Kayli did not dare fire a shot lest she hit Terralt. Even as she came to that conclusion, however, Terralt made a fatal strike and the raider collapsed to the ground, unmoving.

Terralt spared no time to enjoy his victory; he was back in the saddle before Kayli finished repacking her bow. Panting, he snatched up Maja's reins, and Kayli saw blood on his sleeve.

"Are you badly hurt?" she asked, reaching toward him. Terralt shook his head impatiently.

"Just a scratch," he said. "We'd better move on quickly. He couldn't have been alone."

Kayli had to admit the sense of his words, and she made no protest as Terralt once more spurred his gelding to a gallop. Thankfully no other Sarkondish raiders materialized out of the rain, although Kayli could not resist the impulse to glance behind her every few moments.

It unnerved her to ride on and on by night, with not so much as moonlight to guide their way. How could Terralt possibly know where they were going in the darkness and the rain? Surely the night must be nearly over, but the darkness continued; only Kayli's energy was fading. She was grateful for her Bregondish saddle; it had been made for just such long rides, even equipped with special straps to be buckled across the thighs so that the rider could sleep in the saddle if necessary. Now Kayli regretted that she had never developed such skill; a few moments of rest would have been a great blessing. As time passed, Kayli mustered every bit of her temple discipline to hold out just one moment longer, and then one more, and then one more . . . even her cold, wet skin and her helpless shaking were no longer enough to keep her alert. When she thought she could bear not a single moment more, Terralt pulled the horses to a halt under a cluster of trees. Kayli thought he had decided to camp after all, but they paused only long enough to let the horses regain their wind, then rode on. Kayli surreptitiously swallowed a stimulant potion from her pack, but the potion roused only a brief renewal of strength and warmth from a body already drained of its resources. She huddled in Terralt's cloak, clung to the saddle, and endured.

At last a dim gray light appeared behind the heavy clouds, but neither the rain nor Terralt's speed diminished. As the potion she'd drunk wore off, Kayli was forced to buckle the saddle straps across her thighs. After that there was nothing to do but hold the cloak closed, clutch the raised pommel of the saddle—and what, she wondered dully, had become of the lovely hawk Randon had given her?—as she drifted in and out of consciousness, dozing and then jerking upright again.

Maja halted so suddenly that Kayli was thrown forward and would have fallen were it not for the sturdy straps. Even so, she only half woke, blearily realizing that they were surrounded no longer by wetland countryside, but by stone walls, a courtyard of some sort, and that people flocked around them.

There was a confusing babble of voices, but Kayli was too weak to translate the rapid Agrondish and could only sit limply while hands fumbled to unbuckle the straps holding her in the saddle.

She drifted out of consciousness as she was lifted from the saddle but half woke again sometime later when she realized she had been lowered into a large hot bath. The warmth was so delicious that Kayli struggled to stay conscious, but in vain. She roused again only when someone held a cup to her lips; remembering only that she was fasting, she struggled weakly to push the cup away, spitting out the bitter liquid.

She recognized Terralt's voice, and this time she could follow the Agrondish.

"She said she was on some kind of fast. She was drinking potions out of that bag."

A strange voice. "She's half-starved and chilled through. I'm afraid she'll get the choking sickness if I can't get something into her. Still, I don't dare risk poisoning her by mixing potions. What *can* she have?"

"I don't know." Terralt's voice was heavy with irritation. "I was escorting her, not feeding her. Broth. Tea. That's all I saw her take."

Some immeasurable time later another cup was put to her lips, and Kayli smelled rich broth. She drank gratefully; when the cup was empty, she was given more, and she drank that, too. Voices faded in and out, but she paid them no heed. She was safe; that was all she needed to know. She let herself slide back down into sleep, and this time she was in no hurry to wake.

Some indefinable time later Kayli awoke slowly, luxuriously, relishing the soft warmth of the bed in which she lay, the familiar crackling of a fire somewhere nearby. She sighed with pleasure and opened her eyes. The first thing she saw was Endra's face, a deep cut down one cheek and a large purple bruise framing her left eye, but Endra nonetheless.

"Well, good morn to you, lady, or good afternoon, rather." Endra chuckled. "You've had everyone dithering, most of them afraid the fragile lady would drop dead of a simple chill. I knew you were a tougher weed than that, eh, lady?"

"Most assuredly." Her voice was rough and hoarse; Kayli

cleared her throat, and Endra poured her a cup of water from a pitcher on the bedside table. Kayli pushed the cup aside. "How long has it been since the attack?"

"Two days." Endra pushed the cup back into Kayli's hand and gazed at her sternly until Kayli drank. "I lit out close on your trail—what I could see of it in such a storm—with three of the guards. Once they knew you were headed for Tarkesh, we did the same, but you still bested us by half a day."

Kayli swallowed the last of the water and impatiently pushed herself up into a sitting position.

"What of the other maids?" she asked.

"The guards said three rode off toward Bregond," Endra said. "When the last of the raiders fled, Anida and Devra and Brother Santee rode ahead with some of the guards. They've arrived. There's no news of the three who rode west."

"But the other?" Kayli pressed.

"The guards say Dena was taken by the raiders," Endra said quietly. "I'm sorry, my lady."

Kayli knew what that meant. By now Dena would have ended her own life, as would any Bregondish citizen captured by enemies, so she could not be made to betray her country's secrets. In Dena's case, however, a quick death would have spared her other torments.

"I will send word to my father," Kayli said grimly. "Much Sarkondish blood will spill for this."

"Don't trouble yourself, my lady," Endra said gently. "There was nothing any of us could have done. Are you well enough to rise and dress? Lord Randon is eager to meet you."

Kayli nodded, for once glad that there were Anida and Devra and Endra to help her dress and arrange her hair. When she looked in the mirror, she was dismayed at her appearance—there were huge dark circles under her eyes, her lips were dry, and her cheeks were hollow; beneath her golden-brown skin, she was pale and wan. In the Order she had never worn the powders, creams, and rouges some of her sisters used to enhance their beauty, but now she was glad Endra had brought them. As she was, Lord Randon would likely think her diseased and half-dead.

When Kayli was as presentable as Endra and the maids could make her, she opened the door. To her surprise, there were two guards outside her door—was she a prisoner? She was somewhat reassured when both guards bowed deeply to her, and one of them said (in slow, careful Agrondish, as if to a child), "Good afternoon, Lady Kayli. We have been assigned to guard and protect you. May we be of any service?"

Did Lord Randon fear assassins in his very castle?

"I thank you," Kayli said in Agrondish, bowing in return. "I would be grateful if you would escort me to Lord Randon."

"He will be greatly pleased by your recovery," the first guard said, smiling. "Come, I'll take you to him now."

One of the guards remained outside the door to her room (so no assassin could enter? Kayli wondered), and the other led her through corridors and down a flight of stairs. He stopped at a set of large double doors and knocked, then opened the door.

"My lords, the lady Kayli of the High House of Bregond," the guard said, standing aside for Kayli to enter. Kayli took a deep breath and stepped forward.

The room was a study perhaps, for books lined shelves on the walls, and the two men in the room were sitting at a long table strewn with books and scrolls. Terralt was pointing to a passage in one of the books; the tall, slender man beside him with the amazing red-brown hair must be Lord Randon, her betrothed.

Both men rose and came forward.

"Well, here she is, brother," Terralt said, grinning. "Delivered safe and sound, just as I promised you."

Lord Randon gave his half brother a scowl before he turned to bow deeply to Kayli.

"I'm honored to meet you, lady," he said in halting Bregondish. "I'm Randon."

"Lord Randon," Kayli murmured, flushing at the awkward situation. Terralt's presence made it worse. Hesitantly she extended her hand; Lord Randon took it gingerly, as if he did not know what to do with it.

"I'm sorry," he said, pausing slightly before each word. "I've had little time to learn your customs or your language."

"Then we will speak in your language instead," Kayli said, hoping her Agrondish was less clumsy and accented than Randon's Bregondish. "As I am to live in your land, it is fitting that I learn your language and your ways, and not you mine.''

Terralt burst out laughing.

"What did I tell you, little brother?" he said. "Speaks it like one of us. And you should see her ride." He chuckled, making his comment an innuendo. "But doubtless you will."

"Terralt!" Lord Randon scowled. "Enough of that. Go and find the priests, please, and see if they're finished conferring. This is difficult enough for all of us."

Terralt gave an exaggerated sigh, bowed extravagantly to Kayli, and stepped out without another word. Randon turned back to Kayli with an apologetic grin. Kayli noted for the first time that Randon had the same magnetic, sparkling eyes as Terralt, but his were brilliantly green without any of the brown in Terralt's eyes. Kayli was relieved that Randon was more sun-browned than Terralt, probably because of his riding and hunting; it might be normal for Agronds to be so fair, but Kayli could not entirely shake off the impression that these pale folk looked sickly. At least he had a proper mustache, and no hair on his chin.

"Please pardon Terralt," Randon said quietly. "The weeks since my father declared me Heir have been difficult for him. He feels he's been cheated, and I'm inclined to agree. He served Father well for years, and I'm ill-prepared for rulership—and no one knows that better than Terralt." He stopped, sighing and shaking his head. "Forgive me. I'm babbling like a fool. Please, sit down." He saw Kayli's hesitation and added, "Unless you need to send for one of your maids?"

In Bregond it would have been highly improper for Kayli to be alone in a closed room with a man, but that seemed silly when she'd traveled so far to marry him. She smiled and sat down in one of the chairs near the fireplace. Randon hesitated, then sat down in a chair facing hers.

"My instincts nag me to offer you something to drink," Randon said ruefully. "But I'm told you're fasting, much to Stevann's—my healer, that is—disgust. May I ask how long you're expected to continue your fast?"

Kayli flushed. She had not expected to be asked about it.

"Until our wedding night," she told him.

Randon raised an eyebrow, a gesture strikingly similar to Terralt's.

"Do all Bregondish brides starve themselves, or only the noble ones?"

"Neither," Kayli said. She had to smile. "It is a—a custom of my Order."

"Then I trust you won't object to a hasty wedding." Randon cleared his throat. "In fact, it would be best if we were married immediately, if you don't mind. The wedding, my succession, are unpopular with most of the nobility of Agrond, and Terralt has made a formal complaint. We have permission from the advisory council to be married immediately."

Kayli was surprised.

"They have found me suitable without even meeting me?"

"You're High Lord Elaasar's daughter," Randon said wryly. "That makes you suitable." He hesitated, then said frankly, "Stevann examined you while you were unconscious—in the presence of your midwife, of course—and confirmed your virginity. I beg your pardon for that, but—"

"No. I would have expected as much under the circumstances, although in Bregond a midwife would have performed such a task." Kayli flushed with embarrassment, but perhaps it was best; at least she had been spared the indignity of such an examination by a stranger—and a man!—while she was conscious. And at least her fast would soon end. "When would you like to have the wedding?"

"Tonight, if you don't object." Randon shrugged. "I know it's short notice. But if you're well enough—"

"I am well," Kayli said quickly. "But are there no banns to be posted, none of the noble families to witness?"

Randon grimaced.

"We can't be crowned until you've demonstrated that you can bear my heir," he said. "Technically, until that time I could set you aside in favor of another woman, or pass the line of succession to Terralt. By our custom, we'd have a formal wedding when you became pregnant, inviting all the lords to witness both the wedding and the coronation. A private wedding now confirms the alliance between our countries and ensures the legitimacy of my heir." He shrugged, embarrassed. "I'm sorry to speak so plainly. As Terralt is ever reminding me, I've spent too much time among peasants."

"Thank you, but I prefer your honesty." Kayli took a moment to master herself. So, despite having left behind her life, her dreams, she could still be set aside, renounced as a failure if she failed to bear a child with expected promptness? But of course, if Randon's Heirship required a successor, he could not afford a wife who would endanger his claim.

"Very well. I can be prepared for our wedding tonight." Kayli spoke without emotion; in fact she felt empty and numb. "If it reassures you, my midwife Endra and my father's healers have examined me and assure me that there is no reason I should not bear strong and healthy children."

"Stevann said the same." Randon sighed ruefully. "You have no idea how I resent the businesslike nature of this whole arrangement. When Terralt was married to Ynea, at least they'd met a few times at feasts and festivals, and there was no real need for Terralt to hurry about fathering an heir. Not that he was slow about it anyway." He sighed again. "Forgive me, lady. I'm sure Terralt's told you what a dreadful husband I'll make. I can only promise my best effort, and my respect, which will be all the greater if you can bear with me through this nastiness."

He said this in such an earnest, almost pleading manner that under other circumstances Kayli might have laughed. How different he was from the cocky, self-assured Terralt! As it was, she couldn't quite keep a smile from her lips.

"I have no doubt that there will be harsher tests of our mettle than a hasty wedding," she said quietly. "Nonetheless I have spent my life learning to accept and meet challenges presented to me. When failure is unacceptable, the motivation to success is greatest." She chuckled to herself; she'd repeated that adage over and over as she prepared for her first firewalk.

Then she glanced at the door again.

"Where is Brother Santee?" she asked. "I thought you sent Terralt for him."

"Not for him," Randon said. "Your priest was injured in the raid. He'll recover, Stevann says, but he's not well enough to perform the ceremony."

Kayli's heart sank. She'd fully expected to be wed in a proper Bregondish bloodbonding; would her people even recognize some outlandish Agrondish rite? Would her children be considered illegitimate in Bregond?

"I sent our priest to see him," Randon continued. "He'll perform both rituals so that we can be wed by your customs as well as ours. Your Brother Santee insisted that he be carried down for the wedding so he could at least prompt the priest if he forgot anything. Is that acceptable?"

"More than acceptable," Kayli said, relieved. She hadn't realized how much she'd counted on a proper bloodbonding, her one assurance that this marriage was a true one, not merely political prostitution. "I thank you for your consideration."

"And I thank you for the horses," Randon said quickly. "They're wonderful beasts. If not for the circumstances of your arrival, I'd have been in the saddle long before now. I couldn't have asked for a nobler gift. Were they your choice?"

Kayli couldn't suppress a flush of pride at his words.

"They were the finest in my father's stables," she said. "I was so pleased by the beautiful hawk you sent." She sighed. "I fear he was lost in the raid and is likely seeking a mate of his own somewhere between our two countries."

"No matter," Randon said quickly. "I'll take you to the mews and you can choose another." He hesitated. "Lady Kayli, I want to make this as easy for you as I can. Of course I need an heir, but you may keep your own rooms and—"

Kayli chuckled a little bitterly, remembering her own hopes that her husband, like Jaenira's, might not trouble her overmuch. Somehow her attitude had changed in the intervening days. She had given up too much in the name of this alliance. If this marriage must be, she would not let Randon or anyone else make a mere travesty of it.

"In Bregond," she said gently, "it is the custom for husband and wife to share their quarters. I thank you for your kindness, but although I was no more prepared for this marriage than you, it is my intention to honor my vows in every way, and strive to be the best wife and High Lady that I can be."

Randon smiled in relief.

"Thank you, lady. I begin to believe the Bright Ones have blessed me with a most exceptional bride."

Kayli had to smile again. No, she was not so exceptional. But given time, hard work and Brisi's grimoires, she would be.

"I thank you," she said quietly. "Is there time to change my clothing before the ceremony? I had a gown made from the fabric you sent, and I would wear it for our wedding."

"Of course, there's time," Randon assured her. "I'll speak to the council and have everything prepared for the ceremony. It's midafternoon now; can you be ready at sunset?"

In Bregond, weddings would have been performed at dawn or moonrise; a sunset wedding would be considered inauspicious. Obviously the Agrondish thought differently.

"I will be ready at sunset," Kayli said. "Where will the ritual be held?"

"In the great hall," Randon told her. "Ordinarily it would be held on the front steps; it's our custom that the bride and groom step over the threshold of their home together. But that's best saved for the large ceremony later."

Or perhaps best avoided in case the bride must be set aside for another. Either Randon truly believed that Kayli would be the wife to bear his heirs, or he was trying to spare her feelings; either way, Kayli was warmed by the gesture.

"Is there any special preparation I should make for your ceremony?" Randon asked as Kayli rose to leave.

"In Bregond you would have a dagger specially made and consecrated, unless you belonged to an Order and had your own *thari*," Kayli said. "But we can share my *thari*. Such a minor infringement of custom is acceptable."

"Very well, then." Randon took her hand and bowed deeply over it. "Until sunset, lady."

"Until sunset," Kayli said, feeling awkward and stiff once more. She hurriedly retreated, glad to return to her room.

Endra was, to Kayli's surprise, not dismayed to learn how soon the wedding was to take place.

"Better sooner than later," she said practically. "Your gown's loose on you now. Much longer and you'd have fasted yourself down to a pile of rattling bones. Best have it done."

At the sudden realization that the waiting was over, that she was shortly going to marry a stranger and share her bed with him that very night, Kayli felt a flash of panic. Here truly was the end of all she'd known. She looked down; to her disgust, her hands were shaking.

"Oh, Endra, what will I do?" she said quietly, although she wanted to scream. "I am so frightened."

"Why, of course you're frightened, pet," Endra said soothingly, stroking Kayli's hair. "I've never met a new bride who wasn't, unless she'd had a few barn-loft tumbles beforehand. Your sister Jaenira cried and shook before her wedding until I potioned her to sleep. But I have an answer for new brides."

"Oh, please, no more potions," Kayli groaned as Endra set a cup in front of her.

"No potion, my lady, only a cup of broth with herbs to fortify you," Endra said sternly. "Though I've often thought it might be a mercy to give bride and groom both a good dose of Midnight Dew in these arranged matches. Seems like lords and ladies lay a heavy enough burden on their children's wedding nights. Of course they'd never agree to dosing their children with love potions; besides, I doubt if there's enough Midnight Dew in the Three Kingdoms. No, the answer is simpler—just remember that however terrified you are, Lord Randon is just as frightened."

"I fail to see how he could be afraid," Kayli said irritably. "Lord Randon has had more than a 'few barn-loft tumbles' if the rumors are true."

"Well, that's all to the good, too," Endra said placidly. "At least your husband knows the lay of the land, so to speak. A pity *you* couldn't have had your Awakening before now, but there it is, and you'd have been every bit as nervous for *that*. So if it helps, imagine you're going to your Awakening, but in a fancier gown. There you are." She tied off the last lacing.

Kayli surveyed herself critically in the mirror. The rich red gown with its gold trim, the gold collar and earrings with their deep red stones made her dusky skin seem golden itself. The gold combs glistened against the loops of her shining black hair, but the golden glints in her deep brown eyes were brighter still. She took a deep breath and swallowed her fear.

"Is it nearly sunset?" she asked.

"Soon." Endra glanced out the window. "I'll move your things to the lord's room as soon as you go down."

"Oh, no," Kayli said quickly, clutching the midwife's hand. "Please, you must come to the ceremony. Please."

Endra chuckled.

"Very well, then, lady, if you wish, though I don't know how these folk will take to a servant at a private wedding. Go on, then, and I'll give the girls their orders and come down."

Kayli wished desperately that the midwife would walk down with her, but she said nothing. She clutched her *thari* in its sheath and felt a small measure of comfort.

I judge this blade well forged.

A guard waited outside the door to escort her down. She hoped that after the wedding that could be changed; guards waiting at her door and dogging her every footstep would be intolerable, and the need for them spoke poorly of security.

Kayli had not seen Agrond's great hall before, and her first glimpse both impressed and disappointed her. The hall was far larger than that of her father's castle and much more richly ornamented with tapestries, rugs, and expensive metals, but the ceiling was far lower and the room less brightly lit, too, making it seem somehow smaller and meaner. Half a dozen men and women sat at the large table, presumably the High Lord's advisers.

Randon, Terralt, and a tiny, pale woman, heavily pregnant, waited by the door, standing near a litter holding Brother Santee. Beside the litter stood a strangely dressed priest, and a younger fair-haired man, more plainly robed, knelt at Brother Santee's side.

"My lady," Terralt said, bowing and taking Kayli's hand. "Such beauty dazzles me." He turned to the pregnant woman, pulling Kayli with him. "I make known to you my wife, Ynea."

Kayli's cheeks flamed with humiliation, but to pull her hand from Terralt's now would appear as if she had cause to feel guilty, so she simply turned to Ynea and extended her free hand.

"Lady Ynea," she said, giving the deep bow of respect she had not accorded Terralt. "I am honored to meet you."

"I—the honor is mine, Lady Kayli," Ynea said, stammering a little as if surprised. Despite the thinness and pallor that spoke of ill health, the lady was astonishingly beautiful, with large dark eyes and the delicate, fine bones that made Kayli feel gangling and coarse-featured.

Randon took Kayli's hand from Terralt, to Kayli's relief.

"Lady Ynea is of a scholarly nature, like yourself," Randon said. "The two of you might have much to discuss."

"Yes, I—" Ynea glanced at Terralt, flushed, and lowered her eyes. "I'd welcome the companionship."

Terralt turned away from his wife, as if dismissing her, took Kayli's arm again, and turned her bodily toward the robed man near Brother Santee.

"This is Stevann, our healer," Terralt said. "He's been tending your priest—and you, of course, while you were ill."

This time Kayli did pull her arm from Terralt's, occasioning a grin from the lord. Kayli ignored it and bowed to the healer.

"I am honored to meet you, Br—Lord Stevann," Kayli said. "I thank you for your care."

"You're most welcome, lady," Stevann said, his smile lighting pleasant light brown eyes. "But I'm afraid I'm entitled to neither your bow nor the title 'lord.' I'm of frightfully common birth."

For a moment Kayli was silent with confusion. She'd addressed Stevann as "lord" only because she knew that outside Bregond, mages were not trained in holy orders. But surely the mere achievement of sufficient magical skill to serve a High Lord demanded respect even in Agrond. High Priestess Brisi herself had been the daughter of simple herdsfolk.

"Forgive me," Kayli said at last. "In Bregond we honor mages regardless of their birth." She bowed again, this time the half bow of an equal. "May I then address you as Brother Stevann, as I would a Bregondish mage who has left his temple?"

Stevann smiled again.

"I'd find it flattering," he said. "Thank you, lady. Are you well today?"

"Quite," Kayli said quickly. "But Brother Santee, how does he fare?"

"He took an arrow in his back," Stevann said, shaking his head. "He should be resting, but he said he'd sooner die than see this wedding performed improperly. Lords, lady, I'd thank you to hasten the ritual so he can go back to his room."

"Of course," Randon said quickly. "If Calder's ready."

The strange priest looked up from a scroll he was reading and grimaced.

"I think so, my lord," he said. "I've studied the ceremony as best I could. Please forgive me, Lady Kayli, if Brother Santee must prompt me. If you'll come to the hearth?"

Kayli followed Randon to the hearth, surprised that he did not present her to his advisers at the table. They watched her, she thought, rather dubiously; had Terralt, or her own actions, turned them against her? But there was no time to fret now.

Guards lifted Brother Santee's litter and carried it forward so that the priest was beside and slightly behind Kayli. Of course; he must take Brisi's place and give the temple's permission for her to wed.

Lord Calder performed the Agrondish ceremony first; to Kayli's surprise, he spoke not in Agrondish, but some other language of which she understood not a single word. There was a long listing of titles and lands, she guessed that much, but she could only repeat what the priest bade her say, disturbed by the idea that she did not even know what vows she made. But she couldn't refuse, so did the meaning of the vows truly matter?

Kayli was surprised to feel Randon's hand trembling in hers; glancing sideways, she saw that his lips were white and tight.

Why, Endra was right, Kayli thought suddenly. *He is as frightened as I.* She wanted to squeeze his hand reassuringly, but did not; if he shared Tarralt's pride, her acknowledgment of his fear might humiliate him.

The Agrondish ceremony, unlike the Bregondish one, involved an exchange of tokens; after their vows, Randon slipped a bracelet of gold and silver twined together over her wrist and handed her another thicker bracelet, which she then slid over his hand. Likely the twined silver and gold symbolized the joining of man and woman. Was she silver or gold?

At last the long, strange ceremony was over, and Lord Calder closed his heavy book and took out the scroll which seemed to contain the Bregondish ritual.

"This business of the knife—" Lord Calder said hesitantly. "Lady Kayli, you have it?"

Kayli drew her *thari* in its sheath through the slit in her skirt and handed it to the priest, hilt first.

"The blade has been cleaned and consecrated by fire," she

said, "and blessed by the High Priestess of the Order of Inner Flame. As Randon has no *thari,* mine alone will suffice."

"Very well," Lord Calder said. "Then I'll begin."

Kayli gently pulled at Randon's hand.

"You must face me, not the priest," she told him. "We speak our vows to each other."

"I hope I remember what to say," Randon murmured. "Terralt read the words to me at least a dozen times, but—well, I'll do my best."

Kayli had seen many weddings in her years at the temple, as a temple wedding was thought to bring good fortune. The familiar phrases were comforting, although Kayli thought privately that Brother Santee's knowledge of Agrondish was somewhat lacking when he had translated the ceremony for Lord Calder.

At last, Lord Calder said, "By the authority left by High Lord Terendal, I give you, Randon, to Kayli as High Lord to High Lady, as husband to wife, as lover to lover, as man to woman, to be joined before Earth, Wind, Water, and Fire and before the witnesses gathered here. Is such a joining your intention?"

Randon met Kayli's eyes squarely.

"It is my will and the desire of my heart."

Brother Santee spoke weakly from his litter.

"On behalf of High Priestess Brisi of the Temple of Inner Flame, I give Kayli, Dedicate of the Order, permission to wed."

"By the authority of your Order," Lord Calder said, "I give you, Kayli, to Randon as High Lady to High Lord, as wife to husband, as lover to lover, as woman to man, to be joined before Earth, Wind, Water, and Fire and before the witnesses gathered here. Is such a joining your intention?"

Kayli took a deep breath.

"It is my will and the desire of my heart," she said. *Not for love, but for my country, my people, it is my will.*

"Then I bind you by blood and blade." Lord Calder drew the *thari* from its sheath and handed it to Kayli.

Kayli held up her left hand and placed the sharp edge of the *thari* against her palm.

"By my vows and by my blade, I am of one blood with

you," she said. "With this vow you are my family, my home, my lands, my country, my temple." She thought of Kairi and her voice shook slightly. She pulled the blade downward, making a shallow cut in her palm so that the blood welled forth.

Randon bit his lip and took the *thari,* holding it against his palm as Kayli had done.

"By my vows and by my blade, I am of one blood with you," he said, his voice stumbling a little. "With this vow you are my family, my home, my lands, and my country." He did not say "my temple," of course, as he had no Order. He cut into his palm, and Kayli winced as she saw how deeply he'd cut.

Kayli placed her cut hand palm to palm with Randon's; Lord Calder tied a cord around their joined hands.

"Before Earth, Wind, Water, and Flame, and before the witnesses gathered here, I say that Kayli and Randon have joined as one in blood," he said. "With the blade on which their blood joins, I sever all other ties that bind them, leaving only the bond of their blood and their vows." He cut the cord binding their hands together. "Kayli and Randon, as High Lord to High Lady, as husband to wife, as lover to lover, as man to woman, now and for all time you are one."

Lord Calder paused.

"What do I do now?" he asked hesitantly.

Kayli exhaled slowly. *Done. There is no turning back.*

"Now we let Brother Stevann bind Randon's hand before he bleeds to death," she said quietly. "I am sorry, my lord, that I failed to warn you of the sharpness of my *thari.*" She took her kerchief from her pocket and wiped her own hand, then Randon's; by custom they would keep the kerchief, stained with their mingled blood, as long as both lived. She used the same kerchief to wipe clean her *thari* before she sheathed it.

"It's all right," Randon said stoutly as Stevann bandaged his hand. "I'll survive." He turned to Kayli.

"It's our tradition to celebrate with a wedding feast," he said. "Are you permitted to eat now?"

Kayli flushed; how could she explain the details of Awakening before strangers—and especially before Terralt?

"With respect, lord, our custom is to have the feast three

days later.'' Endra's voice startled Kayli; she'd never noticed when the midwife had joined them. Nonetheless, she was grateful for Endra's timely interruption, although the midwife was unabashedly lying; there was no such custom in Bregond.

''It's tradition to let the new marrieds have three days alone to—to become accustomed to each other's society,'' Endra continued blithely, giving Kayli a sidewise glance. ''It's meant for matches like this where husband and wife have had no chance to know each other before the wedding.''

''A sensible custom,'' Randon agreed, although from the way his eyes twinkled, Kayli wondered if he'd guessed Endra's ruse. ''I'll honor it gladly; for three days we're not to be disturbed. Nevertheless, there's one local custom I'll not forgo.'' He leaned forward slowly, giving Kayli time to signal her displeasure if she chose, and pressed his lips softly to hers.

His kiss was gentle, almost chaste, but Kayli was acutely embarrassed to be kissed in the sight of all these others, and she was hard put to keep from pulling away. When Randon straightened again, Kayli forced a small smile, fancying that she saw disappointment in his eyes. Perhaps Agrondish women gave no thought to venting their passions in public.

''My turn now,'' Terralt said, but before Kayli could even draw back, Randon raised a hand, halting him.

''Not every country lets other men kiss the bride,'' Randon said firmly. ''A little respect for the lady, please.''

''Yes, I'll take Lady Kayli upstairs now,'' Endra agreed.

''That's a good idea.'' Randon relinquished Kayli's hand as if reluctantly. ''There are a few documents I must sign. I'll be up shortly.''

Kayli was utterly grateful to escape; between her fast, her illness, and the tension of her wedding, her head was spinning. Endra took her arm as the midwife led her back up the stairs, this time to another set of rooms. Despite her unsettled state, Kayli was impressed by Randon's chambers; besides the bedroom, he had a dressing room, a sitting room, and a small room in which he had placed his weapons and armor. Only the sitting-room door opened to the corridor, so the bedroom was quiet and private. A balcony on the south wall looked out over the huge city of Tarkesh. Beyond the wall of Tarkesh,

Kayli could see the lush green fields for which Agrond was famous.

A small fire had been laid in the bedroom fireplace, more for light than to warm the room. Randon's bed was wide and thick, the covers turned down invitingly, and Kayli wondered how many women he had brought there.

"The girls were quick," Endra said approvingly. "They've put all your things away. Come, lady, here's a robe; let's get you out of that gown before your husband comes back and makes a botch of doing it himself."

Kayli had to chuckle at that, but in truth she'd have liked to keep the armor of her gown a little longer. Nevertheless she let Endra help her out of it and put it away, then unpin and brush her hair.

"I'll be going now," Endra said at last. "Unless you'd like a last cup of tea or broth?"

"Oh, Endra, no, my stomach is sloshing already," Kayli said wryly. "Any more liquid and I will surely be sick."

"All right, then." Endra smoothed a rough hand down Kayli's hair and smiled encouragingly. "I wish you a joyous Awakening, lady."

"Thank you." Kayli tried to regain her lost calm as Endra left, but her heart was pounding—and why not? Here she was alone in the bedroom of a man she'd barely met. Kayli rose from her seat and paced restlessly. At last she pulled some of the furs strewn over the floor to the hearth and sat down, comforted by the familiar heat and light of the flames in the fireplace.

She held her hands as close to the dancing flames as she could stand, but try as she might, she could not muster the concentration to thrust her hand into the fire or touch the burning logs. Ah, but when she was Awakened, all the powers of the Flame would be hers. She'd be able to summon fire, to control it, to—

When she was Awakened? Kayli shuddered. There was no certainty that she would, in fact, come to the fullness of her power at all. The fasting and the potions should have cleansed her body of the last effects of the morning tea she'd drunk ever since she'd entered the Order, the tea which kept her sexual and magical energies safely subdued, but Kayli felt no desire for the coupling to come, only anxiety.

So much rested on a man she had only just met, of whom she knew so little. At the Order there would have been no doubt; any priest she chose would have been trained and practiced in Awakening Dedicates. And even if Kayli was not Awakened the first time, she could try again.

But now Kayli had to trust her Awakening to a stranger who had no notion of the significance of their coupling, only of the importance of getting his new wife with child. And if he failed to Awaken her, would she ever be able to try again?

Kayli heard a muffled knock at the hall door—muffled because the chamber door was still closed. Kayli opened the chamber door a small crack and peered out; it wouldn't do for someone to come in and see her in her robe.

"Yes?"

"It's me." Randon said hesitantly. "May I come in?"

Kayli gaped. What sort of land was it where a lord must ask permission to enter his own chambers? But of course, she realized, he was only trying to be considerate.

"Of course, my lord," she said, her mouth suddenly dry.

Randon stepped quietly into the sitting room—he was carrying a covered tray—and closed the door behind him. He gazed gravely at Kayli's face, peeping from the crack of the bedroom door, and at last said gently, "Am I to stay here, or would you like to open that door, too?"

Kayli felt the blood rush to her cheeks, and she hurriedly stepped back, opening the door.

"Forgive me, my lord," she murmured, hating the quaver in her voice. Why, hardly two weeks ago she'd deemed herself ready for her first firewalk, ready to entrust her life to the forge fire. What had she to fear from this man, compared with that?

Randon laid the tray on the bedside table.

"Forgive me," he said, "but I wish you'd use my name and stop my-lording me." He grinned a little sheepishly. "You're not one of the servants, you know."

"I beg your pardon, my—Randon," Kayli said embarrassedly. By the Flame, how much more of a puling idiot could she make herself seem? "In Bregond, it would—" She stopped. What did Bregondish custom matter? She lived in

Agrond now. She would likely never see Bregond again.

Randon stepped to Kayli's side and took her hands, drawing her into the half circle of firelight.

"Try again," he said, still smiling.

"Randon," Kayli said, forcing a small smile. In the firelight, his green eyes seemed touched with gold.

"I like the way you say my name," Randon said softly. "Kayli. My bride." He lifted one hand and ran his fingertips gently over her cheek. "My very lovely bride. But I suppose many men have told you how beautiful you are."

Only at court, and never unless they thought that saying such a thing would gain them something. And then, of course, Terralt, but Kayli would say nothing of that, either.

"Thank you," she said simply.

Her brief response seemed to perplex Randon, and he frowned slightly, turning to the fire, perhaps to cover his confusion.

"I brought up a late supper," he said. "I thought you'd like something to eat, after fasting so long."

"I—not now, thank you," Kayli said politely. Truth to tell, this moment was the first since she'd left Bregond when she felt no hunger at all.

"You know, Kayli, however anxious my father's ministers are for me to father an heir," Randon said awkwardly, "I'm not so impatient to bed you that we can't spare a few days to let you settle in here, if that makes you feel less anxious. Pardon me for speaking so plainly, but you seem so quiet, so frightened."

Kayli gaped openly at his words, the concerned expression in his eyes. Suddenly the whole situation seemed utterly ridiculous—here she was, standing on the hearth in her nightrail with a man she didn't even know, half-starved and faint with fasting, terrified that he couldn't succeed in Awakening her, Randon fretting that she was afraid of her first coupling, and all the while his brother and his ministers likely standing in the hall with their ears pressed to the door, laying wagers on whether or not the Heir to Agrond would succeed in putting his wife's belly up! Kayli chuckled, then laughed helplessly, tears streaming down her cheeks.

Randon raised his eyebrows, then chuckled, too.

"I beg your pardon," he said gravely. "I'm glad you find my selflessness so amusing."

That made it all the funnier, and sent Kayli into a new fit of laughter; it was some minutes before she was able to speak.

"Please forgive me," Kayli gasped. "I only thought—so many people concerned with the outcome of our coupling, while we stand here not knowing what to say to each other—"

"—while my advisers pray to the gods you'll conceive, and Terralt prays that you won't," Randon finished, chuckling. "Gods, it *is* ludicrous, isn't it? You ought to stand by the window and scream your head off; then the guards standing listening underneath will think I'm doing my job. And then when they're all gathered out there to listen, we'll empty the chamber pot onto their heads."

That set Kayli off again, and this time Randon joined her, the two of them laughing until at last their chuckles died away from lack of breath.

"Well, let them all mutter and wonder," Randon said at last, gazing into Kayli's eyes. "I'll leave the rest of the world outside the door if you will."

Kayli sighed, her amusement gone as abruptly as it had come. For a moment she desperately wanted to tell Randon everything, her fears, the importance of her Awakening—

Enough, she thought suddenly. *Enough. I can bear to fast for one more day. Tomorrow is soon enough for my Awakening. I deserve*—we *deserve*—one night all our own.

"I beg your pardon, my lord—Randon," Kayli corrected hurriedly, smiling. "And I thank you for your consideration. But the truth is that I must fast until we have consummated our marriage, so your forbearance is unnecessary—unless it is your will that I starve to death, that is."

Randon chuckled, but shook his head.

"How unkind of your Order," he said wryly.

"It has nothing to do with kindness," Kayli said defensively. "The fasting and potions are an important preparation. In the Order, my first coupling would have been a very special ritual, most . . . sacred."

Randon smiled and sat down on the furs, drawing Kayli down beside him.

"It will be," he said. "I promise." He took Kayli's hand and traced his finger gently over her fingertips, turning her hand in the firelight to gaze at the palm, then the back.

"Why so many scars on your hands?" he murmured.

Kayli glanced at her hand and cringed a little inwardly. Her hands were crisscrossed with scars, dappled with healed burns. Of those born with the mage-gift, the Order of the Inner Flame received the fewest novices, for the simple reason that the Flame allowed for no mistakes. Her hands were no longer a lady's hands; they were the strong, scarred hands of a novice mage who had paid dearly for her skills. They were Kayli's silent boast, a reminder of all she had accomplished at such a cost.

That sudden knowledge brought a rush of confidence. This time Kayli was able to reach into the fire and pick up a burning stick, bringing it out for Randon to see.

"This is simple for me now," she said. "But it took me many failures to learn."

Randon waited until she put the stick back, then took her hand again, kissing her fingertips.

"Magical hands," he murmured. Randon's lips brushed the thin skin of her inner wrist, just where her pulse beat, and his fingers slid down her forearm to the inner bend of her elbow with a feather touch. Kayli shivered with the sensation, her stomach seeming to shiver, too.

"You're very quiet," Randon said with a smile. "Do you find me so repulsive, or are you so frightened?"

Kayli was silent, unsure what Randon wanted her to say. Repulsive? Clearly he knew better. Frightened? Of coupling? There was always a little pain at first, she knew, but it could not rival the burn of a hot coal when her concentration wavered. But failure, of a lifetime of wasted hopes—

"I *am* frightened," Kayli said honestly. "A bit."

Randon pulled her down to the hearth furs, and the gentle touch of his fingers through her robe, then under it, left tingling trails over her skin.

"I know little enough about being a High Lord, or a husband," Randon murmured gently. "But in these matters, at least, I'm confident of my skill." He bent to kiss her.

The lighting of the fire. The first mystical spark, drawn from the heart of flint and steel, leaps to tinder and flares alight. One moment where the universe hangs suspended, while the Flame, in its most elemental form, is conjured from nothing.

For her own part, Kayli could only gasp and marvel at the wonder of it as Randon's fingers and lips fanned the spark in her body into flame, fanned flame into fire, fanned fire into an all-consuming conflagration. Her Awakening, Randon's heir, their marriage, the alliance between their countries—all those things were consumed and obliterated in the inferno sweeping through her body. It was her first firewalk, and more—she lived in the heart of the Flame itself, and it burned within her body and all around her, a bright and searing pleasure that was a sort of agony itself. Even the brief small pain when Randon entered her body was only fuel for that fire.

For a moment Kayli knew true fear. In the temple she had always been taught that loss of control could mean horrible death. Now she could only helplessly wonder—when she could manage to think at all—what Randon had unleashed within her. She could only surrender completely to that flame, and that very surrender, that heedless immolation, was utterly glorious.

In the wake of the fire, peace. Randon's skin was warm and slippery against hers, the beat of his heart slow and strong. There was a slight, not unpleasant ache between her thighs.

"Not as bad as you imagined, eh?" Randon said gently, bending to kiss the sweat from her upper lip.

"I never believed it would be bad," Kayli said honestly. "But I never supposed it would be so—" She hesitated.

"So what?" Randon grinned. "Magnificent?"

"—so consuming," Kayli finished, smiling.

"It very nearly was." Randon reached to one side and held up his fingers. They were blackened with soot. "The furs are singed all around us. Some sparks must have flown out from the hearth. We're lucky we weren't burned."

Kayli pushed Randon aside and sat up, gazing with dismay at the singed area that surrounded them. She was glad that in the firelight Randon could not see the flush of her cheeks. She suspected that the fire that burned the fur had not come from the fireplace. Well, at least the waiting was over.

"What's the matter?" Randon asked.

"We—we should get up," Kayli said. "There may be more sparks. And I would like to wash, if I may."

"Of course." Randon nodded at the large copper jars flanking the fireplace. "Those are filled with water. It should be warm now. Unless you'd like me to have the servants draw a bath for you?"

"That will be unnecessary, thank you." The thought of servants coming into the room now seemed indecent. Kayli took the cloth that Randon handed her and made a hasty toilet, retrieving her robe when she was finished. She was a little embarrassed to find Randon, robed again also, sitting at the small table and watching her.

"I thought you were starving," Randon said, amused. "As we've 'consummated our marriage,' don't you want to have a little of the supper I so kindly brought up for you?"

Kayli's stomach growled at the very thought, and she joined Randon at the table. No food had ever tasted so good as the cold roast meat and hearty cheese, the fine soft rolls and butter, and the strange new fruits. She ate for several minutes before she realized, to her humiliation, that Randon had eaten nothing; instead he'd been watching her, an expression of amusement mixed with concern on his face.

"Don't mind me," Randon said good-naturedly when Kayli abruptly stopped eating, wiping her lips and fingers self-consciously. "I had plenty of supper. To be truthful, I'm relieved to see you with an appetite after your illness and your difficult journey. Stevann worried at your thinness."

Kayli reached for more meat, this time eating slowly.

"There was no need for concern," she said. "At the Order, fasting was a common practice. I am accustomed to it."

"You've been ill, and you're thin," Randon corrected. "And the anxiety of traveling to a new country under such circumstances couldn't have helped."

Kayli chuckled even as she helped herself to another thick wedge of cheese. What a puling, frail thing he must think her!

"I beg your pardon, my lord husband," she said gently. "But did I seem so weak and sickly only moments ago on the furs before the fire? To hear you speak, one would think me standing with one foot in the Hidden Realms already."

"I beg your pardon." Randon said ruefully. "I'm only trying to be a good husband. If only I knew how.''

Kayli wiped her fingers, then touched his hand.

''I would suggest you have made a fair start at it.'' She smiled, flushing a little as she remembered their passion.

''And we stay here for three days?'' Randon asked, smiling. ''I suppose I'll have time to learn a great deal in those three days. And so will you.''

Kayli lowered her eyes.

''Endra was lying,'' she said. ''Bregond has no such custom.''

''Well, nobody needs to know that, do they?'' Randon chuckled. ''A little time alone together isn't such a bad idea. And truth to tell, I've been so wretchedly busy since Father died, I've hardly had a chance to draw breath. Three days to become acquainted with my new bride and relax in my rooms just suits me. Unless you'll find it too confining?''

Kayli chuckled.

''I have spent most of my days in small, windowless stone rooms and smoky forges,'' she said. ''Compared to that, these rooms are as open and spacious as the wide plains with the wind blowing through the grass.''

''You describe it well,'' Randon said, sipping wine. ''I envied Terralt his chance to see fabled Bregond. Although to hear him talk about it afterward, it wasn't such a marvelous place as our legends said.''

''A marvelous place?'' Kayli smiled at the thought. ''Bregond is a harsh land, I suppose. The soil is poor, rocky, and dry, and water holes are few. Little grows there besides brambles and grasses sharp enough to cut flesh. But it is a great and ancient land with magic in its bones, and at the moment when the sun rises, spilling blood and gold over the plains, when the wind in the grass whispers secrets to those who have learned to listen, I know in my heart that there can be no other place where the spark of life burns more brightly. It is a land that demands much of us, but it gives much in return, even though its gifts are gifts of the spirit, not readily visible.''

''You make it sound very special.'' Randon's eyes sparkled in the firelight. ''All our tales would have the Bregondish a race of warriors and mages and little else. I suppose it must be a magical land indeed to spawn such a folk.''

"I fear I must disappoint you," Kayli said with a sigh. "Merchants from other lands say that there are more mages born in Bregond than other lands, but our Orders have learned to recognize the mage-gift in our children and begin training it early, while in other lands such a gift might pass unnoticed. Most of those born without the gift learn the sword and the bow, true, but most often their arrows are aimed only at the wolves that prey on our herds, or game for supper."

"I think you give your people too little credit," Randon said. "Everybody's heard of the fierce and terrible warriors of Bregond, so deadly with their bows even while riding their wonderful steeds, able to vanish like ghosts into the long grass, able to slay a dozen men each before dying themselves."

"You have an exaggerated idea of our greatness," Kayli said, although his words made her proud. "But I suppose our reputation has served us well, for nobody but Sarkond has troubled us in many years, and your father thought it beneficial to ally our two countries."

"Mmmm. Yes." Randon gazed at her in the firelight. "You talk a great deal about your people, but nothing about yourself. And regardless of alliances, it's you I wed."

Kayli wiped her fingers again and sipped the wine. It was wonderful wine, far superior to the wine at home, although perhaps that was only because it had been so many days since she'd had any wine at all. Then again, with such moist lush soil, Agrondish vineyards must fairly pour forth their bounty.

"I have been here," she said quietly, "awake and aware, only one day, and in that day I have been wed, bedded my new husband, and had my first meal in days. Forgive me, but I am tired, so very tired."

"Of course you are," Randon said hastily. "I beg your pardon. Come, I'll dim the lamps and we'll sleep."

It was strange to lie in the large soft bed and feel the presence of another beside her. Humble and barren as her small cell was at the Order, she had had it to herself. Strangely, Kayli found the sensation of Randon's presence somehow comforting. It was too easy to feel alone, so far from home.

Randon's voice in the darkness startled her.

"Homesick?" he asked quietly.

Kayli sighed.

"Perhaps a little," she admitted.

She heard Randon move closer in the darkness, and then his arms were warm around her. Kayli turned over a little awkwardly and laid her head on his shoulder. She'd coupled with this man only an hour before, but now it seemed strange to seek comfort from him. But thankfully he said nothing more, just held her in the silence until Kayli's exhaustion overcame the strangeness and she spiraled down into sleep.

4

KAYLI WOKE SLOWLY, STRETCHING LUXURI-
antly. The first weak rays of sunlight just touched the
windowsill; at the Order she'd have been awake long
before. She rolled over and gazed at her bedmate—her husband. Randon was deeply asleep on his side, one wrist over
his eyes, the covers pushed down almost to his waist.

How strange to wake next to this man, this naked man sharing her bed. Sharing more than her bed, Kayli reminded herself. Sometime last night she had woken to his kisses and
caresses, her body already burning for him. Sweetly drowsy,
the darkness swallowing any awkwardness or embarrassment
she might have felt, Kayli had astonished herself with her own
abandon. The memory made her blush a little now, in the light
of day.

She glanced at the sheets, the covers. Thankfully there was
no hint of scorching. Whatever power had been released at her
Awakening, at least she apparently need not fear setting the
bed afire every time they coupled. A blessing, for even now,
remembering that hot, secret passion in the darkness, Kayli
could feel the Flame pulsing along her nerves.

Daringly Kayli cupped her hands and focused her thoughts
as she had been taught; almost immediately a small flame
flared alight in the cup of her hands. Its touch on her skin

tingled pleasantly but did not burn. Kayli smiled and banished the small flame; to her delight, the cut on her palm had healed to a white scar. She folded her hands closed as if to hold in a secret.

Randon murmured something in his sleep and rolled over on his back. Kayli slid out of bed, donned her robe, and tiptoed out onto the balcony.

Even in the weak dawn light, Kayli marveled at the size of Tarkesh beyond the castle wall. She could see small figures moving in the streets—merchants going to market, perhaps, or to their shops. Kayli wondered if she might someday see Tarkesh's legendary market. There were villages around her parents' keep, of course, but like most villages in Bregond, the greater part of the inhabitants traveled with the herds, circling the lands in their territories, returning home only to cull the herds, visit with the family members who remained at home, and send their tithes on to the High Lord. Merchant wagons passed singly or in small groups through the villages as they did the High Lord's keep; there were few large gatherings.

Now that Kayli had a better look at the grounds inside the keep wall, she was amazed to see that except for the meticulously tended gardens, lush with greenery, most of the ground had been paved with stones rather than leaving the earth to become trampled and hard. Of course; she was living in the wetlands now, and bare earth would become slippery mud. She wondered briefly where Randon rode. They seemed surrounded by city, at least as far as she could see from the south-facing balcony.

"You're up early." Randon folded his arms around her waist from behind and kissed the side of her neck. "After all you've been through, I thought you'd sleep late."

"I apologize if I disturbed you," Kayli said, leaning back against his warmth. It was an unusual, pleasing sensation. "I am accustomed to waking early."

"I heard the maids put a tray in the sitting room," he said. "Come and have something to eat."

Kayli was glad for the food; she was hungry and the meal was tasty, but even better, it gave her something to do. She felt inexplicably awkward in Randon's presence; after she'd wed this stranger and coupled with him, what could she say to him?

Randon apparently felt none of the same awkwardness; he chatted jovially while they ate, saying nothing of any consequence, seemingly oblivious to Kayli's shyness. Of course, she thought wryly, he was far more accustomed to waking up beside a bed partner than she was. After listening to an accounting of Agrond's harvests last year, the increasing cost of importing tin, lead, iron, and copper, and the regrettable decrease of game near the city, however, Kayli held up a hand, silencing him.

"What you say interests me greatly," she said gently, "but you tell me nothing of yourself. I would like to learn something of the man I wed."

Randon sighed and put down his mug.

"I'm sorry," he said. "This is a little strange to me. To be quite truthful, I don't know that I've spoken—well, meaningfully—to anyone much except Stevann, and Father put an end to that years ago."

"Terralt said your father opposed your studying magic," Kayli said quietly. She could still hardly conceive of such an attitude in any parent.

"I very much doubt it was the magic," Randon said wryly. "I imagine he simply didn't want me so much in Stevann's company. Stevann's a lover of men, you know. I suppose Father was afraid he'd teach me such habits."

Kayli tried not to blush. Obviously Agrond was a much more cosmopolitan country than Bregond. There were men and women of such tendencies in Bregond, Kayli knew, even in her own Order. Officially such practices were forbidden. Unofficially they were ignored, but never spoken of in polite company.

"In any event, I'd have made a terrible mage," Randon said cheerfully. "I'm not the studious sort, and I read and write poorly—undoubtedly you know that from my letter."

"In the Orders that would not have mattered," Kayli told him. "Except for copying the rituals into our grimoires, our lessons are spoken. In my Order there are two priests who are completely blind."

"And what sort of magical talent do you have?" Randon asked eagerly.

Kayli cupped her hands together as she had before. It was easy, amazingly easy to conjure up the small flame.

"I am fire-Dedicated," she said, extending her hands so that Randon could see the flame. The tiny fire danced merrily over her skin, leaving behind an odd, pleasurable tingling.

"How wonderful." Randon bent over her hands, holding out his own hand. "May I?"

Kayli hesitated. It seemed probable that Randon had some trace of the mage-gift, at least, but Kayli was uncertain that she had enough control over her fire yet that she could keep it from burning him if he had no magical affinity to the Flame. But, oh, if he *did*—

Kayli closed her hands, banishing the small flame, smiling at the disappointment in Randon's expression.

"Give me your hand," she said. "No, that one." She gently unwound the bandages, wincing inwardly when she saw how much the cut in his palm had bled, how the cloth had stuck to the wound. "As most healers know, fire has the power to stop blood and close wounds."

Randon's eyebrows drew down a little apprehensively, but he said nothing, letting Kayli expose the cut on his palm, wincing only a little when she opened his hand flat.

Kayli brought forth the dancing fire in her own hand, then, holding Randon's hand steady, spilled the tiny flame into Randon's palm. Randon cried out, more in surprise than pain, and nearly pulled away, but Kayli's grip on his wrist held his hand still. There was a brief odor of burning flesh as the small flame danced across his palm; then the flame vanished.

"It didn't hurt," Randon said hesitantly, staring with a mixture of apprehension and distaste at the charred line across his palm. "But it felt so strange. But look, I'm burned."

"Perhaps. But I think not." Kayli dabbed at Randon's hand with her napkin, then wiped more vigorously. The smudge of burned blood scrubbed away, leaving a healed scar like her own.

"That's remarkable," Randon said, his eyes wide. "How did you do that?"

"*I* did nothing but permit you for a moment to share my

own fire magic," Kayli corrected. "If you had no affinity of your own with the Flame, it would have burned you in truth."

"Then I have the same kind of fire magic you do?" Randon asked, such eagerness in his voice that Kayli was dismayed.

"You saw how the flame died in your hand," she said gently. "Either you possess little of the Flame of your own, or because of your lack of training, you are unable to sustain it."

"I suppose it's too late to learn," Randon said, sighing. "Stevann said mages begin training when they're very young."

"Yes, for many reasons," Kayli said quietly. "But, Randon, the duties of a High Lord would leave you no time for such studies in any wise." She did not add that for Randon to attempt to learn fire magic so late in his life, long after his sexual energies had matured, would be unthinkably dangerous. There was no need to say it; Randon already realized the futility of the idea.

"But what about you?" Randon asked, frowning a little. "I'm delighted to learn my new bride is a mage, and it'll certainly impress my advisory council, but you say you still have learning to do. How can you do that here and now?"

"Learning the necessary concentration and self-discipline was the greatest and most difficult lesson," Kayli said, sighing at the memory. "Now I need only learn the rituals themselves."

"Will you need a study, or perhaps a workroom like Stevann's to read and mix potions and such?" Randon suggested. "There are plenty of chambers I could have converted."

A great wave of relief left Kayli shaken; she had never permitted herself to wonder if Randon might oppose her studies.

"I have only a few books, and I would prefer to ask Endra or Brother Stevann to prepare any potions or powders I might need," Kayli said, smiling. "But if I might ask it of you, I would request that a forge be dedicated to my use—"

"A forge?" Randon said, raising his eyebrows. "Well, I suppose that's not so strange, especially if you want to conjure a fire any larger than that tiny flicker, or juggle coals like you did last night. There's the old palace forge in the cellar, but it hasn't been used since my grandfather's time."

The offer stunned Kayli to silence, and for a moment she stared into Randon's eyes, expecting to see the twinkle that meant he was mocking her. But there was no mockery in his eyes, only keen interest—or rather, thinly veiled curiosity. Well, there was no harm in that; he was her husband, after all, and most of the rituals need not be held secret.

"You're so inscrutable," Randon said, chuckling a little, after a long moment of silence. "You say so little. What are you thinking with such a serious expression on your face?"

Kayli smiled.

"That I am grateful for your generosity and your interest," she said. "But do you truly wish to spend three days locked in these rooms?"

"Mmmm." Randon stood and walked around the table to Kayli, bending over to nuzzle the side of her neck. His tongue traced a tingling path over her skin, and a restless warmth filled her, so that she leaned back against his hands.

"I don't know," he murmured against her neck. "Three days may not be long enough by half."

This time Kayli had no fear or doubt to make her reluctant. In the aftermath of passion, however, her head pillowed on Randon's shoulder, their legs tangled comfortably, she sighed.

"What's the matter?" Randon asked.

"You are so skilled at pleasing me," Kayli said, rather embarrassed. "I think of the women you have lain with, women who were skilled at pleasing you, and I feel—inadequate."

Randon laughed.

"Any man can pay his coins and have a whore as talented at feigning pleasure as she is at giving it," he said. "Believe me, it's pure delight to lie with a beautiful woman and know I'm making her happy, and to be wanted for more than my gold. So don't trouble yourself. No man marries a virgin and expects to find a great courtesan in his bed."

Kayli would have answered, but a timid knock at the outer door interrupted her thoughts. Randon scowled, but donned his robe and disappeared into the sitting room; Kayli could hear muffled conversation, and once a sharp, angry exclamation by Randon. Randon strode back into the room, flinging his robe aside and sighing explosively as he collected his clothes.

"Is something wrong?" Kayli asked, reaching for her robe.

"More or less," Randon said irritably. "Knowing that I'd be conveniently out of the way for three days, Terralt's called a meeting of *my* advisers to discuss all the reasons why my father's choice of Heir should be ignored. Bright Ones, if it weren't for the loyalty of the servants I'd never have even heard about the meeting. They're already in the council chamber. I didn't expect Terralt to force a confrontation so soon."

"Can he do that?" Kayli asked surprisedly. "Call a meeting of the High Lord's own advisers without the High Lord?" Immediately she was embarrassed to have asked; Terralt had done it, hadn't he?

"He has no right, if that's what you're asking," Randon said wryly, struggling with his trousers. "But my advisers are in an odd position—I'm the declared Heir, but not confirmed as High Lord yet, while Terralt's been the High Lord in all but name for years. In their place I might have agreed to the session, too. But to fail to notify me—well, I'll have something to say about that."

"Then I will go with you." Kayli pulled a gown at random from her wardrobe and stepped into it.

"There's no time," Randon protested. "By the time your maids could have you ready, there'd be no use in going."

"Then your council of advisers must learn that your bride cares more for her duties than her appearance," Kayli returned. She brushed her hair hurriedly and pinned it into a simple knot at the back of her head, half laced her slippers, and nodded briskly. "I am ready."

Randon raised one eyebrow.

"You're not wearing any underthings at all, are you?"

"No one can see that," Kayli said. "However, if you wish to wait while I don all of my smallclothes and petticoats—"

"No matter," Randon said hurriedly. "As you say, nobody will know but us." Then he grinned. "But I may find the thought something of a distraction."

This time they walked not to the great hall, but to another room on the ground floor. Two guards were stationed at the door, but they stepped aside as Randon approached, one hurriedly opening the door for them. Randon did not wait to be announced, but strode into the room, and Kayli, taking a deep breath and performing a brief calming exercise in her mind, followed.

This apparently was the council chamber, a smallish room with no windows and only the one door. At the back of the room was a heavy wooden table with a large, ornate chair behind it, and beside that a smaller chair. Terralt was sitting in neither; he was standing instead, leaning against the table.

A short distance from that table and perpendicular to it were two longer tables facing each other. Seated at those tables were the advisers Kayli had seen at the great hall when she and Randon had been married: three men at one table, two women and a man at the other. All six had turned to gaze at Kayli and Randon, and Kayli felt a little of her tension ebb when she saw the surprise and embarrassment on all six faces—and a measure of relief as well. Not a conspiracy, then.

"Fair morning, lords and ladies," Randon said casually, as if he'd met them in the hallway. "I've already presented to you the lady Kayli, my bride; Kayli, I make known to you my advisory council: Lord Kereg, Minister of Agriculture; Lord Disian, Minister of Science; Lord Vyr, Minister of the Army; Lady Tarkas, Minister of Trade; Lady Aville, Minister of Justice; and Lord Jaxon, Minister of Finance."

The ministers stood and bowed as they were named; Kayli noted that Lord Kereg and Lady Tarkas glanced briefly at Terralt as they rose, but whether their glance was to obtain approval or merely to gauge Terralt's reaction, Kayli could not tell.

"You may be seated, lords, ladies," Randon said amiably. "I'm gratified that a formal assembly could be called so soon after my wedding so that my wife could meet you. I'm certain it was a simple oversight that someone forgot to notify me that my own council was sitting in session."

"Why, brother"—Terralt grinned—"have you forgotten that you said that you weren't to be disturbed for three days?"

You have shown courtesy, Kayli thought, tightening her grip on Randon's hand. *Now you must show strength.* But she said nothing; it was Randon who had been challenged, not she.

When Randon spoke again, there was a gratifying note of steel in his calm voice.

"I would have preferred to believe this business an honest

misjudgment on your part, Terralt,'' he said quietly. "I didn't want to believe you'd court treason so far as to disobey Father's orders, to conspire against his chosen Heir, even try to seduce my ministers into treason with you."

"Until you're confirmed as High Lord, they're no more your ministers than they are mine," Terralt said flatly, his grin gone. "And what sort of Heir expects his country to wait for three days while he dallies with his bride?"

"The sort of Heir who respects the customs of a country with whom we've signed a treaty," Randon said quietly. "But that's exactly what this is about, isn't it—what sort of Heir I am. And now's as good a time as any to discuss that."

Randon led Kayli past Terralt as if the latter did not exist, giving Kayli an apologetic shrug as he motioned her to the smaller chair.

"It's my shame to agree that until Father died I had no preparation for rulership." He turned back to Terralt. "But our own grandfather was a common mercenary until his brother's death forced him to take the seat. At least I can read and write, however clumsily."

Randon sat back in the chair, and his knuckles were white where he gripped the arms of the chair.

"You're not pleased, Terralt, with the way I've spent my youth—Bright Ones know you've made your views known to everyone—but my father was the only one entitled to judge my suitability as Heir.

"And you don't like my politics. Strange that you made no complaint when they were our *father's* politics. But a declared Heir can't be set aside simply because his subjects"—he emphasized the word slightly—"aren't happy with his position on foreign affairs. So on what grounds, brother, do you believe that Father's advisory council should—or have the right to, for that matter—set me aside in defiance of Father's choice?"

Kayli could see Randon's white hand begin to tremble; she laid her hand over his to cover it. Startled as if he'd forgotten she was there, Randon glanced at her, and Kayli smiled at him. She felt him relax just a little.

Terralt scowled at Randon blankly for a long moment, and Kayli thought that he had been doubly surprised: first, that Randon had appeared at all to defend his claim; and second, that he had been prepared to speak so strongly on his own behalf.

"You argue well for your claim, brother," Terralt said at last. "If you could rule this land with pretty speech, we'd be better off. But it doesn't surprise me that you speak only of your rights, your power. Those matters were always first with you, before the welfare of the people of this country, and they remain so now, as the council can plainly see."

Randon exploded to his feet, slamming his fist on the table.

"I had everything I wanted!" he shouted. "I had my freedom, all the money I could spend, all the wenches I could bed, my horses and dogs and the open sky, and gods, how you hated and envied me for it, while you set yourself the task of reading Father's papers, writing his proclamations as any scribe could've done, all the while hoping he'd see what a dutiful little son you were and hand you the country like a bone to a favorite dog. It's you who has always wanted the damned power, not me! The Bright Ones know I'd be glad enough to be rid of it!"

Terralt leaned over the table, his face only inches from Randon's.

"Then," he said icily, "give it to me."

Silence. Kayli felt her own hands trembling, stilled them.

Randon returned Terralt's gaze squarely.

"Swear before me and the council that you'll continue with the alliance and all other matters as Father wished," Randon said quietly, "and the seat is yours."

This time the silence was longer. Kayli sat still, scarcely breathing. Randon was playing a dangerous game for high stakes indeed; he was wagering that Terralt's honor was stronger than his ambition. Then Kayli realized that Randon already *knew;* he'd made that same wager when he'd sent Terralt to fetch his bride.

"You know I can't swear that," Terralt growled at last, slamming his fist on the table as Randon had. "What this country needs isn't an alliance with a herd of backward nomads, it needs a mercenary force strong enough to—"

"Enough." The unfamiliar voice startled them all; the tension in the room broke like a string pulled too taut. Kayli saw

Lord Kereg standing. "Enough, the both of you. Sit down and be still."

The brothers glared a moment longer; then Randon nodded slightly and sat down. There was nowhere for Terralt to sit but on the edge of the table; he glowered, but sat.

"Terralt brought before us the suggestion that High Lord Terendal was dying and his thoughts were confused when he named you as his Heir, Lord Randon," Kereg said. He turned to Terralt. "The council discussed that idea long before you broached it—in fact, on the day of High Lord Terendal's death, before we confirmed his choice. High Lord Terendal was weak and in great pain, but his thoughts were whole. He spoke clearly until his death." Kereg glanced apologetically at Randon, then turned back to Terralt. "Most of us expected and favored you to become our High Lord. If ever, even once, High Lord Terendal had previously named you his Heir—even indicated that he might one day choose you—that might have been excuse enough for us to question his choice of Lord Randon. But the High Lord always hoped for an alliance between Agrond and Bregond, and in the last months of his life he worked single-mindedly toward that cause. His choice of Heir was made after great deliberation. We decided that there was no challenging his choice."

Lord Kereg sat back down.

"So long as Lord Randon proves that he can provide his country with an heir, and doesn't show himself grossly unfit to hold the seat," he said, "we have neither authority nor reason to sustain a challenge to his claim to the throne of Agrond." He shrugged. "That being said, I suggest that any further business of this council be postponed until our next sitting."

"No." Randon rose again. "There is one more item I wish to place before the council. And my brother." He laid his hand on Kayli's shoulder.

"This council is appointed to serve the High Lord and Lady of Agrond," he said. "As High Lord presumptive, that's myself and Kayli. The council sits at our order, and ours alone. My brother has no authority to convene this council; you have no authority to convene it yourselves. From now on, the council will sit when *and only when* I or Kayli has ordered it. And my brother has no right to attend or speak at any session of council except at our invitation. Is that quite clear?''

There was a gasp from someone in the council, and the rage on Terralt's face grew to thundercloud proportions.

Lady Aville was the first to stand.

"Your order is clear, High Lord presumptive," she said calmly. "And I shall honor it without fail."

One by one, the other ministers stood and acknowledged Randon's order; Kayli noted carefully the voice and mannerisms of each as they spoke. By the time the ministers had finished, the rage was gone from Terralt's face, and he shrugged.

"Have it your way," he said. "And may the Bright Ones have mercy on our country. But remember, brother, you're not yet confirmed the High Lord of Agrond. Remember that."

Randon frowned, and Kayli thought wildly that another argument would undo all that Randon had accomplished here. She stood, startling Randon once more.

"I will spare Terralt the trouble of telling you that I have had perhaps less preparation for rulership than my husband, and I am hampered additionally by small knowledge of your people and your customs," she said. "Like Randon, I can offer only my best effort. But by the trust and admiration that Randon has expressed to me for each of you, I know that I may rely upon you to help me learn, to correct my ignorance, and to forgive any inadvertent offense I may give."

She turned to Terralt.

"And before my husband and this council, I am pleased to have the opportunity to give my deepest thanks to Terralt for his great courage and honor. By marriage he has become my brother, and like Randon, I could not wish for better." She extended her hand, gazing into Terralt's eyes.

A rueful smile twitched at the corner of Terralt's mouth; then he relented, taking Kayli's hand.

"You speak as eloquently as my brother," he said. "Between the two of you, I'm doomed to appear the blackguard." He bowed a trifle too deeply. "I wish the two of you happiness, if not fertility." Releasing Kayli's hand, he turned and walked from the room.

A little awkwardly, the ministers excused themselves also.

When they had gone, Randon sat down, then slumped forward, his elbows on the table and his head in his shaking hands.

"Bright Ones," he said. "I don't know what I'd have done if—for a moment I thought—"

"You thought they would side with Terralt against you?" Kayli asked gently. "No. They lack the courage for such an action. And some of them, I believe, prefer you to Terralt as High Lord, though their reasons may be suspect."

Randon raised his head and glanced at her.

"What do you mean?"

"There are many reasons they might favor you," Kayli told him. "Terralt's ambitions are too strong, as you observed, and now that the treaty has been signed, Terralt, given freedom of action, might offend Bregond to the point of war. Perhaps some of them favor the alliance, as your father did. But some may believe you more malleable, easier to influence, and therefore more desirable a High Lord." She shook her head. "I know none of them well enough to judge their motives."

"You judged Terralt shrewdly enough," Randon told her, smiling faintly. "After the scene he made, I thought the best I could hope for was open hostility instead of quiet treachery. Bright Ones, what I'd give to have the man as my ally! With his help and his influence with the nobility, there's no limit to what I could do with this country."

Kayli smiled, but inwardly she found Randon's vision unlikely. Terralt was too ambitious, too inflexible in his thinking to be content with a subordinate's role. As Randon had implied, likely Terralt had served at his father's side only in the hope that the High Lord would one day name him Heir. How onerous such service must have been to the proud lord!

"Well, after that, I don't think I could go back to our rooms and play at being newlyweds again, could you?" Randon said ruefully. "What if we change our clothes instead, and you can show me the wonderful horses you brought, and choose a new hawk for you, and tomorrow we'll ride in the country. And when we're done in the stables and the mews, I'll show you the forge."

"That would be most pleasant," Kayli said with relief. She was indeed far too agitated now to return to idleness, and she very much wanted to finish dressing.

When she considered her wardrobe, she realized that she had nothing fit for stable wear except the riding clothes she'd worn on the journey to Agrond. Was such clothing offensive by Agrondish standards? Well, she thought at last, better to find out now while there was nobody but Randon to see.

She need not have worried.

"What a marvelous outfit," Randon said when he saw her. "Perfect for hunting. Terralt told me about the leather leggings, but you're not wearing them now, are you?"

Kayli pulled her jaffs out of the chest and held them up for Randon to see.

"They are not necessary here," she said. "They are only for protection from the high grass."

"Well, you look marvelous. I wonder if Ynea—" Randon sighed. "No. She's never been well enough to ride."

"Childbearing seemed to disagree with her," Kayli said, glancing at Randon as they walked through the corridors. "Endra is a very skilled midwife, trained in one of the healing Orders. I had thought to offer her services to the Lady Ynea."

"Mmm." Randon was silent for a moment as they walked. "Best say nothing to Terralt, or he'll forbid it. Stevann suggested bringing in a midwife after Ynea nearly died bearing her first child. My mother died bearing me, you know."

"No, I did not know." Kayli was silent. Because most novices in the healing Orders not gifted enough to continue in the Orders became midwives, it was rare that any Bregondish childbearing woman or her infant died for lack of skilled care. Kayli knew that mages were less common in Agrond than Bregond, and that Agrondish mages did not specialize in one area of magic and so concentrate their talents, but surely there were midwives of some sort, be it only village wisewomen. What excuse could there be for a nobleman to deny his wife such care? After a moment's worry that she might offend some Agrondish custom, she voiced her thoughts to Randon.

"Most noble households have healers like Stevann, not midwives," Randon told her. "And as you say, our mages don't specialize in healing. My mother had both a midwife and a healer present at my birth, and she died anyway. Father had both the healer and the midwife banished, and it was years before he hired Stevann. Terralt has no faith in midwives, and little enough in mages at all. At least he lets Stevann attend Ynea.''

They were at the front entry now. Randon nodded briefly to the two guards flanking the heavy wooden door, and they opened it. Kayli was not too lost in her thoughts to be grateful that no guards followed Randon and herself outside.

The bricked courtyard felt strange under the soles of her boots, but the fresh air and the wind and sun on her face was wonderful. Even the smell from the stables was almost pleasant in its familiarity. Kayli was pleased to see that despite the unavoidable stink of manure, the stable was clean, the horses well-groomed and healthy. She was concerned, however, to see the small boxes Agrondish horses were kept in. To her confusion, Randon led her through the stables and out the other side.

"Your string have given our grooms a little difficulty," Randon admitted. "As long as the weather's been good, we've kept them in the outdoor pen."

That sounded reassuring, but Kayli was less pleased when she saw the wood-fenced enclosure. It was large enough, but the ground was wet and soiled. Her horses, too, had not been groomed as well as those in the stables—or perhaps they had simply been rolling in the muck.

"As I said, the grooms have had a little trouble with them," Randon said apologetically. "They're not used to horses with so much spirit."

Kayli whistled and Maja trotted over to the fence, the rest of the string following.

"They are spirited, but not mean," Kayli said slowly. "One of my maids can assist your grooms until my parents can send a groom. But this wet ground will ruin the horses' hooves and legs. They are accustomed to drier footing."

Randon nodded.

"I'll have it taken care of," he said. "That's your mare, isn't it?"

"Her name is Maja." The mare snorted in pleasure as Randon's fingers unerringly found her favorite scratching spot behind her ears.

Seeing that Randon was confident with Maja, Kayli coaxed the mare around to the gate so she could bring her out for him to examine. Despite the reputed intimidation of the grooms, Randon handled Maja confidently, admiring her deep, broad chest and muscular hindquarters. Agrondish horses seemed tall and weak and knobby to her; surely Maja looked squat and round to Randon, but he said only, "How powerful she is. I imagine she could run forever on open ground," shaking his head admiringly as Kayli returned Maja to the pen.

Randon agreed with Kayli's suggestion that Carada, a swift but patient mare, would serve best as his own mount. Judging from Randon's bride gift and Terralt's remarks, Kayli had anticipated some common ground between herself and Randon in hunting and riding, and she was glad to have a topic on which they could converse easily and comfortably, their discussion carrying no more import than simple chat. Although Kayli usually hunted with her bow, she knew enough of falconry to talk knowledgeably with Randon when he took her to the mews, although she insisted that he choose her new hawk.

"It was your bride-gift, after all," she excused herself. "I would prefer to fly a hawk that you chose for me."

Any further casual chatter fled Kayli's mind, however, when Randon showed her the palace forge deep in the cellars.

"My great-great-grandfather used to have dungeons here," he said. "That was when Tarkesh was so small that the few cells here could actually hold all the criminals. When the new dungeons were built in the city, Great-Grandfather hired a master smith—he had a passion for fine swords—and had the forges built to the smith's order. There are clever conduits at the walls with levers to open and close them, to let the smoke out. Of course, we don't use the place anymore now; Father thought it was wasteful for smiths to be sitting around the castle idle most of the time. What do you think?"

Kayli gazed around her with awe. The forge had been designed by a master smith indeed. Why, the great inner forge at the Order was no finer than this—and imagine designing a forge inside the castle cellars, with no windows, but still being rid of the smoke! There was a small forge built into the wall, likely for the making of swords, as Randon had said, and that would be of no use to Kayli, but there was also a good old-fashioned open firepit for larger meltings. The stones of the floor, walls, and ceiling were, of course, grimed with a heavy coating of soot, and that, coupled the room's size, meant that Kayli would spend a great deal of time cleaning it properly before consecrating it, but if she had been given her every wish, she could have asked for nothing better than what she saw.

"You needn't say a word." Randon laughed, startling her out of her meditation. "I'm answered by your expression. I'll hire some sturdy lads from the city to scrub the place down and arrange things to your liking. Meantime we'd best go back before Terralt finds a way to have us barred from my own home."

There was, of course, no such difficulty, but a maid was lurking just inside the door, wondering whether the lord and lady would take their dinner in their rooms or the dining hall. Randon glanced at Kayli for confirmation, then told the maid they'd dine in the hall today.

To Kayli's relief, Terralt was not there, nor was the Lady Ynea, and no places had been set for them. Randon told her that Ynea seldom felt strong enough to leave her rooms, and Terralt was sorting through some of their father's papers.

"I really should help him," Randon said hesitantly. "If you'd pardon my absence, that is."

"Of course, you must not neglect your duties on my account," Kayli said immediately. "Can I help you?"

"I don't see how you could," he told her. "It's mostly a matter of sorting out old documents which can be discarded, those to be filed in the archives, and those that contain current business to be reviewed. I'd leave the job to Terralt entirely— it's miserably hard for me to read Father's writing—but I don't think it's wise to let him make too many decisions without me. Again, if you don't object."

"Of course not." Indeed, Kayli felt a sort of guilty relief; she was accustomed to solitude, and in the time since she'd left the Order, she'd had precious little of it. A few hours of privacy would let her explore the effects of her Awakening, glance through Brisi's grimoire, and plan her course of study. Most of the preliminary work she could practice at the hearth fire, until the forge was ready.

As they ate, Kayli noticed a large portrait of a man and

woman hanging over the fireplace. The woman was lovely, tall and fair-haired, and the man bore a striking resemblance to Randon, although he was noticeably older.

"Is that your father and mother?" Kayli asked, indicating the painting.

"My father, yes," Randon told her. "But that's Delana with him, Terralt's mother, Father's mistress before he married my mother. After my mother died, Father had that portrait hung. He loved Delana very much. I imagine he'd have wed her, but he was Heir and Delana was only a coppersmith's daughter." He glanced at Kayli, then looked away again. "She took her own life when my father married my mother. I imagine that's one of the reasons Terralt never cared much for me."

Kayli flushed with embarrassment, wishing she had not asked about the portrait. How unkind of High Lord Terendal to hang the portrait there in open view in the dining hall. Poor Randon would probably never have it removed.

When they had finished eating and Randon returned to his work, Kayli found that the maids had taken advantage of her and Randon's absence to tidy their chambers. The hearth fur had been replaced, and she wondered with a mixture of amusement and embarrassment whether her maiden's blood had been displayed to Randon's advisers as proof of their coupling. Agrond seemed to favor such immodest customs.

Kayli leafed through Brisi's grimoire with some satisfaction. Awakening marked more than merely the rousing of her magical talent; it marked her initiation into the true practice of magic, the transition into a completely different course of study. In her years at the temple, the rituals Kayli had learned were simply a means of developing and focusing concentration or training self-discipline necessary to master her magical energies when they were activated.

The ritual of Initiation, too, was only a formality, a way to mark the passage from the latently talented novitiate to active scholarship. Initiates learned to consciously manipulate the Flame itself, putting to use the control already learned over the power of the Flame as it grew and developed.

Already Kayli could manifest the Flame in its simplest form and direct it to some extent. As an experiment, she brought the small flame forth again. With a little practice she could make it larger or smaller, make it dance over her fingertips, pour it from one cupped hand to the other like water, but as soon as she tried to direct it elsewhere—onto the tabletop or into a clay dish—the fire quickly died. With further practice that would change; Initiates were expected to light candles and lamps, and later to kindle the forge. Brisi could make anything burn, even water or stone. So obviously there was a way to free the Flame from the confines of her own flesh.

Kayli studied as the shadows from the window lengthened, delighted when patient concentration let her light a candle to read by, and in her fascination might well have worked all night if Randon had not walked in, sighing and rubbing his eyes.

"Well, there's a good deal more to be done," he said unhappily. "But it'll wait for another day." He glanced at Kayli. "You look as tired as I feel. Have you been studying all afternoon and evening?"

"Yes." Had it been so long? Apparently so; the sky was completely dark at the window.

"We're a pair." Randon chuckled. "You at your books and me at mine right through supper, and only the day after our marriage. Well, never mind; hopefully there'll be many quiet days to come. Meanwhile I've ordered up supper, enough for us both. I didn't know if you'd eaten."

Kayli only smiled, laying the grimoire aside. How comfortingly like her days in the Order it had been—to become so utterly absorbed in her studies that hours had passed unnoticed. How many times had Priestess Vayavara sternly ordered her and the other Dedicates away from their books or their meditations to eat or sleep or do their chores?

"You're so silent," Randon said, frowning slightly. "Do you want to be left alone?"

"Oh, no, no," Kayli said hurriedly. In truth she'd have liked nothing better than a few hours more alone with her studies, but she was a wife and a ruler now. Her studies would have to wait for whatever time she could spare.

"Forgive me," she said, pinching out the candle she'd lit so proudly. "I had merely become absorbed in my work. I am glad we can sup together, even if it is late."

Although Randon glanced wistfully at the grimoire, Kayli

avoided the subject of her studies. She might invite him to watch some of the rituals if he was curious, but best he accept now that he could not share this part of her life. Instead she drew him into a discussion of the earlier meeting with the council, reminding Randon that she knew nothing at all of these people who held so much influence in Agrond's government.

"There's not much to tell," Randon said, shrugging. "Most of the ministers have held their posts since I was very young. Lord Kereg and Lady Tarkas, though, were appointed more recently. Nothing suspicious about the appointments themselves—Lord Kereg joined the council when Lady Ecenia simply grew too old and frail to hold her post, and Lady Tarkas replaced Lady Besanne when Lady Besanne's husband was crippled in a fall and needed his wife's full attention—but both Lord Kereg and Lady Tarkas spent a lot of time with Terralt at court before their appointments, and I don't doubt that Terralt had a hand in their selection. Of course, I don't mean to say they're corrupt," he added hastily. "Like all Father's ministers, they took an oath of loyalty to the High Lord and to Agrond under truth spell."

Kayli nodded, understanding. Lord Kereg and Lady Tarkas and possibly others on the council were loyal to the High Lord of Agrond—but Randon was not yet confirmed as High Lord and his claim as Heir could still be challenged unless he produced an Heir of his own. They were loyal to Agrond—but they might believe that Terralt would better serve the country than Randon.

"Then we will find a way to convince them that you are not only the legal, but also the sensible choice of High Lord," Kayli said at last. "As Ministers of Agriculture and Trade, Lord Kereg and Lady Tarkas are in the best position to see the benefits of the alliance between Agrond and Bregond. Have they examined the trade goods my mother and father sent?"

Randon shook his head.

"There's been such a bustle since the night you arrived that the stuff's been sitting in storage. I'll have the goods released to Lady Tarkas tomorrow. Maybe the possibilities there will sway her, as you say."

Kayli nodded and poured her dose of High Priestess Brisi's fertility potion, trying not to make a face as she swallowed it.

"What's that?" Randon asked, frowning. "I thought you were done with potions and fasting."

"I am done with fasting," Kayli corrected. "This is a potion to aid in conception." She raised an eyebrow. "Unless you would prefer I not take it."

"No, no," Randon said hurriedly. He handed her a cup of wine to wash away the taste, his fingers lingering against hers, his eyes warm. "But I know a better way to induce conception."

"As my potion is of no use without your method, I could hardly disagree," Kayli said with a smile. "Even if I were inclined to do so."

After pleasure, Kayli lay awake, rubbing her palm thoughtfully over her belly. How long might it be before she conceived, even with the advantages of her fertility potion and Randon's apparent enthusiasm for the task? Endra had warned her against too immediate hopes.

"Potions and purification are all well and good," the midwife had said, shaking her head, "but any girl's workings would be set a bit awry by such upheavals in their life as you're having. I'd not expect you to hold your lord's seed for at least a month or two, when your body settles. And fretting about it will only worsen the matter."

But Kayli could not help but worry as she lay there in the dark, and a pang of guilt followed. Although she'd known how important it was to Randon's claim to the throne of Agrond that she conceive, she had not worried unduly until she learned that *her* future as much as his relied upon that conception—just as on their wedding night she had worried about her own Awakening more than all the concerns weighing on Randon. Why, she'd hardly left the Order, and already she was becoming spoiled and selfish. In the Order, merely another novice, faced daily with menial labor to humble her and a regimen of rituals and tasks to instill self-discipline, she never forgot that she was but a single strand in the web of the Order, the country, the world. As a noble lady and wife to the High Lord presumptive, it was easy to see herself at the center of that web. She was becoming a disgrace to her teachings.

Randon's hand closed over hers, startling her; she turned her head to see him gazing at her in the dim light from the moon and the hearth.

"It's too soon to worry about it," he said gently, patting her belly. "Nobody expects you to conceive overnight, not if you were as fertile as Ynea. Even Terralt took a month or two to put Ynea's belly up; he can hardly deny you the same courtesy. Now, forget about it for tonight, at least, and get some sleep."

Kayli sighed again and closed her eyes obediently, mentally reciting a calming chant. The old habit was comforting in its familiarity, and at last she slept.

5

"WHAT, BY THE BRIGHT ONES, DO YOU think you're doing?"

Kayli glanced up, absently rubbing her sweaty forehead with the back of her wrist, leaving a smear of black soot behind.

"Good morn, Randon. I thought you would still be with Terralt, sorting your father's documents."

"I had to stop. My eyes were twisting up." Randon glanced around the forge. "Couldn't you wait for the boys I hired?"

Kayli laid down her scrub brush and sat back on her heels.

"I felt the need to do this work myself," she said awkwardly. She could well understand the astonishment in Randon's eyes—there was Agrond's High Lady-to-be dressed in Anida's roughest gown, covered nearly head to toe in soot, on her knees scrubbing at the stone floor of the forge with a brush. He would never understand that by her labor, a sort of self-imposed penance, she was cleansing not only the grime from the forge, but the emotional "grime" from her spirit.

When Randon said nothing, Kayli continued, "I hope you will forgive my appearance. I am accustomed to work and activity. It is difficult for me to be idle as I have been."

Randon squatted down next to Kayli, frowning slightly.

"I can sympathize with your restlessness," he said slowly,

"but, Kayli, do you have any idea what Terralt would make of this, if he stood before the ministers and told them their future High Lady was scrubbing the floor in the forge like the lowliest menial? We can afford that sort of muttering when we're confirmed, but not now. Can you understand?"

Kayli swallowed a surge of irritation—who was he to tell her she couldn't clean the very forge he'd just given her? Of course, she answered herself, he was her husband and, in this country, perhaps her only ally. And, little as she liked to admit it, what he said was true. Kayli laid down the brush and stood, waving aside the hand Randon offered for assistance.

"Bad enough that anyone should see *me* in such a state," she said wryly, "much less the Heir. You are right, of course. Please forgive my thoughtlessness."

"It's my fault," Randon said generously. "You new here, and me locked away with Terralt, of course you're bored. But what I'm doing is no more interesting. Perhaps you'd like to take advantage of Terralt's absence to visit Ynea."

Kayli flushed with guilt as she remembered her concern for the frail woman, her intention to make Endra's services available to her—all forgotten in her own selfish boredom.

"I will visit her this very afternoon," she promised. "As soon as I have bathed and dressed presentably." She hesitated. "I know you are busy, Randon, but would there be time soon to show me your city? I saw so little of your country when Terralt brought me here."

This time it was Randon's turn to hesitate.

"I don't think that's a good idea," he said at last. "You know that this marriage, the alliance with Bregond, isn't widely favored. I don't think it would be wise to present you to the public before we're confirmed High Lord and Lady, while Terralt is still a threat. Even in a closed carriage, an angry crowd could become dangerous."

Kayli was keenly disappointed, but she said nothing. Was she indeed a prisoner in this place? For a moment the stone walls seemed to close chokingly about her as the walls of the Order never had—at least in the Order no one actually prevented her from venturing outside.

Then she wondered whether Randon might not have another motive for his refusal. He would not be confirmed High Lord until his wife conceived, and until then, there was no guarantee that Kayli would be his High Lady. Randon might consider it safer to refrain from displaying a bride he might later have to set aside.

That sobering thought kept Kayli pondering as Endra prepared her bath and helped her wash the soot from her skin and hair. Randon had been so considerate that it was easy to forget that he had other concerns beyond their marriage, and that the young man who had fumbled for conversation at their first breakfast was the same lord who had played a very shrewd game of honor with his half brother and manipulated a roomful of ministers. She could not afford to trust him too completely.

Clean and presentable, Kayli found one of the palace maids and got directions to Ynea's rooms. When Ynea's personal maid announced her, she was shown into the room immediately; she was dismayed, however, to find Ynea in bed, still as pale and wan as she'd been at Kayli's wedding.

"I beg your pardon," Kayli said quickly. "I had no wish to intrude if you are ill—"

"Oh, no, please don't go," Ynea said quickly. "These days I fear this is as well as you will find me. Please stay."

A little doubtfully, Kayli sat down in the chair at the side of the bed. Ynea was obviously all but an invalid; Kayli had had no notion the woman was in such poor health.

"I came to visit with you and to offer my friendship," she said slowly. "But I also came to offer you the services of my maid Endra. She is a highly skilled midwife, and my family has relied on her for many years. She is not a mage like Brother Stevann—but neither is Brother Stevann a midwife."

"I'd be most grateful for her help. My parents, too, kept a midwife, for the women of our family always bore with difficulty." A faint flush crept into Ynea's pale cheeks. "I'd prefer Terralt didn't know. If you'd allow, I could send my maid for Endra from time to time."

"Of course." Once again, Kayli found the whole idea ridiculous. "Lady Ynea—"

"Just Ynea, please," the lady interrupted.

"Ynea," Kayli corrected. "Why would Terralt deny you the aid of my midwife? Randon said that Terralt has no faith in healers, but even so, what harm could such treatment do?

Surely he does not believe Endra would do you some ill simply because he and Randon disagree politically.''

"I'm sure he would never believe such a thing," Ynea said quickly. "But neither could he gladly accept aid from Randon—or his wife, either.''

Kayli nodded slowly. "Beliefs are powerful things," High Priestess Brisi had told her. "We build great towers of them, one atop the other. When we wish to believe a thing, we find every possible reason to do so—and when we cannot find enough reasons to suit us, we create more. It is important to question your beliefs, but even more important to question the foundations on which you have built them, for there may be weak blocks which will crumble with time or shatter under pressure, and when the tower falls, you may well fall with it.''

It suddenly occurred to Kayli that perhaps Terralt's pride and ambition were the foundation on which he had built most of his life. He had accepted the humbling role of assistant to his father only so that he could eventually gain the throne of Agrond himself, but what would become of him under Randon's rulership? He could never accept a position subservient to his brother; nor could his pride bear the humiliation of being a hanger-on in Randon's court. So for him there was only one possible choice—he must find a way to keep Randon from becoming High Lord, leaving his own way clear. Perhaps he truly believed that Randon's politics were dangerous for Agrond and that he himself was Agrond's best hope, or perhaps that was merely a block that he himself had created to support his pride and ambition.

"My father told me you and Terralt had several children already," Kayli said, glancing around curiously.

"Derrin is four years old, Avern is three, and Erisa is almost two," Ynea said with a tired smile. "They're with their nurse. Terralt hopes this child will be another son. Stevann thought it likely. If so, Terralt said I need bear no more.''

Kayli kept her peace, but looking at Ynea's thin, pale face, she knew that any midwife in Bregond would have agreed that Ynea should not have borne this child, much less any others.

"Randon said you were something of a scholar," Kayli said, deciding that a change of subject was the tactful course. "I have only studied subjects related to magic myself. In what area of knowledge did you direct your attentions?"

"Plants," Ynea said rather shyly. "I know, Terralt said it was a foolish subject for a woman of noble birth to clutter her time with, but my mother's sister was an herbalist, and she told me so many interesting things that before I knew it I was counting petals and pressing leaves. Do you see those books there?" She gestured at several thick volumes on table across the room. "They are part of my collection."

"Only part?" Kayli stepped over and touched one of the books, glancing at Ynea. "May I?"

"Please," Ynea said eagerly. "Bring it here if you like."

Kayli picked up the top volume and carried it over. Flipping through the pages, she inhaled softly with amazement. The front of each page was covered with neat, skilled drawings of a plant, detailing petal tip to rootlets, with a pressed leaf and blossom, seemingly preservation-spelled, affixed to the page. The back of the page was covered in a fine, neat script, describing the plant, its growing habits and uses.

"How many such volumes have you done?" Kayli asked, awed. Even a single book represented an incredible amount of work, a marvelous eye for detail, and an amazing talent.

"Fourteen." Ynea flushed faintly again. "I'm ashamed to say my work has been neglected since Derrin was born. They are in order, you know," she said hastily, as if to excuse herself.

"Order?" Kayli leafed through the book, wrinkling her forehead. She had some knowledge of the more common flora of Bregond, but these Agrondish plants were strange to her.

"Order of blooming," Ynea explained, showing Kayli the blooming dates. "Flowering plants are grouped in order of blooming; there are separate volumes for spring bloomers, then summer, then fall. Trees are classified the same way, and vines, and brambles. Nonblossoming plants and grasses are grouped by their habitat and leaf shape."

Kayli shook her head again. Sages and herbalists had studied the plants of Bregond, but surely they had no cataloging system as impressive as this.

"Once when Second Circle Priestess Vayavara said that my concentration was wandering," Kayli remembered, "she took me out onto the plains and bade me count all the different grasses which grew there. I found forty-one different grasses in those hours, and though I had walked or rode across those grasses a thousand times, it was as if I had never truly seen that land before in my life. It makes it all magical, somehow— so much hidden from my eyes by my own blindness.''

"Exactly so," Ynea said eagerly, a slight sparkle lighting her eyes. "It's like having a secret treasure, knowing what nobody else knows. Why, your husband, Randon, rides out to hunt over and past these plants and never sees them. Terralt tramples them under his boot soles and never knows it. The assistant cooks gather a few, never knowing how many others they pass by."

Kayli was glad to see the excitement in Ynea's eyes. She remembered her own pride when Vayavara had nodded approvingly as Kayli had laid out each blade of grass, describing the shape of the seeds, the length of the leaves, the thick or narrow ribs. What warmth had grown in Kayli's heart when Vayavara had given her a small smile, saying, "When High Priestess Brisi set me the same task, I found only thirty-four kinds."

"I would be greatly honored if you would allow me to study your books," Kayli said, closing the volume. Ynea had taken enough pride in her work to have some leatherworker make an ornately tooled cover. "All I knew of Agrond was that it was a land of rain, mud, and lush crops, like a fabled paradise. But these books make it real, your words and pictures. I would very much like to share your secret, if you would permit it."

"I would like that," Ynea said shyly. "Very much. And perhaps you would tell me about the plants that grow in Bregond. I'd be interested in knowing how they differ from ours."

"You would be wiser to ask Endra that," Kayli said, laughing. "She knows most of the medicinal plants and herbs, while all I could tell you are the plants to avoid and the forage every child learns—plus, of course, forty-one varieties of plains grass. And I have no skill at all in drawing." Kayli thought for a moment, then smiled. "But Devra does."

"Devra?" Ynea prompted.

"One of my maids." Kayli patted the book. "Do you know, if you have an interest in Bregondish plants, and I wished to instruct you, what would be more natural than that I should bring Devra, who can draw, to assist me, and also Endra, who knows so many more herbs than I do? And how natural, too, that she might bring with her herbs she has brought from Bregond, to show you the leaves and roots and blossoms? And if your husband should ask how we occupied our time, you could show him the pages of the new volume you have begun on the plant life of Bregond.''

Ynea understood then, and she chuckled.

"Terralt said you were cleverer than he expected," she said. "In a way that pleases him, and troubles him, too."

"Pleases and troubles him?" Kayli asked slowly.

"You're the sort of woman he would have wished for his wife," Ynea said plainly, not meeting Kayli's eyes. "He admires the quickness of your wit and speech, your—strength." She folded her thin, pale hands over her swollen belly. "What I know from my studies, from my books, is useless to him. I heard one of the guards tell another how you stood with Randon in the council chamber. I could never have done such a thing, stood up in front of the ministers and found the right words to say. I'm weak in many ways, and I think Terralt despises that weakness."

A pang of sympathy pierced Kayli's heart, and she laid her own scarred brown hand over Ynea's slender white ones. Kayli had trained for years to maintain her composure, and still in the short time she'd known Terralt, he had managed to irritate and disturb her. How much more he must have intimidated gently reared Ynea! Briefly Kayli wondered how Ynea might have blossomed had she wed a gentle, understanding man like Randon.

"You belittle yourself too much," Kayli chided. "You have taught yourself lessons that came hard to me, patience and the ability to see all around you what—"

The door opened, interrupting her. Terralt entered, a wary expression on his face.

"Good afternoon," he said, bowing briefly to Kayli. "Randon said you might come to see Ynea this afternoon. It was kind of you to trouble yourself. As she's usually too weak to leave her room, her days are rather dull."

"It was no trouble," Kayli said, stifling an impatient frown at Terralt's failure to greet his own wife and his way of speaking as if Ynea were not present. "It was kind of Ynea to receive me. I was glad to learn we share so many interests." She turned to Ynea. "Which volumes are concerned with the flowers that bloom now? I would borrow those, if I may."

"The one you hold, and the two on top of the stack," Ynea said a little timidly, glancing at Terralt as if for permission. "And I do thank you for your companionship, Lady Kayli."

"It was my pleasure," Kayli said firmly, squeezing Ynea's hand. "I will come again soon, and we can begin discussing the plants of Bregond."

"Oh, by the Bright Ones, not more plants," Terralt groaned. "Isn't fourteen books of leaves and roots enough?"

"Do you object, Terralt?" Kayli said, confronting Terralt squarely. "I would think that you would welcome any diversion I could bring your wife."

"Oh, do as you please," Terralt said irritably. "As long as *I* don't have to listen to it."

Kayli sighed with exaggerated disappointment.

"Then however it must gall us, we will forgo the pleasure of your presence," she said. "But somehow we will bear the lack of your amiable conversation and doubtless extensive knowledge of Bregondish flora."

Terralt broke into a grin.

"My lady, I fear I've had all too close an acquaintance with the greenery of Bregond," he said, "as my tattered trousers will testify. But I'll gladly leave you women to your bushes and weeds, and I'd do so now except that Stevann wants to call upon Ynea for her daily pokings and potions—much good they've done, as you can see. And as Randon was groaning for his supper, doubtless he'd appreciate the return of his bride."

Well, as much as she liked Ynea's company, Kayli had no desire to sup with Terralt. She quickly took leave of Ynea and hurried back to her rooms to stack the books on the table. She had thought that surely Randon had already gone down to supper, but he was there waiting for her, and his smile when he saw her (although it may have only been eagerness for his supper, as Terralt had said) brought an answering warmth to her heart.

"There you are!" he said. "Crept away on me again. Visiting Ynea, were you?"

"Of course," Kayli said, surprised. Hadn't Randon himself suggested it?

"How is she?" he asked after a moment's hesitation. "At our wedding it seemed as if she was doing poorly."

"I am no healer, nor midwife," Kayli said slowly. "But I have seen no healthy woman, even advanced in pregnancy, so pale or weak. Stevann was coming to her even as I left, but I must see that Endra has the chance to examine her." She shook her head. "Terralt said you were wanting your supper."

"I am, and so should you be, after your busy day." Randon grinned. He took the books from Kayli and laid them down on a table. "Ynea's books of plants. She must have liked you very much to lend them to you." He took her hand and led her to the door. "You know, if it would help, I could keep Terralt busy in the study from time to time. There are always plenty of tasks for him, work important enough that his pride wouldn't let him refuse. Poor Ynea would be all the better for your friendship, however little Terralt might like it."

Kayli so enjoyed her supper in Randon's jovial company that she felt a little guilty—Ynea was sweet and kind, but her very delicacy and weakness made Kayli uncomfortable. Even her sister Laalen, sickly by Bregondish standards, was no invalid. Kayli did not know how to behave with such a languid, frail person; why, she had spent so little time in court in the last few years that she could hardly manage polite conversation, and that was one of the thirty-nine arts that all marriageable Bregondish ladies of noble birth were expected to master.

Randon, however, was another matter. He may have preferred hunting and riding to scholarship, but apparently he'd enjoyed court enough to excel in polite chatter; he could seemingly talk forever, effortlessly slipping to another subject whenever her interest began to wane, entertaining her so skillfully that only occasionally did she even realize that he rarely said anything of consequence.

At first Kayli had wondered at his courtly manner when Terralt had said that Randon was unpopular among the nobility. As Randon spoke of his friends at court, however, she realized that most of them had come from the guild houses and craft halls of Agrond rather than from the gently born noble families. She had heard of Agrond's intricate and rather confusing guild system—the Bregondish structure of guilds was far less formalized—but it seemed to her that the guilds had great political influence in Agrond. She wondered whether Randon had considered the possible leverage of his guild alliances.

Kayli knew, too, the supreme importance of Agrond's agricultural industry. She'd heard stories of what a fertile land Agrond was, the soil rich with water, green things springing up from every inch of earth, but she had never actually understood how the cultivation of plants could be the very lifeblood of a whole country. Of course it would have to be so; Agrond's population was so great, the whole country would have to be covered with herds to feed so many, and its lush greenery would quickly be grazed down to the bare earth. The sheer importance of agriculture in Agrond explained to Kayli, too, how Lord Kereg had come to act as the spokesman for the ministers despite his short tenure among them. That boded ill for Randon, if Lord Kereg favored Terralt.

Kayli suddenly realized that Randon had stopped talking and was gazing at her somewhat ruefully.

"I've done it again, haven't I?" he said with a sigh. "I'm sorry. I just don't know what to say to you, the way you sit there so quietly, gazing at me as if you were drinking my words like wine. Then I realize I'm gibbering like a mistwitted beggar."

"I beg your pardon," Kayli said quickly. "Often I feel that I know nothing of the matters of which you speak. It seems easier to let you talk and learn from what you say than to speak when I have nothing to contribute to the conversation but my igorance. I hope I have not offended you."

Randon sighed, and Kayli felt that she had somehow disappointed him by her answer.

"Not at all," he said with a smile. "Have a little more of the soup. Oh, and we'll have to cancel our ride tomorrow. We're in audience in the morning."

"Audience?" A sensation very like panic made Kayli's stomach flop over. "You—we—are in audience, although we are not confirmed as High Lord and Lady?"

Randon gave her a rueful grin.

"Agrond trudges on, whether we're confirmed or not," he said. "My father is dead. That leaves you and me to sit in audience—or Terralt."

"Has Terralt been sitting in audience since your father died?" Kayli asked, appalled. How presumptuous could Terralt be? And how could the ministers, however much they favored Terralt, have permitted it?

"No." Randon shook his head. "The most pressing matters have been heard by the ministers, but most business has been postponed. There's quite a backlog waiting to be heard, and Lord Kereg quite properly reminded me of my duty—*our* duty—as presumptive rulers."

"Are you certain you wish me to sit beside you in these audiences?" Kayli asked. By the same logic by which Randon would not take her into town, it might be an embarrassment for her to appear publicly in audience. A sudden unexpected empathy for his difficult position forced her to give him a polite escape. "My ignorance of Agrondish law and custom would make any opinion of mine questionable at best."

Randon raised one eyebrow.

"Then it's also a fresh viewpoint, something I might find very useful indeed. Besides, I haven't done this any more often than you have. Do you think I want to go out there and face those people alone?"

He grinned and raised his goblet.

"Besides, it'll let some of the people have their first good look at their new High Lady."

Startled, Kayli glanced at him, wondering if he had somehow read her thoughts. His eyes were sparkling at her as if they shared a joke, and she thought wryly that perhaps they did.

Still her stomach fluttered and she had lost all appetite for her food. Her wedding had been such a hasty thing, she'd had little enough time to brood, and what time she'd had, she had worried selfishly about her marriage and her husband, not about her duties as High Lady of a country with which she was completely unfamiliar. She had rarely observed her mother and father in audience, and even then she had paid more attention to the cases and the decisions her parents had rendered than she had to the *process* by which the High Lord and Lady of Bregond had made those decisions. How, she wondered dismally, had her mother and father come up with so much wisdom?

"Do you worry," she said softly, "about what sort of High Lord you will make?"

Randon chuckled.

"Only about ten times an hour, day and night," he said. "I can't even remember the last time I saw Father in audience. I always thought that tiresome stuff was something I'd rather leave to Father and Terralt. Then suddenly that tiresome stuff is *my* responsibility, and it's frightening. Terralt's right—I'm like a new rider who stupidly thinks he can hop onto the fieriest horse in the stables and ride it without taking a fall. Only if I can't ride this particular horse, I won't be the only one taking a fall; I might take my whole country with me."

Kayli reached over to clasp his hand.

"Then we must hope that two can hold on more tightly than one," she said with a calmness which surprised her. "I wonder why, if Terralt takes the welfare of Agrond so seriously, he, too, does not feel such fear."

Randon raised an eyebrow as if the thought was new to him.

"While Father was alive he was really only Father's assistant, however much he could act like the High Lord himself," he said at last. "Terralt's never actually sat in the seat when his decisions were entirely his own, so he's never felt that weight. It only hit me sooner, I suspect, because my life changed so drastically, while Terralt's gone on just as he always has. I suppose he thinks it would be no different if he was High Lord in truth."

Later in their quarters, lying comfortably in her husband's arms, Kayli remembered the rather wistful tone in which he had answered her question. Did Randon envy Terralt his self-assurance, even if it arose from ignorance?

The memory of the speaking crystal tucked carefully away pricked at Kayli's mind. Oh, how she wished for Brisi's wise counsel right now! Perhaps Kairi, too, would have some advice, or at least reassurance, to give her. But she could no longer lean on her mentor or her family for guidance. And it would be questionable at best for her to seek advice in Bregond on the governing of Agrond.

Kayli sighed and relentlessly disciplined her mind into calm. She'd be of no use to Randon or Agrond in her present confusion. Whether or not she actually felt confident in her role as High Lady, she must at least seem so for Randon's sake.

At least it could be no more difficult than journeying to a strange country, being beset by Sarkondish raiders, marrying and bedding and being Awakened by a man she'd never met. That thought gave her comfort even as it drew her down into sleep.

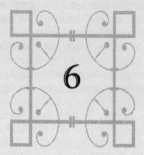

6

BY MIDMORNING, KAYLI DECIDED SHE HAD BEEN
half-right. Sitting in audience as High Lady of Bregond
was, in fact, no more difficult than journeying to a
strange country, being beset by Sarkondish raiders, marrying
and bedding and being Awakened by a man she'd never met;
however, it was far more disagreeable.

In Bregond each of the clans had at least one adjudicator,
studied in Bregondish law to settle ordinary disputes. Small
towns and villages relied on the adjudicators of the clans that
passed through with the seasonal circuit of the herds. Some
cases were, of course, too large for the adjudicators' authority;
other matters fell on the gray line where the law was unclear.
At times adjudicators might feel they were biased and should
not rule on a case; sometimes, too, two or more adjudicators
might hear a case and disagree amongst themselves. Those
matters only were brought before the High Lord and Lady.

In Agrond there appeared to be no adjudicators. The noble
houses themselves judged many cases in the lands which they
held, but they had no special training in the law and often
their own interests were involved, making their decisions questionable. Larger cities had a system of governors and judges,
but their concentration was on punishing crime rather than
settling civil disputes. So, apparently, these cases came before

the High Lord and Lady. After listening to Randon rule on two farmers' squabble over six bushels of turnips harvested from a patch of disputed field, Kayli wondered how the royal house of Bregond had any time for rulership. When the farmers left, she quietly asked Randon as much.

"Don't worry," he whispered back. "I'm told we only have to do this two mornings in each sevenday. We'll sit a bit oftener, though, until some of this backlog is cleared up."

Unfamiliar with Agrondish law, Kayli preferred to sit quietly and nod at Randon's judgments; several times she noticed that if she'd ruled by Bregondish principles, the result would have been quite different. Near noon, however, a case arose which interested her. Two lords had come with a dispute over a large area of land which included a good-sized town and many farms. Each had brought surveys, maps, and deeds to prove their claim, and a spokesman from the town had come, too.

After studying the documents, it was plain that a simple mistake had been made long ago when the course of a river which had marked the division of the lands had been diverted to irrigate the farms. By Agrondish law, both lords had a legal claim to the land. The dispute had never been resolved, but the two noble houses had shared governorship of the land and the town, dividing the taxes and harvest tithes equally. Because of last year's poor harvest, however, the land had yielded little income to the lords and the previously amiable disagreement had dissolved into hostility.

Randon was stymied, but Kayli had heard at the Order of a similar case, and she gestured to the townsman to come forward.

"Until now, both houses have shared in the income provided by your farms," Kayli said. "How have they shared in their responsibilities? Who provided protection for the people?"

"Lord Ethen and Lord Reive have always divided the duty, High Lady," the man said a little hesitantly. "But last year's harvest was poor, as they've said, and when we couldn't pay the taxes due, Lord Reive withdrew his men."

"But Lord Ethen's guards have continued to protect the village?" Kayli asked.

"Yes, High Lady." The man hesitated almost imperceptibly before speaking the title.

"Then, Lord Ethen, the lands and town are yours," Kayli said, inclining her head to the lord. "Duty is not the servant of profit, and a lord who will not protect his lands and people in poverty as well as plenty does not deserve to hold them. The deeds and title to the land will be rewritten accordingly."

Lord Ethen and Lord Reive glanced from Kayli to Randon and back again, and for an anxious moment Kayli thought Lord Reive would protest, but at last both lords bowed and turned silently away, and she breathed a silent sigh of relief.

"You may have won us an ally," Randon murmured as the lords took their papers to the court scribe. "Lord Ethen is influential with other nobility in the area, and he's always supported Terralt."

"And Lord Reive?" Kayli asked as quietly.

"Well, he supported Terralt, too," Randon admitted. "But to tell you the truth, I think you impressed him a bit. As you did me," he added. "That case had me puzzled."

His praise warmed Kayli's heart, and the reception of her first decision as High Lady of Agrond bolstered her confidence. For the remainder of the morning she took a more active role in judging the cases brought before them. When the servants closed the doors for dinner, however, Kayli was vastly relieved, surprised to discover how tense and anxious she'd been.

She was surprised, too, when Terralt joined them at the table for dinner.

"I sat at the back and watched most of the hearings," he said between bites of roast fowl. "Not bad for your first audience, although I doubt the clenched hands and white knuckles impressed anyone."

"I'm sure it reassured them to know that I didn't take my judgments casually," Randon said, grinning. "I'll be satisfied if I ever become accustomed to the job enough that every new case doesn't set my stomach to twisting. I think Kayli has more talent for this sort of thing than I do."

Terralt glanced up from his plate, his eyes twinkling mockingly.

"I'd be inclined to agree," he said.

Randon, however, refused to take offense.

"Then you'll have to teach me," he said to Kayli. "Laws vary from land to land, but justice at least remains constant."

"Or injustice," Terralt muttered, but Kayli chose to ignore the remark.

"I promised Kayli a ride in the country, and I believe I'll take her this afternoon," Randon said at last. "The Bright Ones know we could use a little fresh air. Would you care to come, Terralt?"

"Thank you, no," Terralt said, shaking his head resignedly. "Maybe you can spend an afternoon in idleness, Randon, but I can't. You gave me those figures to check against the stores, remember? And then Lord Ethen and Lord Reive have invited me to supper while they're in town."

"Well, that should be pleasant," Randon said, chuckling. "If they're speaking to each other at all after this morning's judgment, that is."

"It's a pity the quarrel ever had to come this far," Terralt said, shrugging. "Their houses have lived in peace for generations." He turned to Kayli. "If you'd simply ordered Lord Reive to live up to his half of the responsibility for those lands, the town would've been that much better off and *both* lords would've walked away smiling. Reive's son was due to wed Ethen's daughter this summer anyway, so that would've solved the whole problem. Now the wedding will likely be canceled, at least until Reive stops sulking, which may take a year or two."

Terralt's statement troubled Kayli deeply. Suddenly she was ashamed of her pride in her decision. She'd made a judgment without knowing all the facts, and the peace between two noble houses would suffer for it.

"Terralt, Kayli hasn't had time to toss sweetmeats to the nobility as you have," Randon said patiently. "She'd hardly be expected to know the family situation of every noble house in Agrond, or even to remember them in her first audience if she did. The Bright Ones know *I* didn't know about the wedding, so it's hardly common knowledge. And you can lay a fair share of the blame on yourself, too. Lady Aville came up to advise me on points of law at least a dozen times; you could've put a quiet word in Kayli's ear or mine, and we'd have thanked you for it.''

"Really?'' Terralt drawled. "I thought you wanted me to keep my mouth shut except by your express invitation.''

Randon set down his goblet and faced Terralt squarely.

"If it gives you pleasure to exercise your spite in silence and inaction, do so,'' he said levelly. "But don't come to me or Kayli later and blame us for not possessing information you could have—*should* have—given us. Kayli, if you've finished your supper, I suggest we go. I'm suddenly inclined to leave Terralt to his figures and his social maneuvers.''

Kayli felt it wisest that she not intervene this time between Randon and Terralt, so she said nothing, only followed Randon quietly back to their rooms, where she changed into her riding clothes. When she emerged from the dressing room, Randon had already donned a simple tunic and trousers.

"I had to arrange for guards to ride with us,'' he said ruefully. "I never needed them when I was only Terendal's ne'er-do-well younger son. Now, though, as High Lord presumptive, it's not safe for me to ride out alone, especially if you're with me, I'm afraid. Well, I see you're ready. Why don't you help me saddle the mare—Carada, I think you called her—and I can try her paces.''

Maja was glad to see Kayli, and Randon handled Carada so confidently that Kayli was certain the mare would give him no trouble. He had a little difficulty with the high Bregondish saddle, and it took him a little practice to master the long single rein and the foot and knee commands Kayli showed him, but at last he got himself settled comfortably.

Kayli was a little dismayed by the size of their escort—there were eight guards, all fully armed and armored—but she fairly trembled to get out of the walled castle and see Agrond, to feel fresh wind through her hair. Maja danced in her eagerness to stretch her legs, and it was with some impatience that Kayli fell in behind the four guards riding in front of her and Randon.

When the palace gates opened, Kayli thought eagerly that she'd get a good look at Tarkesh, but although they emerged into the city, the guards turned quickly, almost hastily, onto a small side road which reached one of the city gates in a surprisingly short time. Even the brief glimpse of Tarkesh, however, impressed her with the vast size of the city. Most of the buildings were of wood, which in itself was a wonder; Bregondish buildings were made of bricks of mud and dried grass or, less frequently, of stone. There was an amazing proliferation here of businesses, both shops and mobile vendors hawking their wares from small stands, carts, or baskets. Kayli stared at the unfamiliar fruits and vegetables so longingly that Randon could do nothing but call the whole procession to a halt and buy her a small basket of bright red berries to nibble as they rode. The merchant would not accept Randon's coin, only smiling proudly as he pressed the basket into Randon's hand, but he gave Kayli a glance that was far less friendly. As they rode on, Kayli saw a good many more hostile expressions, some directed at Randon but more at her. Perhaps Randon had spoken the simple truth about the dangers of riding through the city.

The guards at the gate seemed surprised to see their High Lord arrive unexpectedly in his riding clothes, but they opened the gates, and Kayli sighed with relief. Somehow she'd half expected to be confined to the city, just as the citizens of the city seemed determined to keep her prisoner in the castle.

Before her stretched the fields of Agrond, and Kayli could only sit silently gaping for a moment, awed by all that green just as she had been when she'd first left Bregond. But this was not wild, unsettled lands; these were the famed fields of Agrond, lush and green and tall already, even though it was only the end of spring, and all that greenness would one day be food. Kayli was astounded by the sheer enormity of it all. It seemed incomprehensible that she could be utterly *surrounded* by food. Why, surely what she was looking at alone could feed most of Bregond through the cold season!

"Impressive, isn't it?" Randon said, interrupting her thoughts. "And that's just the first harvest of the year. We'll get another in mid-autumn if the weather's good."

"Two harvests?" Kayli said, very quietly. "You can grow all this food from this land and harvest *twice* in a year?"

Randon chuckled.

"We can thank Bregond and Sarkond for that, although the farmers seldom do," he said. "The worst of the weather seems to vent its fury on your plains and Sarkond's foothills and moderates before it reaches us. Flooding's a bigger problem.''

She could well imagine. Everywhere she looked there were small streams or large streams, muddy or running clear over gravel. She wondered if she'd ever seen so much water at one time in her life, except possibly the stormy night she'd fled with Terralt across Agrond. To Bregondish plainsfolk, all this water was a treasure even greater than the fields.

"It is beautiful," she admitted. "But, Randon, where can you possibly hunt in all this settlement?"

"We'll be out of the fields very shortly," he told her. "As soon as we cross the Coridowyn, there are no more farms; because of the levees on this side, the land floods too often there, so it's clear riding all the way to the forest."

They passed fields and more fields, and it shocked Kayli to the depths of her spirit to realize that this was only a small part of the farms around Tarkesh, and the farms around Tarkesh were only a small part of the farms throughout Agrond. What a wonderful and terrifying prospect—so much food, enough to feed a huge population, and yet a system so delicate because it depended on the whims of the weather. Why, a drought here could be even more devastating than in Bregond. Water holes and streams on the plains were few, but the plants and animals (and people) of Bregond had accustomed themselves to a harsher, drier climate.

Kayli had looked so eagerly for the Coridowyn, hungry for her first glimpse of a real river, that she was disappointed when she finally caught sight of the thin line snaking across the land, edged with a straggly fringe of brush and saplings. The river itself was less than a dozen man-heights wide, and that, Randon told her, was as big as it usually got, due to the recent rain. The water was muddy, too, and even the plants at the river's edge were heavily silted. Altogether it was a draggled and unimpressive sight.

The bridge, however, more than made up for Kayli's disappointment in the river, for it was a marvel of engineering the like of which she had never imagined. The huge stone-and-beam structure straddled the little river like a giant dipping its toes in the muddy water, and it made Kayli a little breathless to ride over it so casually. She wondered whether anyone had dared to bridge the fabled Dezarin, and when she asked Randon, she was a little chagrined to see that he laughed heartily.

"The Dezarin? I doubt if there's enough stone in the country for that task," he said. "And anything we built would wash away like twigs at the first flood. Nobody even lives too close to the Dezarin, for she bursts out of her banks regularly and sweeps away everything she touches. Someday I'll take you to meet the lady herself. I'm sure you'll find her far more interesting than this little whelp."

When they crossed the river, true to Randon's word, there were no more farms or fields, only open land and, far ahead, the dark green fuzz of a forest. But this was no plain such as Kayli had known all her life; this was what Agrond called open country, full of brush and wildflowers and low-growing green things. A thousand new fragrances overwhelmed Kayli's nose.

Randon leaned over so he could speak to her softly.

"These guards have been leading long enough," he said, grinning. "Want to see if they can keep up with us?"

Kayli smiled back and, without replying, gave Maja's sides a gentle squeeze with her knees, leaning forward as she did so. Maja immediately launched herself forward, full out, passing the guards as if they were stones at the roadside; to her delight, Randon was not far behind her. Kayli laughed at the shouts that faded with gratifying rapidity behind her. Even Randon gradually lost ground, as Maja had a lead and Kayli was a lighter load. At last, however, she heard him calling her, and she signaled Maja to slow and stop, letting Randon catch up.

"Remind me never to race you again," he said, laughing. "And I thought Terralt was exaggerating when he said it was your mare dragging his along, not the other way around. But better stop for a moment. The guards are in a panic back there; their horses tired out long ago under all that weight."

Kayli sighed and waited for the guards to catch up, after which she and Randon received a lecture from the captain as to why the High Lord and Lady should never leave the range of the guards' protection, and why the High Lord and Lady should never race along at such dangerous speeds anyway.

The guards were thwarted in their overprotectiveness, however, for Randon and Kayli had several good runs over the level ground. Kayli wished wistfully for her bow, for she saw any quantity of small game, but Randon assured her that there would be many other opportunities, and someday soon they'd go boar hunting in the forest. They rode until even Maja and Carada were tired, then made their way slowly back to the castle.

There was no time to bathe and dress before supper, so Randon had a tray sent up to their quarters and they ate just as they were, smelling of leather and horses and laughing over their meat buns and boiled tubers. After supper they had their baths, and they were not too tired to end the evening in each other's arms in front of the fire.

"So, our first audience," Randon mused, stroking Kayli's hair. "Now we've been through the fire."

"What?" His choice of phrase startled her, and she raised herself up to look at him.

"Well, it wasn't too bad, was it?" Randon said, not understanding. "I suppose it will get easier with time."

So he had viewed this morning as a sort of firewalk indeed, a proving of his worthiness. Kayli sighed, remembering that she had been denied her first firewalk. Her own worthiness had never been tested. Now that she had been Awakened, she could still make a firewalk, and would, but it would not be the same as the wonderful, terrible ritual for which she had prepared so painstakingly, entrusting herself to the flames while, as a novice, she still had no immunity to their fiery embrace. She would have to be careless now, her concentration fail her utterly, for a firewalk to do her harm, and for that very reason, it could never mean as much to her. She would never know that moment of purest faith again.

And Randon would never have the chance to know it at all.

"What do you believe?" she asked him.

"Hmmm?" Apparently surprised by the change of subject, Randon turned over to face her. "What do you mean?"

"You speak sometimes of the Bright Ones," she said by way of explanation. "Are they deities that you worship?"

"Hmmm. Worship? I don't know about that," Randon said slowly. "We call them the Bright Sisters, too. It's the moon and the sun, of course. By day, the sun makes the plants grow; by night, her sister the moon controls the change of the seasons. The farmers make offerings to them, and the family has a few token public rituals, but I can't say we *worship* nowadays, not for a few generations, at least. What about you? You speak of fire sometimes as if you worshiped it.''

"The Flame?" Kayli hesitated, wondering if her knowledge of Agrondish was sufficient to explain. ''The Flame is not a god, not a . . . consciousness, in the way you speak of your Bright Ones. The Flame is a force, a power. Of all things, it was the first that came into being when the universe was born. First there was the great darkness, and in the heart of that darkness, a single spark that grew slowly into the Flame. And the Flame flung its sparks far and wide, and some of those sparks cooled and became Earth—such as our world—and from the womb of Earth, Water and Wind were born. Other sparks burned on, and in the sky we can see them, especially in the darkness of night. The sun is such a fire, giving us light and warmth. And even in our cooled world, the Flame lives in fire. A memory of it lives in stone and metal, else how could fire be struck from flint and steel? And it burns in some people, in their flesh and in their spirit, and in Bregond, those people are taught to use that power for the good of our people. We have rituals, but they are not worship, more like a—a focus of concentration, perhaps.''

"A spell?" Randon suggested. "Like Stevann uses."

"Words and gestures to focus his power?" Kayli asked.

"Yes."

"A spell, then, yes." Kayli brought into life again the small flame in her hand, showed him its dancing light. "As I learn more, I will need such rituals only for complicated magics. So my rituals are not worship as one would worship a deity. And we may ask the wind to bring us rain, or the earth to yield us food, but we are not speaking to a deity so much as—as to a power within ourselves.''

"Mmmm." Randon rolled over suddenly so that Kayli lay on her back, his face just above hers. "And suppose *I* wanted to speak to something within you. How would I go about that?''

Kayli laughed a little.

"Then I would suggest," she murmured, "that you use a language without words."

The next days fell into a pattern that Kayli feared would represent the rest of her life. Every other morning there were audiences until midday, sometimes later. If there was no audience, she would spend her morning studying. In the afternoon she would visit with Ynea, or study if Randon was still sorting his father's old business; if he was free, they might discuss the day's judgments, or they might sit down with Terralt or one or more of the ministers to discuss the complexities of Agrondish law or to sign documents and proclamations that needed their approval. Sometimes work continued at the supper table, where Terralt might or might not join them.

After supper, however, Randon insisted, to Kayli's relief, that the High Lord and Lady had retired for the evening, and he and Kayli would have their time together uninterrupted. Unfortunately this usually meant retreating to their quarters, locking the door, and ignoring the knocks that inevitably came. Kayli appreciated the quiet time, but when days passed and she realized that she had set foot outside the castle only once since she arrived, she almost despaired, wondering how Ynea could bear such confinement.

But bear it Ynea must. Endra returned from her first visit with the frail lady very troubled.

"She should never have borne this child," Endra said without preamble. "I suspect she should not have borne the three before it. If I'd seen her sooner, I'd have given her a potion to lose the child, if she were strong enough, which I doubt. If she follows my orders strictly and this mage of hers is quite good, she may live. And then again, she may die." Endra shook her head disgustedly. "She's only ten years and seven, did you know that? Hardly two years out of her first decade when her husband put her belly up. Shame to the father who would barter off his daughter to bear at such an age, and shame to the healer who let it happen, and shame to the husband who couldn't keep his manhood in his trousers long enough to let his wife grow out of childhood. And I'd say so and more to him if I was let."

"Then he would say you were not to see his wife again," Kayli said patiently, "and Ynea, who will not speak against him, would lack your care altogether. So curb your temper, I beg you, and help Ynea as best you can. And whatever medicines you require, if Stevann cannot procure them for you, I will send to Bregond for them.'' Kayli thought, but did not say, that she would be just as glad if Endra kept a full stock of all her medicines, in case Kayli herself should suffer such difficulties.

Something in her expression must have revealed her thoughts, however, for the midwife laid a hand on her arm and smiled reassuringly.

''You'll have no such trouble, lady,'' Endra said. ''Believe me. Your cycles are regular and you have health and strength, and if I tell you you must drink blackroot tea between your children to prevent you from bearing too close together, you and Randon have the sense to listen.''

Kayli thought wryly that she had little enough use for blackroot tea. The arrival of her courses proved that she had not yet conceived, and although Randon had assured her that it was of no consequence, that nobody expected her to conceive so soon, she had been disappointed and knew that he was, too. She had asked Endra whether she ought not try a different fertility potion, but Endra had only shook her head and said that whatever High Priestess Brisi had prepared, it was likely far superior to anything she could mix together. Kayli took the potion faithfully every night, even though it made her feel a little ill afterward and sometimes her stomach cramped painfully.

Ironically, although it was her Order-trained self-discipline which sustained her, Kayli wondered whether that same training had not spoiled her for life at court. Although her days at the Order had been as busy and her free time as scarce as now, there had been a general tone of accomplishment, of peace, of—well, order—to her time. Here she felt hurried and frustrated and often ignorant, and even the decisions she made gave her no sense of accomplishment, usually leaving her worrying for hours whether she had made the right judgment.

Randon was kind, and she knew he would understand her worries, but she could confide in him least of all. The Flame knew he had worries enough without the addition of hers, but more than that, despite their marriage, Randon remained essentially a stranger to her, someone with perhaps very different goals and purposes. She was his wife, but she was also, of necessity, a means to an end for him—and a replaceable means, too. That knowledge, and the importance of the child she must bear, remained a wall between them.

When her courses ceased, Kayli went to Stevann to ask whether he knew any spells to aid in fertility.

"There are no spells I know," Stevann told her, "to assure pregnancy. Healers try not to interfere with the natural process; I've heard that in the savage west there were once powerful magics used to speed the growth of an unborn child, but it was found to be too dangerous to mother and child."

"High Priestess Brisi gave me a fertility potion," Kayli said, handing Stevann the flask. "Is not the conception of Randon's heir worth some risk?"

"Mmm." Stevann sniffed the vial, frowned, and shook his head. "It doesn't smell like any of the fertility potions I'm familiar with, but then the herbs in Bregond would be different. It's usually not a sound practice to mix potions by two different mages. Give your potion time to work. If you haven't conceived in a few months, we'll see what can be done."

Kayli was not satisfied with his answer, but there was little she could do to change his mind, especially when Randon agreed with the healer. So she did the only thing she could do: she waited, and she fulfilled her duties as best she could, and she tried to master the speaking crystal.

It took, in fact, several days to learn the simple twist of her thoughts to activate the crystal. Once she had the trick of it, she was surprised at the simplicity of the technique. She chose to try the crystal in late afternoon, when she knew the High Priestess usually set aside time to meditate, and was gratified by the immediacy with which her mentor's face appeared in the crystal. Even more gratifying, however, was the calm lack of surprise with which Brisi recognized the caller.

"So you have mastered the speaking crystal," she said serenely. "You look well, my student, although I had word that your caravan was set upon. Your parents were frantic with worry when two of your maids returned to tell of the attack. A fire-scrying told me you had escaped, but were gravely ill, and the country was in an uproar until High Lord Randon's envoys arrived to say that you were safe and had recovered, and that the wedding had taken place. Your mother and father have dispatched another caravan to Agrond, as I understand.''

"I thank you for the tidings of my family," Kayli said, relieved to learn that her maids had escaped. "But what has transpired at the Order since I left?"

"But for your absence, little has changed," Brisi told her. "But all will be glad to hear your tidings."

Kayli hardly knew where to begin, so much had happened since she left home, but High Priestess Brisi listened patiently until she had finished. When she was done, however, she was surprised when Brisi laughed gently.

"And you worried because you were unable to make your first firewalk here," the High Priestess said, smiling. "Kayli, you have completed a firewalk the likes of which few of our novices ever dream. If the Flame were to find you unworthy after such trials, no living soul could be deemed fit. Continue to study as you are able, and have no fear on that account."

"My greatest concern is another matter," Kayli said hesitantly. "As you know, it is urgent that I bear Randon's heir. Yet despite the potion you gave me, I have not yet conceived, and—"

Brisi chuckled.

"Kayli, you are hardly a month out of the temple," she said. "Only a miracle could make you conceive so quickly. The people of Agrond must simply be patient for a little longer. Continue to take the potion I gave you; I have sent a further supply to your parents, who will send it on with their caravan. And practice your meditations more often. I have heard it said that excessive worry can prevent conception."

"Yes, High Priestess." Kayli was no more satisfied than she had been by Stevann's and Endra ressurances, but there was nothing to do but obey. Brisi seemed pleased with her progress in her studies, which cheered her somewhat; she'd expected to advance far more quickly after her Awakening. She was reluctant to say good-bye to her teacher, and when Randon knocked on the door, she was only just putting the crystal back into its pouch.

Randon glanced around puzzledly when he entered the room.

"I thought I heard voices," he said. "I thought perhaps one of the maids was in the room."

"No, I was speaking with High Priestess Brisi of the Order of Inner Flame," Kayli said, showing him the crystal. "She gave me this speaking crystal before I left, trusting that I could use it later. With it I can speak to any mage in Bregond who holds such a crystal. I hope to reach my sister Kairi in the same manner soon."

She was surprised by Randon's frown as she spoke, but his reply left her stunned.

"Kayli, you mustn't use that thing again," he said slowly. "Promise me you won't."

A surge of irrational anger—what right did have to make such a demand of her?—nearly blinded her for a moment. With difficulty, she calmed herself, although she clutched the crystal in its pouch possessively.

"How could you ask such a thing?" Kayli said, forcing her voice to evenness. "*Why* would you ask it?"

"Kayli, you have no idea how precarious our situation is," Randon said earnestly. "The treaty with Bregond won't be final until you and I are confirmed and crowned. In the meantime I need every bit of support and help I can get, and there are already those who mutter simply because they've learned you're a mage. Do you know what Terralt would make of you having magical communication with Bregond, secret communications anytime you liked? He'd make you a spy sent here under guise of the treaty to learn state secrets, the strength of our military—who knows what the ministers would believe? Even the best of them would have some suspicion. Worse yet, what if word got out to the people? The supporters I have would turn against me, and Terralt would seem justified. No, Kayli. I've supported your magical studies up to now, but this is too much."

Kayli once more repeated a calming ritual to herself, forcing herself to consider Randon's words carefully, but shook her head at last.

"No, Randon," she said slowly. "I cannot agree. What you say is reasonable, and if you say I must, then I will not mention the speaking crystal to anyone and will use it only in the privacy of the forge when it is locked. But there is no harm in my communications with my mentor or my sister, and if needed, I would swear it under truth spell. But this is a part of my training, something that lies at my very heart. Terralt and the ministers may not trust me, but I must know that you do.'' She met Randon's eyes squarely as she spoke.

This time it was Randon's turn to stop and consider. At last he sighed.

''I don't like it, and I wish you'd change your mind,'' he said. ''But if you won't, you won't. Just please, as you said, make sure no one else learns of it!''

His words and his expression made Kayli realize with a sinking heart that in some way, at least, she had not yet earned his trust. A moment later she pushed aside her dismay. She could hardly expect more from him than she was willing to give.

''I understand your worry,'' she said, laying her hand on Randon's. ''But it is without cause. And the speaking crystal may serve to your benefit in time—why, from the High Priestess I learned that my parents are sending a second caravan to Agrond—and I know that Brother Santee, who resides at the castle, must surely carry a speaking crystal. So when he returns home, should great need ever arise, I could send a message for you to be delivered to my father and mother.''

''You're right, that could be useful.'' Randon smiled, but the smile seemed forced. ''The men finished cleaning the forge yesterday, did you know?''

''Yes.'' Kayli did not tell him that she had had to clean the forge herself all over again after the men had gone; apparently the men had a different notion of ''clean'' than the one Kayli had learned at the Order. ''I will consecrate it tomorrow at dawn. You may watch if you wish,'' she added, seeing his wistful expression, ''but it is only a simple consecration. Most fire magics are much more impressive.''

''All the same,'' Randon said with a cheerful grin, ''it's an excuse to see something I've never seen before. Besides, if there are any more mutterings about your magic, it might be helpful for me to be able to say I know what you're doing.'' The twinkle in his eyes made his statement a sort of joke between them, and Kayli appreciated that, although it stung her that there was an element of truth to what he said. She quietly put away her speaking crystal, privately resolving to call Kairi as soon as possible, and let Randon believe what he would.

Her conscience, as always, was her own.

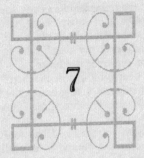

7

KAYLI ROSE WELL BEFORE DAWN THE NEXT DAY in order to ready the forge for consecration. Randon, sleepy-eyed but eager, lurked in the doorway watching her every movement, and Kayli told him to inform her when the sun was beginning to rise. Randon ran back up the stairs frequently to check the sky so that Kayli could work unhindered until he reported that the sky was beginning to lighten in the east.

A little thrill shot through Kayli's heart. This consecration would be her first important ritual as an Initiate. She composed herself—somehow it was simple here in the forge—and gestured to Randon, indicating a corner where he might sit and watch more comfortably. She stepped to the torch she'd placed in its sconce on the east wall.

"As the fire of the sun lights the sky," she said in Agrondish, for Randon's benefit, "as the Flame lights the center of the world, so I bring the Flame to this holy place and welcome it inside." She touched the end of the torch with her *thari*, suppressing her pride as the torch flared alight. She'd worked hard to perfect the technique for this ritual.

She repeated the summoning at the torches mounted on the north, south, and west walls, then walked to the forge itself, dropping her robe behind her. Randon was forgotten now, her concentration focused on the task before her. She knelt at the edge of the forge.

"I summon the Flame from the heart of the world, from the center of the sun, from the depths of my soul," she said. "As an Initiate of the Order of Inner Flame, I summon the Flame to bless and consecrate this holy place and dwell therein, to light the forge and serve my will." She raised her head and extended her *thari* out over the forge.

Kayli felt the heat building in the hard black coal in the firepit and knew her success long before the first orange-amber flame flickered upward. The fire spread slowly, but at last the whole firepit was alight.

One by one, Kayli consecrated her tools, extending them into the flames; after she poured a little oil on the anvil and carried a coal from the firepit to light it, she carried the coal to the corners of the room, touching it to the stone of the walls and floor. Impulsively, and to Randon's amazement, she took his hand and passed the burning coal over it, so quickly that he had neither time to pull away nor to be burned.

"I summon the Flame to dwell in this holy place," she said. "Live in each stone, in the air, in our flesh. Dwell in memory, burn unseen in darkness until I summon you forth."

She focused on the coal in her hands. This was the difficult part, for she must quell the fire in the forge, yet leave the torches burning. She felt the Flame all around her in its smallest manifestations. Each torch on the forge walls was a sort of pleasant itch at the back of her consciousness; the firepit itself was a more powerful sensation, drawing her forward as if luring her to immerse herself in the flames. Kayli dismissed the fire almost hastily, gratified that although the torches guttered slightly when the flames in the firepit subsided, they quickly recovered.

Kayli replaced the now cool coal in the firepit, then sighed and let herself collapse to her knees on the stone, suddenly aware how tired and drained she was by the ritual.

"Fire feeds on wood or coal," Brisi had told her. "But the Flame feeds on you. In time only the greatest rituals will tire you severely, but it is important not to overreach your skill. One who summons more of the Flame than she can feed or control will surely be utterly consumed."

Kayli rested where she was, amused to find her loins hungry despite her weariness. Well, she'd been warned of that, too, as the fires of magic and the flesh mingled so closely together. When Randon hesitantly approached with her robe in his hand, she gestured to him to sit beside her.

"Are you finished?" he asked. "Are you all right?"

"Yes, and yes," Kayli said, leaning back against him. "Only a little weary. But that is to be expected."

"You surprised me with that coal," Randon said, rubbing her shoulders. "I thought I was just watching."

Kayli frowned. Once or twice observers had attended consecrations in the temple, but only novices were usually included in the ritual as she had impulsively included Randon. Now she wondered whether her action had been unwise. Randon had at least a trace of the fire magic, after all, and she technically *had* invoked the Flame in him. Well, it was only a simple consecration; surely there was no harm.

"Well, you have been consecrated with the forge," she said lightly. "Now you may observe my rituals sometimes. You must, after all, keep track of my possibly seditious magic."

"Kayli—" Randon protested.

"Oh, hush." Kayli turned in his arms to face him, her lips too hungry for his to wait another moment. Randon seemed a little taken aback as she pulled impatiently at the lacing of his shirt, then gave up and concentrated on ridding him of his trousers instead, but he quickly matched her eagerness and they coupled there on the hard stone floor of the forge.

When passion finally cooled, however, Randon laughed at the coal dust smudging the tunic he had never managed to remove, and liberally dusting his own and Kayli's hair and skin.

"The servants will never understand if they see us," he said, grinning ruefully. "But if Terralt himself catches us on the stairs, it was worth it. But wasn't that a little—well, sacrilegious? I mean, if this is a consecrated place—"

Kayli laughed.

"All the Awakenings in our temple take place in the forge," she said. "Of course, a pallet is placed on the stone to make it more comfortable." She did not add that like the singed hearth fur of her wedding night, those pallets often withstood only a single use. "Sexual and magical energies mingle closely, and one most often feeds the other."

"Then Stevann must be more circumspect than I thought," Randon said, chuckling. "Whenever I saw him casting spells, he seemed far more exhausted than—well, otherwise."

Kayli flushed as she remembered what Randon had said of Stevann's inclinations.

"Perhaps Stevann's magic is of a different sort," she said. "What I was taught may only be applicable to the elemental magics. Well, at least this forge has certainly been properly prepared for fire magic," Kayli added, chuckling. "But if we sit in audience today, it is water I must seek."

"No audience." Randon reached for his trousers, clucked amusedly over the broken lacing, and handed Kayli her robe. "I didn't know how long this ceremony might take, so I canceled everything for the day, thinking that if you liked, we might pack a lunch and go rid—hey!" Randon protested, but he laughed as Kayli dragged him to his feet and pushed him toward the door, barely pulling the robe around her own shoulders.

"Well, at least if anyone sees us, your people will know that I, as well as you, am doing my best to provide this country with an heir," Kayli said amusedly as they crept up the backstairs. Then she sighed. "It is a great pity that in our own home we must forever worry what others are thinking of us."

"I know," Randon said, nodding a little sadly. "It annoys me, too. I'm so accustomed to doing what I please that it's an effort to remember that my life's not my own anymore."

Kayli made a hasty toilet and donned her riding clothes, taking her bow and quiver with her; by the time she was ready, Randon had already ordered their lunch basket and had the horses saddled. The guards were waiting, too, and at the sight of them, Kayli's enthusiasm ebbed a bit, but Maja was no more frisky and restless than Kayli herself, and she fidgeted impatiently in the saddle until the guards led them out through the castle gates.

This time Kayli fancied she saw less hostility in the stares directed at her, although an increased number of peasants muttered excitedly to each other as the group rode by. Kayli urged Maja a little closer to Carada and asked Randon about it.

"Well, nobody really knew what to expect from the daughter of the Bregondish High Lord," Randon told her. "Half the rumors had you a barbarian with bones in your ears and rings in your nose, and the other half had you figured for a pretty but useless—pardon me for saying it quite that way—lady like Ynea. I'm sure that after Terralt's stories, a lot of folk thought I wouldn't be any use in the seat, either. After a few audiences, I imagine we corrected that impression. From what Kereg's told me, your decision on the case of Lord Ethen and Lord Reive was the talk of the city for days. As you've never shown yourself in public with bones in your ears and rings in your nose, I'm sure your image has improved."

Kayli smiled. Perhaps someday soon Randon would be able to take her into the city, even if in a heavily guarded carriage.

Randon must have had similar thoughts, for when he spoke again, he said, "You know, I think it's time to let Tarkesh get a look at its new High Lady. When we're crowned, I'll throw a grand festival. In the meantime I'll arrange for us to visit some of the lords in town. That'll give you a glimpse of the city, at least, and give the city a glimpse of you, too."

Randon's words warmed Kayli's heart, but she sighed quietly to herself. The idea of visiting nobles who likely resented her and Randon, too, was not what she'd wanted. Randon probably enjoyed the prospect no more than she did.

"You have mentioned a number of guildmasters of your acquaintance," she said after a moment's thought. "Surely it would be slighting them and the importance of their guilds if we neglected to visit them as well, especially since they have supported you so loyally."

"There's a thought," Randon said, raising his eyebrows as if the idea pleased him. "Yes, you could safely visit most of the guild halls, and that'll give you a chance to learn a little about Agrond's industries. It's a capital idea. Oh, good, there's the gates." He glanced at Kayli, and his eyes twinkled mischievously. "How rebellious are you feeling?" He tilted his head at the guards ahead of them.

Kayli chuckled.

"Very rebellious indeed," she murmured back.

"Very well, then. Shall we show them just how much trouble we can be?" Randon dared her.

"Indeed I shall show them," Kayli returned, tossing her head. "And you as well." She nudged Maja with her knees, and the mare immediately bolted forward, dodging the guards and their mounts adroitly and galloping down the road at a speed that startled even Kayli. She dropped the rein loop over its peg and threw her arms out to the sides, laughing as the wind tugged at her clothes and hair; then she pulled the pins from her hair and let her long braids uncoil behind her. Dimly she heard Randon calling behind her, but this time there was no stopping her or Maja, either; peasants on the road drew back, staring incredulously as their High Lady thundered by. It wasn't until Kayli had crossed the stone bridge that she slowed Maja to let Randon catch up.

Before Maja had completely stopped, however, she startled a middle-sized piglike creature out of a low thicket; almost by reflex, Kayli reached behind her and drew her bow and an arrow, instinctively signaling Maja to pursue. By the time she had nocked her arrow, the creature was plainly in sight, and her arrow was true to its mark.

Randon, to his credit, was not too far behind her, but the amusement in his expression was tinged with irritation as he reined Carada in beside her.

"Well, so much for convincing the people that their High Lady isn't a barbarian." He chuckled wryly. "*That* spectacle will be the talk of the city longer than your first audience. They probably thought you were fleeing back to Bregond."

"Then they have not sense enough to realize that Bregond lies in the opposite direction," Kayli returned serenely. "Come, Randon, do not be angry. Now if the guards chide you, you can tell them you were forced to leave them behind to pursue your wayward lady. Only see what a fine kill I have made, and what a perfect spot I have found for our luncheon." They were on the knoll of a small hill covered with wildflowers, with a lovely view of the river and the city in the distance.

"Well, it *is* a beautiful spot," Randon admitted, sliding down rather awkwardly from the Bregondish saddle. "And congratulations on your kill. That was a neat shot from horseback."

To Kayli's chagrin, she discovered that she'd brought no knife other than her *thari* and the belt dagger she used for eating, neither of which she wanted to use for butchery. Fortunately, Randon carried a hunting knife in his boot, with which he cut Kayli's arrow free.

"That was a clever guess, hitting it right under the ear," he told her. "It's hard to drop a speckled boar with one shot, they're so muscled. Was it just luck?"

Kayli shook her head.

"I have often hunted tusk boars on the plains," she said. "They are fierce, especially when wounded; an eye shot or below the ear are the only targets for a quick kill."

It was pleasant to dine out in the fresh clean air, the breeze fragrant with the smell of wildflowers, but Kayli's enjoyment was tainted by the nine guards nearby, each of them glancing at her or Randon every few moments. It was impossible to relax under such scrutiny. To distract herself, Kayli turned to gaze at the green edge of the forest so close by.

"Randon, would it not be possible to go for a walk in the forest?" she asked presently. "Just you and I."

Randon glanced at the guards dubiously.

"They won't want to let us out of sight again, especially after your wild ride," he said. "But if you really want to go for a walk in the forest, I can have them hang well back, and I know a place where they'll leave us alone for a while."

Kayli had never seen a forest except in passing on her journey to Tarkesh. She had never suspected the trees could actually be so large; what tremendous amounts of water they must need! And if she'd been impressed by the verdure and variety of plant life on the open hillside, she was now utterly awed by the diversity of growth that sprang up from the earth. Surely one would immediately become lost in a place where it was impossible to see more than a few paces ahead. But Randon showed her a path leading back into the forest, and Kayli followed him with less eagerness than she had felt when she'd suggested the stroll.

"I come here to hunt often," Randon said. "And to visit the place I'm going to show you."

"Why such a mystery?" Kayli asked him. "What is this place?"

"There's no mystery," Randon said, glancing at her. "I only wanted to surprise you. Look, here we are."

Kayli's eyes had grown used to the lesser light in the forest, and she was a little dazzled when the path opened abruptly into sunlight. The path ended in a large clearing, and in that clearing was a pond the size of the largest water hole Kayli had ever seen, dozens of man-heights across, at the foot of a tall cliff cut out of the side of the hill behind it. But unlike the muddy water holes that spotted Bregond's plains, the water of this pond was clear and clean, falling sparkling into the pond from a waterfall tumbling off the cliff.

"What a marvelous place," Kayli said, nearly breathless with delight. "I have never seen the like of it."

Randon turned to the guards.

"Go back down the path and stay there," he said. "We'll call if we need you."

The guard captain frowned.

"But, lord—"

Randon gestured expansively.

"Captain Beran, we're in a *forest*. Alone. You'll hear us if there's any trouble. Please go."

Captain Beran shook his head, but he turned and motioned to the other guards to walk back down the path with him. When the guards were gone, Randon turned to Kayli and smiled triumphantly.

"There," he said. "Better?"

"Much." Kayli chuckled. "But why would they leave us alone here and nowhere else?"

"Well, they can hardly stay and watch while we swim, can they?" Randon was already pulling his tunic over his head.

"Swim?" Involuntarily Kayli glanced at the pond, and her stomach flipped over in realization. "In there?"

"Of course, in there," Randon said. He attacked the lacing on his boot, then sat down on the ground to finish the job, glancing up at Kayli. "Don't you want to? I thought you might enjoy it after all that soot this morning."

Kayli stared at the pond. The water might be terribly deep.

"But—you mean to take off your clothes and—and go all the way into that—that water?" Kayli asked in a small voice.

Randon pulled off his other boot, then gazed up at her.

"What's the matter?" he said. "You *do* know how to swim, don't you?"

Kayli swallowed hard and shook her head. Know how to swim? She could hardly *conceive* of it. She knew that Kairi and other Initiates at the Order of the Deep Waters frequently immersed themselves completely in ceremonial pools, and it was rumored that they taught themselves to breathe underwater, but that was a secret of their Order. Certainly Kayli had no such protection.

"Oh." Randon appeared perplexed by her answer. "Well, no matter. I'll teach you. Come on, it's warm out and the cool water will feel good."

Reluctantly Kayli removed her clothing. It felt unseemly to be naked outdoors, even—no, *especially* with all these huge trees around her. Why, someone could easily hide behind that great tree over there and spy upon them. She shivered and clasped her arms over her breasts, imagining the gaze of unseen watchers crawling over her skin.

"Come on." Randon held out his hand. "It's simple, truly. You'll soon get used to it."

Kayli allowed him to lead her into the shallowest part of the pool, where it emptied out into a small stream. When the water decently covered her breasts, however, and Randon appeared quite intent on leading her even deeper, she balked.

"No further," she begged. "I feel as if my feet would leave the bottom."

"Well, that's the idea," Randon said, chuckling. "Just watch me. It's simple." He released her hand and propelled himself right out into the deep water using strange motions of his arms and legs. The sight so unnerved Kayli that she retreated back into the shallows, shivering now. At last Randon swam back to her.

"Now you try it," he said.

Kayli tried, and tried again, telling herself that it was no different from a bathing tub—a very *large* bathing tub—but after several sputtering failures she admitted defeat and returned to the bank to let the sun dry her.

"I am no fish," she told a disappointed Randon. "Perhaps you were born with gills, but I was not."

When they dressed and walked back, Captain Beran said that he could smell rain in the air, and besides, Kayli's boar should be brought in from the heat, so he insisted they return to the castle immediately. The road was full of horses and wagons; as it was late afternoon and rain was threatening, the market was emptying rapidly. Kayli and Randon had hardly passed the city gates, however, when a small, ragged figure broke from the crowd of peasants watching them pass and flung itself practically under Maja's feet. Well-trained Maja halted immediately, and several of the guards leaped from their mounts, swords drawn; but Kayli had caught a glimpse of brown skin and black hair among the rags, and she was already on the ground, shielding the child with her own body.

"Stay back!" Kayli commanded, her icy tone brooking no disobedience. "It is only a child."

She stroked matted black hair back from a very dirty face indeed. A young girl, she thought, Bregondish as she'd suspected, of about twelve or thirteen years of age. The child twisted free of her hands and pressed her face to Kayli's boots.

"Priestess, lady, I beg the sanctuary and protection of the Flame," a whispered voice said in Bregondish.

A shock ran through Kayli—how had the child known her Order?—but the plea could not be denied.

"I have no temple to shelter you," she murmured, stroking the thin shoulders, "but such sanctuary and protection as are mine to give, you are granted." She turned to find Randon and four of the guards standing beside her, shock on all their faces.

"By the Bright Ones, it's a Bregondish child!" Randon exclaimed. "A slave, too. See?" He pointed to an iron band around the child's neck.

A hot, hard anger surged in Kayli's heart.

"How can such a thing be, that one of my people is here, a slave?" she demanded.

Randon hesitated, glancing at the peasants watching them.

"This isn't the place to discuss it," he said at last. "We'll talk about it when we're back at the castle. What are you going to do with the child?"

"Take her with me, of course," she said hotly, her eyes daring Randon to refuse her.

Randon raised his eyebrows, but only sighed resignedly.

"High Lady, you can't mean it," Captain Beran protested. "The creature's a slave, and filthy as well."

"The 'creature' is a child of my people, and under my protection," Kayli said, so furious that her own hands shook as she gathered the small body to her. "What is your name, little one?" she murmured to the child in Bregondish.

"Seba, Priestess," came the reply, still in a whisper.

"Very well, Seba, you will ride with me." Ignoring the stares of everyone around her, Kayli helped the child into her saddle, then mounted herself. Seba clung as fiercely to the saddle as she had to Kayli herself, and Kayli could feel the child shaking still; her own anger was so great that she could hardly bear to look at Randon, much less the staring peasants muttering as she passed.

Randon said nothing as they rode back, but when they reached the castle stables, he slid down from Carada's back and stepped to Maja's side. He held up his hands, but when Kayli would have handed Seba down to him, the child whimpered and clung even more determinedly to the saddle. Kayli shook her head at Randon and dismounted; only then would Seba let Kayli lift her down.

"Well, now you've got her, what are you going to do with her?" Randon said patiently. "She stinks like an open cesspit, Beran's right about that much."

"She will be bathed," Kayli said. "Anida and Endra can find some clothing for her. May I leave Maja in your care?"

Randon agreed, and Kayli led Seba up by the backstairs to avoid a confrontation with the servants or, worse, Terralt. She reached her quarters without incident, and Anida and Endra, no less stunned than Kayli at finding a Bregondish child under such circumstances, immediately set about preparing a bath and clean clothing for the girl. To Kayli's relief, Seba appeared willing to go with the Bregondish women, giving Kayli some time to recover from her own shock.

A Bregondish child, a slave in Agrond's capital city? How could such a thing happen, and why? Only those convicted of severe crimes in Bregond could be enslaved to serve their victims or their victims' family; the only other slaves in Bregond were captured Sarkondish raiders. It had never occurred to her that Agrond permitted slavery as a common practice. And *Bregondish* slaves—Kayli shuddered to think what her father would say or do when he learned of it, and Kayli meant that he should learn of it very quickly indeed.

"The storm gathering outside isn't nearly as impressive as the one on your face," Randon said mildly, closing the door behind him. He sat down beside Kayli. "Has she told you yet how she came here?"

Kayli shook her head, forcing herself to calmness.

"No. She is too frightened. I left Endra to coax it out of her, if she could."

Randon shrugged.

"I can pretty well guess what she'll have to tell," he said. "You know, don't you, that there's been a few merchants trading illegally between Agrond and Bregond for many years?"

"Of course." Kayli sighed. "Else I would never have learned Agrondish, more than likely, nor my father learned the news of Agrond."

"But do you know those same merchants sometimes trade with Sarkond, too?" Randon raised his eyebrows at Kayli's stunned silence. "Don't look so shocked. If they're willing to break the laws of two countries, why not both at once? There's the source of your slave trade, my lady, not Agrond raiding across the border, if that's what you've been thinking. When Sarkond raids a village, they take what they want, kill most of the adults, and sell the children as slaves to the merchants, who take them across the border to sell. There are likely a few Agrondish citizens wearing iron collars in Bregond, I'd wager."

"There are *not*," Kayli said hotly. "It would never be permitted."

"Mmm. It's not permitted *here*," Randon said pointedly. "Neither is trading across the border, but it happens."

Kayli faced him squarely.

"And what justice will you offer that child?" she demanded. "How will you punish the one who kept her?"

"He'll likely go unpunished," Randon said, holding up a hand to prevent Kayli's outburst. "Even if the child can identify him, nobody will testify against him. His friends and neighbors will deny that he kept a slave at all. Remember that in their eyes, he hasn't committed any crime. She's Bregondish, an enemy. I couldn't condemn anybody on only the word of a child, no matter how much I might like to.''

A gentle knock at the door prevented whatever reply Kayli would have made, and Endra peeped in.

"May I come in, lady?" she said. "The child's having a bit of supper, and then Anida will put her to sleep in my room.''

"Yes, come in," Kayli said hurriedly. "Is Seba well? Have you learned how she came to be here?''

"Well enough, I suppose, and yes, but you're not going to like it much," Endra said, glancing at Randon.

"Go ahead," Randon told her. "I'd like to know, too.''

"Mm. She was born in one of the horse clans," Endra told them. "Orphaned a few years ago in a Sarkondish raid, but a very few of the clan escaped. One of the healing temples took her in—she's not certain which village it was nearest—and kept her long enough to be certain she'd no mage-gift, then settled her in the next horse clan that passed the temple on its circuit. Then *that* clan was raided. She's been sold a couple of times since then, before she ended up with an herbalist in Tarkesh.'' Endra glanced at Kayli, her lips narrowed. "Been violated, too—by her first master, though, not the last one.''

Kayli shuddered but said nothing. What could she say? *Why* had her parents never told her of such things happening? How could they ignore such horror as if it did not exist?

But what else could they do? she realized. The borders were patrolled as thoroughly as was reasonably possible. Sarkondish raids were prevented, or at least avenged, whenever possible. What more could be done? Only make a treaty with Agrond in the hope of preventing further incursions. And that, too, had been done.

"I'll go back to her now," Endra said after the awkward pause. "I've still to mix the mite's sleeping draft. She'll need it, poor babe.'' The midwife ducked her head in lieu of a bow and backed out the door.

"What will you do with her?" Randon asked Kayli. "Send her back to Bregond?''

"Send her where?" Kayli asked helplessly. "She has no kin left to take her in, and without the mage-gift I cannot send her to one of the temples.'' She stopped there, not wanting to add that no one else in Bregond would have her—a captive of the Sarkondish who had failed to take her own life as was her duty to Bregond. It sounded heartless even to Kayli; she knew Randon would never understand.

"No," she said at last. "I will keep her here. It is, after all, my duty, as she asked for my protection." She glared defiantly at Randon. "I will find some work for her."

"All right, now, calm down," Randon said, laying his hand on her arm. "*I* didn't abduct the girl. And I scarcely expected you to throw her out into the street again. What more do you want from me?"

"I want justice for Seba," Kayli countered. "And I want measures taken so that this will not happen again."

"All right, I'll try," Randon said, shrugging. "If I can find any way to do it, whoever owned her will be punished. But how do you expect me to stop a trade that's already outlawed?"

Kayli thought for a moment.

"Issue a proclamation that anyone dealing in slaves, either buying or selling, will be put to death," she said. "And that any testimony against such traffic will be generously rewarded. Then those around them will cease to protect them."

"That last is a good idea," Randon admitted. "But if I have people put to death over Bregondish slaves, the resentment against Bregond—and you, Kayli—will only increase."

"Then make the guilty slaves themselves," Kayli pressed. "Let them serve others as a reminder that evil caused to others will one day return upon them."

"Fine," Randon said patiently. "Then those who already own slaves will either abandon them or kill them so as not to be caught with them. And what do you expect to become of these ex-slaves, or do you want to keep them all like Seba?"

Kayli said nothing, only gazed steadily at Randon. How would he react, she wondered, if he had stumbled across Agrondish citizens being held as slaves in Bregond? What action might he have demanded be taken?

"All right." Randon sighed at last. "All right. We'll think of something. I'll talk to Terralt in the morning. He may have some ideas. In the meantime I'll call a smith to cut that collar off the girl."

It was impossible to be angry when Randon gave her that wry grin. Kayli smiled gently in return and laid her hand over his.

"I am sorry I became so angry," she said, a little embarrassed. "But when I thought of that child, torn from her home and made a slave in a strange land—"

"—you reacted the same way I would," Randon finished for her. "Kayli, I'm sorry. Of course you're outraged. I wish you'd sit down with me tomorrow and help me write a message to your father telling him about the problem. If he's been more successful than we have in controlling illegal slave trade, I'd appreciate any suggestions he can offer."

That was neat, very neat, Kayli thought with a weary cynicism. By telling her that he was personally going to notify her father, he effectively prevented her from making her own report, and at the same time by his honesty and apparently prompt action he forestalled any protest the High Lord and Lady of Bregond might make. Kayli sighed to herself. Would she spend the rest of her marriage questioning the motives behind Randon's every word and deed?

Randon twined his fingers through Kayli's.

"You've been in a poor temper these last few days," he said gently. "Stevann says you've been worrying because you haven't conceived. Are you afraid I'll set you aside, take another wife?"

Kayli forced an expression of serenity she did not feel. What could she say? If she was honest and said *yes, I am afraid of being set aside, but I am just as afraid of being here in this country that sometimes horrifies me, afraid of these responsibilities I have been set, and I ache to my very soul for privacy and freedom,* what comfort could Randon give her? There was no reassurance he could give that was not a lie.

"I am not so worried as all that," Kayli said as lightly as she could. "Stevann and Endra, too, say it is too soon to be concerned. I only hope that your advisers feel the same."

"Mmm. Every day we sit in audience they grow more willing to wait," Randon told her. "You've surprised and impressed everyone, lords and commoners alike, by the active role you've taken in decision making. I won't say it hasn't helped me, too. A number of lords who wouldn't support me before, thinking I had no training in rulership, are more willing to give me a chance with an active High Lady at my side. I think it's time you became more involved in other ways, too— the paperwork, and making policy with me. The sooner the people come to accept the two of us as their rulers, the happier everyone will be—except Terralt and his followers, that is.

"That being said," Randon added in a lighter tone, "I've invited the heads of several of the guilds to dinner tomorrow. It's past time they met their new High Lady, and you them. And as you've said, they've been my staunchest supporters."

A sudden surge of panic wiped out the last of Kayli's anger. Dinner with the leaders of the guilds only a day away, and she wholly unprepared! Why, she had no idea even how to address such figures, much less how to comport herself with them.

"Then you must help me," she said quickly. "Give me their names and titles, and describe them each, and what their guild does, and any recent events of import to them so that I may address them personally."

"But it's late already," Randon protested. "And we've had a busy day."

Kayli shook her head.

"You have earned the guilds' loyalty through years of friendship," she told him. "I must accomplish the same in a few hours of talk."

"All right, all right," Randon said resignedly. "But how are you going to remember all that from one night's briefing?"

"I have a good memory," Kayli told him. "I have trained it extensively. Please, begin." She sat down at the small bedroom table, motioning to him to join her.

At midnight Randon finally waved a hand dismissively.

"No more," he said firmly. "You've got everything *I* can remember. If you can remember all that, you'll surely dazzle them all tomorrow, and if not, there's no good in wasting any more of our time. I'm desperate for sleep."

In the morning Kayli rose early and let Endra and the maids do their best for her with scented bathing oils, perfumes, jewels and other adornments; still she had time to meditate before dinner and to sit quietly sipping the wine Seba brought her, so that she went down to dinner with a calmer and clearer mind. Randon met her at the foot of the stairs; he seemed calm, too, as he took her arm and led her to the dining hall.

Of course. These people are his friends and allies. For him this is no test.

As was Agrondish custom, the men and women were already seated at the dining table, but they rose as Randon and Kayli entered. Randon introduced each of them, and Kayli could not suppress a small surge of pride as she recognized them from his descriptions, and managed to address a small personal comment to each of them—to Master Dyer Lidian, praise for the new shade of purple that was the talk of Tarkesh; to Master Weaver Odric, congratulations on the birth of his first grandchild; to Guildmistress Ravena of the House of Scribes, a sympathetic hope that her shoulder, recently broken in a wagon accident, was well mended. The guildmasters and guildmistresses seemed astonished at Kayli's small store of knowledge, and Kayli smiled quietly to herself as she sat down beside Randon at the head of the table, knowing her study and worry had been well worth it if she had earned some respect from these people.

She was grateful, too, that Randon's talk of the night before and the audiences they had shared let her converse intelligently with them and not seem ignorant of affairs in Agrond. She found herself warming to these people, surprised to actually enjoy a dinner of state. But then, she realized, why should she not enjoy their company—these folk were commoners who had made their place through hard work and accomplishment, as had those at her own Order, and they were Randon's friends besides; their society lacked the velvet-and-dagger dance of courtly manners of which Kayli had already grown so tired. She was surprised, however, when Randon shifted the conversation from rising grain values with an abruptness that left her gaping.

"I'm sure by now you've all heard what happened yesterday," Randon said.

"The business of the slave girl," Guildmistress Ravena said, nodding. "Already the guilds are fair buzzing with it."

Randon sipped thoughtfully at his wine.

"And what tone," he asked slowly, "did the talk take?"

Guildmistress Ravena only frowned a little, but it was

Smithmaster Erinton who answered forthrightly, although he glanced at Kayli and flushed as if uncomfortable.

"It wasn't a popular act, lord—High Lord, I mean, confiscating somebody's slave like that, and it's raised some worries. We all know keeping slaves hasn't been precisely *legal* for nearly a decade, but—"

"—but until now it's been tolerated," Master Tanner Crinna finished, twisting her stained fingers nervously. "At least the guards've overlooked it. Why, the tax assessors always listed 'em on the accounts and taxed us on 'em same as barrels or carts, and nothing ever come of it. What's folk to think now?"

"Folks are to think that changes come with the ascension of a new High Lord and Lady, just as it's always been," Randon said patiently. "My father was opposed to the slave trade, but while Bregond was still our enemy he saw no need to apply drastic measures to stop it. Now, however, Bregond is our ally, and that alliance is fragile enough without the added strain of Bregondish citizens kept here as slaves. What troubles me most, though, is that the trade puts us in league with Sarkond; by providing a market for these slaves, we're tacitly supporting them and encouraging their raids. It's got to stop now. My advisers will make their recommendations, but you all have a closer view of the problem. I wanted to hear what you have to say."

There was a moment of silence around the table as guildmasters and guildmistresses glanced uneasily at each other. At last Smithmaster Erinton spoke again.

"You mean all slaves, High Lord, or just the Bregonds?"

"All of them," Randon said, glancing briefly at Kayli. "I don't see how we could reasonably enforce the law otherwise. The question is how to implement a law that's been on the books for years, but never really enforced. I want an immediate stop to the purchase and sale of slaves in Agrond, and I want the presently held slaves to be given justice, not tossed out penniless on the street or worse. What would you suggest?"

Ravena leaned forward.

"What you need," she said slowly, "is a period of immunity from punishment, when slave owners can free their slaves, giving them enough money to make their way home—''

''They will not return to Bregond,'' Kayli interrupted.

''—or get a start here,'' Ravena finished, raising her eyebrows at Kayli's statement. ''*Then* have the guards begin enforcing the law vigorously.''

''Not enough,'' Randon told her. ''We're not changing a law or writing a new one; we're punishing a *crime*. The law against slavery was proclaimed nearly a decade ago. No matter that the guilty parties haven't been punished; a murderer who hasn't yet been caught is still a murderer. Kayli's told me a little about how Bregond might handle the matter. Your period of immunity, though, Guildmistress, is a good idea. Kayli, can you make something of that?''

Kayli was surprised at Randon's abrupt question, but after her discussion with him after Seba's rescue, she had given the matter a good deal of thought and was able to answer promptly.

''If I were to decide,'' she said carefully, ''it would be thus: that any slave owners have a period of time—say one moon cycle—to free their slaves and give them money in reparation, as Guildmistress Ravena suggested. However, if the slave feels he has not been fairly compensated for his enslavement and his treatment thereafter, he may bring his owner before us in audience. And after that moon cycle, anyone found buying, selling, or owning an illegal slave in Agrond will himself be indentured. And any whose report of such a one leads to his capture will be well rewarded.''

''Harsh, but fair,'' Randon said thoughtfully after a moment's pause. ''Slaves could extort a good sum from their masters under threat of bringing a case before the Bregondish High Lady, but that could be a fitting punishment. It'll mean extra audiences, though.'' He paused. ''Guildmasters, Guildmistresses, I'd ask that each of the major guilds choose a representative to join us in those audiences in an advisory role. Your people have most likely known or dealt in the past with most slave owners.''

Kayli sipped her wine quietly, wondering what Randon was doing. It was a daring move, to take such a step before he was confirmed as High Lord. Surely he would lose some of his support; the very fact that he had brought the matter up at this dinner indicated that the guilds might well be the worst offenders, the largest purchasers of slaves—of course they would be; slave labor was cheap, and slaves were not accorded the benefits and rights of guild members. Why, then, did Randon risk alienating the guilds, who were his staunchest supporters?

As Kayli looked down the table, however, many of the men and women nodded slowly, and she saw a cautious relief on several faces. Abruptly Kayli realized her mistake. These were commoners who had worked their way to a good position but who largely depended for their livelihood upon other commoners. The guilds fared best under a firm and orderly government, and would thrive in a country in which the law gave full justice even to slaves. Randon had made a subtle statement that he valued his responsibility as High Lord above his popularity with his friends, and by doing so, won only their respect.

Kayli was gratified by the warmth with which the men and women took their leave when dinner was concluded, and even more pleased by the numerous invitations she received to visit their guilds. Her joy was marred only by a gnawing ache in her stomach, likely caused by her anxiety, or perhaps the unaccustomed variety of vegetables and grains disagreed with her. Still, she was glad to return to her quarters with Randon when the guests had left, and put away her finery and jewels and ask Endra to fetch her a mug of minted water. Then she thought she could relax, but to her disgust she found her hands shaking. She clenched them resolutely and hid them in her lap.

"You surprised me with your choice of conversation," she told Randon, sipping the minted water. "Will your advisers not resent that you consulted the guilds instead of them?"

"Doubtless they will." Randon shrugged. "After what you said about them likely thinking me more easily influenced than Terralt, I thought it wise to show them otherwise. Besides, as I told our guests, I think they're closest to the problem. The nobility, so far as I know, isn't greatly involved with the slave trade. The mercantile houses won't sully their reputations by dealing in Sarkondish captives, and the landed nobility won't tarnish their names by buying them. Outland slaves are usually bought for menial work, and that means city businesses—the crafts and guilds, small inns and taverns and the like. The ministers are just too remote from the goings-on at that level of society. It's one reason the trade has gone on as long as it has—because the nobility just don't take any interest."

"But you should have warned me," Kayli told him. "I was hard-pressed to answer when you asked for my recommendation."

"You did well enough, I'd say." Randon smiled at her. "But to be truthful, I *wanted* you a little off balance."

Kayli said nothing, swallowing her anger with her mint water. Neither rested easily in her aching stomach.

"You gave me a fiery speech yesterday," Randon told her gently, "but that won't go far in dealing with these people. If I'd told you last night what I was going to talk about, you'd have come up with even harsher penalties and a thousand arguments to justify them, and come to the table with your mind made up firmly. I wanted you to think on your feet, as it were, *after* you'd heard what the others had to say about it. And you made a wise recommendation."

Kayli frowned and clenched her hands more firmly.

"You wrong me if you think me so inflexible," she said a little more coolly than she meant to. "After our discussion yesterday I thought on what you had said, and the recommendations I made were the ones I had already planned to give you. I was surprised when you agreed."

"Mmm. I'm sorry, then." Randon reached across the table and stroked her arm. "I meant that as a gesture of trust, inviting your suggestion in front of my friends. I suppose sometimes I don't know who I'm dealing with—my wise bride, or the High Lord of Bregond's loyal daughter."

"Well, as you wed both, you must deal with both," Kayli said, her anger fading slightly. "Forgive me, too, my ill temper. So often I feel tested—by you, by others—that sometimes I question every word and deed. It is unfair of me."

"Hah! There *is* mistrust in every word and gesture," Randon said wryly. "But mostly it's directed toward me, not you. However insulting you may find it, nobody expected much of you. As long as you bore my heirs and didn't run

screaming down the streets with a sword swinging, you'd do.
But me—"

"Oh, we must stop this," Kayli said crossly. "We both are
whining with self-pity, and there is no excuse for it." She was
horrified by her words as soon as they had left her lips, and
she stood, holding out her hand to Randon. "Oh, Randon, I—"
Abruptly the room seemed to drop out from under her feet,
and she grabbed desperately at the edge of the table, crying
out involuntarily as sharp cramps doubled her over.

"Kayli!" Randon rose; Kayli only dimly felt his arms
around her, guiding her to the bed. She retched helpessly,
alarmed to see that the vomitus staining her pillow was red.
A river of heat, of pain, ran through her veins—

And at the end of the river, silence.

8

CRASH OF THUNDER. KAYLI FORCED OPEN
crusted eyelids. The room was dark but for the embers
of the hearth fire. She rolled her head to the side; there
was Randon in a chair beside the bed, his head down on his
folded arms on the coverlet.

"Randon?" Kayli's voice came out a harsh, weak croak,
but Randon's head jerked up as if he had been stabbed.

"Kayli. Thank the Bright Ones." He took her hand, pressed
it gently to a cheek rough with stubble. "Don't move, Kayli.
Don't speak. Just be still until I get Stevann."

Kayli was too weak and tired to do anything but obey. It
seemed only a moment later that Stevann appeared at her bedside, Endra with him; had she fallen asleep again?

"Well, good evening, lady," Stevann said cheerfully. "Or
good morn, rather, as it's nearly dawn. You had us all well
frightened, I don't mind saying. I'll make you a bargain—if
you can swallow another of my nasty brews, you can have all
the broth and cream you want. No, don't try to sit; let us do
all the work for you."

Randon's arm was warm and strong under her head and
shoulders, and Kayli dutifully swallowed another potion,
choking a little at its sickly-sweet flavor. Then, thank the
Flame, there was thick soup, rich with butter and cream, to

banish the sweetness and soothe her sore throat.

"That's better, isn't it?" Stevann slid more pillows behind her head and shoulders so Kayli could look around her. "How do you feel?"

"Tired." It was a weary sigh. "My throat aches. And my vitals."

"I'm not surprised." Stevann laid his hand against her forehead, nodded, then felt the beat of her heart. "We thought we'd lost you, lady. You were poisoned with *arrabia*."

Poisoned! The word brought only a dull surprise through her weariness. But what else could it have been? No disease could have struck so quickly. *Arrabia,* though—that was a Sarkondish poison, often fatal.

"You're made of strong stuff, lady," Stevann said more soberly. "But you can thank your midwife in part for your life. I didn't know that mesinica root was used in Bregond to treat *arrabia* poisoning."

"It wasn't me, Brother Stevann," Endra said forthrightly. "I've had no experience with poisons. You can thank Seba instead. Kayli, child, you've never seen the like. No doubt the border healing temples have seen Sarkondish poisons, and Seba learned of it there. The child was describing a plant I didn't know, so I took her to those books from Lady Ynea, and she found it in a minute. We had riders combing the hedgerows by lantern light. Fortunately we found some."

Kayli turned to Randon.

"Was anyone else poisoned?" she rasped.

Randon shook his head.

"Only you. I've racked my brain trying to remember what you ate, what I ate. But by the time I thought to send someone down to the kitchen, all the plates and cups were emptied and washed. There was some wine left in the pitcher we'd both drunk from, but we gave it to one of the dogs and it suffered no harm. All I can think is that the poison was put directly into your cup or plate. Stevann says *arrabia* is a slow poison—it could have been anytime during the meal."

He hesitated, glancing at Stevann.

"I've already had the kitchen and serving staff questioned under truth spell, although I had to bring in a mage to do it—Stevann needed all his power for you. None of the staff were involved. Our guests—'' A look of such pain crossed Randon's face that Kayli squeezed his fingers as hard as she could. "I don't know how any of them could have had the opportunity to do it. I don't think any of them were ever alone with the food.'' His voice was heavy. "And I don't have enough evidence to justify questioning them under truth spell."

"No!" Kayli started upright, then grimaced and fell back weakly, the strength running out of her like water from a leaky cup. "No," she said as firmly as she could. "You must not. Promise me you will not do that." Unless Randon believed there was a wholesale conspiracy among the heads of the guilds, and surely he could not believe that, even at worst some of their guests must be wholly innocent. If Randon antagonized them, he would lose the only powerful support he had. Surely he must understand that.

"Shhh." Randon smoothed her forehead. "Don't worry yourself. I'll do nothing for now, if that's what you want. I promise. But you must rest."

Kayli was too weak and tired to do anything but obey, glad when Stevann and Endra left her and Randon alone. Randon stretched out on the bed beside her, sliding his fingers very gently along her arm as if he was afraid to touch her.

"It's strange," he murmured. "Until I thought I'd lose you, I didn't really realize how I'd come to—to value you. And now you may be the only one I can trust."

His words troubled Kayli profoundly, but she was too tired to answer; she could only smile at him as the last embers of her strength burned down into darkness.

The next day Kayli was a little stronger, the pain in her vitals less, and Endra sternly banished Randon from the room.

"She'll mend in her own time and no sooner," the midwife said firmly. "Meanwhile you look worse than your lady, and you've neglected your duties. And I would most respectfully suggest a bath and clean clothing, High Lord, before you sit in audience today. I'll make certain nobody disturbs your lady's rest, and not a drop or morsel will cross her lips but what Brother Stevann and I have approved. Now go."

When Randon reluctantly allowed himself to be shooed out the door, Endra brought in Anida and Devra, and two other Bregondish women whom Kayli did not recognize.

"This is Silva, and this is Minda," Endra said, indicating the two new maids. "Your mother sent them with the caravan that arrived a few days ago. Between the five of us, doubtless we can manage to get you into a tub to soak."

"Days?" Kayli's voice was still a harsh croak, but surprise and dismay lent it strength. "How long?"

"Four days." Endra slid her arm under Kayli's shoulders and muscled her upright. "No, lady, just lie quiet and let us take care of you." Almost magically the woman whisked Kayli out of bed and into blessedly hot water.

"Yes, it's been four days," Endra continued, motioning the other maids to change the bed linens while she gently washed the sweat from Kayli's skin. "The caravan arrived the day after. It's still here, too; Brother Santee wouldn't leave until he could take word back that you were going to be all right. Let's see, what else? Your mother and father sent the girls, as I mentioned, and a groom for your horses, and all sorts of gifts and trade goods. There's boxes for you, too, from your parents and from the temple. But all that will wait until you're stronger." Thunder crashed and Endra set her hands on her hips, pursing her lips with annoyance. "Storming again. Bregondish don't call this 'wetlands' for naught. Three days already of rain and noise, and no sign of it stopping, either. A good thing it wasn't pouring down the night you were poisoned, else nobody could've found that root."

Kayli said nothing, letting Endra's talk wash over her in a flood more soothing than the hot water. A package from the temple—that must be from Brisi. And a groom—the facts seemed to slip through her mind like water through her fingers; she couldn't seem to grasp them. But one thought pushed its way to the forefront.

"Seba," Kayli said, suddenly strengthened by the memory. "Endra, I must speak with her."

Endra set her hands on her hips and raised both eyebrows.

"Now? All right, but we'll get you out of the tub first. Minda, fetch the child, will you? And while you're out, tell the cook we're ready for the soup."

Kayli was dried, comfortably wrapped in a clean robe, and settled snugly into her bed when Seba crept into the room, carrying a tray.

"Priestess, I have soup and tea," she said timidly. "The lady midwife asked me to bring it."

"Soup? Tea?" Kayli sighed as she lifted the covers from the bowl and cup. "It seems I am fasting again." She tasted the soup and grimaced; once again the thick broth was overly rich with cream and butter and eggs.

"*Arrabia* burns from within," Seba murmured. "It will take time for the flesh burned from your throat and vitals to heal. The enriched broth is soothing as well as nourishing. Please drink, Priestess, I beg you."

"I am no priestess," Kayli said, but she swallowed the thick soup, sip by tiny sip, until it was gone. Soon she wished she'd saved a little for last, for the tea was so thick and sweet with honey that she could barely swallow it. She choked the last of it down, however, and by that time Seba had poured blessedly cold, clear water for her.

When she had finished, Kayli patted the edge of the bed at her side and, when Seba hesitated, gazed at her sternly. Reluctantly Seba sat down, and Kayli took the small, callused hand in her own.

"Your knowledge and quick action saved my life," she said. "For that I am in your debt. No—" She held up her hand to silence Seba's protest. "You have saved the daughter of the High Lord of Bregond, and the High Lady of Agrond as well, and you have earned the gratitude of two countries.

"Soon the caravan will depart for Bregond," Kayli continued. "You should return to Bregond with it. Brother Santee, and the letter I will send, will tell my parents of the service you have rendered me. My parents could reward you with a herd of your own, if that is what you wish, or lands and a permanent home near their castle."

Seba's face fell.

"You are sending me away?" she murmured, stricken.

Kayli sighed.

"Little one, listen to me. My position here is not secure. Any reward I grant you could be taken away if I am set aside, and you might once more find yourself alone in a strange country. You deserve better than I can offer you here."

Seba would not raise her eyes from the floor.

"I can't go back, Pri—mistress. I could have the best herd

of horses in the land and nobody would buy from me. I could have the largest house and nobody would sit at my table.''

Kayli sighed. She wanted to argue, but could not. A Sarkondish captive was dead in the eyes of kin and country, to be mourned, yes, and avenged if possible. A living captive was a traitor to betray her people, a hostage to cripple and bleed them, a suffering victim to haunt their dreams. No. The captives were dead, honorably and cleanly by their own hand, as was their right—and their duty.

And if not, they would come to wish they were.

No, Seba was right. It was monstrously unfair, as unfair as the raid which had left a child alone and enslaved in a foreign country. But there was nothing to do but hope that the alliance of Agrond and Bregond would finally drive Sarkond back beyond the borders forever.

"Please, mistress, don't send me away," Seba whispered, her fingers clutching desperately at the blankets.

"No, Seba. I will not send you away." She could, she supposed, give the child money, lands, a house here in Agrond. But she had no assurance that such gifts would be honored if Kayli were set aside as High Lady—and likely, too, that the citizens of Agrond might turn on the poor child in such a case. And Seba had been a slave for many years; although Kayli was disappointed that Seba would rather remain in service to her than take the risks of freedom, it was understandable. Perhaps it was best that the girl stay with her, at least for now, where Kayli could protect her. Later, when she'd borne Randon's child and secured her own future, when Seba's broken spirit had grown strong again, there could be other rewards.

"No, child, you may stay if that is truly what you want."

The naked relief in Seba's expression troubled Kayli, but she only squeezed the small, hard fingers and said nothing.

"I'll serve you well, mistress, I swear," Seba breathed. "But for now you should rest again."

The child was gone as quietly as she'd come, whisking the dishes with her. Kayli lay back, banishing the numerous worries that pressed for her attention, and let herself drift into sleep, hoping that Randon would be there when she woke.

When she opened her eyes, however, she was surprised and a little alarmed to see Terralt's silhouette, not Randon's, in the dim light of the fire. Kayli started to push herself upright, her head swimming, when she spotted Endra hovering at the open door, glancing from her to Terralt as if undecided whether to stay as chaperon or send for the guards to haul the visitor away. Kayli waved Endra over and let the midwife push more pillows behind her; then Endra withdrew as far as the window, where she pulled up a chair and pointedly sat down.

Terralt chuckled and stepped to the bedside.

"Your maid doubtless believes I poisoned you, and I've come to finish the job," he said. "Can you reassure her?"

"I have no idea," Kayli rasped, trying to discern his expression in the dim light. "Can I?"

Terralt was silent for a moment. Then he chuckled again, but it was a rather weary chuckle, Kayli thought.

"Unless you believe Stevann is conspiring against you as well," he said. "He chose the mage who questioned the kitchen staff, and I demanded to be the first tested. So you can rest assured I'm not here to see my evil deed completed."

Kayli did not know what to say. She turned away.

"Endra, would you bring me something to drink?"

Endra clucked reprovingly, but she left, closing the door behind her, leaving Terralt to draw up a chair to the bedside.

"In fact," Terralt said, as if they were in the middle of a pleasant conversation, "I came to bring Ynea's regards. Stevann won't let her out of her bed, but she sent more of her flower books to entertain you."

"One of those books helped to save my life," Kayli retorted, hating Terralt's condescending tone. "In that book they found the plant that counteracted the poison."

Kayli could not be certain in the darkness, but she thought Terralt smiled.

"I'll tell Ynea," he said. "It'll cheer her no end. She's not the type to gloat, but I suppose she's earned it this time." He leaned a little forward. "I'll even apologize for ridiculing her hobby."

"Then make your apology to her, not to me," Kayli said. "For she has earned that, too, many times over."

Terralt leaned back again, and when the fire flared briefly, Kayli could see his familiar grin.

"You'll not be satisfied until you lay the whip to my back

with your own hand, will you?" he said wryly. "Very well. Ynea will have her apology. Rest well, my lady, and I wish you a swift recovery. Good night."

Terralt left Kayli with a thousand questions burning in her mind. If he was not behind her poisoning, who could it have been? Kayli dreaded the thought that one of Randon's friends might have been responsible. But who else could it be?

Endra brought more rich soup, more oversweet tea, but little sympathy as Kayli choked down the liquids.

"Be glad you're alive to drink it," the midwife said sternly. "Now, if you can sit up, I'll comb your hair. Your husband should be here soon."

The storm raged outside, and Kayli drowsed and woke, drowsed and woke again, but still Randon did not return. Perhaps he was meeting with his advisers. Perhaps he was working with Terralt.

Perhaps he did not want to come.

When Randon arrived at what Kayli guessed must be nearly suppertime, he was neatly dressed and appeared better rested than when she had last seen him, but no less harried as he sat down in the chair by the bedside.

"Endra said you were stronger today," he said, clasping her hand. "But, if you'll pardon me saying so, you look worse than the night you arrived here. Can I get you anything?"

"Some water, please." Kayli managed to smile despite the dull, cramping emptiness of her belly. "It seems I am back to soup and tea."

"Stevann told me." Randon grinned, too. "Well, it won't be for long." He helped her scoot up higher on the pillows, then handed her a cup of water. "Drink up. I've sent for your supper. I've been so busy, I just ate while I worked."

"Busy?" Kayli prompted.

"Oh, Bright Ones, I don't know who I *didn't* see today," Randon groaned. "Guards are looking for anyone selling or buying *arrabia*. All the mercantile houses, it seems, have sent envoys to swear that none of their caravans could possibly have carried in Sarkondish agents or poisons. My advisers are in an uproar." He sighed. "Then there's the slaves."

"Slaves?" Kayli rasped.

"Four days ago we made our announcement to the heads

of the guilds, or don't you remember?'' Randon told her. ''I think every craft hall in the city's sent someone to ask about it. I finally drafted an official announcement today, and though I haven't sent it out yet, already a dozen slaves have appeared mysteriously on my very doorstep—some with money, others with nothing, half speaking no Agrondish, all confused and terrified. Your Brother Santee has been helping to translate. Bright Ones, what a mess.'' He shook his head ruefully.

''I am sorry.'' Kayli squeezed his fingers. ''Sorry for starting this, and then not being there to help you.''

''Well, blame whoever poisoned you, then,'' Randon said flatly. ''In the meantime don't let it worry you. I gave Terralt charge of tracking down the owners and so on. Interestingly, he finds it a worthwhile cause.''

''He was here,'' Kayli said when Randon paused.

''He was? When?'' Randon asked, surprised.

''Near noon, perhaps.'' She sipped a little more water. ''He assured me that he had not poisoned me.''

''I never thought he did.'' Randon sat back thoughtfully. ''His complaint is with me, not you. Besides, his pride wouldn't let him take the seat of Agrond by murder.''

''Then who?'' Kayli whispered.

Randon gazed at her soberly.

''I don't know,'' he said. ''The guards swore under truth spell that nobody was in the dining room but the servants and our guests. The servants were also cleared. I don't want to blame any of my friends, the Bright Ones know, but who else is there?''

''You must not accuse them,'' Kayli said as firmly as her ravaged throat would allow. ''They may all be innocent. At least some of them must be. You cannot lose their support.''

''I don't need the support of traitors,'' Randon said, but he wore a troubled expression.

''There is no proof that they are traitors,'' Kayli pressed. ''Until you know otherwise, you must believe they are innocent, your friends. And you need friends in this time.'' *But on what friends shall I rely?* her mind cried.

''I don't agree.'' Randon sighed. ''Unfortunately my advisers do. They say that without evidence to bring the guild heads in for questioning, I'll gain nothing by antagonizing them." He shook his head. "But on one point I'll not be swayed: until our confirmation, every morsel you put in your mouth will be tasted by a servant first."

"That would be of no use," Kayli said gently. "With a slow poison such as *arrabia,* many hours might pass before any effects would be noticeable."

"Then I'll talk with Stevann about some kind of magical protection," Randon said, undaunted.

Kayli only smiled at Randon's concern. If the citizens of Agrond truly wished her dead, no food taster or spell could protect her forever.

"How have the people reacted to the news?" Kayli asked.

"I've been surprised," Randon admitted. "The city guards report more outrage than I expected. Of course it's frightening to the peasants to realize that their rulers are vulnerable, but it goes beyond that. Do you know, peasants are coming forward to expose lowlifes selling poisons in the alleys, and one of the city's wisewomen sent a silver charm that's supposed to turn black when it touches poison. Stevann says there's not a grain of truth to it, but it's a kind thought."

Randon's words warmed Kayli's heart. At least not every citizen of Agrond hungered for her blood. But one, nevertheless, hated Kayli with a fearful passion. She'd never thought she need fear for her life in the castle itself.

"You're so quiet," Randon said gently. "I thought my news might cheer you."

"It was good news," Kayli said quickly. Then she sighed. "I tried to send Seba home. But she wants only to serve me."

"Chains are easily struck from the hands of a slave," Randon said, nodding. "It's harder to strike them from the heart. In part, that's what I feared in releasing all these slaves—that they don't know how to live free."

Kayli was silent for a moment, remembering the day when a small group of beggars had knocked on the door of the temple.

"Give a beggar coins, and you fill his belly once," Brisi had said. "Give him work, and you feed his spirit with self-respect. But teach him a trade, and you feed both body and spirit for life."

"We were wrong," Kayli said at last. "And I most of all.

I was so blinded by the wish for—for revenge, I confess, against the wrongdoers that I forgot the needs of the victims."

Randon sighed, too.

"Well, I admit I thought more about politics and economics," he said. "I didn't want to recognize that I have a duty toward every resident of Agrond, no matter how they came to be here. But I don't know what to do about it."

"You say you have not yet sent out the proclamation," Kayli said after a moment's thought. "Perhaps, instead of giving the freed slaves money, they might instead be apprenticed at some trade. Thus the slaves, Agrond's economy, and justice are all served."

Randon raised his eyebrows, then grinned.

"Apprenticeships! I should've thought of that myself. By the Bright Ones, I'll do it, and the guilds will love me all the more for it." He patted Kayli's hand. "Only just awakened from near death, and still the wise High Lady. Terralt was right—I *have* been luckier than I deserve."

Randon answered a quiet knock at the chamber door and returned with a tray. He watched sternly while Kayli finished her soup and tea, grinning at her reluctance.

"Back to a liquid supper again," Randon chuckled. "Well, Stevann says you'll be on your feet again in a few days, although the effects of *arrabia* tend to linger, and then I'll have a grand feast to celebrate your recovery."

"Well, just as well I had not yet conceived," Kayli said with a sigh. "For such poisoning would have cost a child in my womb its life, or at least done it great harm."

Randon sighed, too.

"That's true," he said. "I suppose it's just as well, even though—" He stopped abruptly.

"Even though?" Kayli prompted. "Randon, what?" she pressed when he did not answer immediately.

"Stevann said—" Randon hesitated. "Stevann said that a poison that lingers in the body like *arrabia* usually renders women barren for some time. But try not to worry. There are potions, spells that Stevann can try, but later, when you're stronger, much stronger."

Kayli said nothing, but she could see that *he* was worried.

Surely the council was worried, too. No wonder Terralt had been so cheerful.

"Look, all that's important now is that you regain your strength," Randon said stoutly. "The Bright Ones know there's nothing to do in such weather *but* stay home and relax." As if in agreement, a great peal of thunder shook the castle.

"It was storming yesterday when I first woke," Kayli remembered.

"It's been storming," Randon corrected, "since you were poisoned. Early summer storms aren't rare, but I admit the timing was amazing. There's a rumor circulating through Tarkesh that the Bright Ones were angered by the attempt on your life."

He smiled as he spoke, but his words troubled Kayli. In Bregond such a storm was a powerful omen and, despite the life-giving rain, not a good one. A thunderstorm was an unlikely alliance of Wind, Flame, and Water against Earth, and for it to linger so in one place must hold great meaning. Had Kayli become so much a part of Agrond's destiny that harm to her brought such dire punishment upon Tarkesh?

"Has the storm done much damage?" she whispered.

Randon shrugged uncomfortably.

"The river's risen," he said. "If the rain keeps up, it could drown acres of crops. Luckily only this part of the country is affected, or so Stevann says. If the rain doesn't stop soon, he'll work with weather mages, turn the storm north into Sarkond. Now stop fretting, and we'll get some sleep. That, at least, we can do in foul weather as well as fair."

Well, but she had done nothing but rest for days, and even when Randon snored beside her, Kayli found that sleep eluded her. At last she slid unsteadily from the bed and sat on the hearth. The fire had been banked for the night, but she used the small bellows to fan the coals alight. The dancing flames comforted her, and the radiance of the fire drove some of the weakness and ache from her body. Kayli reached out impulsively, thrusting her hand into the brightest part of the flames.

A shock ran up her arm, neither pain nor pleasure; more the snapping jolt she felt in dry winter air when she touched metal. Energy flowed up Kayli's arm and into her body in sharp, almost painful waves, and she nearly pulled back instinctively. Of course—she was an Initiate now, her body attuned to fire energies. Just as she fed those energies from within herself, so they fed her, too, from outside. Kayli sat still until the last of her weakness passed, and with it the constant gnawing ache in her vitals. She banked the fire, took her speaking crystal from its pouch, and crept out of the room and into Randon's small armory as silently as she could.

Perhaps because of her illness, it was some time before Brisi's face appeared in the crystal, and the High Priestess raised her brows in gentle surprise when she saw Kayli.

"Well met, young one!" she said. "I am glad to see you well, and of course I am always pleased to talk with you, but what has happened to make you call at such an hour? I had sought my bed an hour past."

"I beg your pardon, High Priestess," Kayli said humbly. "But a great trouble has come upon me, and I desperately need your wise counsel."

Brisi listened silently, only the expression in her eyes betraying her horror when Kayli spoke of her poisoning. When Kayli finished, she shook her head slowly, her lips tight, and Kayli was surprised to see the High Priestess betray even that much emotion. Her story must have indeed shaken her mentor to the very depths of her spirit.

"What a terrible thing, child," the High Priestess murmured. "And how fortunate that someone nearby knew the remedy for *arrabia* poisoning. But how can I help you? Poisons and their remedies, that is more a matter for a healer than a priestess of the Flame."

"Randon's healer has done his best for me," Kayli told her teacher. "No, what I would know is this: I have seen how the Flame can strengthen and heal. I know that fire is cleansing as well. Is there a ritual by which the Flame can cleanse this poison from my body, perhaps a ritual to ready my body for the conception of the child I must bear?"

Brisi was silent for a long moment. When she spoke, her words were slow and measured.

"Young one, you are a clever student," she said. "And in honesty I must tell you that there is such a ritual in the grimoire I sent with you. But as your teacher, I ask that you trust now in what I say. The Rite of Renewal is beyond the level of skill to which you could possibly have progressed since your Awakening. In time you will master the ritual, I do not doubt, but I pray that you remember the folly of reaching beyond your ability.''

''Then can you offer me another solution, High Priestess?'' Kayli asked, fighting down despair.

''Kayli.'' Brisi sighed heavily. ''My student, if you have one fault, it is that your nature is too close to that of the Flame itself—burning fierce and hot and heedless. Curbing that impatience has been your greatest battle. You must remember that lesson. Even those in Agrond who oppose your marriage cannot cast you aside for the results of a poisoning by their own people. They will give you time to mend.''

Brisi changed the subject firmly, telling Kayli of the small events at the Order, but Kayli had no interest in news that once would have brought her joy. She was relieved when the High Priestess said her good-byes and the crystal darkened.

Kayli returned to bed and slept rather uneasily, waking immediately when Randon slid out of bed.

''Are you in audience again?'' she asked with a sigh as Randon donned his dressing gown.

Randon shook his head.

''Meeting with my advisers,'' he said ruefully. ''Then a private session with a few of the guard captains over the new proclamation. *Then* lunch with Terralt while he explains the new tax laws Father enacted last year. But I've cleared the whole afternoon. Unless Brother Santee needs me again, or there's another representative here to ask about the new proclamation or—''

He sighed and shrugged helplessly.

''Yes. Of course.'' Kayli stifled a sigh of her own. Randon could hardly let his country wait while he sat at her bedside. Besides, if she had read his disheveled appearance and weariness correctly, he'd already spent several days and nights doing just that. And, she realized, it might be good that she had time alone, to consult her grimoires.

Endra appeared shortly after Randon's departure with more soup and tea for Kayli's breakfast. Stevann politely waited until Kayli had had time to bathe and put on a clean gown before he came to examine her. After he had felt her pulse and smelled her breath, he frowned and shook his head.

"You've improved remarkably in such a short time," he admitted. "You may try a little bread in your soup at dinner, and you may walk about the chamber a bit, but you mustn't weary yourself. Rest is what you'll need most for some time."

"The fertility potion," Kayli said hesitantly. "How soon may I begin to take it again?"

Stevann gazed at her sternly.

"If your cycles resume when they should, a month after that. If not, a month after they *do*. But you mustn't—"

"—trouble myself," Kayli finished with a sigh.

As soon as Stevann was gone, however, she pulled out Brisi's grimoire and began leafing through the spells. She was dismayed to find the Rite of Renewal far into the grimoire, among the most difficult rituals. The procedures seemed simple and straightforward enough; most of her novice rituals had been far more complicated. But the very simplicity of the ritual itself, she suspected, was deceptive. Only a priest or priestess of great skill would not require the progressive deepening of focus accorded by an elaborate ritual.

Any mage's greatest tool was the force of her will—to focus her concentration during the preparatory stages of the ritual, but even more importantly, to keep from being overwhelmed by the raw power of the Flame. The only difference between the High Priestess and the rankest Initiate was the strength of her will—and her discipline, born of experience, in applying it.

Strength of will.

Kayli spent the morning studying the ritual, and at dinnertime, savoring the promised bread, she sent for Seba. The young girl crept in as timidly as she had before, head down as if she expected a beating. When Kayli motioned her to sit at the table, Seba perched on the edge of the chair as if her touch would somehow soil it.

"Seba, you spent some time at one of the Temples of Healing," Kayli said, noting the child's immediate slight relaxation as no rebuke seemed forthcoming. "Did you witness many of the rituals performed there?"

"Many," Seba murmured. "The temple was near the border, an area frequented by Sarkondish raiders. Many came to our temple for healing or shelter. I was permitted to serve the temple in small ways—arranging the ritual instruments, preparing the inner temple for ceremonies, other such duties. I hoped to be allowed to stay, to cook or clean, perhaps.''

Kayli sighed and patted Seba's hand comfortingly. The poor child must have had not so much as a glimmer of the healing gift. Novices at the Healing Temples were fortunate that there was need for even those with very little of the gift, as midwives, herbalists, and so on. Elemental magic was not nearly so forgiving; either a novice had enough of the gift to train as a mage, or she did not.

But why had the temple not kept Seba on to study as an herbalist or an assistant to one of the traveling healers? Perhaps the priests and priestesses thought Seba had a vocation better realized among the horse clans.

"Seba, I wish to perform a very important ritual in the forge," Kayli said slowly. "An assistant would be helpful. It would be simple work and there would be no danger to you, but I wish to keep the ritual secret until it is completed. Would you be willing to assist me?''

Seba ducked her head in a quick nod. That was all, but the glow in her eyes spoke eloquently.

Randon did not return as promised after dinner, and Kayli decided finally that she could not bear the inside of her chambers one moment longer. Resolutely she crept out into the hallway after making sure none of the servants were about. She would find Randon at whatever administrative work he was doing. He would chide her for disobeying Stevann's orders, but he would let her stay, and perhaps she could read papers for him. Anything was better than another afternoon in bed.

After dodging around corners a dozen times to avoid detection, Kayli resolutely squared her shoulders and walked openly down the stairs. She occasioned a number of surprised stares, but no one came to herd her back to bed. And why should they? She was their mistress and their High Lady.

To her surprise, Randon was neither in the study where she expected to find him nor in the library. Kayli feared that he had had to sit in an afternoon audience after all, but a look out the front windows showed no carriages waiting outside, nor peasants waiting their turn. At last she made her way to the council chambers and, with more assurance than she felt, waved the guards away from the door. When they had retired, rather reluctantly Kayli thought, she opened the door just a crack. If Randon was alone, she could still join him.

When she peeped through the crack, however, she was dismayed to see that the full council in session. She had already started to shut the door when the sound of her name froze her where she was.

"I tell you, there's no need to argue about the matter now," Randon said. "Three days ago Kayli had one foot in the Dark Realms, and all because *we* failed to protect her—we who asked for this wedding in the first place."

"All I'm asking, High Lord presumptive," Lord Jaxon's voice insisted, "is that you give the matter due thought. Every month that passes places you both at greater jeopardy."

"I think you're wrong," Randon said. "I've seen it in my audiences. I've heard it in rumors from the city, in the reports of my guard captains. The people are coming to accept Kayli. Those who disapprove of the match are being won over."

"And one of those people who are growing to love our new High Lady poisoned her," Lord Kereg said gently. "She can't bear your heir anytime soon—perhaps never—and she's in constant danger of further attempts on her life. What will it gain either of you if she costs you the throne of Agrond?"

Randon was silent for a long moment, and that very silence almost broke Kayli's heart.

"If I sent Kayli back to Bregond," he said at last, "I might as well give up the throne to Terralt and be done with it. My father named me as Heir to make this alliance between Agrond and Bregond at last. What do I have to offer Agrond without that alliance? Terralt's more prepared for this work than I am, I can't deny it. No, whatever I can give my country as High Lord depends on Kayli as my High Lady. Together, we *do* have something to offer. I'll take my chances with her."

His words should have comforted Kayli, but it was with a heavy heart that she closed the door and made her way back to her room. By the time she regained her chambers, removed her gown, and crawled back into bed, she was tired beyond any illness, tired to her very soul. From the day she had arrived in Agrond, she had tried in every way she knew to be a good wife to Randon, a good High Lady. Now it seemed that all that was not—might never be—enough. And there was nothing more she could do.

Well, no. There was one thing more. And that step, too, she would take. Because it was her duty.

And because it was her only hope.

9

KAYLI ROSE IN THE COLD, EMPTY HOURS BEFORE dawn, the noise as she slid out of bed covered by the continuing storm outside. She retrieved her grimoire from the table and slipped quietly out into the hall. When Randon awakened, he would not be surprised to find her gone; she had left a letter for him, telling him that she would be meditating in the forge.

It was not a lie. Not wholly, at least.

Kayli easily eluded the few servants in the halls and made her way to the forge, where Seba waited. How the child managed it, Kayli had no idea, but she had brought down a bathtub and enough water for a proper purifying bath. Seba had not kindled a fire in the firepit—it was vital for the ritual that Kayli light that fire herself—but she had lit the small forge in order to heat the water, and she had laid a bed of fresh coal ready in the firepit.

The familiar scent of cleansing herbs and unguents calmed Kayli even as they refreshed her, allowing her to focus on her preparations. Even so, she could not help thinking of Randon asleep in their chambers, and felt a pang at the thought.

It was past suppertime when Randon had returned to their chambers, but Kayli had asked Stevann for a sleeping potion and was so deeply asleep that she had only half roused at his return. The potion guaranteed her rest before the ritual, but better yet, sleep spared her the necessity of talking to Randon. She did not want to hear his explanation of why he had not returned earlier; she thought she could not bear it if he lied to her, as he surely must.

Seba, bless her, knew better than to distract Kayli with talk. She quietly made sure that everything Kayli might want lay within easy reach, then retired until Kayli might need her for another task. She emerged from her corner only long enough to help Kayli braid her hair and coil it up under the protective leather cap; then she melted back into the shadows.

When Kayli was satisfied with her preparations, she knelt at the edge of the firepit. Her skill had increased since she'd consecrated the forge; now she lit the coal almost casually. She felt a brief pang; she should never have had to dare a firepit for the first time alone. There should be other priestesses to kindle the flames for her firewalk.

But this was no simple firewalk. Kayli did not let the fire burn down to coals; instead, she prodded the flames higher, Seba moving unobtrusively to operate the large bellows as Kayli had instructed her.

The flames burned hotter, feeding on the coal, on the air from the bellows, on the power within her, until they burned so bright she could scarcely look at them, so hot that the stone floor around the edge of the firepit glowed red. Kayli held her arms out over the flames and began her chant.

The fire burned even more brightly in the firepit, and Kayli felt an answering flame growing within her, building quickly until she wondered whether it was the Flame within her, not the fire outside, that would immolate her. Then there was a moment of utter stillness, of incredible precise balance in which the backfire within Kayli's soul equaled exactly the flames in the firepit before her. In that instant of complete clarity, there was no room for fear or doubt; Kayli spoke the last words of her chant and stepped forward into the fire.

There was pain, incredible pain as Kayli felt herself consumed utterly—but was it from the inside or the outside that the Flame devoured her flesh, her spirit? And in the wake of that pain, even as surely as the flesh crisped and fell from her bones, her bones charred and crumbled to ash, came a wild, excruciating pleasure as she burned red-hot, white-hot, molten, and was forged anew, every nerve and fiber singing with the Flame. It fed her even as it consumed her, filling the last corner of her spirit as her power, in turn, fed it.

Kayli collapsed to her knees (*Knees? I still have knees?*), then fell to her back, crying out (*Voice? I have a voice, and ears to hear it?*) as the Flame filled her, consumed her, dissolved her and resurrected her, knew her as no lover could. Fiery fingers stroked their way up her nerves, through her veins, down her spine, filled her womb, and curled around her heart. She cried out again, frightened and at the same glad that she was losing control—no, no, that was not the truth, the truth was that she was lost, utterly lost, that she belonged to the Flame now, that even the tiny inner core that was *Kayli* was consumed. She was losing herself, and at the same time she wanted that dissolution, to be one with the Flame and burn forever—

But a tiny, stubborn core of her will refused to give in, and it was finally that small nagging core that made her raise her head and slowly crawl from the center of the firepit, sobbing as she forced her leaden limbs to move. Was the fire cooling slightly around her, relinquishing her as reluctantly as she pulled away from its heart?

Her fingertips touched hot stone, and Kayli crawled, fingerwidth by fingerwidth, from the firepit. Hot stone gave way to warm stone to cool stone to cold stone, and at last she rolled to her back and panted, whimpering as the fire within her subsided only slightly.

Seba abandoned the bellows, and the fire in the pit of exhausted coal, with neither Kayli's energy nor the gusts of air to feed on, subsided. Seba dampened a cloth in a bucket of clean water and gently washed most of the ash and cinders from Kayli's skin, but Kayli could be still no longer. She pulled the leather cap from her hair and flung it aside, pulled her robe impatiently around her, and half ran to the door.

"Send a maid for my husband," she said breathlessly, striving to think over the pulsing heat in her body. "Tell him he must come to our chambers immediately. Immediately."

This time, although Kayli kept to the backstairs as before, she did not care in the slightest when some of the servants saw her; she did not care how they stared at their mistress dashing up the stairs, her hair tumbled and her feet bare, her gown barely closed and her eyes burning. Kayli dashed into her chamber and flung her robe heedlessly aside, kindling the fire in the hearth with the merest wisp of casual thought. As the hearth fire flared alight, she almost screamed as her awareness of it raced up and down her nerves. But no matter how hotly that fire burned, she burned hotter still, and she paced impatiently, clasping her arms around herself as if to hold back that fire within her.

It seemed an eternity before Randon burst through the door, worry plain on his face, his fingers stained with ink, and a pen still clenched in his hand. He saw Kayli at the hearth and knelt beside her, dropping the pen.

"What's the matter?" he said breathlessly, frowning at her nakedness. "Has your fever come back? Should I send for Stevann? I was told—"

"Not Stevann," Kayli gasped through the tumult in her mind, her body. "You are all I need." His tunic tore under her desperate grip as she tried to pull it from his body by main force. Flame flowed through her body, into his and back again in a wave that was almost painful in its intensity. Words. Why must there be words now?

Randon seized her wrists, a scowl of mixed puzzlement and anger gathering on his brow. Even that slight contact made her blood sing.

"Damn all, Kayli, I was in council signing important documents. By the Bright Ones, what did you think—"

"Don't speak," Kayli said urgently, pulling him to her. "Don't speak."

"What—" Randon began, but she stopped his words with her lips, her momentum toppling them both to the hearth fur.

Randon did not react for a moment, as if utterly amazed by Kayli's insistence, but then the heat of her body kindled his as a spark might kindle dry grass. And like that same grass fire, the flames swept heedlessly through them both, burning hot and furious. And when the fire had spent itself, Kayli and Randon lay panting on the hearth furs among the rags of Randon's clothing, too tired to move.

It was some time before Randon spoke, rather breathlessly.

"Well! I'm sure this won't be the last time I'm called out of a council session, but I wonder if the other occasions will be so pleasant an interruption. Still, I don't know what got into you, Kayli. That was an important meeting. And besides, however well you might feel, I doubt Stevann would have approved of such—well, such vigorous activity for you."

Kayli leaned her face into his sweaty shoulder. No, she would not tell him yet. Not until she was certain. She did not owe him the full truth now, not while he discussed her fate with the council behind closed doors.

"I beg your pardon," she said softly. "Please forgive me. I have felt—very lonely. Very confined."

Randon sighed, and his hand smoothed her hair.

"I know," he said. "I'm sorry. Look, if you're well enough for this, I don't see why you should stay in your room. I'll talk to Stevann. And I suppose it was my fault, after all. I promised I'd spend the afternoon with you yesterday."

"Do you need to go back?" Kayli asked quietly. "To make your excuses to your advisers."

"Too late," Randon said, chuckling. "I'm sure they've gone by now. I'll send a messenger around to apologize, and by the next meeting I'll think of something to tell them."

Randon dispatched the messenger and sent a maid to fetch up dinner. Kayli tried not to look at Randon's food while she soaked up her soup with sodden bread, but the meal depressed her, the more so because there was now no need for her to bear this liquid fast, and there was no way to explain that without causing more trouble. Randon and Brother Stevann, rather than being relieved by her recovery, would no doubt be incensed at the risk she had taken, even though they had no idea of the full extent of that risk. Kayli remembered the searing touch of the Flame and shivered.

"Must you work this afternoon?" she asked Randon, but she rather hoped he would. She had no desire to pass the afternoon in his company while a coal of resentment still smoldered in her heart after what she had overheard. She felt a guilty relief when she saw the regret in Randon's expression.

"I'm sorry," he said, "but I'm going to work with Terralt and Brother Santee with the freed slaves. I'm hoping Terralt can take over completely when Brother Santee is gone. His

Bregondish isn't good, but he's a better administrator than I am, and the responsibility will placate him. But I'll meet with the advisers very early tomorrow, and I *swear* I'll be done before dinner and I won't let *anything* disrupt our afternoon, not if the blighted castle is burning down around us.''

When Randon was gone, Kayli pulled on a dressing gown and slipped back down to the forge. She was surprised and dismayed to find the forge spotlessly clean, every tool in its place, fresh coal laid in the firepit, the tub removed—even the water barrel filled with clean water. How poor Seba must have worked to finish so quickly!

Kayli returned to her rooms and lay down, her hands folded thoughtfully over her belly. If she had conceived—and if she had performed the Rite of Renewal properly, she had—by tomorrow Stevann should be able to detect it. In the meantime a nap to recoup her strength would at least pass the time.

She had only just closed her eyes, however, when she found herself back in the heart of the fire, flame searing its way along her nerves. Light and warmth filled her, consuming her, her spirit burning bright as the sun—

Kayli jolted awake, shaking, her body drenched with sweat. She slid out of the bed, wrapping her arms around herself, and walked to the window, unfastening the shutters. A gust of cold wind and rain blew in, startling her; she'd forgotten the storm raging anew outside. Still, the cool rain felt good against her flushed face, and she leaned out the window, letting the wind run icy fingers through her sweat-damp hair.

A brilliant flash of lightning reached down from the sky to touch the horizon, and an answering wave of heat flashed through her loins, and she gasped and clutched the window ledge as her knees almost gave way under her. Fear seized her heart. Had the Rite of Renewal attuned her so thoroughly to the Flame that even lightning affected her? Brisi's notes on the Rite of Renewal had mentioned no such effect, but she *had* lost control of the ritual. What might the raw power of the Flame have done to her?

But no. Surely it was only a lingering sensitivity induced by her recent poisoning and her present weariness. Surely that sensitivity would fade as she recovered her own energies.

Kayli stood at the window until she was cold and wet. Each

flash of lightning seared through her body, but she had to marvel at the sheer quantity of water pouring down upon the land. Surely the river must be overflowing its banks by now.

When she was chilled, Kayli closed the shutters and curled up by the fire with one of Ynea's flower books. Thunder crashed, wind howled, and rain pounded against the castle; the storm in Kayli's body at last quieted somewhat despite her heightened awareness of the hearth fire, and she drowsed pleasantly until Randon opened the door.

"Good, you've been resting," he said, sighing with relief. "Do you know, after I left, I started wondering whether what happened wasn't a sort of lingering effect of the poison. I worried about it all afternoon."

Kayli smiled and laid the book aside, holding out her hand and letting Randon pull her to her feet.

"I was more wearied than I thought," she admitted.

"And the fire was pleasant with such a storm outside."

"Yes." Randon glanced at the shuttered window.

"The storm," Kayli realized. "That is why you have been so busy of late."

"Well, between the slaves and all this rain, I'll admit I've had all I can do and more," he said with a sigh. "But I told them all that at dinner tomorrow the High Lord disappears and becomes a husband."

"Thank you." The lines of weariness and concern on his face thawed Kayli's resentment. In truth, Randon had had more to occupy his time and attention than fretting over whether or not to set his wife aside in favor of another—and, she was ashamed to admit, the same should have been true for her. "Although this is no weather for a hunt, or even a pleasant ride in the country."

"No, I'm afraid it's not much weather for farming, either." Randon sighed. "The north side of the Coridowyn has flooded completely, and the south bank will go soon, there's no doubt of it. Dozens more fields were washed out by the rain. If the storm keeps up more than another day or two, there's not going to be a planting left in the area. The farmers can replant, but then there'll only be one crop this year."

"But only this area is affected, is it not?" Kayli asked him. "Other areas will produce their crops as always?"

Randon shrugged.

"It won't cause a famine, if that's what you mean," he said. "But that won't be much comfort to farmers who lose a whole planting, half their year's income."

"Well, then the rains must stop," Kayli said. "Where are your cloud herders?"

"Our what?" Randon raised his brows puzzledly.

"Air-Dedicates or water-Dedicates who specialize in using the wind to move the clouds," Kayli told him. "In Bregond they bring rain when there has been a long drought, but I see no reason why the opposite should not work."

Randon nodded.

"We have no cloud herders, as you call them," he said, "but we have mages who specialize in weather magic, and tomorrow they'll do what they can. Stevann's afraid there's magic behind this storm in the first place, and I admit I'm starting to wonder. But let Stevann and his mages worry about that." He put his arm around Kayli's waist and squeezed gently. "If you'd like to get out of the room, we could eat in the dining hall. Nobody but us, I promise."

As they walked down the stairs, Kayli wondered whether the guards had told Randon that she had listened at the door when he was meeting with his advisers the day before. Surely not, or he would have mentioned it; at least he could not have acted so naturally with her if he knew that she'd heard the advisers' recommendations. Why had the guards not told him?

But why should they? She was their High Lady; it was her right to *be* in the council chamber, and there was nothing strange in her peeping in to see if Randon was there, to listen for a moment to the business discussed. The guards themselves had been too far from the door to hear what was being said. Likely they thought no more of it after she had gone.

Randon had evidently thought ahead about their dinner, for Kayli found that their places had already been set at the table. She was surprised to see well-minced roasted fowl in her soup; Randon winked when she glanced at him in surprise.

"I won't tell Stevann if you won't," he said with a grin.

He had another surprise for her, too, for when they had finished their food, the servants brought small bowls of finely scraped fruit ices. As the cold, sweet-tart delicacy melted on her tongue, Kayli thought blissfully that surely there was no finer flavor in the universe.

"Since you're up and dressed," Randon remarked when they had finished, "I thought you might want to see what we're doing with the slaves who show up on our doorstep. Unless you're too tired. Stevann wouldn't approve."

"Oh, no," Kayli said quickly. "Now that I have already incurred his wrath, I may as well enjoy my misbehavior."

Randon drew a cloak around them and led her through the storm to one of the outbuildings behind the castle. As they shook the rain from their hair in the entryway, he explained that the building was a guard barracks.

"It wasn't half-full," he told her. "So I moved the guards to quarters in town. Mind you, most of the slaves are here just long enough to note their grievances, if they have any, and to find out what their skills are so that we can send them on to the appropriate guild."

When Randon opened the door, however, Kayli was both cheered and dismayed. The building was comfortable enough—fires warmed the place well, and the cots were thick with warm bedding. What stunned her, however, were the numbers of men, women, and children who glanced up with only dull curiosity as she and Randon stepped inside. Most appeared healthy enough, but some showed marks of recent beatings, and a few were so gaunt that their sunken cheeks and hollow eyes wrung her heart.

Brother Santee came to greet them; to Kayli's surprise, he held a tiny baby.

"Greetings and welcome, High Lord, High Lady," he said, glancing at Kayli with some surprise. "I had no idea the High Lady was yet up and about."

"Well, I am not," Kayli said, smiling. "At least as far as Brother Stevann is concerned. But what child is this, Brother Santee?"

"Ah, this handsome lad is Lesett's new son," Brother Santee said, smiling down at the infant. "She bore it only yesterday. Her master's, she says."

"Then her master will be questioned under truth spell," Terralt said, joining them. "And if the child is his, he'll be made to provide for them both." He glanced at Randon mockingly. "You agree?"

"Of course," Randon said, unperturbed. "I told you you were quite capable of handling this matter. I only came to show Kayli how her folk fared."

"Come in, my lady," Terralt said, bowing elaborately to Kayli. "I'm certain your country folk are eager to throw themselves at the feet of their savior."

But in fact the barracks's inhabitants only stared dully at Kayli as she walked through. So many! And these were only the few slaves sent to the castle already. Doubtless some had already gone on to the guilds. And Tarkesh was only one city in the country of Agrond—Kayli had wanted so much to believe that Seba's case was a rare incident, but the men, women, and children here gave lie to that hope. She could offer them nothing better than a trade in the land that had enslaved them, a life among strangers. But at least their children, like the babe in Brother Santee's arms, would be born to freedom.

To Kayli's surprise, although men and women from countries other than Bregond were present, there were no Sarkondish in the barracks. She asked Terralt and Randon about this anomaly, but the two men only shrugged.

"I doubt you'll find any anywhere," Terralt said indifferently. "It's Sarkondish captives who are sold as slaves. The Sarkondish themselves we only meet in battle. And we've never taken any of them alive."

A knife twisted in Kayli's heart. She had believed that Bregonds, too, could not be taken alive. Had these folk been too cowardly to take their own lives? Kayli could not humiliate them by asking, any more than she could so hurt Seba. But how many more Bregondish citizens, believed dead by their kin, had survived to find themselves in such straits?

A hand on her shoulder startled her out of her thoughts; surprised, she turned to face Randon and found his eyes warm with understanding and compassion.

"This is too much for you, your first day out of bed," he said gently. "I shouldn't have brought you out in the rain. Look, you're shaking. Let's go back now."

Kayli nodded, but turned to Brother Santee.

"Please, may I hold the child?" she asked.

"Why, of course." Brother Santee carefully transferred the small bundle to Kayli's arms. The baby was red and rather mottled looking, but not unappealing for all that. Living at the Order, she had never held an infant, but he was warm and fit neatly into her arms. One day she would hold her own child so; one day her child would root at her breast and stain her tunic with spittle. Kayli chuckled and handed the boy-child back to Brother Santee. The Flame willing, her own time would come soon enough.

Terralt fell into step beside her as Randon gently led her toward the door.

"As you're feeling so well, perhaps you'd have time to dine with Ynea in the next few days," he said. "Stevann—and your midwife, by the way, in case you thought you were fooling me—won't let her out of her bed, and she's lonely." He gave Kayli a mocking grin. "I'm sure I can find other duties to occupy me so you'll be spared my distasteful presence."

"Thank you for your invitation," she said gravely, ignoring his last comment. "Randon has claimed my time tomorrow, and I his"—no, nothing was going to prevent Kayli from telling Randon of her pregnancy once Stevann had confirmed it— "but the next day I will give the whole of my day to Ynea, if she can receive me."

"*And* providing Stevann doesn't object," Randon added sternly. "No more word games with Kayli today, Terralt. She's exerted herself too much already."

Terralt chuckled rather nastily.

"So I gather," he said. "Really, Randon, if you don't want the whole castle knowing you've been rumpling the furs with your lady, you shouldn't go out smelling of your rut."

Kayli's face flamed, but Randon must be humiliated; why, he had been with his advisers. And, yes, now that she focused her mind on it, she could smell the dried sweat of their passion on her skin and his.

"Well, my advisers have been talking of nothing but the necessity of conceiving my heir," Randon said with a joviality that relieved Kayli. "So I'm sure everyone is happy with the effort Kayli and I have been giving to the task."

Thankfully Terralt did not follow them out into the rain,

and Randon squeezed Kayli's arm comfortingly as they walked.

"Don't pay Terralt any mind," he said. "If you saw how hard he's worked with these people, you wouldn't begrudge him his little pokes. And if those stodgy old advisers have forgotten what men do with their lovely wives, it's time they were reminded. Now stop fretting. You're shaking like a new-born foal."

When Kayli woke in the morning, it was to an odd silence. At last she realized what was missing—the thunder outside had stopped, and the constant tap of the rain. Kayli slipped out of bed and padded over to the window, opening the shutters. Bright late-morning sunlight left her blinking, and she leaned out the window to breathe in clean, fresh air and greet the day. Ah, bright and joyous day, and the Flame willing, there would be yet another reason to rejoice!

Kayli dressed hurriedly in a simple gown and trotted off to find Stevann. She had never actually seen the mage's workroom, but she found it easily enough.

"Well, good morn to you," Stevann said, grinning when he answered her knock at the door. "Not much use in asking how you feel this morning; I can see you're friskier than any person should be only a few days after *arrabia* poisoning."

"Mages heal quickly, do they not?" Kayli countered.

"Only if they can perform some kind of magic to heal themselves," Stevann returned, his expression somber but his eyes twinkling. "And thereby violate their healer's orders by over-taxing themselves. But there's no point in lecturing you, as whatever you did has certainly improved your health. So I can guess why you're here. Yes, you may eat what you like, unless your stomach starts to pain you, and you may get about as you please. Will that suit you?"

"Indeed it will," Kayli said, "but in fact it was another request that brought me to you." She clasped her hands to stop their shaking. "I wish to ascertain whether I have conceived my lord's child."

"You know that's impossible," Stevann said gently. "If you'd conceived earlier, you'd certainly have lost the child. And while I don't know anything about Bregondish magic, I doubt there's anything you could do to conceive so soon after such a serious poisoning. But I'll cast the runes again for you, if that's what you truly wish.''

"Forgive me, but I must ask you to humor my whim," Kayli said. "Please. If I have asked in vain, I promise I will not trouble you until you believe a suitable interval has passed."

Stevann sighed again, but he resignedly lit his brazier and pricked Kayli's finger with a silver needle, letting three drops of her blood fall into his silver scrying bowl, then chanted a short spell and poured a little quicksilver into the dish. Immediately the liquid flowed to form a peculiar symbol.

The mage's eyes widened; then he scowled and emptied out the bowl, cleaning it thoroughly before he repeated the spell. When the quicksilver responded as before, Stevann, visibly excited, spoke a longer incantation and laid one hand over Kayli's belly. When he took his hand away, he grinned broadly.

"Well, your eyes say you already knew what I have to tell you," he said. "You're indeed with child, although it's too soon to say whether it's a son or daughter." He chuckled. "I should announce it to the High Lord and his advisers, but you'd never forgive me if you couldn't surprise Randon, and *he'd* never forgive me if he couldn't surprise Terralt. So I'll keep my peace—for just a little while," he added sternly. "This news is too marvelous to keep secret."

"If you will only wait until Randon and I have a chance to dine together at midday," Kayli said humbly.

Stevann only nodded, and Kayli saw for the first time how weary the mage looked. There were great dark rings under his eyes, and his table was stacked with scrolls and books.

"I believe I have fared better these last days than you," she said gently. "Was it your magic that ended the storm?"

Stevann smiled tiredly.

"No, we owe that to a weather mage named Gerowan, Gated all the way from Keplin's Downe. No, I'm afraid it's Lady Ynea who's been occupying my time, and your midwife's, too, in case you've missed her presence."

"Terralt said you had confined Ynea to bed," Kayli remembered. "Has her condition worsened?"

"*I* haven't confined her to her bed," Stevann corrected, shaking his head. "The plain fact is that she's too weak to leave it, goes white when she stands up. Endra has her on a hideous concoction of raisins and beef liver that seems to help—builds up her blood, or so Endra says—but I think it's too late to do her much good. I wish Terralt had listened to me years ago when I said she should never bear another child."

"Surely something can be done for her," Kayli protested.

Stevann shrugged.

"I suggested to Terralt that we bring in other healers to consult. When High Lord Terendal employed me, he wanted a sort of jack-of-all-trades mage who could mix up a potion for his aching joints, forecast the fall harvest, and cast preservation spells on the hams. But that also means that I'm not a specialized healer, and my knowledge of childbearing is limited. Usually midwives handle that hereabouts. But Terralt won't hear of consulting anyone else, and I doubt anyone would come anyway. Ynea's case is too chancy, and nobody wants to risk Terralt's anger if she—if all doesn't go well."

Pride again. Kayli clenched her hands, struggling to keep silent. But what could she say or do? At least Terralt let Endra tend his wife, although Kayli suspected that he permitted that only so he could gloat about discovering Kayli's ruse.

But even her concern for Ynea could not dampen Kayli's happiness. She took her leave of Stevann and hurried back to her quarters to prepare for Randon's arrival. Thus when he appeared a little before noon, he found Kayli elegantly dressed and coiffed, the covered dishes of their dinner laid ready on the table. He raised his eyebrows and smiled.

"Well, you look beautiful," he said. "But what's the occasion? I'd have thought you'd rather get out of the room."

"Brother Stevann has told me I may eat what I please," Kayli said, smiling. "Is that not cause to celebrate?"

"Well, that's true," Randon admitted, sitting down. "All right, let's enjoy your first solid meal in days, although for me it's celebration enough that you're here to eat it."

He laughed when Kayli reached for her third venison-and-mushroom pasty.

"Making up for lost time? If I hadn't believed you fully healed, I'd know it now," he said, grinning. "Anybody with an appetite like that must be healthy."

Kayli smiled back at him.

"And Brother Stevann tells me my appetite will only grow," she said. "Over the next ten cycles of the moon."

"Mmm." Randon sipped his wine; then his eyes widened and he sputtered, spilling wine down the front of his tunic.

"Ten moon cycles?" he repeated, very carefully. "Do you mean to say—"

"I mean to say that yesterday, on the hearth furs, I conceived your child," Kayli said, reaching across the table to clasp his fingers. "Brother Stevann has confirmed it. But I wanted to tell you myself."

Caution warred with amazement in Randon's eyes.

"But Stevann said it wouldn't be possible for some time, maybe months," Randon said slowly. "Because of the poison."

Kayli flushed, but there was no evading his question now.

"Yesterday at dawn, I performed a potent ritual," she said quietly. "I used the Flame to purify myself and ready my body for the conception of a child. The ritual could not *make* me conceive, but it did place me at the peak of my fertility. I knew you would forbid practicing such potent magic, so I said nothing of it."

Randon's eyes searched her face.

"Was it dangerous?" he asked slowly.

Kayli took a deep breath.

"For one new to such magic, it was dangerous," she admitted. "I could have been consumed by the Flame, body and spirit alike." She did not tell Randon just how close she had come to such a fate. Nor did she tell him how seductive, how exquisite she had found the touch of the Flame. Somehow it embarrassed her, as if she had committed an infidelity.

Randon was silent for a moment, then he sighed.

"I want to say I wish you hadn't tried it," he said. "But I'd be half lying. I know why you took such a risk, and in your position I might have done the same. So I'll thank you instead of lecturing you and say no more about it."

"Thank you for understanding," Kayli said, relieved. "I assure you, High Priestess Brisi, my mentor, will be far less charitable when she learns what I did."

"Well, it's hard to scold when I'm so happy." Randon stepped around the table, gave her a fierce hug, then dropped to his knees to press his ear to her belly.

Kayli laughed.

"You will not feel anything now, or for many weeks to come," she said, amused. "Your child is a tiny spark of life only just kindled."

"Well, this little spark is going to light a big fire in Agrond," Randon said, patting her belly contentedly. "I suppose Stevann's already told the ministers?"

"I told him he could not deprive you of that pleasure," Kayli said, smiling. "Just as I must have the pleasure of telling you."

"Hmmm. Too late to call them back now, I suppose," Randon said regretfully. "They'll all have gone home for dinner. But I'll ask them to supper, and Terralt, too, and of course Stevann. We'll make a grand occasion of it."

He fairly ran out of the room, leaving Kayli chuckling beside their abandoned dinner; it was not long, however, before he returned.

"I've got messengers and servants scampering around like frightened rats," he said with a chuckle. "But for once nobody knows what's going on but us."

"I have not even told Endra," Kayli said, a little surprised herself. "She has been spending most of her time with Ynea." She told Randon what Stevann had said, and his brow furrowed with concern.

"I had no idea it was so bad," he said. "I'll try to persuade Terralt to let Stevann bring in other healers." He hesitated. "Are you sure you won't have troubles like that?"

"Endra says I should bear with no difficulty," Kayli assured him. "I am not small and frail like Ynea, nor am I too young, nor will I bear my children so closely as to sap all the strength from my body."

Randon looked even more worried.

"What, you mean that now you've conceived, you're going

to ban me from your bed for the next three years?''

"Of course not," Kayli reassured him. "But there are teas and powders to inhibit conception; the Orders in Bregond have used them for centuries. Surely your own healers have them; did you think all your whores barren from birth?"

Randon grinned a little abashedly.

"Do you know, I never thought about it," he said. "I suppose it's unlikely that so many healthy women all happened to be barren while a frail thing like Ynea is so fertile."

He shook his head.

"And Ynea has all my sympathy. But right now I'd rather think about you. And me." He pulled Kayli warmly to him. "Want to celebrate?"

Kayli slid her arms around Randon's neck, brushing her lips lightly over his.

"Yes," she said simply.

After pleasure, remembering Terralt's comments, Kayli insisted on a bath. Then she resignedly chose one of her simpler gowns (there was no hope of getting back into her formal gown with only Randon to help her), musing rather bitterly how her own attitudes had changed since she left Bregond. In the Order she would never have fretted over the formalities of cosmetics and dress.

"Not that." Randon cupped her shoulders from behind and laid a kiss at the juncture of her shoulder and her neck. "Wear that outfit you wore when you arrived that first night."

"My riding clothes?" Kayli protested, laughing. "Why?"

"Because they're more *you* than anything else," he told her. "And consequently you look more beautiful in them than in anything else. You're going to be their High Lady, and you've worked hard adjusting to us. Let them start adjusting to *you*."

" 'Them'?" Kayli chided gently.

"All right, all right." He surrendered. "Us."

Kayli gazed into his eyes, and saw an openness there that pleased her. For the first time since she had arrived in Agrond, she thought, *Yes. This is right.*

"Very well," she said, and the expression in Randon's eyes said that he understood she was agreeing to something more than the choice of her clothes. Some essential gulf between them had been bridged in that instant.

As Kayli folded her gown away and donned her riding clothes instead, she realized that Randon had understood something she had not—that the familiarity of her clothing made her feel more confident and comfortable. By the time she laced her boots, her movements had taken on their old efficiency and firmness, and she no longer felt like a performer on a stage. She braided her hair in a single plait, regretting that there was no time for the thirty-nine thin braids to which she was entitled. Well, that would wait; nobody at dinner would be impressed by their symbolism anyway.

Thus when she took Randon's arm to walk down to the dining hall, her step was lighter and freer than it had been since she had arrived in Agrond. And if a few eyes went wide when they stepped into the dining hall, if muttered conversations came to an abrupt halt, what did that matter?

"Good evening, lords, ladies, Terralt, and Stevann," Randon said rather grandly, giving them all a brief bow. "Tonight we're dining together to celebrate the recovery of my wife, Kayli, your High Lady—and the mother of my child."

Silence. It was a crucial moment, and Kayli's eyes darted to each of the advisers, noting their reactions. Lord Kereg and Lady Aville schooled their faces to impassivity immediately. Lord Jaxon did not bother to stifle his broad grin, nor Lady Tarkas her thin-lipped skepticism. Lord Disian seemed mildly annoyed. At last Kayli glanced at Terralt, expecting to see anger or at least dismay in his reaction. To her surprise, he gazed directly back at her with a sort of resigned amusement. As their eyes met, Terralt gave her a wry smile and bowed his head briefly in acknowledgment.

The brief moment of shocked silence passed quickly, followed almost immediately by an uproar, the advisers clustering around Randon or firing rapid questions at Stevann. For a moment Kayli felt almost forgotten. Then Terralt rapped the hilt of his dagger sharply against the wooden table.

"Lords, ladies!" he said sternly. "This is, I believe, a joyous occasion which requires due celebration. And I'll make the first toast." He raised his goblet. "To High Lord Randon and High Lady Kayli—congratulations on the lady's swift recovery, and on their joyful news.''

Randon led Kayli around to their places at the table, but when she started to lift her goblet, he touched her wrist, halting her. He glanced over at Stevann, who gave the barest hint of a nod. Randon took his hand away, smiling at Kayli, and raised his own glass.

There were questions, as Kayli had known there would be, and her supper was more an inquisition than a celebration, but she had expected that, too. She kept quiet and let Randon and Stevann explain while she concentrated on swallowing her second solid meal in a week.

''With respect, High Lord''—Lord Kereg hesitated—''and High Lady, a public wedding should be held as soon as possible. The banns should be posted immediately, and some sort of festival planned as well.''

''You're right about that.'' Randon was silent for a moment. ''We'll have the wedding day after tomorrow. Forget the usual formalities; Gate the messengers to the outlying cities and towns if you must, and Gate back any nobles you think will be mortally offended if they can't attend.''

Randon's announcement surprised Kayli as it apparently did the others, and for a moment she was too confused to follow the hot outbursts that followed.

''High Lord, you can't possibly be serious,'' Lord Kereg protested. ''A wedding of this magnitude must be conducted according to the proper protocols. I must insist—''

''No, *I* must insist,'' Randon said firmly. ''Lord Kereg, put yourself for the moment in the shoes of High Lord Elaasar. Since he sent his daughter to marry me, she's been attacked by Sarkondish raiders and poisoned by our own people, both while we were supposedly protecting her. The announcement of her pregnancy is going to cause even greater conflict. So long as she's pregnant but not yet confirmed High Lady, she's still a target. So the wedding will take place at noon—''

''At dawn,'' Kayli said gently.

Randon glanced at her, then smiled.

''At dawn day after tomorrow,'' he said. ''With feasting and frolicking to follow. Then Brother Santee can return to

Bregond with the news that High Lord Elaasar's daughter has been properly confirmed High Lady of Agrond.''

''How can we possibly prepare for a festival in two days?'' Lady Tarkas asked patiently. ''Mages can Gate in the nobility, true, but they can't conjure up a feast, musicians—''

''Nonsense,'' Randon said. ''Plenty of performers are already in the city for the midsummer festival in a few weeks. They'll be glad of the extra work. As for the feast, send messengers to the bakers and butchers in town. Hire them to prepare food and bring it to the feast. Right now it's important to let the people get used to the idea that Kayli's here to stay, and the alliance is here to stay, too.'' He raised his hand. ''No more argument. Now let's eat, please. This was supposed to be a celebration.''

As the advisers murmured among themselves, Randon leaned over to murmur into Kayli's ear, ''I asked Stevann to check all the food and drink for poison. And until we're confirmed High Lord and Lady, he'll continue to check every drop and morsel to cross your lips.''

Kayli winced at the thought, but she could not argue, although she found Randon's reasoning dubious. True, the confirmation would end any hope that Randon would repudiate his bride and nullify the treaty with Bregond. But if she were to die before her child was born, Randon must remarry, and the treaty could then be broken, if Randon was prepared to risk the war with Bregond that would follow. No, Kayli and her children would not be safe until she had gained popular support or the citizens of Agrond had become accustomed to the idea of the treaty. Involuntarily, she pressed her hands protectively over her flat belly and waited for the uncomfortable meal to end.

In their rooms later, Randon waved aside Kayli's concern at his advisers' reception of his news.

''Of course it's a shock to them,'' he said. ''And they don't like surprises. But I plan to keep surprising them. Neither one of us can afford to be thought their puppet—by the people or by them, either.''

Randon sighed, and Kayli twisted in his arms to look at

him. He was massaging his temple with the fingers of his free hand, his face twisted with pain.

"Randon, are you unwell?" she asked.

"It's nothing." But Randon withdrew his arm from her shoulders and leaned forward, one hand pressing his left temple, the other covering his left eye. He twisted away from the light of the fire.

"Randon? What is the matter?" Kayli knelt before him, trying to pry his hands from his face. "Shall I call Stevann?"

"No—" His voice was weak. "There's a potion."

He waved his hand vaguely at his chest at the foot of the bed.

Kayli opened the chest. At first she saw nothing but Randon's clothes, but as she pushed them heedlessly aside, she uncovered a small metal flask. She pulled out the stopper and carried it back.

"Is this what you wanted?" she asked.

Randon groped for the flask as if he did not see it, and in the end Kayli had to guide it to his lips. As soon as she had laid the flask aside, she pulled the tapestry screen in front of the fire, blocking its light, and helped Randon hobble over to the bed. His face relaxed slightly; Kayli hoped that meant the pain was easing as well.

"Randon, is there nothing further I can do for you?" Kayli asked gently, smoothing his hair away from his forehead. "Are you certain I should not send for Stevann?"

"Ice," Randon muttered. "Ask the kitchen to send up crushed ice in a cloth."

Afraid to leave him alone, Kayli rang for one of the maids. When the girl heard her request, she nodded.

"Got one of his headaches, has he?" the girl asked sympathetically. "I'll have the ice up straightaway, and I'll have cook brew up that clover-and-mint tea he likes. Always settles him after."

True to her word, the maid was back with the ice in a cloth after only a few moments.

"Just put that on his head where it hurts, over his eye," the maid said. "He'll be right again in a bit. I'll just bring the tea to the sitting room and leave it."

Randon had turned on his side, away from the screened fire, and his wrist covered his eyes, but he seemed to relax a little more. He let Kayli gently move his wrist away, and he shuddered, gasping with a mixture of pain and relief, when she laid the icy cloth over his left eye and forehead. His right eye opened and focused on Kayli.

"I'll survive," he said, and his voice had some of his old cheer in it. "My father had headaches like this, too, from time to time, and so does Terralt. It passes soon."

"Has it been like this all your life?" Kayli asked, worried despite Randon's reassurances. She had known novices at the Order who had such headaches, but when pain struck, one of the priests or priestesses took them away for special rituals which apparently helped them. Unfortunately Kayli had no idea what sort of spell might have been used; that seemed more a matter for healing magic than the power of the Flame.

"Well, since I was fourteen or so," Randon mumbled. "Look, Kayli, it's nothing. A good night's sleep'll put me to rights." He was silent for a moment, then: "Kayli, would you mind sending for some tea, clover, and—"

"And mint?" Kayli smiled. "Wait a moment."

The tray was already waiting in the sitting room. Kayli poured Randon a cup, then helped him sit up to drink it, still holding the cloth over his eye. By the time he'd drained the cup, his uncovered eye was half closed.

"I'll sleep now," he said thickly, letting the empty cup tumble from his grasp. "Just . . . sleep." His head lolled to the side and his hand fell away from the icy cloth.

Kayli lifted the cloth away, but Randon did not stir, nor did he rouse when she slipped off his boots. She left him in his surcoat and trousers and simply pulled the covers over him; better to let him sleep than risk disturbing him.

Kayli, however, was too shaken to sleep. She undressed and lay down beside Randon, watching him in the dying light of the fire. She had thought that the news of her pregnancy would bring joy and celebration. Instead, she had passed an evening as tense and miserable as any since she'd left the Order.

Kayli sighed and began one of the meditations to bring sleep. For at least the next two days, she would need all her faculties about her, and a weary mage, High Priestess Brisi had taught her, was a mistake waiting to be made.

10

"**T**HERE, THAT'S PERFECT." ENDRA MINUTELY adjusted the last jewel-tipped pin in Kayli's hair. Kayli swallowed a groan. Endra and the maids had braided fine gold chains into each of her thirty-nine braids, which were now unbearably heavy. And then there were the pins, to hold her braids in the complex loops and whorls traditional for a noble wedding in Bregond. Then there was her heavy wedding gown, the petticoats to hold the skirt out, and the jewelry Randon had given her, the oddly long and narrow (and overly tight) gold-embroidered formal slippers—and, of course, the necessary creams, powders, and perfumes. By the time Endra deemed her ready, Kayli felt stiff and heavy and awkward, like a walking doll.

"Where is Randon?" she asked her maid distractedly.

"Likely already down at the entryway," Endra told her. "There appears to be some ridiculous Agrondish custom that the groom shouldn't see the bride until the ceremony—never mind that the two of you are already married twice over. I'm to take you down the backstairs and through the kitchens so he won't catch a glimpse of you, and you're to wait in the great hall until he's outside. Then Brother Santee will take you out to him when the ceremony starts."

The older woman patted Kayli's shoulder reassuringly.

"There, there, this'll be the last of it," she said comfortingly. "Why don't you go have a peep out the window? You'll be amazed at the front court."

Kayli tottered to the window and peered out, then gasped. The eastern sky was only just beginning to blush pink, but already the courtyard was filled with tables, and the tables were rapidly filling with food. Some came from the kitchens—Kayli could see baskets and trays being brought out—but more came, apparently, from the city. Carts rattled in at the gate, and small figures below unloaded the carts and wagons onto the tables. Kayli could see Stevann wandering to and fro, probably casting his spells to assure that no poisoned food or drink could endanger the royal couple.

Kayli sighed. In Bregond, noble marriages were not public spectacles, especially when the marriage was made after a child was already conceived, and most particularly when the fact of the child's prior conception was known outside the household. The very notion was unseemly. Kayli was embarrassed already.

Anida joined her at the window and sighed, too.

"Seems they've tried to make it as nasty for you as they could ever since you arrived, lady," she said, shaking her head. "Wouldn't surprise me much if they insisted on parading you down the streets in your shift in a few months so the peasants could see the swell of your belly."

"I have tried to honor Agrondish custom as best I could," Kayli said, "but I fear I have reached my limits today. What a spectacle I shall be." She shuddered.

Devra leaned her head in the door.

"Lady, they're nearly ready," she said breathlessly. "You're to come down now."

Kayli took a deep breath, then nodded to Endra. She followed the midwife down the backstairs, hoisting her heavy skirt higher after she stumbled twice. If Agrondish weddings demanded such feats as scurrying around backstairs and corridors, then brides should be allowed to dress accordingly.

Despite the bustle outside, the kitchens were empty; doubtless all the kitchen staff were already working at the great tables. A crowd of servants clustered around the half-closed front entry, however, peering out through the opening. Brother Santee hurried forward, taking Kayli's arm.

"They're almost ready," he said. "Your lord made a speech before they started; I think he wants to make sure the crowd won't turn ugly when you come out. There's guards enough out there to conquer a small nation."

The servants moved aside to let them through. Brother Santee peered out through the opening, waited for what seemed an eternity. Kayli could hear voices droning outside—Randon, Lord Calder. At last Brother Santee nodded to someone outside the door and led her forward.

Randon was there, stiff and awkward in his best surcoat and cape, standing before Lord Calder at the top of the steps. She stepped to meet him, clasped the hand he extended.

Mutters from the crowd held back by the line of guards at the foot of the steps. A few cheers. A few hisses. Kayli ignored them both, her eyes locking with Randon's.

The words of the ceremony. Kayli barely heard them; the phrases she parroted when Lord Calder prompted her seemed distant, dim. What did all of it matter, really? There was her, Randon, and the child growing in her belly. That was all.

More words, and now Kayli became confused. Had she made these same promises before? The ceremony seemed longer now, possibly because she felt so awkward and uncomfortable. Her feet ached wretchedly in the horrible slippers. Had more language been added to the marriage ceremony because this was the formal ritual? To her surprise, Randon was turning her away from the castle, to face the courtyard. Were they to speak their vows now with their backs to the priest? What kind of ridiculous custom could that be?

Movement beside and behind her; Kayli had to steel herself to keep from flinching. A cool pressure settled on her brow, and she could not help lifting her free hand to touch it. A slender, smooth metal band encircled her head. She glanced at Randon; someone had placed a plain gold band on his brow also. So she had just stood woolgathering through her own coronation. The thought was utterly amusing, Kayli standing stiff and doll-like in her finery, already pregnant, daydreaming through her coronation. Suddenly it was very hard to stifle laughter.

She glanced sideways at Randon and saw the same stifled laughter in his eyes, and that cheered her. If he saw the ridiculousness of the situation, if they shared that much, then there was hope.

"I present to you," Lord Calder said, "Randon and Kayli, High Lord and High Lady of Agrond."

Silence. Long silence. Then a lone pair of hands clapping. Another. Another. At last there was enough hesitant applause that Kayli could ignore the few grumbles and hisses that reached her ears. Then the time for words was over, and Randon kissed her gently, to the obvious delight of many of the onlookers; now there was a little cheering and a few good-natured "Give it to her, your lordship!" calls.

"Say a few words to them," Randon muttered quietly into Kayli's ear. "I think they're ready for that."

Ah, but was she? Such a possibility had never occurred to her. Kayli took a deep, cleansing breath and released Randon's hand, stepping forward. A hush gradually fell over the crowd.

"Some of you have seen me in audience, or riding," she said at last. "Others are seeing me for the first time, as I am you. Some of you welcomed my arrival; others did not." There were a few angry mutters; was her poisoner there?

"I did not wish to come here," she said bluntly. "I did not expect happiness. I did not expect to fall in love with my lord at the moment my eyes first met his. But although I have not been among you long, I have come to value this land." She reached for Randon's hand again. "And this man I have wed. Likewise I do not expect the folk of this land to love and accept me immediately. Trust is earned, not granted. And if I cannot earn your trust and your respect, I pray that you will believe that it is I alone who have failed you, not my lord, who helps me to understand this land and its ways, and not my people, who sent me to make peace between our land and yours. I can only promise that I will try not to fail them, and you."

Another moment of silence, then more applause—Kayli dared to hope more than before. Hurriedly she retreated to Randon's side.

"What do we do now?" she asked him quietly.

"*We* do nothing," he said, grinning. "*I* do this." To Kayli's amazement, he swept her up into his arms, regardless of her finery, and carried her grandly over the threshold. This time the applause behind them was loud and unrestrained.

As soon as they were out of sight behind the door, Randon set Kayli back on her feet with a sigh of relief.

"Thank goodness," he said, panting most unflatteringly. "Kayli, I do believe that rig you're wearing doubles your weight. Come, my lady, and let's take our appointed places for the rest of the morning's tiresome duties."

"There is more?" Kayli asked, trying to hide her dismay.

"Oh, yes," Randon said ruefully. "Now we sit on our thrones and make pleasantries while all the lords and ladies present us with gifts and make their oaths of allegiance. Then we show ourselves around the courtyard to make the people happy. Then, by custom, we sign pardons releasing all those in the prisons. Then, if we're fortunate, we may get some dinner. If it isn't time for supper by then, that is. Come on, let's get it done with, shall we?"

Kayli expected to return to the great hall where she and Randon had held audience, but to her surprise, the two thrones had been moved to a platform (fortunately under a canopy, as the sun was already hot and her heavy gown nearly stifled her). Flanked heavily by guards, Kayli and Randon assumed their seats, and Kayli stifled a sigh of relief as she took her weight off her aching feet. Noble lords and ladies were already forming a line at the base of the platform.

Kayli expected that Terralt, as Randon's brother, would be the first to offer his oath of fealty, but to her surprise, Ynea stood at his side. Kayli was horrified to see how fragile and gaunt her friend had grown in the few days since she'd seen her; Ynea seemed nothing but wisps of skin stretched tight over bone and the bigness of her swollen belly. A fierce, hectic color burned in her cheeks but did not warm the almost bluish pallor of her lips.

Terralt helped his wife walk slowly forward with a solicitousness that surprised Kayli, but she looked at the six steps Ynea must climb to the platform and thought with horror, *Why, she can never do it!*

She was on her feet without thinking; when she turned, she found that Randon had reached the top of the steps before her.

She hurried after him to meet Terralt and Ynea at the bottom of the steps. Terralt glanced at them with obvious relief. Ynea's own eyes were glazed, and Kayli wondered what potions Stevann had given her so she could come at all.

Kayli expected some mocking comment or innuendo from Terralt, but he gave his oath almost grimly, his lips pressed to a thin white line. Kayli could not bear to see Ynea stand there growing paler and paler through the customary well-wishing, and Randon firmly motioned the litter forward while Ynea was still swearing her fealty.

"Stop fretting and start watching the people," Randon murmured in her ear when they resumed their thrones. "I'll want your impressions later."

Kayli realized the truth of Randon's words and forced her attention back to the waiting nobles. Many of these powerful lords and ladies lived far from Tarkesh. This was the first—and perhaps the only—chance that she and Randon would have to assess their loyalty, and Kayli's best chance to win their favor by taking an individual interest in them.

It might have been an impossible task. To Kayli's surprise, however, she found her court training immeasurably useful here. Trained from childhood in the art of reading the "unspoken language," she found it easy to see annoyance in the subtle downward turn at the corner of a mouth, unease in the slight lowering of a brow, insincerity in the tension of a shoulder.

Kayli found, too, that her memory training in the Order was an asset here. Those lords and ladies she had met previously, however briefly, she could greet personally. She had absorbed an amazing variety of information—names, titles, cities and villages, regional crops and crafts, events of importance— from the council meetings, audiences, and supper conversations. When the heralds announced Lord Ostuan and Lady Naeste, Kayli was able to congratulate them on the recent marriage of their son; when Lord Kerrar presented them with forty barrels of his finest wine, Kayli commiserated over the recent curly-leaf-rot problem in his vineyards. From time to time Randon gave her an approving grin; occasionally Terralt would glance sideways at her, lift an eyebrow, and nod slowly, his eyes twinkling although he did not smile.

Despite her concentration, the morning crept on at a snail's pace. The sun edged higher and higher, and with it the heat; no breeze stirred the banners on their poles. Once more Kayli's temple training helped her; even in her heavy dress, cinched so tightly around her waist that she could hardly breathe, the golden chains in her braids slowly pulling every hair from her scalp, immobile for hours on her throne, she maintained her calm. Whatever torments were inflicted upon Agrondish rulers, they were nothing compared with hours spent kneeling on a stone floor and meditating on a candle flame, or with the pain of searing her hands again and again and again as she fought to master her own recalcitrant flesh. Why, this was less disagreeable even than the long ride from Bregond, even without the addition of torrential rains and Sarkondish raiders. And of course the nobles waiting to pay their respects, standing all this time in the hot sun instead of sitting under the canopy, were more miserable than she.

By mid-afternoon it had grown even hotter, but the end of the line of nobles was in sight. Finally Randon and Kayli greeted the last lord and lady, signed the final pardon, and Randon sighed as the steward carried the scrolls away.

"By the Bright Ones, I thought they'd somehow managed to Gate in every man and woman in Agrond," Randon muttered. "Come on, let's look at what's left of the festival, shall we?"

Just standing on her feet after hours of sitting was pure pleasure despite the torturous slippers. Kayli tried to ignore the guards that fell into step around herself and Randon (and, to her dismay, Terralt) as they walked away from the platform. This was her first chance to meet the citizens of Agrond face-to-face instead of looking down from a throne or a saddle, and she was determined to make the most of it.

The feast tables were thronged with nobles and peasants alike, but Randon shook his head sternly when Kayli would have turned her steps in that direction.

"Oh, Randon," she protested. "Soon I will surely starve. How can there be any danger when I saw Stevann testing the food earlier?"

Terralt, who had positioned himself opposite Randon at Kayli's side, chuckled.

"He's not afraid you'd be poisoned," he said rather patronizingly. "By custom, you and he are providing this feast for the citizens of Agrond—paying for it, at least—not for yourselves. It's to symbolize the selfless dedication of the High Lord and Lady to their people. Don't fret about it; the merchants have booths along the wall, and they'll be delighted to push their finest delicacies into your hands so they can boast that the High Lord and Lady stuffed themselves silly on their wares."

An astounding variety of merchants had set up stalls and carts along the entire inner wall of the courtyard. True to Terralt's predictions, Kayli and Randon nibbled their way around the grounds, tasting the fresh fruits, baked goods, skewered meats, and sweets that the merchants thrust into their hands.

"Don't fill yourself up before the best part," Terralt told her, taking her arm so firmly that Kayli could not pull away without making a scene.

"The best part?" she asked with some dismay. What more could there be?

"Just a surprise I arranged for you—for both of you," Terralt added after a pause that was a brief second too long.

"What kind of surprise?" Randon asked, and Kayli could hear a slight edge creep into his voice.

"Around at the side," Terralt said vaguely. "I didn't want either of you to see it out the front windows."

Kayli tightened her grip on Randon's hand, but allowed Terralt to guide them around the east side of the castle. Even before she turned the corner, a strange aroma drifted to her nostrils, a cooking sort of odor that was slightly metallic, yet at the same time spicy and appetizing. Kayli had never smelled its like, but Randon recognized it immediately.

"Dragon!" he exclaimed, sniffing the air with delight. "Terralt, you scoundrel, how in the Bright Ones' names did you manage to find a dragon in time for the wedding?"

"I didn't, of course," Terralt said dryly. "Less than a week after your lady arrived in Agrond, one of my friends told me one had just been killed in his territory. So I bought the whole thing, had it preservation-spelled and stored to wait for your confirmation. It's good luck for a pregnant woman to eat dragon; supposedly it assures a strong child who will make a good warrior." He grinned mockingly. "The Bright Ones know any spawn of Randon's needs all the help it can get."

There was no way to dig a firepit in the stone-paved courtyard, but a sort of raised brick hollow had been built there. A huge spit, supported on thick crossed beams, held the largest slab of meat Kayli had ever seen over the coals. Rich fat dripped off to sizzle on the embers, and several young boys slathered dark sauce from buckets over the roasting meat.

Dragon. Kayli had heard tales of the gigantic winged reptiles, seen pictures in scrolls and tapestries, but she could never have imagined a creature so huge that the awesome slab of meat roasting over the coals could be only a portion. Although dragons were rarely seen in Bregond, they were known in the Orders as a powerful union of Earth and Flame. It took many great hunters to kill a dragon, Kayli had heard, and many times it was the dragon, not the humans, who feasted. Had this dragon ever killed and eaten humans?

No such concerns apparently troubled Randon, for when one of the boys handed him a skewer of dripping meat, he bit into it without hesitation. Kayli looked at her own skewer with some doubt, but the spicy aroma was just too tempting, and she tore off a bite of the tough flesh with her teeth. The meat tasted even more hearty and spicy than it smelled, and Kayli had worried off several more bites before she realized that she no longer cared what the dragon had been eating.

"Thank you, Terralt," Randon said, and Kayli was ashamed that she had made no thanks of her own. "It's a wonderful gift, and one I'm certain we'll all appreciate in the dining hall for some time to come. Have you sent some up to Ynea?"

"Your lady's midwife laid claim to the liver and heart the moment she found out we had it," Terralt said a little irritably. "Said they'd strengthen Ynea's blood, however she supposes *that* would happen when Ynea can't seem to keep the smallest morsel down long enough to do any good."

"You look tired," Randon said, putting his arm around Kayli's waist and ignoring Terralt's comments. "We've made our obligatory appearances, and it's expected that I'll make off with you sometime to consummate our marriage. It would make a likely excuse, if you'd like to retire now."

"Only an excuse?" Terralt mocked. "Why, brother, have

you changed so much in the last few weeks? The Randon I've always known would've ducked his guards and pulled the lady into the barn to flip her skirts up, no doubt. Or have you grown fastidious since you wed?''

''Well, there's your difference,'' Randon said good-naturedly. ''A quick tumble in an out-of-the-way spot's all well and good, but my exotic Bregondish lady has taught me the value of a more prolonged encounter.'' He guided Kayli away from Terralt. ''You should try it sometime, brother.''

Almost inaudibly behind them, Terralt laughed.

''Perhaps you're right,'' he said. ''Perhaps I should.''

Suddenly fire flared in Kayli's heart and she turned, releasing Randon's arm to face Terralt squarely.

''Would you care to repeat that more loudly?'' she said deliberately. ''There are perhaps a few passersby who did not hear your insult. Perhaps you would like to address everyone at the festival. I am sure they would be much impressed by all the clever insults you have made from the day we first met. Come, play no more muttering games. Say what you will, and say it now so we all can hear you.''

The mocking grin faltered slightly. Then Terralt's lips thinned and and he bowed elaborately.

''I most humbly beg the pardon of my High Lord and High Lady for my impertinent and insulting manner,'' he said loudly. ''It was inexcusable, and I will see that they are troubled by it no longer.'' He bowed again, even more extravagantly. ''If I may be dismissed, of course.''

Randon stepped forward, one hand extended.

''Listen, Terralt, there's no need to—''

There was no yielding in Terralt's steel-hard eyes.

''If I may be dismissed,'' he repeated coldly.

Randon dropped his hand and turned away.

''Very well,'' he said, no emotion at all in his voice. ''You're dismissed.''

''Thank you, High Lord. High Lady.'' Without another word, Terralt turned and strode back to the castle. As soon as Terralt was gone, however, Randon rounded on Kayli.

''By the Bright Ones, what did you do that for?'' he demanded, taking Kayli's arm and dragging her out of earshot of the gathering circle of onlookers.

Hurt astonishment momentarily stunned Kayli silent. *What did you do that for?* In Bregond no lady would have stood for such insults and innuendo as Terralt had made since they had met; no husband would tolerate it, either.

"Perhaps you are accustomed to his slurs upon your honor," Kayli retorted angrily. "Perhaps they do not trouble you. But that does not obligate me to tolerate them as well, not when he has all but undressed me with his words!"

"So he's offended you," Randon snapped. "Is your dignity more important than the good of this country?"

"Apparently it is of less import than Terralt's freedom to say whatever foul thing he likes," Kayli replied. "And why, might I ask, should that be so?"

Randon averted his eyes for just a moment, and in that instant Kayli wondered whether she had seen the barest flash of guilt in his expression; when he faced her again, however, his anger was as unyielding as before.

"Since the moment my father proclaimed me Heir instead of Terralt, I've had to pander to Terralt's pride, flatter him, argue with him, all but *beg* the man for his help," Randon said flatly. "He knows the business of ruling this country, and *I need that knowledge.* I need the years he spent at Father's side. The games I've played to get that cooperation! And now how am I to expect any assistance from him, now that you've humiliated him in public?"

His fingers dug into Kayli's arm, and she halted.

"Release me," she said quietly.

Randon glared at her. "What?"

"I said, release me." Kayli met his eyes squarely. "You are my husband, not my master. I will not be dragged like a recalcitrant dog. Nor will I be admonished for defending myself against offenses I have borne far too long already. If you wish to let Terralt insult you at every opportunity, that is your affair, and if I choose otherwise, that is mine."

"Damn all, Kayli," Randon said angrily, "the man's lost what he thought was his birthright, and his wife may be dying." Again that flash of guilt. "You could afford to be a little more charitable."

"Why, because he has lost the throne of Agrond, while all I have lost is my home, my kin, and my vocation in the Order?'' Kayli retorted. "As to Ynea, I have done all I could to help her, rather than cosseting the pride of the man who withholds aid that might save her. And pray tell me, my lord, how many healers you summoned while Terralt was in Bregond?'' Not waiting for Randon's answer, Kayli pulled her arm free and walked back to the castle as quickly as she could, relieved beyond measure when neither the guards nor Randon followed.

The servants scattered in astonishment when Kayli strode through the doorway. She started upstairs to her rooms, but then changed her mind and turned to the forge instead. At least there was one place in this castle, in this accursed country, that was *hers,* where she might expect privacy.

As soon as she was through the door, Kayli yanked pins and chains from her hair, scrabbling at the fastenings to her elaborate gown. For a time she feared there was no getting out of the thing by herself; at last she tugged, wriggled, and, she feared, ripped her way out, dropping it and her jewelry into the corner. Her slippers, petticoats, and hose followed; then, clad only in her chemise, her braids hanging down her back, she dipped a bucket of water from the barrel and scrubbed her face and neck again and again until every last trace of powder and coloring was gone. She sat down in the corner, drawing up her knees and resting her forehead on her folded arms, and fought to keep from weeping.

How naive she'd been to think that a child in her belly would solve all her troubles! The sacrifice of her life at the Order, her journey to an alien land to wed a stranger, the risk of her life several times, even the risk of her soul itself in the Rite of Renewal—none of it was enough. And there was nothing more she could give.

Suddenly Kayli sat upright, her heart sinking as she realized the enormity of what she had done. Yes, she had humiliated Terralt in public, shattered the tenuous bond of cooperation probably beyond repair—but far more terrifying was the reason *why* she had done it. Kayli had acted blindly, impulsively, out of anger and—far worse—the petty desire for revenge, the malicious wish to inflict suffering in return for her own wounded pride. How much worse her own action than anything Terralt could have done to provoke it, for to him such behavior was only a manifestation of his own inner frailty, while Kayli had had a lifetime of training that should have let her shrug off such insults effortlessly. No, there was no possible excuse for such a breach of her self-discipline, nor for the smallness of soul to want to do such a thing.

Kayli remembered her loss of control in the forge during the Rite of Renewal. That failure had nearly cost her her life and her soul; her lapse today might, as Randon said, hurt the country she had sworn to serve. Her self-control had failed her so many times since she had left the Order. Could it be that some fundamental flaw in her character had merely waited dormant in the orderly world of the temple, only to betray her under the pressure of her new position and responsibilities?

Kayli shivered at the wave of despair that chilled her to the depths of her soul. There had been so many warnings of just such a possibility since she had left Bregond. If that was the case, she had been more fortunate than she knew to escape the Rite of Renewal intact. How could she ever dare perform any of the powerful rituals now? Why, dared she even attempt a firewalk now, especially with a child in her belly?

Kayli dropped her head again, suddenly tempted to light the forge and let the Flame judge her, one way or the other. Now that she had alienated Randon, she was utterly alone in this strange place. Death, even a fiery death in the heart of the forge, seemed the kinder alternative.

But she carried in her womb an innocent life which she had no right to cast away with her own. And even were that not so, she knew that she could never surrender to despair. After dedicating her life to grueling training, all to be consummated in one act of faith, gambling her life against the strength of her will—no. There was no surrender in her. Fear, disappointment, even despair—these were old enemies whom she had faced and defeated before.

Kayli threw back her head suddenly and laughed.

"I will walk through the fire," she said aloud. "Let it consume what it will, and what remains is Kayli."

She stood, wondering at the sudden lightness of her heart, and returned to the bucket to wash tear tracks from her face. There was no hope of donning her gown without assistance, but she found her robe where Seba had folded it neatly in the corner. She wadded her clothing and jewelry into the best bundle she could manage and carried it upstairs in her arms, ignoring the stares of the servants she passed on the staircase. She had padded through the castle in her robe before and likely would again; best they get used to the sight now.

Kayli dreaded that Randon would be waiting in her room, but to her surprise it was Endra who greeted her. The midwife smiled at her and, to her surprise, embraced her comfortingly.

"Come in, child, and sit down," Endra said, taking the bundle of Kayli's clothes. "I've mulled you a mug of wine. If you'll pardon my boldness, I've had the maids move your lord's things to another room. The both of you need a day or two's peace without your tempers striking sparks off each other. Now drink that and settle yourself down."

Kayli sighed with relief and let Endra ply her with the hot wine and crumbly pastries, even though she was neither hungry nor thirsty. The midwife's solicitude fed another kind of hunger, a hunger of the heart for sympathy and caring that Kayli had not even known she felt.

"I feel such a fool." Kayli sighed, shaking her head. "If you only knew—"

"What, how you took Terralt's words, chewed them up, and spit them back at him?" Endra chuckled. "Or about your spat with your lord? My lady, I'll wager I'd heard the lot before you closed the forge door. It's the talk of the castle. Don't trouble yourself. A High Priestess might've uttered a harsh word or two by now. And just as well your lord and his brother learn that the fine lady has teeth and and claws of her own."

"No." Kayli shook her head decisively. "I will not allow myself to become so provoked again."

Endra chuckled knowingly.

"Ah, my lady, there speaks the temple-raised child who's had no dealings with childbearing before starting her own. Ah, my lady, don't look so astonished; I talk with Brother Stevann every day, and shame to you that he had to bear me the news. In any wise, flares of temper are the least of the odd twists you'll feel in the next months, so best you and your lord resign yourselves to it."

Kayli sighed.

"But I did a terrible thing, Endra," she said. "I humiliated Terralt, and before many onlookers. I fear he will withhold the assistance Randon needs from him."

"I'd have to agree," Endra said reluctantly. "He's got the servants packing his things to move into the city."

Kayli bolted up out of her chair, fear spearing through her.

"But he must not do that!" she said, horrified. "Randon needs him. And Ynea, she must not be removed from your care and Brother Stevann's!" She took a deep, steadying breath. "No. I will speak with him."

"I don't know as that's a wise idea," Endra said slowly. "I'll wager his own temper's burning hot right now."

"I lit that fire, and I will be the one to extinguish it," Kayli said firmly. "Help me dress. Whatever good Randon thinks of his brother, I will not appear before him in my robe."

Only a few moments later she knocked on Terralt's door. She had had some difficulty locating it; she knew Terralt kept rooms separate from his wife, but she could not bring herself to ask the servants for directions.

Terralt opened the door. Kayli saw surprise in his eyes, but his expression did not change; he merely opened the door wider and stepped aside to let her enter.

Endra had not exaggerated. Although it was little more than an hour since the argument in the courtyard, the open trunks around the room were half-full of clothes. Several maids halted in their packing, stared at Kayli in surprise, and fled the room even before Terralt could wave them away. Kayli wondered miserably what new rumors the High Lady's visit alone to Terralt's bedchamber might occasion.

"Whatever more you've come to say," Terralt said without prelude, "I don't especially want to hear it."

Kayli took a deep breath.

"I came to apologize," she said quietly. "What I did was inexcusable—not what I said, for the Flame knows it was true, but why I said it, and when, and where. I have disgraced myself and shamed my teachings, and I ask that you forgive me."

"Did Randon send you?" Terralt said rather bitterly. "To see that his valuable assistant doesn't leave the High Lord to fend for himself, I suppose."

"Randon," Kayli said steadily, "is furious with me, as I am with him, and he did not send me. Whatever troubles are between you and Randon are your own, and my poor conduct is my own responsibility and not Randon's."

"Mmm." Terralt folded his arms and gazed at her consideringly. "So you're saying that I shouldn't leave simply because I'm angry at you."

"Yes." Kayli met his gaze squarely.

"And what," Terralt said slowly, his eyes narrowed, "makes you think you understand anything about why I do anything?"

"But—"

Kayli was not allowed to finish whatever she might have said; without warning, Terralt seized her shoulders and covered her lips with his.

Kayli froze, stunned at first by the outrageousness of his action, and then, even more astonishingly, by the sudden surge of fire that shot through her body, burning her will to ashes. At last Terralt released her, turning abruptly away.

"You'd best go now," Terralt said, rather coldly, still not facing her. "I have a great deal of packing to supervise." He glanced at her, then away again. "I'm leaving Ynea here. And I've already left word for Randon that I'll be here tomorrow. To work." Now he faced her again, and all the old mockery was back in his eyes. "Or did you truly believe I'd place my injured pride ahead of the welfare of my country? You wound me to the quick, my lady." He opened the door and stepped aside, plainly dismissing her.

Kayli, too bemused to think of any response, made her escape as quickly as she could. She hurried back to her quarters, helpless to prevent herself from glancing over her shoulder every few steps. As she crept into her room like a thief slinking away from her crime, she wondered whether she had looked to see if the servants had observed her leaving Terralt's room—or if she looked to see whether Terralt was watching her go.

Her room was empty, and while otherwise Kayli would have appreciated the solitude, now she felt an uneasy desire for company. Well—

Fortunately when Kayli arrived at Ynea's door, the maid

who answered her knock told her that Ynea was awake.

"She'd be grateful for the company." The maid nodded, smiling. "She's fair chewing the blankets."

Ynea was pale and wan after the morning's exertion, her lips an alarming blue color, but she sat upright, an untouched tray of food beside her. Her thin face lit in a smile when she saw Kayli in the doorway.

"Oh, Kayli, I'm so glad you've come," she said with a sigh. "And how kind of you to make the time on your wedding day. Can you sit for a little while?"

"Gladly," Kayli said, almost dizzy with relief. "But only if you will eat your supper. Endra would never forgive me if I made you miss your meal." She glanced down at the tray, wincing inwardly at the bowl of broth and chopped raw liver. It looked altogether too much like what she had been served while she was fasting, or sick.

Ynea followed Kayli's gaze and smiled.

"I told Endra and Stevann that I am so tired of cow's liver, especially uncooked," she said. "So today I have the liver of the dragon Terralt killed, and broth from its flesh. A small change, but a pleasant one." Her eyes twinkled at Kayli. "Were you pleased with the dragon?"

"Very pleased," Kayli said honestly. "I had never tasted it before. It was a magnificent gift." She hesitated, wondering what Ynea had heard of the argument in the courtyard. Surely Terralt was not leaving without informing his wife?

Ynea laid her thin white hand on Kayli's strong brown fingers and smiled sympathetically.

"You mustn't allow my husband to wound you with his gibes," she said gently. "I swear to you he was kinder when he believed life treated him less harshly. I'm afraid he's become accustomed to saying what he will without anyone taking him to task for it. He's a good man, but sometimes his goodness is hard to see through his anger."

Kayli sighed.

"Randon is very angry with me as well," she admitted. "And he is right. I shamed myself with my vengefulness."

"Well, if that was shaming yourself, then I hate to imagine how you'd judge it if you had slapped his face, which any woman worth her salt would have done," Ynea said with a sigh. "And I doubt that Randon is truly angry at you. More likely he's angry at himself. Men are like that—he's ashamed that he's tolerated Terralt's insults, to him and to you. But he tolerates it because he believes he must, and tries to forget that he's ashamed. So he becomes angry with you, because you dare to speak out when he doesn't. Men are easily pricked where their pride is concerned. Poor Terralt, I think, is constantly chafed raw."

Kayli was silent. How could Ynea defend this man who had treated her so poorly? And would she continue to defend him if she knew how Terralt had behaved toward Kayli in his room?

"But there's another matter I'd like to discuss with you," Ynea said. She pulled the bell rope at her bedside; a moment later the same maid Kayli had seen before peered in.

"Bring in my children, please," Ynea said.

Ynea had mentioned the children before, but Kayli was seeing them for the first time. The eldest, that was Derrin, perhaps four years old, and heartbreakingly serious looking for a boy so young. The three-year-old would be Avern, and the little girl, still unsteady on her chubby legs and clinging to the maid's hand, that would be Erisa. Erisa and Avern were dark-haired like Ynea and big-boned like Terralt, but Derrin was slighter of build, his hair a glorious dark auburn.

"Children, this is High Lady Kayli, High Lord Randon's wife," Ynea said, beckoning them forward. "Come and greet her; by marriage she is your aunt."

Silently they came forward, the boys bowing soberly, little Erisa trying awkwardly to curtsy. None of them said a word.

Kayli hesitated; she'd had no experience with young children, but these stiff, silent children almost broke her heart. She dropped to her knees on the floor and smiled, extending her arms.

"I am so pleased to meet my nephews and my niece," she said warmly. "In Bregond children embrace their kinfolk. Or are Agrondish children afraid of their aunts, when they are so fearsome as I?"

The children exchanged dubious glances, and finally it was little Erisa who toddled forward and slipped her fat little arms around Kayli's neck. The boys hesitantly followed their sister's example, and Kayli felt a pang when they gave Ynea an equally perfunctory embrace and left as silently as they had come.

Ynea sighed when the children had gone, and Kayli was alarmed to see how much of the animation had drained from the young woman's face. Her eyes had sunk far back in her head, surrounded by dark rings of exhaustion, and Kayli thought Ynea was clinging to consciousness by will alone.

"I've had so little part in their lives," Ynea murmured, as if to herself. "I couldn't even nurse them. Terralt chose the governesses and tutors who raised them. I feel I've done them a terrible wrong, but perhaps it's for the best. Perhaps when I'm gone they won't feel much loss."

"Ynea—" Kayli began, fear stabbing at her heart.

Ynea raised one hand.

"Please," she said gently. "I'm no fool. Stevann smiles and makes fine-fine noises when he examines me, but I can see the truth in his eyes. Your maid Endra is more honest, thank the Bright Ones. I'm tired of kindly meant lies. And I've felt the presence of death growing within me as surely as I've felt my child grow there. I pray to the Bright Ones I'll live to see the face of my last child, but I don't hope for more than that."

"Oh, Ynea," Kayli said, dread settling like shadows around the room. Ynea had said in plain words what Kayli had not let herself acknowledge. "You must not believe—"

Ynea held up a hand again, gazing into Kayli's eyes.

"No," she said quietly. "I want our friendship a true one, with no lies spoken between us even to give comfort. That's the second greatest kindness you can do me. But I have one other boon to ask of you."

There were many things Kayli wanted to say, but when she met Ynea's eyes, she simply clasped her cold, bony hand instead.

"Ask me what you will," she said. "If it is within my power, I promise you it shall be done."

"My children." Ynea glanced with that same resigned longing at the door where they had come and gone so quietly. "Please, watch over them. See that they have love and a chance to be happy. My spirit can find peace if I know that you and Randon will see that they're well cared for."

"Ynea, I will do what I can," Kayli said awkwardly. "But Terralt is their father, and he is not receptive to my advice."

Ynea chuckled weakly.

"He has never borne alone the responsibility for four children," she said. "I've left a letter for him containing my wishes, and I know he'll be grateful for your assistance and advice. He has great respect for you, however little he shows it." Her eyes bored into Kayli's. "Promise me."

"I cannot speak for Randon, but for myself, I promise," Kayli said, her heart sinking. Yes, she could see death in those large, dark eyes, feel it in the faint pulse of the blood in Ynea's cold hand. It was as if the child had sucked all the life out of her, leaving her with nothing.

"Thank you for that. As for Randon, I have no concern." Ynea sighed and closed her eyes; in only a moment, her slow, deep breathing told Kayli she was asleep.

Kayli tiptoed from the room as silently as she could, leaving the door ajar rather than waking Ynea with the squeal of the hinges. When she returned to her room, the fire was lit, and now she was glad of the solitude. There would be little sleep for her tonight, but she was glad to be alone with her thoughts.

For in the end, everyone was alone.

Even on their wedding night.

11

KAYLI SLID THE LAST BEAD OVER THE END OF her braid and pinned it almost defiantly. She had looked over her gowns that morning and chosen the one which most differed from Agrondish styles, giving orders to the seamstresses to prepare, with the aid of her maids, garments according to her specifications. Meanwhile, Kayli had debated with herself how to wear her hair. She was entitled to the elaborate knots and coils of a married noblewoman, but such a style required the services of her maids and long preparation, and her temple upbringing cringed from such vanity. So in the end she had kept the thirty-nine braids, as was her right, but worn them in the simple style of an Initiate, with a small coil at the back of her head, but the beaded ends hanging down her back. She wore her *thari* openly at her hip, but laid aside her jewelry (with the exception, of course, of her temple ring), and she had pushed the perfumes and powders to the back of her dressing table. She would not require them any longer.

When she finished, Kayli gazed at herself soberly in the mirror. No Initiate would wear such a gown, but it could not be helped; she could scarcely appear in audience in a temple robe. But that was as far as she was willing to compromise. Her boots clicked confidently on the stairs as she strode down to the main hall, and the beads on her braids clacked at her back, as if in answer. As she stepped into the main hall, Kayli thought, *Today I would almost dare the fire again.*

If Kayli had anticipated a grand entrance, she was disappointed; the hall was still completely empty. She sighed. Of course, when there were no guards at the door, she should have known that the others were still at breakfast and, judging from the fact that the outer doors were still closed, would be for some time.

Kayli's stomach rumbled at the thought of breakfast, but although she did wish to confront Randon this morning, she did not want it to be in the dining hall while the others were still chatting over their breakfast. She slipped quietly around to the kitchen instead, horrifying the kitchen staff with her sudden appearance. She fought down laughter as everyone scuttled around clearing a place for her to sit, and she scandalized the servants by requesting plain bread and cheese to break her fast. Little did the wide-eyed scullery maids know that Kayli had chopped carrots and scrubbed the hearth in the Order's kitchens. Little, too, did they know that crusty toasted bread with melted cheese and a foamy cold mug of cider were more to her liking than the rich cream pastries and almond milk pudding sent to the lord's table.

After Kayli had eaten her fill, however, she excused herself and made her way back toward the main hall. On her way, she glanced out one of the front windows, then stopped and looked out again. There was a long line of peasants and nobles at the door awaiting audience, but what had drawn her attention was a large caravan of wagons that was departing through the main gate of the courtyard. Surely that must be the caravan returning to Bregond—yes, there was Brother Santee in one of the wagons—but what amazed Kayli was the size of the guard contingent accompanying it. Surely there could not be less than a hundred guardsmen falling in behind the wagons, and she could see more outside the courtyard wall waiting to join the procession. Was the danger of a Sarkondish raid so great that Randon thought it necessary to send a small army to guard the caravan?

The guards had assumed their posts flanking the door to the main hall, their expressions carefully impassive as they stood by to let Kayli enter. Thankfully Randon was there, just settling himself in his seat, and just as thankfully Terralt was *not* there. Randon was engrossed in a scroll on the table before him and did not notice Kayli until she was halfway across the room, but when he saw her, the surprise and relief in his eyes sent an answering wave of relief through her. He *did* want her, then, at his side.

As Kayli slid into her own seat, Randon reached over and squeezed her hand.

"I'm glad you came," he murmured. "I was afraid you wouldn't."

"My place is here," Kayli said simply, squeezing his fingers in return. "I saw Brother Santee's caravan leaving. Is there some trouble, that you send so many troops?"

Randon shook his head.

"No; actually it was Terralt's idea, and a good one. I'm setting up a garrison at the border. Most of the troops will go on to see the caravan home safely, and I'm inviting your father to send troops of his own to help me secure the border. It's time to yank the reins on these raiders once and for all, and between the two countries, I believe we can do it, now that neither side is going to shoot at the other's troops the moment we see them."

Kayli sat back, pleased at Randon's words, although she would have preferred that the idea came from another source than Terralt. What game was the lord playing? He had no desire for peace with Bregond; what did it profit him and his cause if the border was secured to enable travel and trade between the two countries? But she could not say this to Randon now, not after yesterday's argument.

Kayli was surprised at the huge number of peasants who suddenly had grievances to bring before the High Lord and High Lady that day; by dinnertime, however, the manner of the petitioners and the surprisingly simple nature of the conflicts brought before them made Kayli realize that curiosity more than conflict had brought most of the petitioners.

When Randon motioned to the guards to close the door so he and Kayli could snatch a little dinner, he grinned at her and said, "Do you know, I think most of them just wanted a look at you, now that we're formally confirmed and all the rumors have had time to make their way around the city."

Kayli grimaced.

"Then the reputation of the Bregondish people has been much diminished since I came."

"I'd be inclined to think the contrary." Randon waved to the servants to bring in the trays laden with his and Kayli's dinner. "Have you noticed that now the folk speak to both of us instead of trying to ignore you? And I don't think you've received a single sour scowl all morning."

"You forget the farmer whose bull strayed and mounted all the heifers in his neighbor's field," Kayli reminded him. "He gave me a scowl fit to wither all the grass on the plains."

"Well, he was furious that you didn't award him so much as one of the calves," Randon said, chuckling. "Doubtless he'll call it outlandish Bregondish justice. Never mind that I'd have made the same decision if you hadn't said it first."

Kayli smiled, but she could not bring herself to care too much about straying cattle. It was hard to sit beside Randon all morning with matters so unsettled between them. And there was still Terralt. How was she ever to deal with the man now?

"I had an idea, if you're up for it," Randon said to her. "I've heard nothing from Master Dyer Lidian or any of the others since you were poisoned. I think they're waiting, too, to see what I—what we'll do. But almost every one of them invited us to visit the guilds; I think this is a good time to accept those offers. Their manner with us—with you, especially—might tell us a great deal."

Kayli glanced at Randon, troubled by the anxiety in his eyes. The guildmasters were his friends and staunchest supporters. How it must have galled him all this time, wondering which of them might have tried to assassinate his bride at his very table. And how he must hate this new game even as he contemplated playing it.

"Do you know," she said slowly, "perhaps it was not one of them. Others might have had access to our food, and many of the guildmasters and guildmistresses brought their servants, who could have been suborned by another. I wonder if your friends are not all innocent after all."

Randon raised his eyebrows, a cautious hope in his eyes.

"Why do you say that?"

"If I had been one of them, and guilty of such a crime," Kayli said after a moment's thought, "I would make an effort to make myself appear innocent—implicate a business rival, hint that one of the others at the table might have a motive or access to poisons. Perhaps I would even volunteer to be questioned under truth spell, knowing that once I, your friend, had made such an offer, you could not in good conscience accept. But none of them have made such protestations. I think it likely that they are merely waiting, as you said, to see whether you will trust them or not. So your idea, to show such trust by visiting them, is a good one."

Randon smiled with relief.

"All right, then," he said. "I'll send a messenger immediately. Which one first, do you think?"

"Master Dyer Lidian," Kayli told him. "He is your closest friend in the guilds, is he not?"

"How did you—" Randon stopped, then grinned ruefully. "I forget how you can almost pick the thoughts out of a man's head. You'll have to teach me the trick of that sometime. Lidian it is, then."

The afternoon's audiences were not much different from those in the morning, and when the guards closed the doors again at sunset, Kayli thought privately that she had likely seen every citizen of Tarkesh this day.

When they rose from their seats, Randon laid his hand on her arm.

"Endra said you needed time alone," he said. "I can't say it surprised me. But would you have supper with me?"

Kayli wanted to decline, wanting nothing more than quiet and sleep, but after all, sooner or later she must talk with Randon, and likely there would be no rest for her until there was peace between them.

But was this the way to gain that peace?

"I will sup with you tonight and every night you wish," she said slowly. "And contrary to Endra's advice, I do not wish to be alone. But the matters on which we disagree will not be mended by words, at least not truthful words. So I would ask that until such a time as one or the other of us should change our feelings about the matter, we belabor it no further."

Randon sighed, but Kayli fancied there was a little relief in the sigh.

"As little as I like to admit it, you're right," he said. "All right, then, if that's what you want, we'll say no more about it." Then he gave her an entreating grin. "But may I please move myself and my belongings back into what were once my own rooms? It's a hard thing, barring a groom from his bride's bed on his wedding night."

"No harder than for the bride to spend her night in that lonely bed," Kayli said, smiling despite herself. The night before she'd been glad enough to be alone with her thoughts; tonight, however, she would be glad of companionship to keep those same thoughts at bay.

Supper was quiet and awkward, the sparse conversation carefully limited. Kayli thought to herself that in fact she had known Randon for only a short time; it was hard to mend a quarrel with someone still so much a stranger, and now, like Randon, she had secrets to keep. After some consideration, however, she decided that she should tell him of her promise to Ynea. Randon's expression grew grimmer and grimmer as she spoke.

"Do you think she's right?" he asked, his voice leaden. "Do you think she's going to die?"

"I have not directly asked Stevann or Endra," Kayli said slowly, covering his hand with her own. She had come to love Ynea in the short time she had known her, and Randon had known her since she had married Terralt. "But if Endra told her that her chances of survival are poor, I must believe it. If she had not borne so young or so close together, or perhaps if she had been tended by great healers—"

"We'll bring the healers," Randon said quickly. "Now that Terralt's not here, it will be easy."

"Then bring them, by all means," Kayli said with a sigh. "But I think there is little they can do now but give her comfort and ease. Still, even that would be a blessing. And all I can do for her is to promise kindness to her children." She glanced at Randon. "I hope I did not presume too much."

"No, of course not," Randon said remotely, gazing into the fire. "We'll see that they're well cared for and happy. I would have anyway, at least as far as Terralt will let—No, you have to be wrong," he said more firmly. "There has to be something the healers can do. Why, I've heard in the west they have mages who can raise the dead."

Kayli shuddered at the thought of such desecration, but she said nothing. Privately she doubted there was any healer powerful enough to save Ynea, not so late in her pregnancy, but there was no harm in letting Randon believe what he would. Besides, what did she know? Perhaps there was magic mightier than she had ever heard.

"Then you must bring those healers quickly," she said, nodding. "But you might comfort Ynea most by visiting her from time to time. I am sure your company would please her greatly."

Randon stared into the fire moodily, and Kayli could almost feel his guilt. He could have defied Terralt as Kayli herself had done; he could have brought in a healer surreptitiously to visit Ynea as Kayli had sent Endra. But for whatever reason he had thought good—whether because he doubted his ability to keep the secret from Terralt, or whether he believed Terralt less likely to forgive his own brother than a stranger for interfering—he had not done so, and he would not soon forgive himself for it. Now Kayli regretted her words in the courtyard even more bitterly. Terralt had at least warranted a rebuke, if not such a public one, but Randon was merely the victim of her ill temper.

"Your thought to send troops to secure the border, that was a good one," Kayli said, hoping to distract him.

"It wasn't my idea, it was Terralt's," Randon said ruefully. "He said if we were going to have this alliance, we might as well do it properly. He said we should slowly stock an encampment at the border, but I took it a step further and sent the troops with the caravan. Terralt also suggested that we might want a permanent garrison at the border to watch for Sarkondish raiders. Mind you, I imagine he's thinking as much of Bregondish warriors creeping over our borders as Sarkondish ones, but the idea's still a good one. A permanent fortress would make a safe stopping point, too, for messengers and caravans traveling between Agrond and Bregond. Primarily, though, I just wanted to show your father that we were doing something about the problem immediately." He shook his head. "If two attempts on his daughter's life aren't enough for him to declare the alliance null and mount a war against us, I don't know what is."

"My father's word is written in stone," Kayli told him. "He values me, yes, but he would not place my well-being above the welfare of our country." She knew that only too well. "He will be delighted to learn that we have conceived a child." In fact he would likely be outraged by the strange Agrondish custom of the wedding and confirmation after the conception. But there was no need to trouble Randon with that information; there was little else he could have done.

Randon turned and glanced at her.

"Kayli, what happens when your parents die?" he asked suddenly. "To the alliance, I mean."

"It depends on which daughter they choose as their Heir," Kayli told him. "Mother and Father will choose a daughter and her husband whom they believe will best rule Bregond in the manner they wish."

"Might he choose you?" Randon asked her gravely.

"Perhaps," Kayli said slowly. "It would be a daring move, for then our two countries would become one, under you and me as High Lord and Lady, and after us, our child. But I do not know that my father would risk such a choice. To ally with Agrond, that is one thing; to become one people with it is another. It might mean a great future for our people, but many would see it as a betrayal, as a loss of our sovreignty, our very identity." In fact, Randon's question troubled her. Did he hope to rule Bregond as well as Agrond? Such ambition seemed more characteristic of Terralt than of him, and Kayli had never thought that her marriage might not only cement an alliance, but subject Bregond to the rule of another country.

"Perhaps it is best that such great changes happen slowly," Kayli said gently. "A great herd moving across the plains slowly and steadily is a comforting sight, but when they all race uncontrolled, the danger is great."

Randon sighed.

"You're right," he said. "Since you've come I've marveled at how different our peoples are in their ways, when we actually live so close together. I suppose I thought most of the people in the world were pretty much alike. Why, even to the far west in Allanmere—"

"You have been to Allanmere, where water wells up from the earth into every home, and where elves live side by side with men?" Kayli asked, awed. In Bregond, the great city of Allanmere was more myth than truth, touched only through the often conflicting stories of merchants.

"Yes, I was there once," Randon said, grinning at the wonder in Kayli's expression. "I sailed down the Dezarin with some merchants, then back up the Brightwater. It's a marvelous city, all right—larger than Tarkesh probably by half again. The water doesn't bubble up into every home except in the rich areas, though there are plenty of public fountains—and the fountains only spout water, not fine wine, and the streets aren't paved with silver, and peasants don't drink from ruby cups. But it's true the elves there do live side by side with men. Not always happily or well, but some of them own homes and businesses right in the city. You can sit down in a tavern and share a bottle of wine with one—although you may not end up getting much of the wine. But I always thought that if Allanmere could keep the peace between two such different peoples within the same city, there's no reason we can't do it when Agrond and Bregond have so few opportunities to bother each other."

"No sparks are drawn when the flint keeps separate from the steel," Kayli said, quoting Brisi, and Randon had to laugh.

"Well, that's a good thought, since we're trying to prevent a fire that will burn both countries to ash," Randon admitted.

Gazing into his troubled eyes, Kayli felt a sudden warmth in her heart. It was impossible to resent one who cared for so very deeply for his people—and now, by extension, for her own.

"What are you thinking, with such an expression?" Randon asked her with a smile.

"I was thinking of another sort of fire," Kayli said, smiling back. "And how much I would like to kindle it. Unless you wish to be the High Lord all night."

Randon's eyes sparkled, and some of the worry left them.

"I think," he said, "the High Lord has retired for the evening."

In the morning, Kayli and Randon woke early to the sound of a sharp, impatient knock on their door.

"Come in," Randon called, but instead of a maid with their breakfast, it was Terralt who strode in, his face set and tense.

"Better get up, High Lord of Agrond," Terralt said sarcastically. "Your people are rioting at your gates."

"Rioting!" Randon bolted upright. "What's happened?"

"You, as usual," Terralt growled. "Bright Ones, Randon, you couldn't take a good idea and leave it alone, could you? You just had to do it your way, and now look what's happened."

"What are you talking about?" Randon asked impatiently, sliding out of bed and grabbing his robe. Kayli stayed where she was, under the covers. Terralt's eyes flickered to her almost involuntarily, and she pulled the covers a little higher.

"The guards," Terralt said. "I told you to send troops to the border, not parade them through the city with that Bregondish caravan. There are rumors everywhere—that you're sending our troops to defend Bregondish lands from raiders, that the troops aren't there for the raiders at all, but to prevent a planned Bregondish attack. Worst of all, word's gotten out that you've invited Bregond to station troops on *our* border. The people are in a panic, and what did you expect?"

"Well, what did *you* expect?" Randon retorted. "I couldn't mass a garrison of troops at the border without asking High Lord Elaasar to join the effort; otherwise he'd have thought *we* were preparing to invade. And by the time I could have smuggled the troops out of the city quietly, in small groups, they'd have been no use to the caravan. The Sarkondish raids have increased since Kayli arrived, or hadn't you heard?"

"I heard," Terralt said irritably. "And if you'd mustered the force slowly and quietly, as I said, you could have done something productive about it without frightening your own people. Now you've got hundreds of terrified peasants clamoring at your gates. Go out there and deal with them."

"Bright Ones," Randon muttered. He disappeared out the door, presumably going to his dressing room to pull on some clothes before he confronted Tarkesh's irate population.

Terralt stood where he was for a moment, still gazing darkly at Kayli. At last he turned and followed Randon out of the room, closing the door quietly behind him.

Kayli was already half-dressed by the time her maids arrived to help her. As soon as she was clothed, she ran down the hallways after Randon; at the door, however, Stevann stopped her.

"Randon asked me to keep you inside," the mage apologized. "I don't think it's very safe out there right now."

Kayli peered out the door. The courtyard was empty but for guards, most of whom had clustered near the courtyard gates. An ugly crowd had gathered outside the wall, and there was a good deal of shouting and cursing that carried all the way to the castle. She could hardly believe that many of these same people had gathered here so peacefully only two days before to celebrate her wedding.

"Where is Randon?" she asked anxiously. "I do not see him."

"He's up at the gate, where no doubt some assassin's dagger or some peasant's rock will find him," Terralt said, joining Kayli at the door. "I told him to send a messenger out, but there's no reasoning with him. Better stay back. If they catch sight of you right now, it'll only make them angrier. The guards have all they can do keeping those peasants from climbing the wall or battering at the gates now."

Now Kayli could pick out Randon's rich red-brown hair shining in the morning sunlight. Apparently he was trying to reason with the crowd; she could see his head bobbing as if he spoke, and his arms waved. But the roar of the mob continued unabated, and she saw with alarm that true to Terralt's word, there were indeed missiles flying—rocks, or perhaps clods of dirt or offal. Kayli stepped involuntarily forward, and Terralt grabbed her arm, halting her.

The touch of his hand on her arm seared through her, but this time Kayli refused to succumb to embarrassment or confusion, and she rounded on Terralt squarely.

"Do something to help him," she demanded. "Or I shall." When Terralt still hesitated, she added icily, "He is my *husband.*"

Terralt jerked his hand from her arm as if burned, muttered an oath, and strode angrily out the door. When he reached

Guard Captain Beran, the two men conversed for a moment, then disappeared around the corner of the castle.

Meanwhile, at the gate, there was a sudden break in the angry shouting, and for a moment there was a hush, quickly replaced by a rather confused murmur. By the time Captain Beran led a large company of troops around the wall to break up the mob, most of the peasants scattered quietly. Kayli's heart did not slow, however, until she saw Randon walking back to the castle, still protectively surrounded by a dozen guards.

"Are you all right?" she asked as soon as he was through the door. "I saw them throwing stones."

"Well, it was a nasty crowd, there's no denying it," Randon admitted, glancing over his shoulder.

"What was it you told them?" Kayli asked. "Something you said calmed them."

"I don't think it calmed them," Randon said, sighing. "Just gave them something to think about and decide whether they like it or not. I told them you'd conceived my heir."

"But they knew that already, did they not?" Kayli asked, surprised. "The delay of the wedding—"

"I'm sure they'd heard rumors," Randon said, nodding. "But as far as they knew, the wedding had been delayed by your own poor health—your illness when you first arrived, then the poisoning. There was no official confirmation. Well, now they know I'll have an heir, which means the both of us are here to stay, and it'll take them some time, I hope, to decide what they think of that. A child commits you more firmly to Agrond; I hope that eases some of their fears."

"I wonder how my own people are reacting to the alliance," Kayli said, troubled by the thought. Bregond had far more to lose than prosperous, cosmopolitan Agrond. The Bregondish had fought so hard, so long, to hold what remained of their land and their customs. Now the alliance with Agrond meant mingling with strangers who had been their enemies, who had stolen the best of their lands. Now the influx of goods from Agrond would mean that Bregond was *buying* the products of that stolen land, products that would compete with their own trade goods in the market. And Kayli would be only the first to bear a child of mixed blood.

"Likely your parents won't have the same trouble," Randon said comfortingly. "They're long-established rulers. The people are always more doubtful of a newcomer, especially one they weren't too sure of in the first place." He grinned wryly.

But Kayli wondered. Bregond was not ruled as stringently as Agrond apparently was. The nomadic clans largely went their own way, governed by their clan leaders, having no contact with the country's High Lord and Lady for years at a time. The Orders, too, kept to themselves, seldom looking to the High Lord and Lady for resolution of conflicts or protection. The people of Bregond were proud and independent—and stubborn, too. They would be suspicious of any change as quick as drastic as the alliance—and in Bregond, suspicion could quickly flare into anger.

"There's a lot of troops outside the wall," Randon said in surprise, glancing out the door. "Did you call them?"

"No, Terralt spoke to the guard captain," Kayli answered. "But I urged him to help. He would not let me go to you."

"And thank the Bright Ones he didn't," Randon said, sighing. "That lot would have been over the wall in a breath, throwing bricks instead of pebbles, and at you instead of me. Come on, we'll let the guards get rid of the last stragglers, and we can finish dressing for breakfast."

Food was Kayli's least concern, but she followed Randon back to their quarters, then down to the dining hall for a silent and unhappy breakfast. Then, unsurprisingly, there was a meeting with the advisers to discuss the riot, its causes and aftereffects—and what could be done to prevent another.

"Nothing will reassure these people but time," Lady Tarkas told them. "Now that the border's open—*legally* open—the first Bregondish goods will soon appear in the market. Once folk see that the benefits promised by the alliance are real, they'll come around, especially if the Sarkondish raids stop. There's always been rumors that Bregond secretly allied with Sarkond."

Kayli heard this last with vast astonishment. Bregond? Allied with barbaric *Sarkond*? Why, it was well that no Agrondish negotiator had mentioned such a rumor to her father, or the insult might have precipitated the very war they wished to avoid.

"Surely this can't be news to you, High Lady," Lord Vyr said, noting Kayli's affronted scowl. "The Sarkondish raiders fight from horseback, after all, like Bregondish warriors, and in fact their horses are very like yours."

"Their horses are like ours," Kayli said coldly, "because they steal our breeding stock when they raid the horse clans. And they fight from horseback because they could scarcely travel leagues to raid the borders on foot, not when our warriors would pursue on horseback. And I would note to this council that some of the Sarkondish raiders use the Agrondish horizontal bolt-shooter, not our longbows, and they wear armor and metal helms as Agrondish soldiers do. And if the Sarkondish were allied with Bregond, their raiders would scarcely take slaves for sale, knowing that *we* would never purchase them!"

Lord Vyr flushed and rose to his feet, opening his mouth to retort, but Randon rose; too, holding up his hands.

"Kayli! Vyr!" he said sharply. "The enemy's far to the north, not sitting here in the chamber."

Kayli took a deep breath and reined in her temper with difficulty; Lord Vyr clenched his teeth, but sat down again. Randon glanced warningly at both of them before he spoke again.

"We know the rumors about Bregondish dealings with Sarkond are ridiculous," he said, "so we'll move past that, please, and on to something more useful. Vyr, I want two additional companies of guardsmen in the city, three more on notice."

Lord Vyr's eyebrows shot up, but he said nothing.

"Lady Tarkas, I want those Bregondish trade goods scattered through the market as quickly as possible. That leatherwork and those furs are enough to tempt the most discerning nobleman, and the perfumes will be the rage of the city within a sevenday. The gemstones, too, are exceptional."

Lady Tarkas shrugged.

"I will do as you say, of course, High Lord," she said. "And the citizens of the city will, of course, adore the new trade goods; they are as fine as you say. However, instead of angry peasants beating at your gate, you'll then have Master Tanner Crinna, Master Perfumer Zada, and Master Gemcutter Trelanna besieging the castle. There's been grumbling ever since I showed some of the goods to the mercantile families. Master Weaver Odric is already fuming over the cloth samples that came with the first caravan. Never mind, at least the guilds won't riot, and as you're supping with Master Dyer Lidian tonight, you can discuss the guild situation with him.'' At Randon's blank look, she raised her eyebrows. "You *did* send him a message yesterday, didn't you? Didn't Terralt deliver his reply to you this morning?''

Randon let out an exasperated sigh.

"Well, I suppose he forgot about it in the confusion of the riot, and I didn't see him afterward, but rushed right down to eat and meet with you," he said. "Never mind. But if we're to visit with Lidian, Kayli and I need to leave now. And I may know a way to pacify Lidian—and through him, some of the others."

To Kayli's surprise, Randon asked her to arrange their carriage and guard escort while he disappeared into the cellars. When Randon joined her at the carriage, a servant followed carrying a large box; when Kayli glanced at the box, however, Randon only smiled mysteriously.

They arrived at the Dyers' Guildhouse a little after midday, but Master Dyer Lidian, who came out to meet them, seemed unperturbed by their lateness.

"Welcome, welcome, High Lord, High Lady!" he boomed, waving his dye-stained hands enthusiastically as he bowed. "Welcome to my humble guildhouse. After what I heard of this morning's fracas at the castle gate, I feared I'd miss the pleasure of your company altogether, but I still had my cooks do the best they could. And here you are. Come in while the food's still hot, and then we'll trot through the place and see if I can't dazzle the High Lady with my people's talents."

Kayli had no appetite whatsoever, having belatedly broken her fast only a short time before; to her dismay, however, Master Dyer Lidian had ordered an extravagant dinner, and she could hardly insult him by abstaining, not when they had come to show their friendship in the first place.

"I make my toast to the High Lord and Lady of Agrond,"

Lidian said, his voice suddenly formal. "Long may they reign, in happiness and good health." He emphasized the last two words subtly, but his gaze on Kayli and Randon had sharpened.

Randon reached for his own goblet without hesitation, and Kayli raised her own as well.

"I make my toast to the guilds," he said, "and the truest friends I've ever had." He drank deeply.

Despite their repast not long before, Randon helped himself from every platter as if he'd eaten nothing for days, and Kayli perforce followed his example. Seeing them eat and drink without hesitation, Lidian gradually relaxed and chatted amiably with Randon, both of them pausing frequently to explain some facet of the dyeing process to Kayli, or to recount some story of a shared adventure or mishap. Gradually titles fell away, and the High Lord and the Master Dyer became simply Lidian and Randon again, and Kayli's heart warmed as she saw Randon more relaxed than he'd been in days. It was hard to picture the aging, dye-stained, and rather coarse Lidian as the friend and companion of a nobleman, but somehow Kayli could more easily picture him sitting in a tavern, sipping ale, telling ribald stories, and flirting with the serving wenches than she could Randon.

"But enough of our reminiscences," Lidian said suddenly, turning to Kayli. "Tell me, are the rumors true that our lovely and wise High Lady is a mage as well?"

"Well, I am a mage, and I am not," Kayli answered hesitantly. "It is true that I trained at one of the magical Orders in Bregond. But I was only the rankest novice, and despite my study since I have arrived in Bregond, I would never presume to name myself a true mage."

"Ha!" Randon shook his head. "She doesn't do herself half justice, Lidian. I tell you, it'd make your blood run cold to see Kayli thrust her hand into the fire and pull out glowing embers. Go on, Kayli, show him something, won't you?"

Kayli was a little embarrassed by the request, but she could hardly refuse, and at last she summoned a small flame to dance over her fingertips, to Lidian's delight.

"Well, call yourself a mage or not, *I'm* impressed," Lidian declared when Kayli had banished the small flame. "And now, if you've both finished, we'll see if I can't impress the High Lady with the sort of magic my guild can perform.''

Kayli had no knowledge of the dyeing industry; she had naively assumed that one took a piece of cloth, dipped it in a color essence, dried it, and that was that. She was astonished, therefore, to see how elaborate a process it really was, with preparatory solutions, dye baths, fixatives, bleaches—and even more astonishing was the amazing rainbow hues produced. Bregondish clothing tended to be utilitarian, and plain earth and grass colors were more practical than the flashy hues that seemed popular in Agrond. She remarked on the amazing variety of color to Lidian, and he beamed proudly.

"You won't find better in all of Agrond, and I'd daresay far beyond," he said triumphantly. "We've developed some of the best shades in the market, such as that purple you remarked on, and we've got a beautiful orange gold in the works, too." Glancing at Kayli for permission, he turned the collar of her protective robe back slightly to examine the shade of her dress, and frowned critically.

"I'll send over a few bolts for you to try," he said. "With your lovely dark skin and hair, you should be wearing rich reds and golds and dark orange, don't you think, Randon?"

"My lovely lady," Randon said warmly, "would do justice to your best, but she'd look beautiful in plain sackcloth."

"Well, sackcloth notwithstanding, an exquisite picture is worthy of the finest frame you can buy," Lidian said wryly. "But come, my friend, are you going to leave me curious all day, or do I get to see what you're hiding in that box you brought?"

"I thought I'd let you look at a little Bregondish artistry," Randon said. He opened the box, took out several plain cloth samples, and handed them to Lidian. "Bregondish dyers don't produce all the colors we fancy, so I thought you'd be interested in bringing in raw cloth and dyeing it."

"Mmmm." Lidian examined the cloth thoughtfully, sliding it through his stained fingers, pulling at it in different directions, and teasing at the edges of the weave. "Interesting stuff. Light and fine as a spiderweb, but tough. Good and sturdy, I'll wager, but it breathes. What is it? It's not flax, nor wool. . . ."

"*Ikada* wool," Kayli told him. "*Ikada* are a herd animal we raise for milk, meat, leather, and hair. They are hardy and can be sheared twice during warm weather."

"Interesting, and useful. Animal hair takes a color differently than plant fiber." He tugged at the weave again. "Odric would be sick with envy. This is a good, tight weave, but very different than his pattern. I'd wager you good money he'll be wanting to hire a few weavers over to teach him the trick of it, and then maybe arrange to buy bales of the wool to weave himself. Me, I'd be interested in the cloth, whether he weaves it or they do. If it holds a color true, I could sell this dear in the market."

"So far we only have the samples," Randon apologized. "But you're welcome to keep some of them to show to Odric and to test with your dyes, and I'm sure we can get more soon."

Lidian nodded.

"I'd be interested in buying a small amount, say a wagon-load or so, just to test," he said, his eyes sparkling. "And the first batch is going into my personal wardrobe. I have no doubt that Odric would fill out the order, to try to duplicate the weave." He glanced sideways at Randon. "But there's another matter we'd best discuss, and not in front of all my apprentices."

He led them back to a room empty but for a table and chairs, and then fetched wine for them. When they were comfortably settled, Lidian spoke boldly.

"Ever since the High Lady was poisoned, I've expected the city guard to come knocking on my door," he said, "to haul me up before that mage of yours. I'll tell you same as I'd say under truth spell: from the moment I walked in, neither I nor anybody I saw tampered with any food or drink, nor do I know any at that table who'd have done such a thing on the evilest day of their lives. Whoever wished your lady ill, I know nothing of it, nor do I know anybody who does. And I'll say the same before your mage if I must."

Randon extended his hand; after a moment Lidian took it.

"If I'd had any doubt of you," Randon said, smiling, "we'd not have drunk your wine and eaten your food. And I had no end of trouble believing that my most loyal friends could sit at my table, smile politely at my face and poison my wife. No, you'd all say just what you thought in good plain words, and that would be the end of it.''

Lidian grinned.

"You going to see the rest of 'em?" he asked.

"Eventually," Randon said, sighing. "It's a sad day when I haven't time to enjoy the company of my friends, but the truth is I can't spare many afternoons. And I'm afraid my lady deserves more of my attention than she's been getting.''

Lidian only smiled wisely and glanced at Kayli's belly; his expression said more plainly than words, *But apparently she got enough attention to conceive your child.* Kayli flushed, but pride and more than a little gratitude mixed with the embarrassment. Apparently rumors traveled quickly indeed in Tarkesh, but at least Lidian was kind enough to refrain from openly mentioning her pregnancy. Kayli supposed that even in cosmopolitan Agrond, a woman did not like to hear that her bedchamber activities were the talk of the city.

"Well, that went better than I expected," Randon said when they had returned to their coach. "I believed what he said about the dinner." He glanced at Kayli. "What do you think?"

"That he was not responsible for the poison, yes, nor knows who was," Kayli said slowly. "And he is certain none of the others there were responsible. At least one he knows, however, does not support you—or does not any longer, perhaps. I believe our policy on slavery was less accepted than we thought. But his voice hardly faltered, and I believe he felt more irritation than true worry, so while one of your friends has not expressed disagreement, perhaps because of your friendship, I think there is no true disloyalty or danger in it.''

"How *do* you do it?" Randon demanded. "Does your magic let you pluck the thoughts right out of people's minds?"

"Nothing of the sort," Kayli said, laughing a little. "Learning to read the 'unspoken language' of expression and gesture is one of the thirty-nine arts required of every accomplished Bregondish woman of marriageable age. From your friend's voice, the way he moved, the direction in which he turned his eyes—those told me more than his words.''

Randon sighed again, and the tension drained from his shoulders as he slumped back against the seat.

"It's Odric, I'd wager my last Sun," he said wearily. "Remember Lady Tarkas mentioned he saw cloth samples from the first caravan, so he's had time to think about the competition from Bregondish weavers. And his guild's one of the worst offenders in owning slaves. He used them for the worst jobs—weaver's cough, you know, from the fiber dust."

Kayli knew little more of weaving than she had of dyeing, but she said nothing, only gesturing to Randon to continue.

"Odric and Crinna, of my friends at least, stand to lose the most business to Bregondish trade," Randon said thoughtfully. "Bregondish weaving is as good as, or better than, anything Odric's guild can produce, and the leather shames anything in our market—soft as a feather, but sturdy as our toughest hides. I have a suspicion, too, that if any of your bowyers decide to start selling their work here, our sale of crossbows is going to drop. And the horses—"

Kayli had to laugh.

"Randon, you cannot expect my folk to trade everything they own! Our longbows take much work and time to make, and horses take time to breed. We have no surplus of either. And it is a little soon, I believe, to plan the whole of the trade between our countries when there is not yet even one good road crossing the border. Let us not anger your friends at the guilds any more than we must yet."

But even as she spoke, she wondered if the damage was already done.

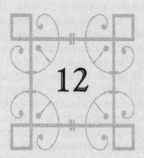

12

LADY TARKAS'S WARNINGS QUICKLY PROVED TO be prophetic. Over the next days, curious peasants requesting audiences were rapidly replaced by worried tradesmen and indignant guildmasters. Only the mercantile houses seemed happy; they did not care whose merchandise they sold, so long as it commanded a good profit, and the prospect of marketing Agrondish goods in Bregond, and Bregondish goods in Agrond (at inflated prices, of course, while the novelty lasted) set their mouths to watering. For every unhappy craftsman pleading for trade restrictions and import taxes, there were two merchants willing to brave Sarkondish raiders if they could get permission to cross the border, all for the privilege of being the first to import the new goods.

"I can't take much more of this," Randon said wearily after their eighth straight day of audiences, public and private. "I'm more than half-tempted to gather together all the guild heads and the heads of all the mercantile houses, lock them in a room together—preferably *with* weapons—and let them fight it out. Survivor wins. About the only thing they can agree on is the new proclamation about the slaves—neither side likes it."

He fell silent, and Kayli knew what troubled him. He had already run afoul of Master Weaver Odric, Master Tanner Crinna, and Smithmaster Erinton over the slaves. Freed slaves from all three guilds had lodged complaints of ill treatment, and Randon had been forced to levy fines against his friends. Kayli had offered to judge the complaints herself, but Randon had refused.

"There's no need to give them one more problem to blame on you and Bregond," Randon had said sourly. "Besides, it's well known they're my friends. It's best to show from the start that they won't receive special favor."

Kayli knew, too, that there was a deeper issue involving Randon's friends. If none of them had poisoned her—and from Lidian's word, it would seem not—then whoever *had* slipped the poison into her food or drink meant Randon to believe that one of his friends was guilty. It seemed likely to Kayli that the poisoning was a deliberate attempt to alienate Randon from his most faithful supporters. Any of Terralt's supporters would profit by the deed, but within the security of the castle, Terralt himself remained the most likely suspect. Kayli knew that Randon did not want even to consider that possibility.

Terralt had kept busy handling the processing of the freed slaves, for the most part, and Kayli was deeply grateful that he seemed to avoid her. She wondered, however, that he continued to live in the city; Ynea was no stronger, and her birthing time was nearing. Randon had quietly brought in several healers, but even they held out little hope.

"If I had attended her earlier, she might have been strong enough for a potion to lose the child," one mage had said, gazing warily at Randon. "I have my doubts of even that. But as matters stand . . ." He shrugged helplessly. "I've heard there's a mage in Erestan who specializes in birthing magics."

The mage from Erestan, an ancient woman, had replied tersely to Randon's message, sent via a merchant ship down the Dezarin. She most certainly could *not* undertake a journey all the way upriver to Agrond, not when the High Lady of Erestan and her own granddaughter were soon to give birth.

Terralt, unaware of these efforts, visited Ynea every day but did not linger.

Also absent, for the most part, was Seba. The girl had approached Kayli several times, asking if she needed her help in the forge. Kayli had not dared pursue her magical studies since the Rite of Renewal, and had gently turned Seba away. She hadn't seen the girl often since then, and had supposed that perhaps Seba was helping Endra with Ynea, where Seba's knowledge of herbs might be useful. She learned otherwise, however, when the Bregondish groom approached her one afternoon.

"I wondered whether you'd sent the child or she'd come of her own, lady," the young man, Brant, said, "but she's got the way of it and no mistake. She rides as if she grew a-horseback, and they answer to her as sweet as they would to the lead stallion of the herd. If you don't need her inside, High Lady, I'd be beholden if you'd let her go on working with me."

And that was how Seba had gone from ex-slave, lady's maid, and temple menial to assistant groom. Looking out the west windows of the castle, Kayli could often see her exercising the horses, tending them as lovingly as a mother might tend a child. Seba was obviously happy in her work, and Kayli was more relieved than she dared admit that the girl had found a position less dependent upon Kayli herself.

Fortunate, too, that Kayli had Seba and the groom to exercise the horses, for she had no time to ride now. Randon had promised that once she conceived and they were confirmed High Lord and Lady, there would be more freedom for them, but it quickly proved otherwise. There were slave complaints to deal with; there were frightened craftsmen and angry guildmasters and greedy merchants; there were peasants and nobles frightened of an imminent Bregondish invasion; and then, besides the *ordinary* day-to-day business of governing an entire country in turmoil, there was still a backlog of work dating from Terendal's death.

It was more than a month after their wedding that Randon finally said one evening, "I just can't take one more day of listening to complaints and signing documents. Let's be lazy tomorrow and go on a small hunt, just us and a few guards, before the weather gets hotter."

Kayli agreed enthusiastically; she'd hesitated to suggest such an outing herself while there was so much to be done. They spent a glorious morning hunting, although they shot only one plump deer. When the noonday sunlight became too hot, they left their horses with the guards and walked to the small pond in the forest, where Randon gave her her second swimming lesson. The cool water was refreshing, but inwardly Kayli preferred her submersions limited to the safe confines of her tub.

When she and Randon rode back through the castle gates at sunset, laughing together, they did not at first notice the strange silence in the courtyard or the subdued manner of the guards at the gate. When Kayli dismounted, however, and Seba did not materialize at her side to take Maja's reins, she noted for the first time Brant's downcast eyes.

"Where is Seba?" she asked him. "Has something happened while we were gone?"

"Seba's gone to help Endra," Brant said, avoiding her gaze. "The midwife called for her soon after you left, lady."

Kayli met Randon's worried glance, and they both ran for the castle as fast as their feet would carry them. At the top of the stairs, however, they met Endra, and the midwife's expression answered Kayli's question before she could ask it.

"There was nothing you could have done, child," Endra said quietly, taking Kayli's hand. "Her heart just had no strength left to beat. It was very peaceful, and I swear she felt no pain." She glanced over her shoulder and lowered her voice. "I wouldn't go back there just now. Terralt's there and he's 'most unhinged. We cut for the baby after she died. It's a healthy girl, but he won't so much as look at her. The children's governess sent for a wet nurse."

A sharp arrow of grief lodged itself in Kayli's heart, but she pushed her pain aside. Mourning and guilt would wait. Taking a deep breath, she turned to Randon.

"You should speak to Terralt," she said gently. "Ynea would want us to think of her daughter now, not to be blinded with grief for what cannot be helped."

Randon clasped her hand tightly, but turned away.

"I doubt if that's a good idea," he said, his voice remote. "I'm the last person he wants to see right now."

A wave of impatience almost brought a harsh retort to Kayli's lips; what kind of man would not comfort his brother in such an hour? Then she swallowed her anger as she had her grief and released Randon's hand.

"Then I will speak to him," she said, and before Randon could reply, she had left him behind, walking as quickly as she could before she, too, found some reason to leave Terralt alone with his pain.

Kayli stopped at the nursery just long enough to look at Ynea's daughter. She was a large baby, black-haired and black-eyed, and her lusty howls bespoke a strong spark of life. The wet nurse had arrived and handled the baby competently, so Kayli did not linger.

Terralt was sitting in Ynea's room in the same chair in which Kayli had sat at Ynea's side, his head on his folded arms on the bed. Thankfully the servants had removed the stained bedclothes and cleaned, clothed, and arranged Ynea's body, but the room still smelled of illness, of blood and birth fluids.

Kayli did not hesitate, but moved to Terralt's side, laying a hand on his shoulder. Terralt jerked as if burned, and his head shot up; when he saw Kayli, however, his red eyes narrowed.

"If you've come to tell me all the things I did wrong, I don't want to hear it," he said, his voice cold and tightly controlled. "I'm sure I've thought of them all already. I should have had a midwife here from the start. I should have brought in mages to examine her. I should have let her be after the first hard birth. I should've been more of a husband and less of a lord."

Kayli knelt on the floor beside his chair so she could gaze into his eyes.

"Were you here when she died?" she asked softly.

"Only by chance," Terralt said bitterly. "I'd come to see Randon, and when I learned he'd taken the day for his own pleasure, I thought as I'd nothing better to do, I had no excuse not to visit my wife." He ran both hands roughly through his hair, then swiped his sleeve impatiently across his eyes. "She started to gasp for air and I called for Stevann." He glanced up at Kayli, and the bewilderment in his eyes made her heart ache in sympathy. "It happened so quickly. She was just— just gone. As suddenly as that."

"Then you were with her to bid her good-bye," Kayli said softly. "That was a great gift."

"A great gift," Terralt said contemptuously. "Of all the

things I could have done for my wife, my great gift was to sit beside her and watch her die.''

There were a thousand words of blame Kayli wanted to say, but what was the use? Adding pain to pain served no good and would not bring Ynea back. She squeezed Terralt's shoulder comfortingly instead.

"Terralt . . .'' She hesitated. "After you left the castle, Randon and I had mages brought to see Ynea. They said there was nothing to be done for her. They said if they had seen her earlier''—she gazed into Terralt's empty eyes and decided—"that it would have made no difference.''

Terralt closed his eyes, and some of the hard lines eased from his face. For a moment Kayli thought he might weep, but he quickly mastered himself, reaching back to pat her hand on his shoulder. A shock ran up Kayli's arm, but she ignored it as best she could.

"Thank you,'' he said quietly. "My pride says you shouldn't have interfered, but to the Dark Realms with my pride. Thank you for trying.''

Kayli smiled.

"In Bregond we believe that we leave a part of our spirit with those we love,'' she said. "We can feel it in our hearts when we remember those who have made the spirit journey, and we can see it in the faces of their children. Your daughter carries a part of Ynea now, and I know that Ynea would want the two of you to comfort each other. And you must give your daughter a name, to tie her spirit to the earth.''

"What, so it won't float away with Ynea's?'' Terralt said tiredly, but he stood. "All right. Let's see this daughter that Ynea died to bear.''

Kayli feared from his words that Terralt would hate the baby, blaming her for Ynea's death, but the expression in Terralt's eyes as he gazed upon his daughter reassured her. He gently fingered the infant's raven hair and smiled, letting the tiny hand clasp his finger.

"She's full of life,'' he said proudly.

To Terralt's dismay, Kayli picked up the baby and deposited her in his arms.

"Then give her a name,'' she said firmly. "And tell her how you will cherish her.''

Terralt held the baby awkwardly, but his kiss on her forehead was without hesitation.

"I haven't been much of a husband, or a father, either," he said. "But I'll do better by you . . . Kalendra." He glanced at Kayli. "So we'll never forget how hard both of you tried." He sat down, still cradling the baby, but he spared Kayli another glance as she tried to slip out the door.

"Wait a moment," he said. "Tell Randon he'll have to do without me for a few days." He smiled sadly. "My children need their father. Better late than not at all, I suppose."

He was silent for a long moment, but Kayli hesitated, certain he had not finished what he wanted to say. At last Terralt cleared his throat awkwardly.

"And tell my brother he should come and see my new daughter," he said at last, very slowly. "Anytime he likes."

When Kayli returned to her quarters, she found Randon already halfway through a bottle of brandy. She was shocked; she had known him only for a few weeks, but in that time she had never seen him drink to excess, although Lidian's stories hinted that he had sometimes overindulged in the past. Kayli hoped that Terralt's words would cheer Randon, but when she told him what had happened, he only sighed and filled his cup again.

"Kalendra, eh?" he said. "Well, that was flattering of him. And very surprising. So what does she look like, little Kalendra?" He took a deep gulp from his cup, his hands shaking.

Kayli smiled.

"I often hear folk say that the new baby resembles the mother, or his eyes are like his father's," she said. "I myself think all newborn children are red, wrinkled lumps of flesh who do not much resemble anyone human. I think she will have Ynea's straight black hair, however, not Terralt's curls, and her eyes are dark like Ynea's, though that often changes with time."

Randon said nothing, only sighed raggedly and ventured deeper into his cup, and in the silence, a disturbing thought grew in Kayli's mind. She pulled up a chair and laid her hand on his arm; when he still would not meet her eyes, she took a deep breath.

"Randon," she said slowly, "is she yours?"

"I don't know," he said dully. "From what you say, perhaps not. But Derrin almost certainly is."

Kayli was shocked to silence, and when she said nothing, Randon took a deep breath and continued grimly.

"She was so unhappy when her father sent her here. Terralt wasn't very understanding. He was angry when she didn't conceive in the first few months after she arrived, and when he wasn't taking her to his bed, he left her alone. She was so lonely, and we'd talk sometimes, and—well, there's no need to say more. Stevann joked that Derrin had our father's looks, but I'm afraid my father wasn't to blame.

"I felt terrible about what I'd done, especially when bearing the baby weakened her so much. She was never the same after that. Stevann said she shouldn't have any more children, but she had Avern and Erisa so soon. And as Terralt spent more and more time working with my father, he seemed to forget Ynea entirely. One evening I found her crying. She said that she wanted to die, that now that she'd borne him three children, she was worthless to him." Randon shook his head. "I couldn't bear to see her weep like that. And she conceived Kalendra almost immediately. But in the meantime Terralt had decided he wanted one more child, too. So Ynea had some use to him again."

"Oh, Randon." Kayli sighed, not knowing what else to say. "Does Terralt know?"

"I think he's suspected ever since Derrin was born," Randon said miserably. "I didn't know which would hurt him worse, to tell him the truth or keep silent. Then I thought how angry he'd be with Ynea, so I said nothing." He met Kayli's eyes. "I swear to you that I never touched Ynea again after she conceived Kalendra, and that was well before I knew about my father's plans for our wedding. Why, I hardly even saw her, not even in public."

Kayli felt an unwilling twinge of sympathy for him. What a burden of guilt he must carry, to have lain with another man's wife, and to have fathered the child that had hurt Ynea so much, the child she had borne too young. And possibly, Kayli reminded herself, the child Ynea had died bearing. In Bregond penalties for adultery were harsh, and girls rarely married before their moon cycles had been regular for at least a year. There were violations of both rules, of course, but not often.

"You must not blame yourself," she said at last. "Whether the seed of her first child was yours or Terralt's would have made no difference, and no skilled midwife would have permitted her to bear so often, so young. But you could not have changed what happened."

There were other things she might have said to comfort him—that he had likely given Ynea the only happiness the poor girl had known since she married Terralt, that it was Terralt who had forbidden the healers who might—possibly—have made a difference in the outcome of events. But although her selfishness shamed her, she thought to herself that Randon had no right to expect comfort from her at this moment. No more had Terralt, but while it might be selfish and even cruel to allow Randon to berate himself with guilt, it would be unthinkable to let Terralt neglect his newborn daughter as he had neglected his wife and his other children. But in both cases, a little guilt was not necessarily a bad thing. Kayli herself would have to live with her own guilt that selfish pleasures had kept her from her friend's deathbed.

Kayli looked up and found Randon gazing at her soberly.

"Kayli, you have my promise," he said, "that as long as you live there'll never be another—"

Kayli held up her hand.

"All the promises I want from you, you made on our wedding day, as did I," she said. "If we cannot trust each other to honor those promises, then there is nothing to be gained in making more."

Randon said nothing, only sighed raggedly and gathered Kayli into his arms. He held her silently, but she could feel hot tears soaking through her tunic at the shoulder.

Not too surprisingly, Randon awakened in the middle of the night with one of his strange headaches; when Kayli had given him his potion, however, and ordered his ice and tea from the kitchen, she insisted on summoning Endra. The sleepy midwife asked Randon a series of seemingly irrelevant questions, gazed into his eyes, sniffed at his potion, and clucked disapprovingly.

"Nothing but a glorified sleeping draught," she said scornfully. "To cure an ill like this, you have to pull it up by the root, not just trim the leaves off at the top."

"But what can be done?" Kayli asked her. "Surely such cases were seen at the healing Orders."

"Well, they were," Endra told her. "Mind you, I didn't tend them myself; I didn't have enough of the gift. No, the healers had a ritual that gave them ease for a time, but quick as they were fit to ride, they were sent to one of the temples for testing. Was he ever tested for the mage-gift, do you know?"

"He said Stevann wanted to train him," Kayli remembered. "But his father refused permission."

"Well, there you are," Endra said, shaking her head. "All those magical energies with nowhere to go, so he turns them inward on himself. Pity it's too late to take him in hand for proper training now. Well, at least he can learn to ground those energies. The Fire temples don't teach grounding, do they? No, the ephemeral magics can't be grounded, that's what I've heard. Don't worry, I'll show him the trick of it myself."

In the morning, Kayli crept quietly out to the kitchen to break her fast so as not to disturb Randon's sleep, but to her embarrassment, she was met on the stairs by a messenger bearing two scrolls bound for Randon—and one carried a seal that made her heart leap, the seal of her father's house. Only the greatest of self-discipline kept her from opening the scroll where she stood; surely Agrondish custom demanded that she break the seal in Randon's presence, if not before his advisers. Fortunately, by the time the servants had prepared a tray of food and Kayli had carried it and the scrolls back up to their quarters, Randon was awake and moodily sipping cold tea beside the rekindled fire.

"This will cheer you, I hope," she said. "Two messages: one from my father, and one from your garrison at the border. Need we summon the council?"

Randon shook his head, his expression brightening as he accepted the scrolls.

"Just what I've been hoping for," he said. He broke the seal on his garrison's message, then hesitated, handing the scroll to Kayli.

"Just read it for me, would you?" he asked rather embarrassedly. "It's dim in here, and my eyes still ache."

" 'To High Lord Randon and High Lady Kayli,' and the usual endless titles and honorifics. 'Greetings,' " Kayli read. " 'As you commanded, we saw your caravan safely across the borders of Bregond, where we parted company with the wagons. We then turned north along the border and have established our troops at the border of Bregond, just north of the village of Jaylind. We have constructed a wooden barracks and stable with the assistance of the villagers, who are delighted at our presence. Since our arrival we have engaged no less than four bands of Sarkondish raiders, three approaching from the north and one from the northwest. Two bands we slaughtered altogether. Another we killed all but two, who escaped by riding northwest through Bregond. As we had no authority to cross onto Bregondish soil, we did not pursue. The last band, larger than the previous three, turned back to the north as soon as they sighted our troops. Since these victories, the people of Jaylind have taken to leaving gifts of food just outside the stockade. This generosity is embarrassing in view of the poverty of this village, due to its being continually raided before our arrival.

" 'Eight days before my writing of this message, we sighted what appeared to be a considerable force of riders approaching from the southwest. These riders stopped across the border and three envoys approached, calling out in halting Agrondish to ask permission to meet with me. Although we conversed with some difficulty, it became apparent that these troops were sent by High Lord Elaasar of Bregond at your invitation to assist us in guarding the border. We were grateful for their presence in view of the raiders who had approached and fled across Bregondish land. These troops quickly constructed large tents of poles and hide, rather than wood buildings, barely in sight to the west. They brought with them what looks to be over two hundred head of cattle, both to feed them and to serve as bait for Sarkondish raiders. This was a good thought as the fat herd may tempt the raiders away from Jaylind and a Bregondish village which I am told lies southwest.

" 'They are good men but very stiff and strange. We do not invite them to our fires, nor they us to theirs, but we meet at the border every day, and once we made a large fire between the two garrisons to converse and try to learn each other's tongues more fluently. They freely share their slaughtered cattle and the cheeses they brought with them. In return I have taken the liberty of giving them several bags of grain and bushels of turnips and beans and dried apples. From these soldiers I have word that there is difficulty in Bregond, groups of nomads threatening to kill merchants crossing from Agrond, and threats to Bregondish craftsmen planning to ship their goods east.

" 'Yesterday another riding party approached from the west. These riders were envoys from High Lord Elaasar sent to inspect the encampment and to deliver to my hand a message from the High Lord to you. I am sending this message with my report. I sent back with the envoys a gift of good black tea from my own stock for the High Lord and Lady of Bregond, with my personal thanks for the friendliness of his troops.

" 'All in all our progress has been encouraging in every way. With the doubled force at the border, I have no doubt that we could withstand all but an outright force of war from Sarkond. I have a good stock of messenger birds, and should the need arise for speedy communication, you should receive word from us very quickly. With the greatest of optimism, I remain loyal in your service. . . . ' and all the usual closing pleasantries." Kayli handed the scroll back to Randon.

"Excellent news." Randon sighed with relief. "I couldn't have hoped for better. Still, four raids in less than a month! Have your folk ever known so much activity at the border?"

Kayli sighed, too, but with irritation.

"Unfortunately at the Order we were isolated from such news," she said regretfully. "My father, of course, would be better informed. Four attacks within one moon cycle, that sounds unusual. Perhaps his message will tell us more."

Randon was sufficiently cheered that he squinted over the second scroll himself, pausing so long before he spoke that Kayli longed to tear the scroll from his hands.

"Besides the usual pleasantries, he congratulates us on our confirmation," he said. "He also thanks me for the invitation to station his troops at the border and hopes that our two forces can work amiably together toward the common goal of—

ha!—'wetting the soil with goodly quantities of Sarkondish blood.' And listen to this, Kayli:'Brother Santee informs me you have had the presumption to get my daughter with child before wedding her in the sight of the people. I will pardon you this dishonor as my daughter is a woman of great accomplishment who can well decide when to permit her betrothed between her legs.' By the Bright Ones, your father's a plain-spoken man! What's this?'' Randon was silent again for a long moment, his brows shooting up as he read.

"He suggests that if matters continue successfully at the border, that a meeting be held there, that he and his lady can meet with us to celebrate midsummer. Bright Ones, that's not a bad idea." He paused thoughtfully. "It'll mean additional troops, of course, but if we meet far south of Jaylind, it should be safe enough, I'd think. But what do you say?"

Kayli drew in a sharp breath. To see her family again, perhaps even Kairi!

"Oh, Randon, it would be wonderful," she said softly.

"Then I'll call a council session," Randon said. "This news shouldn't wait."

The advisers were pleased by the news from the border garrison, but to Kayli's surprise, they showed less enthusiasm for her father's suggestion for the midsummer meeting.

"Forgive me, High Lord, High Lady," Lord Kereg said cautiously, "but this moves far too fast. Why, we've not sent nor received the first trade caravan, and now High Lord Elaasar wants to drag the entire royal family and retinue to the border, where there's not so much as a civilized hostel!"

"I'm not proposing to drag anyone anywhere." Randon laughed. "No, what I'm contemplating is a small affair, just our two families. We won't need much of a retinue for that. I doubt any of us will begrudge the rough conditions for a few days in exchange for the first meeting between Agrondish and Bregondish royalty since—well, since Agrond came into being."

Gazing at Lord Kereg's face, Kayli realized with a shock that he simply did not want Randon to meet directly with her father—and glancing at the others, she saw the same reluctance echoed in their eyes as well.

"And what about the High Lady?" Lady Aville said. "Are

you prepared to endanger her life hardly a month after she was nearly assassinated?''

"The High Lady can well answer for herself," Kayli said sharply. "Was I safe here in this very castle, at my own table? And if I and my unborn child are not safe with my husband and my own parents, and the combined troops of Agrond and Bregond, there is no safety to be had in this world.''

That produced a momentary silence while the lords and ladies eyed each other uneasily, and in that moment Kayli saw Randon's eyes sharpen. Good; he had seen it, too.

"We're not asking *permission,*" Randon said with deceptive mildness. "What I want is your suggestions on the best and safest way to do this. We'll need guards, of course. We'll need servants, tents, food, gifts. In fact," he added, "this might be the opportunity to send the first trade caravans into Agrond and invite the first Bregondish traders here, both with plenty of guard escort to accompany them.''

More confused glances. Kayli thought Randon's suggestion more than canny; it was a stroke of genius. This was perfect opportunity for the caravans to return to the capital cities under heavy guard and in the presence of the High Lords and Ladies of each country.

"I think the idea has merit," Lady Tarkas said smoothly. "I've no shortage of merchants who would line up with their best goods for the first caravan.''

After some urging the remainder of the advisers accepted, if not approved, the idea of the meeting. When he felt he had wrung all the cooperation out of the ministers that he was going to get, Randon turned the conversation to a more difficult subject.

"Ynea's funeral," he said quietly. "I want her to have full state honors and a place in the family tomb.''

"I would have suggested the same, High Lord," Lady Aville said quietly. "It's a difficult matter because of Terralt's—the circumstances of his birth, and for that very reason such kindness on your part will mean a great deal to the people.''

Kayli was glad to hear that Ynea would be given full respect in the Agrondish death rituals, but as she learned more, she was astonished and a little disgusted. Why should the whole city mourn when none of them even knew Ynea? A city sharing in that grief as a mere obligation somehow cheapened it, and the idea of giving the dead no permanent rest, of interring the body in a stone box so that it could never return to the elements that had given it life, seemed selfish and cruel. But these were the beliefs by which Ynea had lived, and Kayli could not object.

There was other business, far more routine, to be discussed, but between her grief over Ynea's death and her joy at the prospect of seeing her family again, Kayli had no interest in such matters. She was glad when they all adjourned for dinner, and Randon was easily persuaded that there was no need for further work that afternoon. After stopping by the kitchen to order a private dinner, however, when they returned to their quarters, Kayli and Randon found Terralt standing awkwardly at their door.

"I can't hide in my rooms forever," he said, not meeting their eyes. "So I thought I'd see if you needed help."

"Yes, come in and dine with us," Randon said a little awkwardly. "We've ordered our meal sent up. It'd be good to have the chance to—to talk."

Terralt hesitated, glancing from Kayli to Randon, but followed them into the rooms. Over rich venison stew, soft buns, and wine, he listened to the news of the two messages more calmly than Kayli would have expected.

"So your plans are going well, little brother," he said rather indifferently when Randon had finished. "A midsummer festival at the border. I'd never have imagined the like. Your caravan idea, that's a good one. So. Do you want me to go?"

Randon's eyebrows shot up.

"I didn't think you'd want anything to do with it," he said.

"I don't." Terralt sighed. "But at the moment I can't manage to care very much. So if you want me to go, I'll go."

"As it happens, it's probably best that you stay here," Randon admitted. "If the citizens react to this festival the way they reacted to the border garrison, I'd rather leave you here to see to things while we're gone."

Kayli carefully schooled her expression to impassivity despite her astonishment at Randon's words. Trust Terralt with the throne of Agrond while Randon was so far away, when

Terralt might well have been the one to poison Kayli? At the very least he openly contested Randon's claim to the throne. There was no doubt that in Randon's absence, Terralt's rulership of the city would lead only to renewed controversy when Randon returned.

Terralt gazed narrowly at Randon.

"What game are you playing now, little brother?" he asked slowly. "I'm not up to it today. I tell you, I'm not."

Randon squeezed Kayli's hand under the table.

"Rein in your gut for a moment, Terralt," he said. "What else am I going to do? There's no one else qualified to keep the country running while I'm gone. And with me at the border of Bregond, sitting at table with the High Lord of Bregond himself, this city's going to boil like a kettle of tea over a hot fire. What if there's another riot? I need somebody here to keep my people from killing each other. Besides, you need something to occupy your time and attention. This once, I think our interests coincide. Is that a game?"

Terralt stared at Randon a moment longer, then shook his head wearily.

"Whatever you say," he said. "I'll nursemaid your throne while you consort with our enemies. But I'm damned if I have any notion what you think you're doing."

"Well, you'll have nearly a month to puzzle it out," Randon said patiently. "In the meantime we should discuss Ynea's funeral."

Once again, Kayli was appalled. How could Randon even think of discussing Terralt's wife's funeral at the table as a casual follow-up to political maneuvering? To her surprise, however, Terralt seemed untroubled, even pleased by Randon's arrangements.

"That was kind of you," he said, and his voice had lost some of its distance. "Ynea's family will be honored, too." He smiled a little. "You should've told me this first."

Randon made a little apologetic gesture.

"I didn't want it to seem like a bribe," he said. "You've already done more than I've had a right to expect."

"Hmmm. I won't dispute that," Terralt said with a hint of his old insolence. "All right, then." He rose and bowed. "By the way, I've told Ynea's maids that they're to serve Kayli now. Ynea left a letter about it. And her books. I'll have them sent over." His voice roughened on the last words, and he hurried out the door, closing it a little too hard behind him.

"Oh, Randon, what will I ever do with more maids?" Kayli said unhappily. "Mine already sit idle more often than not."

"Well, then they'll all have a little more idle time, for the present, anyway," Randon said resignedly. "We have a duty for the welfare of our servants. Anyway, you might find the extra girls useful when you grow larger, and especially when the baby's born. The Bright Ones know you work too hard already. But is that really what's bothering you? I can't imagine a few extra maids occasioning the scowl you gave me."

Kayli sighed.

"I had no wish to protest in Terralt's presence," she said quietly. "But how can you entrust him with your throne as matters stand? Can you be certain that when you return, your seat will still await you?"

Randon waved his hand negligently.

"Terralt wouldn't have the seat if the only way he could get it was to usurp it from me," he said. "I agree that the notion of Terralt taking my place, for however short a time, will only incite more uproar in the city—some hoping he will simply keep the throne, others afraid that he will, still others simply outraged that I'm meeting with your father. But there's no avoiding it if we're to go, and I don't see how we can miss this opportunity. What do you think?"

Kayli could not quite dismiss the feeling that indeed Randon was playing another of his political games—not only with Terralt, but with her, his advisers, and even the very people of his country.

"I think this meeting is important," she agreed cautiously. "Of course I wish to see my family, but even more importantly, they should meet you. My father always said he could not wholly trust a man until he had looked into his eyes."

"Well, if we're going to do it, midsummer's the time," Randon told her. "Once the harvest starts, I don't see how we could leave the city, and the weather's unpredictable after that. Next spring there's planting season and spring floods, and besides, you'll be getting unwieldy yourself by that time. No, if we can't make midsummer, I don't see how we can arrange it until after the baby's born, and we'd lose a whole year.''

"Then we will go, and worry no more about it," Kayli said with a sigh. Her father would be subject to the same problems, though for different reasons—in autumn, the herds were brought in for culling, and that was the season in which the clans were most likely to fall to squabbling. No sizable caravan could cross Bregond in winter, and in spring, foaling season for the horses and fawning season for the *ikada,* the clans would once again need close supervision. No, Randon was right; there really was no alternative.

"Then before we go, best you make your peace with Master Weaver Odric," Kayli told him. "You will need the support of all your friends at home."

"And how do you suggest I do that?" Randon asked wryly.

Kayli smiled.

"I have a thought," she said.

Master Weaver Odric's normally ruddy face was pale when he stepped out of the barracks.

"I had no idea," he mumbled. Then he turned to Randon and met his eyes squarely. "I tell you, I had no idea."

"The slaves who came from the Weavers' Guild weren't as bad as that," Randon said kindly. "But Kayli and I wanted you to see a little of what these people had been through. Remember that they're not prisoners of a war, nor condemned criminals; these were free people stolen from their homes, their families either killed or sold."

Odric sighed and shook his head.

"I never thought much about it," he said. "All I knew was that I was sparing the lungs of our own people. And then when you demanded they be freed, it seemed like you cared more for the welfare of outlanders than our own folk. That draught didn't go down easy."

"Well, the next dose may taste a little sweeter," Randon told him. "Have you see the cloth samples I gave Lidian?"

Odric grimaced.

"You call that sweeter?" he said. "The fibers are good— better than some of our domestic stuff—but that weave's going to push my guild out of the market in time. Our looms won't produce anything like it, and I have no idea how to build one that will.''

''Then you're in luck,'' Randon said, grinning. ''Because I happen to have three freed slaves who used to be weavers, and they're sorely in need of board and employment. Under a properly appreciative guildmaster, I don't doubt that they have a lot to offer. And maybe a few things to teach, too.''

In fact, fewer slaves appeared at the castle now. Randon believed that many owners were now placing their former slaves as apprentices in the guilds, or simply mollifying them with a fat purse. Kayli wondered how slaves in other parts of Agrond fared, but Randon waved aside her concern.

''Tarkesh is the largest city near enough to the border to make the slave trade profitable,'' he said. ''This is the guild seat, too, so most of the merchants would bring their slaves here. Whatever slaves may be scattered around Agrond, where Tarkesh goes, the smaller cities and villages will follow.''

Kayli hoped that was true in many senses. In the few days since she and Randon had decided to accept High Lord Elaasar's invitation to meet at midsummer, word had somehow swept through the city; she wondered whether one of Randon's advisers had spread the rumors. Now every merchant in Tarkesh congregated on the castle steps, each convinced that he or she *must* accompany the High Lord to the border.

Preparation for midsummer had filled Kayli's days. Besides sitting with Randon in audience and in council, she was soon pressed into the role of tutor to Randon and his advisers, who were suddenly all a-hunger to learn proper Bregondish language and manners. Kayli found this sudden change ironic; certainly they'd had no interest in learning Bregondish customs to accommodate *her*.

And certainly some Agrondish customs mystified her. In the week that the city had mourned Ynea's death, no musicians could sing or play; all dancing and gambling was forbidden; no whore could ply her trade, and, strangest of all, every man and woman of the city was expected to wear a cap or scarf on their heads and refrain from strong liquor. Kayli understood none of it. What mattered it to Ynea now?

Kayli herself made time to mourn Ynea properly, burning the bedding from her deathbed in lieu of Ynea's body in the forge and meditating on the life of her friend while the fire consumed the cloth. Later she rode to the open fields where Ynea's beloved wildflowers bloomed, and scattered the ashes on the wind, bidding Ynea's spirit farewell as the flakes drifted away.

Meanwhile plans for the usual midsummer festival in Tarkesh proceeded apace. The festival would take place, as customary in Agrond, on the day and night of the new moon, ten days after the meeting at the border. Fortunately, in Bregond, midsummer was celebrated at the full of the moon instead. That would leave Randon and Kayli time to return to Tarkesh, even at the pace of a large caravan, in time for Agrond's festival.

"It'll be the first time I've ever celebrated midsummer twice in one year," Randon told Kayli, chuckling. "But tell me, do you think I could have outfits like yours made by then?"

He was commenting, of course, on the Bregondish riding clothes which Kayli had taken to wearing whenever she was not at an official function. She'd had several such outfits made, although of Agrondish fabrics. Even at formal occasions she wore her Bregondish-style gowns. If Randon was offended at this small act of defiance, he never said so.

When he made his request, however, Kayli shook her head.

"I will have Bregondish riding clothes made for you if you wish," she said gently, "but I would advise against wearing them when meeting my father. He would deem it presumptuous at best, a mockery at worst. You are not a Bregond, and pretending to be one will not impress him."

Sometimes Kayli wondered, too, what impression *she* would make on her father and mother and whatever priests or priestesses might accompany them. She had disgraced her teachings, indulged in the most undisciplined and selfish behavior, disobeyed her High Priestess—of course they didn't know this, but *she* knew, and she wondered if they could see it in her eyes.

Every few days Kayli would make the long walk down to the forge. She would look at the bed of coals laid ready, her books, her tools; she would draw her *thari* and finger the sharp edge of the blade. Then she would put her *thari* away and walk back upstairs again, with the sour taste of cowardice in her mouth. A hundred times she pulled out her speaking crystal, only to put it away again. What could she say to Brisi or even to Kairi, her own sister? That she, an Initiate of the Temple of Inner Flame, had grown afraid of her own magic? That she no longer dared so much as set a candle alight by her own power, that she fled from the hearth fire out of fear that her caressing awareness of the flame would dissolve what little control she had left? And what could they say in return?

Only a sevenday before her planned departure with Randon to the border, Kayli woke and slid out of bed, walking over to the basin as usual to wash her face and hands. This morning, however, she took only a step or two before sudden nausea seized her, and she barely made it to the washbasin before she vomited wretchedly into it. Unfortunately the sound woke Randon, and then nothing would do but that he carry Kayli back to bed and summon Endra and Stevann to attend her.

Stevann politely stifled his amusement at Randon's concern; Endra, however, made no effort to hide her laughter.

"Best keep the basin by your bed, lady, for you may spew every morning for weeks." The midwife chuckled, grinning sideways at Randon. "It's only the babe, High Lord, playing hob with the lady's vitals."

"But should she travel now?" Randon asked anxiously. "It'll be a long trip, and uncomfortable."

This time it was Stevann who chuckled.

"There's no need to compare Kayli to Ynea," he said kindly. "Kayli's healthy and strong, and the journey won't be all that rough, either."

"In the horse clans, ladies with child ride till their birth spasms begin," Endra added. "I myself don't encourage such a thing, but there'll be no reining in my lady until her belly becomes a misery to her. Don't worry, High Lord, I'll tend the lady as carefully as if she was my own daughter. So don't start troubling yourself now, else you'll have a worrisome few months ahead of you both."

But if Randon had his way, Kayli would have lain in bed, cosseted like Ynea. He ordered all their meals brought to their quarters, and if she so much as reached for a goblet, he would dash to place it in her hand. At first Kayli found this amusing, then irritating, and finally intolerable; at last she fled Randon's company whenever she could, slipping out to the yard to exercise the horses with Seba, chatting with Endra and her maids, or merely brooding in the forge. But she did *not* go near the barracks where the freed slaves lived, nor the wing of the castle where Terralt had resumed his residence with his children.

On the night before she left, however, Kayli could not resist the temptation to see Kalendra once more before beginning her journey. She told herself she would only visit the baby briefly and go, but Kalendra was awake and cooing, her rags fresh and her stomach full, and Kayli could not keep from holding the tiny new life, admiring the miniature fingernails and the whorls of one pink ear.

"She's beautiful, all right." To Kayli's dismay, Terralt stood in the doorway, leaning against the door frame.

"I beg your pardon," Kayli said uncomfortably. "I should have asked your permission—"

"What, to hold my daughter?" Terralt chuckled. "What manner of fool would deny you? As long as you don't steal her entirely, you're welcome. More than welcome." He gave her a lingering glance that brought a flush to her cheeks. "You look good with a baby in your arms."

"Well, soon enough I will have one of my own." She laid Kalendra back in her cradle, using the opportunity to put it between Terralt and herself. "I only pray that I will bear children as fine and healthy as yours."

Terralt reached over the cradle and laid his hand over Kayli's; a surge of flame raced up her arm and straight to her loins.

"I'm sure they'll be as beautiful as their mother," he said.

Kayli snatched her hand away too quickly for politeness, but thankfully Terralt did not pursue her around the cradle.

"I must go," she murmured. "Randon must be looking for me."

A shadow of irritation passed swiftly across Terralt's face, followed by a sort of shame.

"Yes, you'd best go," he said, his expression closed once more. "And good journey to you both."

Kayli retreated down the hall, only to collide with her husband. Randon stopped, gazing at her rather doubtfully.

"There you are!" he said. "What in the world are you doing here?"

"I was visiting Kalendra," Kayli said, aware that she was still flushed and, to her disgust, her hands were shaking. "It will be many days before I see her again."

Randon glanced down the way she had come, and his expression darkened. Kayli heard a door close and knew without looking that Terralt had stepped out into the hall; surely he was standing there with that mocking expression she so hated, daring Randon to think what he would.

"Go on back and finish packing," Randon said, his voice cool now. "I need to give Terralt some final instructions before we leave."

Kayli almost ran back to her room, burying her confusion in activity as she supervised her maids packing her trunks. The supervision was absolutely necessary; since Ynea's maids had began serving her, she'd found to her dismay that more servants meant more work, not less. The six Bregondish maids resented the newcomers and their lack of acquaintance with Bregondish dress, hairstyles, and customs; the ten Agrondish maids, who had been longer in the castle and were now in the majority anyway, fancied themselves the more knowledgeable and experienced and forever attempted to "civilize" the others. The two groups could agree on nothing, it seemed, and Kayli was aghast at the amount of time she spent mediating squabbles between them. At last in despair she'd run to Endra, and once again the sturdy midwife had proven equal to the challenge. Now the girls sorted and packed the clothing, exchanging nothing more barbed than sullen glances, although once Kayli caught one of the Agrondish girls trying to substitute lace petticoats for the breechlike Bregondish small-clothes.

"Bregondish ladies ride astride their horses, and our gowns are cut to permit this, for even on formal occasions we often ride out to hunt," Kayli said as patiently as she could to the horrified maid. "Petticoats might be fine for court, but my thighs would soon be chafed raw in the saddle, and it would be horribly immodest, too, were I thrown from my horse."

"Which of the girls will you want to take with you?" Endra asked abruptly, to Kayli's dismay. She'd hoped to discuss the matter with Endra in private, for while the idea of taking any of the dainty Agrondish maids was preposterous, they'd certainly protest at being left behind.

"Well, Randon would never forgive me if I left you behind," Kayli said at last. "And I will take Seba, too, to tend the horses and assist you. But it will be a rough journey and an uncomfortable one. Food on the road will likely be poor, and I know from my own journey to Tarkesh that there are no inns on the way. So as I thought I would take only two maids, I will let them choose for themselves who will go and who will stay." She glanced at the maids, then added, "Of course, they must be able to ride horseback, as the road is too rough for carriages and the wagons must be lightened periodically after such flooding as Agrond has had lately."

The maids exchanged glances, and to Kayli's relief and amusement, the Agrondish girls were more than happy to let Anida and Devra make the journey.

By the time Randon returned, the packing was complete, the trunks were carried downstairs, and a good supper awaited them. Endra glanced at Randon's brooding expression and hurriedly shooed all the girls from the room, following them out.

Randon did not so much as glance at the supper laid out on the table, but walked directly to Kayli, gazing narrowly into her eyes.

"Is there anything," he said, "you'd like to tell me?"

Kayli set her hands on her hips, breathing deeply to calm herself.

"Regarding what, my lord?"

"Terralt." Randon's eyes searched hers. "And you."

"Then yes, there is," Kayli said deliberately. "And it is this: For what you are thinking, you are not only a fool, but a villain as well. And that is *all* I have to tell you."

Before Randon could reply, she strode past him and out of the room, slamming the door behind her with unnecessary force. For a time she was too furious to think, and her anger had carried her up the stairs to the roof battlements before she knew where she was going. Only two guards walked patrol on the roof, and when they saw their High Lady's expression, like Endra, they chose flight as the safer course. Kayli picked a good vantage point and stared out over Tarkesh, saying nothing, but she ground her teeth till her jaws ached and clenched her hands until her nails bit into her palms.

How dared Randon suspect her of infidelity when he himself had sired at least one bastard child on his brother's wife! How dare he think such a thing when she had left her home and ambitions behind to marry him and endangered her life—no, her very soul—to bear him the child he needed? Any offense he had ever offered her paled beside this calumny.

Yet why then did Kayli feel guilt, even through her anger? She had done nothing wrong. Nothing. Yet there was that fire when Terralt touched her. And there was the kiss. Kayli had done nothing to provoke it, of that she was certain—but she had kept silent instead of telling Randon. And her silence was a lie of sorts.

Footsteps behind her. Kayli sighed and was silent; she recognized Randon's tread, and regardless of whatever guilt she might feel, the Flame would burn her to ash before she was the one to apologize. Whatever wrong she *had* done—if, indeed, any wrong *had* been done—was nothing beside Randon's implicit accusation.

Randon leaned against the battlements a little distance from Kayli, and for a long time he said nothing, only staring out at Tarkesh just as she did.

"I'm sorry," he said at last, and his voice was weary, very weary, and tinged with shame as well. "At the same time, you have to understand something. We're not an ordinary husband and wife. If I have one doubt, my council has six doubts, and the city of Tarkesh has thousands."

Kayli recited a calming ritual in her mind before she spoke.

"If the citizens of Tarkesh or our advisers have a concern about my fidelity, that is one matter," she said. "But you sleep at my side every night and then believe I would betray you. You entrust your half brother with your throne and yet believe he would lie with your wife. Is trust nothing but a game, a test to you? Well, I will not play this game, Randon. I will not take this test. Believe what you will, and when our child is born, perhaps the color of its hair or its eyes will reassure you."

"All right." Randon sighed. "All right. I suppose I earned that. But I was born a High Lord's son, Kayli, and raised at court. Games are a way of life, and trust is hard to come by. I'm still learning."

"At least you try," Kayli said, sighing. "I have not given my temper such rein since I was a child." She shook her head. "Strange. When I left the Order, I thought it would be the duties of a High Lady that would tax me. I had never thought it would be so strange, so difficult, to be a wife."

Randon chuckled.

"Do you know, I've had similar thoughts," he said. "But to be honest, I wonder if we find it so difficult only because we've had so little opportunity to practice. Perhaps with time it'll get easier."

Kayli nodded, but inwardly she thought that Randon was wrong. High Priestess Brisi had always said that outward change, no matter how sweeping, could only begin from within. And nothing would be resolved tonight, here on the roof of the castle.

"Let's go in," Randon said at last, rather awkwardly, when Kayli remained silent. "Our supper's no doubt cold by now, but it's the last good kitchen-prepared meal we'll have for some days." A little hesitantly, he offered his arm; after a slight hesitation of her own, Kayli took it.

To Kayli's amusement, supper was not cold, but gone; someone, probably Endra, had had it taken back downstairs. But almost as soon as Randon touched the bell cord, a maid appeared with a fresh tray and a flask of wine. Cook had surpassed himself, and somehow the sweet wine and the dainty meal cheered Kayli immensely. Cook was saying, in his subtle way, that they would be missed, and Kayli was deeply grateful for that kindness.

There were too many thoughts between Randon and Kayli to allow for lovemaking that night, but late in the night, still helplessly awake, Kayli slid her hand across the covers, where it met Randon's hand moving to reach for hers. They lay silent in the darkness, not looking at each other, only their hands joined together in the night, and Kayli thought that in many ways that said it all—that they both lay in darkness, fumbling for each other's hand. But as long as they both were still reaching, she thought with something like satisfaction, they would find a way to touch, no matter how far apart they lay.

13

"BY THE BRIGHT ONES, I STILL CAN'T IMAGine how your menfolk manage these things," Randon said irritably. "Show me one more time, will you?"

Kayli chuckled and, for the third morning in a row, showed Randon how to lace the supple hide jaffs over his trousers.

"But why trouble yourself?" she asked practically. "There are no sharp grasses here to cut your legs, and the weather is too hot to wear leather if you need not."

"Well, you told me your father would likely want a hunt," Randon said, swearing as he picked at a hopeless tangle of lacing. "And where will the High Lord of Bregond want to hunt? In Bregond, of course. So I'll be riding through Bregondish high grass. So unless I want my legs cut to ribbons, I've got to wear these things. And unless I want to look as inept as a lad at his first bedding, I've got to learn how to put the damned things on properly *before* the High Lord sees me. So I need practice."

"Your dagger would draw more easily," Kayli said solemnly, "if you did not lace the jaffs over it." She fought down a giggle as Randon realized his mistake, swore bitterly, and began unlacing the jaffs again.

"Somehow I think I'd embarrass myself less if I simply

told your father I was too incompetent to ride and shoot," Randon muttered grimly. "Never mind, the damned thing's staying on, and that's a victory of sorts. Well, at least I've had time to learn to ride that mare properly."

Kayli had to admit that Randon's mastery of Bregondish horsemanship had been swift. He now rode as if Carada was an extension of himself, as easy in the Bregondish saddle as Seba, who rode as if she had grown out of a horse's back. He learned quickly, too, to shoot the bow Kayli had given him, although she suspected that he still preferred the Agrondish crossbow and was using her gift only to please her. In the same vein, Kayli flew the hawk Randon had given her but could not share his enthusiasm for falconry. No matter; she enjoyed simply riding again, and her spirit lightened with every hour.

Kayli had seen little of Agrond's countryside in her helter-skelter flight through the rain to Tarkesh, and now she wondered at its lush beauty. The recent rains and the warm summer sun had brought forth plants in such variety that she wondered how Ynea had ever hoped to catalog even a small portion of them. Flowers bloomed in such a profusion of scent and color that Kayli understood why the people of Agrond dressed in such gay shades; when the earth itself sent forth such colorful exuberance, how could the people help but follow suit?

In the days since they left Tarkesh, the farms had thinned out and gradually disappeared as the caravan approached the border. Kayli wondered at this, for the land was good and apparently did not flood so severely as the farms farther to the east. Randon assured her that it was not fear of Bregond that kept farmers from settling here.

"For one thing, Sarkondish raiders become more of a problem close to the border," he told her. "And for another, it's a long trip to take crops and livestock to market. As long as there's still good land closer to the cities and towns, there's no reason to settle the wilds. Besides, these lands aren't held by any of the lords. That means no protection for the farmers."

Kayli wondered at folk who would rather live under the hand of a lord, depending on his protection and surrendering a part of their crops in return, than claim the best land in

Agrond and live free. Bregondish were not much given to farming; the land was simply too poor. But Kayli believed that any of her people would gladly take the good land all the more gladly for their independence.

As they had left the more heavily settled part of Agrond, game, too, was present in gratifying variety, although Kayli and Randon quickly learned that if they wished to hunt, they must range ahead of the noisy caravan. Seba often joined these hunts after Kayli spied her gazing wistfully after them, and although Seba had no bow of her own and refused the use of Kayli's, her proficiency with a sling was amazing. The child could fire with deadly accuracy from a full gallop, bringing down anything smaller than a large deer or boar.

Kayli had feared that it would rain, as it had when she first journeyed to Tarkesh, but the weather remained bright and warm, perfect for riding. She let her braids down to stream behind her in the wind and she raced Randon whenever the guards would let them out of sight long enough for a good run. Each evening when they camped, Kayli would help Seba and the maids rub down and comb the horses, and in the morning she would rise before dawn with Seba and run through the dewy grass hunting rabbits. Her morning nausea had vanished as suddenly as it had come, and she thought wistfully that perhaps she had never been so happy. Even in the Order her days had been filled with tasks and studies; surely she'd never had so much time and freedom to ride and enjoy herself. And ahead of her lay the even greater joy of seeing her family again.

Even as Kayli enjoyed each day, however, Randon grew more worried.

"It's easy for you," he said one evening as they sat staring into the fire. "He's your father. But to me he's the ruler of a country that's been our enemy for generations. It's so damned important that I make a good impression."

"At least," Kayli said amusedly, "you do not have to marry him. And you have Lord Kereg, Lady Tarkas, and Lord Disian to advise you."

To Randon and Kayli's dismay, the advisers had solved the dilemma over whether to remain in Tarkesh to oversee Terralt's rulership or journey to the border to advise Randon by splitting the council. Lord Kereg, Lady Tarkas, and Lord Disian, whose areas of knowledge were most applicable to establishing trade with Bregond, would accompany Randon; the others would remain to assist Terralt. Kayli was glad that at least Lord Vyr, Minister of the Army, had not chosen to accompany them; her father might well have seen that as a veiled threat. Thankfully the ministers did not enjoy the rough travel and kept to themselves in their own comfortable wagons, not troubling Randon or herself overmuch except for the endless questions over dinner—and could Kayli please tell them how to say *this* phrase, or *that* one, just one more time?

More worrisome, however, was evidence of past Sarkondish raids. Occasionally the caravan passed ruined and burned-out houses, and once an entire burned village, although Randon assured Kayli that the ruins must be at least half a century old. Still, even though it was nearly sunset and clouds were gathering ominously overhead, Kayli insisted that they continue out of the area of the ruins before camping. It was the worst ill fortune to sleep where the dead had never received the proper rituals, for such spirits often lingered, bringing terrible dreams.

It seemed, too, that the village was the ill omen that Kayli thought it, for they had only just stopped to camp when the first drops of rain fell and thunder grumbled through the clouds. By the time the tents were pitched, everyone was drenched, and Kayli eagerly retired to her tent to change into dry clothes. So much for the beautiful summer weather.

"Well, here's the wood," Randon said, bringing in an armload of branches and dumping them into the small pit at the middle of the tent. "It's pretty wet, I'm afraid."

He glanced at Kayli thoughtfully.

"Why don't you just light it?" he suggested.

Kayli hesitated. She could not explain to Randon her reluctance to use her magic. How could he understand her fear of lighting one branch when she'd walked through a blazing fire-pit? At last she picked up two of the branches, but for safety's sake, she moved to the opening of the tent.

She focused intently on the first piece of wood. For a moment her magic refused to answer to her summons; then the power surged out of her with lightning force, sending a sharp spear of pleasure through Kayli that nearly toppled her. The branch blazed up in a wave of white-hot light, and startled, Kayli cried out, dropping it; she heard Randon cry out also, somewhere behind her. She stepped back hurriedly, lest her loose trousers catch fire, but when she looked down, she was amazed to see that the branch had shivered completely to ash, instantly consumed by the fire she had conjured.

For a moment Kayli fumbled for some excuse to make to Randon, but that was foolish; he'd seen clearly enough what had happened. Instead she focused more tightly on the second piece of wood, calmed herself as best she could, and tried again. This time, with careful self-discipline she was able to kindle the wood without unleashing such power as she had before. Oh, but she would have to speak to Brisi, to ask the High Priestess what had gone awry within her, and what could be done to remedy it!

To Kayli's surprise, when she walked back into the tent and thrust the burning branch into the stack of wood in the firepit, she did not see Randon immediately. Glancing around the tent, she finally located him in a corner, huddled on the floor, clasping his head as if it would burst.

"Randon?" Kayli asked worriedly, falling to her knees beside him. "Are you unwell?" The fire was catching, and there was a little more light; to her alarm, Randon's pupils were contracted to mere pinpricks, and a thin trickle of blood ran from his nose.

"Bright Ones," Randon mumbled. "I don't—"

"Where is your potion?" Kayli asked when he said nothing more.

"Left it at home," Randon grunted. "Endra said I wouldn't need it."

"Well, did she not teach you how to deal with this?" Kayli asked him.

"Trying—I'm trying," Randon snapped. "It doesn't work."

"What did she tell you?"

"She said—" Randon took a deep breath, as if trying to gather his thoughts. "Said to picture the pain as a light at the top of my head, force it down through my body and out the soles of my feet. But every time I try, it won't go into the ground. It just goes back up.''

Kayli shook her head helplessly. She had never heard anything of the sort, but of course she had never had to deal with a problem such as Randon's. If only Stevann had come with them! But in view of the spring floods, would-be assassins, and riots, Randon had reluctantly decided that his trusted mage was more urgently needed at the castle.

Not knowing what else to do, Kayli took a cloth outside, let the rain wet it thoroughly, and brought it back in, kneeling to wipe the blood from Randon's upper lip. The moment she touched him, however, a snapping sensation ran up her arm, and Randon rocked backward, crying out in pain. Kayli reached for him instinctively, only to draw her hand back in confusion.

Stunned, she rubbed her hand, which still tingled slightly. Of course! Endra had not seen the obvious, but then, neither had Kayli.

Randon had Awakened Kayli; she knew that he had at least a trace of the fire magic. Those were the energies Randon turned inward upon himself. *And the ephemeral elemental magics, air and fire, were not grounded.*

"Randon, listen to me," she said, steadying her voice and speaking slowly. "What Endra told you was wrong. Do as I tell you and all will be well. Put out your hand—no, do not touch me. Yes, like that." Kayli extended her own hand until her fingertips were mere hairbreadths from Randon's. "Think of how you strike a spark from flint and steel, how that spark leaps to the tinder. Take the light in your head and send it to your hand, and see it jump, like a spark to the tinder, to my hand. Strike it free, as you would that spark."

For a long moment nothing happened, and Kayli wondered whether she had been wrong, whether Randon could not focus his concentration sufficiently. Then a small flash of light seemed to leap from his hand to hers with a shock of pleasure that made her gasp. Randon fell back again, but this time his gasp was one of relief, not pain.

Kayli wanted to go to him, but she forced herself to stay where she was. Untrained, Randon was vulnerable to her magic, and her touch while he was completely unguarded only charged him with more energies he could not control. She closed her eyes and breathed deeply as Brisi had taught her, banking down the Flame inside her so that it burned quietly deep within her, ready at her command but controlled. When she was certain of her mastery, she opened her eyes again and gingerly laid her hand on Randon's shoulder. When nothing happened, she allowed herself her own sigh of relief before she retrieved the wet rag and wiped his face gently with it.

"Are you all right now?" she asked gently. "Please forgive me. I think your pain was my fault this time."

"I don't see how it could be," Randon said, forcing a chuckle although his face was still white and drawn. "I've been having those headaches for years, well before you came. But whatever you did to stop it, you certainly have my most heartfelt thanks. Even Stevann's potion never worked that quickly." He took a few deep breaths, then glanced at Kayli.

"Can you tell me what that was you did?" he asked eagerly. "I'd like to remember the trick of it for next time."

"Your headaches," Kayli said slowly. "Did they begin after your first sexual experience?"

Randon's eyebrows raised, but he nodded.

"In our Orders," Kayli told him, "we take a tea to calm our bodily energies until we have progressed far enough in our studies to control our magic, for magical and sexual energies are closely entwined. Then when we are Awakened, we have mastery over that magic. In your case, however, you were never trained, but I believe that at some time you were Awakened, your latent magical ability made active. As you had no way of controlling such energies, they turned inward, causing you pain."

"But what happened when you touched me?" Randon asked her doubtfully. "That's never happened before."

Kayli sighed.

"When I performed the Rite of Renewal to conceive your child," she said reluctantly, "I was overcome by the energies I brought forth. Since then I have been—sensitized to the fire magic, and my control has suffered. You saw how I burned the branch when I first tried to light it. And you are vulnerable to that magic, as your own body draws in those energies. So when I used my magic without properly controlling it, just as a carelessly built fire may throw sparks out to dry grass around it, some of those energies leaped to you. But by the same token," she added quickly, "you can rid yourself of them. I do not know how much of the fire magic Stevann has, but perhaps he could have done as much for you, if he knew how."

"So you mean anytime I have one of those headaches," Randon said with dawning happiness, "you can get rid of it, as easily as that?"

Kayli nodded, wincing inwardly. Randon only saw quick relief from pain that had plagued him most of his life, ignoring the danger she had placed him in. Well, she would simply have to keep her magic tightly reined, using it only with the greatest care, and preferably not at all in his presence. Perhaps Brisi would know some way to protect Randon from those energies. She sighed in irritation. How *could* any parent have been so negligent as to leave a mage-gifted son unprotected against his own power? And now it was too late.

Captain Beran leaned his head into the tent.

"Your pardon, High Lord," he said apologetically. "I heard the two of you talking, but I've got your things still out here. Say, how'd you manage to get that wet wood started so quick? Mind if I take a stick to light our fire? We haven't been able to get the blighted thing going."

Kayli and Randon exchanged glances, their eyes twinkling.

"Help yourself, Captain," Randon said, chuckling. "I think that between Kayli and me, we've got more fire than we know what to do with."

By the time Endra brought rabbit pie and stewed turnips and carrots, the storm was venting its full fury on the camp, and Kayli and Randon had to erect a shield above their fire so that the rain coming in at the tent's smoke hole would not douse the flames. The tent itself, however, appeared admirably watertight, and Randon told Kayli that Stevann had cast a waterproofing spell on it. Kayli was awed; nobody in Bregond would have ever thought of such a thing, not that it was often needed!

"Tomorrow we'll reach the border, providing the storm doesn't keep up," Randon said, cuddling Kayli close under the furs. "It must be Stevann and his weather mages. I told him I was hoping for clear skies for the meeting, so likely he took it on himself to have mages scry out any bad weather at the border and try to move the rain somewhere else. Simple bad luck that we rode right into it. If we're delayed, your father will wait, won't he?"

Kayli chuckled.

"Randon, our two countries have waited hundreds of years for this meeting," she said. "My father will not throw it away because we are a day late."

But Randon's worries were needless. The storm passed in the night and the new day dawned bright and clear. The ground was muddy, but Randon had chosen the high, sturdy wagons against just such an eventuality. Maja and Carada, still displeased by the previous night's rain, danced restlessly, but Randon and Kayli were forced to hold them back because of the poor footing. By midday the caravan passed through the one part of Agrond that Kayli remembered—that narrow band nearest Bregond where rains were seldom, where Agrond's forests slowly melded into Bregond's arid plains. Here the ground was hard and free from ruts and the wagons moved easily, and Randon and Kayli at last let their horses have their heads, racing well ahead of the caravan.

Thus it was that Kayli and Randon were the first to see the buff-colored hide tents just across the Bregondish border, the soldiers patrolling the large camp, the dun-and-gray horses grazing in the tall grass. Randon immediately reined Carada in, waiting for his guards who were even spurring their mounts to catch up, but Kayli would have none of it; she gave a glad cry and urged Maja forward. The mare wanted no encouragement; seeing the familiar plains and smelling her own kind, she ran as though wolves nipped at her heels.

Maja had hardly slowed before Kayli slid from her back. Guards had gathered at her approach, but by the time Kayli dismounted they had lowered their bows and hurried to meet her.

"Lady Kayli!" Captain Jadovar tossed his bow to one of his fellows and bowed deeply. "High Lady, I should say! How wonderful to see you again! Come, I'll take you to your father."

Kayli hesitated, torn between desire and duty.

"I should wait for Randon," she said reluctantly.

Captain Jadovar gazed eastward, shrugging.

"It looks as though he's staying where he is," he said.

Kayli turned to look. The caravan had stopped on the other side of the border, and Randon had stopped with it, heavily surrounded by his own guards. He beckoned frantically to her to come back.

Kayli scowled. What was he waiting for, an official invitation? Likely exactly that, afraid that if he crossed the border of Bregond there would—

"Kayli! At last." Kayli whirled at the familiar voice and threw herself into her father's arms, fighting back tears as she embraced him fiercely, then her mother. Then there was Kairi, and Danine and Melia and Kirsa all clustering around her and laughing even as Kayli laughed and drowned in their chatter, all of them speaking at once and making no sense at all. For a moment she thought that this happiness was too much, that she would simply fill up and then burst altogether, but she glanced at Kairi and hurriedly composed herself.

"Thrice welcome, you and your husband with you," Kairi said, embracing Kayli warmly. "But he appears hesitant to join us. Do you suppose he thinks us Sarkondish raiders in disguise, waiting in ambush?"

"Sarkondish raiders do not embrace their victims," High Lord Elaasar said with a trace of a smile. "No, Kayli, your husband only shows proper caution. This is a delicate matter, not to be leaped into headlong as you have. You should have stayed at his side." He glanced at her sternly. "That is where you belong now."

"The day I must wait for permission to greet my own father and mother, I will know that all our efforts are for naught," Kayli said stoutly. She sighed. "Never mind, I will return nicely to my husband. May I at least give him word that we will all sup together tonight?"

"Very well." Elaasar gave her hand a last squeeze. "But for tonight, only you and your husband, agreed? For advisers and guards and official talk, tomorrow is soon enough."

Kayli rode back more slowly; halfway she realized with a start that Kairi had worn the soft buff robes of a priestess instead of her gray Initiate's robe, and Kayli had not even noticed, much less congratulated her. For a moment she felt a pang of bitter envy, and she forced it down. There was no turning back from her path now.

Kayli knew a rebuke awaited her when she crossed back into Agrond, but to her surprise it came from Lord Kereg, not Randon.

"High Lord, I must protest!" the minister said angrily. "There are protocols to be observed, procedures to be followed in so delicate a situation as this."

Kayli felt a flash of anger, but she quickly suppressed it as she dismounted, handing Maja's reins to Endra.

"I beg your pardon, Lord Kereg," she said politely. "I was precipitous in my actions, as you say. But I knew that we and my father would be forever sending messengers back and forth to carefully negotiate our first meeting, and wanting my supper before midwinter, I appointed myself messenger instead."

She turned to Randon, who was grinning good-naturedly.

"My father has invited us to supper," she said. "Only Randon and myself," she added pointedly.

Lady Tarkas's face went red, and Lord Kereg's turned positively purple.

"High Lord—" he began ominously.

Randon held up a hand.

"What do you want me to do?" he asked mildly. "Refuse the High Lord of Bregond's kind invitation, or merely tell him that we don't trust our own safety in his company? I think not. You'll have your day, lords, Lady Tarkas. We'll have a grand dinner tomorrow, and that'll be soon enough for politics, I think. Now let's make camp, if you please, so that my lady and I can have a tent to wash and change our clothes in, or would you prefer we meet the High Lord of Bregond for the first time looking like vagabonds and smelling of the road? And put together those gifts, too—the box I put in our wagon, not the others."

When Kayli had bathed and dressed, however, and she and Randon had sent the maids and attendants away, she said quietly, "You should not take the gifts tonight."

"Oh?" Randon looked surprised. "Why ever not?"

"Because those are official gifts, and tonight is not for official business," Kayli told him. "Tonight we are not High Lord and Lady of Agrond, we are kinfolk."

"Well, these particular gifts are the *unofficial* ones," Randon told her, grinning. "The sort of thing a man might give his wife's family. Don't worry. I haven't been High Lord long enough to completely forget how to treat friends."

Lord Kereg insisted that the guards accompany Kayli and Randon, and the two attendants carrying the chest, to the edge of Elaasar's camp, where his own guards would meet them.

"I'm not happy about this whole thing," he said. "Even you, High Lord, must appreciate what an ideal opportunity this would make for an assassin—Agrondish, Bregondish, or Sarkondish. With all that high grass, an army could hide right under our noses."

"That"—Kayli chuckled as she and Randon walked—"is exactly how Bregond has managed to hold its lands. And why, of course, our land ends with the tall grass."

"And that," Randon replied amusedly, "is why nobody lives on the far west edge of Agrond where the forests end. Your folk keep to the tall grass; mine keep to the cover of the trees."

Randon gazed a little dubiously at the Bregondish camp, and Kayli knew what he was looking at—there were few firepits, and the fires in them were very low indeed; the Agrondish camp was bright with fires and lanterns, and in comparison the Bregondish camp was hardly lit at all. But Randon did not know the rapidity with which the tall grass could ignite, nor did he appreciate how much more easily raiders could see the Agrondish camp in the darkness. Peat for fires, too, was expensive and hard to haul long distances; one could not simply pick up handy deadfall here as Randon's folk did.

Captain Jadovar and four men met them at the edge of the camp, bowing but saying othing, gazing rather sternly at the attendants and the guards until the two attendants lowered the chest to the ground and they all retreated.

"Welcome, High Lord Randon, High Lady Kayli," Jadovar said, bowing again. "Please follow me."

He conducted them to a large tent at the center of the camp, more brightly lit than the others. The two guards with the chest entered first; then Jadovar held open the tent flap, announcing, "Randon and Kayli, High Lord and Lady of Agrond."

"I thought you said this wasn't a formal occasion," Randon muttered as he stepped into the tent with Kayli. "I didn't wear my surcoat."

Kayli only smiled. Randon had listened to her recitations of Bregondish etiquette, but he had memorized rather than understood it. He did not understand the difference between a formal political occasion and the ritualized courtesy showing respect to a guest.

She was surprised to see that her father had actually brought a table all the way to the border for this occasion, or perhaps he had borrowed it from one of the villages on the way. Unlike Agrondish tables, Bregondish tables were low, to accommodate the diners sitting on cushions on the floor instead of chairs—that and the short legs conserved the precious wood. Her family still stood, of course, all dressed casually except for Kairi still in her priestess's robe.

"Randon," Kayli said, "I make known to you my father and mother, High Lord Elaasar and High Lady Nerina, and my sisters Kairi, Danine, Melia, and Kirsa. My family, I make known to you my husband, High Lord Randon of Agrond."

Randon half extended his hand, then withdrew it rather awkwardly, bowing to each member of the family instead. Kayli knew it was hard for him to remember that Bregondish did not touch in greeting, and was grateful when her father stepped forward, clasping Randon's hand firmly.

"Welcome to Bregond, or to the edge of it at least," Elaasar said amiably. "Come and sit beside me as my son and share our meat."

Randon was not awkward in seating himself at the short table; he'd had no table at all since they had left Tarkesh, and Kayli had warned him that they would most likely sup at an eating cloth, which was still traditional through most of Bregond. Kayli was proud, too, that Randon showed no surprise when Elaasar took the first sip and bite from each plate before he passed it down the table.

"It is an ancient custom," Kayli had told Randon, "from the time when Bregond was only a group of independent clans.

The head of the clan tasted all food first, to assure visiting clan leaders that they were safe from poison.''

Kayli noticed that Elaasar had somewhere acquired Agrondish-style forks and knives, with which the table was set. Forks were used in Bregond by the nobility, who could afford them, but eating daggers were still worn at the hip, not placed on the table as in Agrond. Randon had raised his eyebrows when Kayli told him that in Bregond it was polite—indeed, necessary—to lift his bowl of soup to his lips after the solids were eaten, and sop up the remaining liquid with bread. After months in Agrond, Kayli herself might have been more comfortable with a spoon.

By custom conversation was left for after dinner instead of during the meal; Kayli knew her father would have been shocked to learn that in Agrond politics and business were discussed while eating. Randon seemed unnerved by the silence, and Kayli wondered whether he had ever actually had the opportunity to enjoy a meal in peaceful quiet in his entire life. As a High Lord's son, likely not.

When the plates were removed, however, and steaming cups of bitter *cai* passed around, Elaasar lit the perfumed candle at the center of the table, signaling that conversation could begin. Randon sipped the *cai*, and Kayli could see that he barely stifled a grimace, but he quickly took another sip.

"I'm pleased to see, daughter, that you look well," Nerina said in slightly awkward Agrondish. "When we learned you had had"—she colored slightly—"joyous news, we feared for your health after your misadventures."

Kayli smiled. Her mother must be powerfully curious; to speak of Kayli's pregnancy, even in veiled terms, was not really polite.

"Endra assures me that I am positively alight with good health," Kayli assured her mother. "Randon pampers me shamefully. If I suffer, it is only from laziness."

"And we can speak Bregondish," Randon added in that language. "Kayli told me that Melia and Kirsa hadn't learned Agrondish yet, and while I'm not as fluent in her language as she is in mine, I can make myself understood."

"You speak well," Elaasar said, nodding approvingly. "And the *cai*, do you like it?"

Randon glanced down at his empty cup with surprise.

"I can't say I liked the first taste," he admitted. "But it seemed to get better as I went along."

"Honesty. I like that," Elaasar said, nodding again. He turned to Kayli. "Jaenira, Fidaya, and Laalen send their love. Laalen's chest is paining her again, so we saw no need to drag her so near the wetlands. Fidaya's wedding was a great occasion, and Jaenira has been blessed with a healthy son."

Kayli felt a sudden pang of homesickness. Would she ever see her sister's child? Most likely not, nor would Jaenira ever see hers.

"Kairi, too, has reason to celebrate," Nerina said, gesturing at Kairi's robe. "We were permitted to attend her ascension less than a tenday past. We're hoping that her temple will permit her to serve her vocation at our castle."

"Mother, you know better," Kairi said with gentle reproof. "A water-Dedicate could no more serve her vocation at the High Lord's castle than a peat cutter on the steppes. I would best serve Bregond by moving with the nomads through the driest lands, where I am needed."

She turned to Kayli and smiled. "I wish some of the grazing trails passed nearer the border," she said. "There was a good rain in the making here. I hated to turn it aside."

"Oh, that was you?" Randon asked, impressed. "We ran into that storm; I blamed my weather mages." Then he raised his eyebrows. "That's quite a feat, turning a storm like that by yourself. From what Stevann has told me, it generally takes two or three weather mages working together."

Kairi smiled slightly at the praise, and Kayli explained, "Agrondish mages are not . . . specialized as ours, but learn many different types of magic."

Kayli's comment loosed a veritable flood of questions about Agrond, its mages, the rivers, the rain—Kayli could see the amazement in her father and mother's eyes when Randon spoke of the quantities of vegetables and grain produced every year, and near disbelief when he told them of the terrible flooding which had caused so much damage recently.

"Can you imagine," Nerina said softly. "*Too much* rain."

"Someday I would like to make a pilgrimage to Agrond," Kairi said suddenly. "To study these wonderful waters."

"You'd be doubly welcome," Randon told her. "I could arrange a ship to sail down the Dezarin to the ocean itself; you can't find much more water than that."

Everyone was silent for a long moment, and Kayli knew they were trying (and most likely failing, like her) to imagine a body of water so huge as to have, in all practicality, no end. Kayli shivered at the thought; how could there be so much water in one part of the world and not enough for Bregond?

"Well, we've got water, but no horses like the ones Kayli brought," Randon said. "Hunting on Carada is like riding the wind."

Nerina smiled and flushed, and Elaasar laughed.

"My lady won't take credit for her accomplishment," he said. "She founded our stable at the castle, spent over a decade crossing the best lines in Bregond. Your brother told us Kayli had guessed right what would please you." He glanced rather calculatingly at Randon. "We'll speak tomorrow of our countries. But in the afternoon I'd ask you and my daughter to join us hunting the great plains boar. If the earth favors us, we'll feast on his flesh for supper."

Randon laughed easily.

"I've been looking forward to hunting with you," he said. "But I can't possibly allow you to host me for two suppers one after the other. So tomorrow night, why don't we let my cook impress you instead?"

This was agreeable. Randon used the opening to remind Elaasar and Nerina that he had brought gifts that had yet to be presented. To Kayli's relief, Randon had indeed thought carefully before making his selections, and Kayli realized with wonder how much attention he had paid to her stories of home. For Elaasar he had brought a handsome pipe carved of Agrondish rosewood and a pouch of southern pipeweed to fill it; for Nerina there were seeds of the most colorful and hardiest flowers from the castle gardens. For Kairi there was an elegant silver bowl for water-scrying, and for Danine, Melia, and Kirsa there were boxes of sweets and cunningly carved wooden toys. Randon had brought a selection of the wonderful Agrondish rainbow-hued silk threads for Laalen's embroidery, and while Nerina promised to give Kayli's sister the gift, she said she was so envious of her own daughter that Randon had to laughingly promise her a similar collection, to be sent by messenger at the first opportunity.

To Kayli's surprise, Elaasar and Nerina had gifts for them also—two wonderful cloaks of the finest amber-red plains-wolf pelts and lined with hide even softer than the velvety fur. Kayli did not know if Agrondish winters were as harsh as those in Bregond, but she would wager that the wonderful thick fur would withstand even an Agrondish downpour.

"I never imagined my first meeting with the High Lord of Bregond going so well," Randon said contentedly as they walked back to their own camp. "I felt as comfortable at his table as at Lidian's. Maybe more; I never had to worry that your father might've tried to have you killed."

Kayli laughed.

"You and my father are much alike," she said. "You are both cunning in putting someone at their ease when that is what you want. I think the two of you will get along famously."

Randon suddenly stopped, causing the guards behind them to backtrack hastily.

"Look at those stars," he said wonderingly. "I don't know that I've ever seen the sky so clear."

Kayli gazed up, too. Clouds always seemed to fill Agrond's sky. The stars were old friends whose faces she had sorely missed.

"There you are!" She could not make out the face of the figure approaching them in the darkness, but Lord Kereg's voice was unmistakable. "What happened at the supper?"

"We ate," Randon said, irritation sharpening his voice. "We spoke of horses and hunting. Do you want to know how many mouthfuls of bread High Lord Elaasar took, or how many times he chewed them?"

After a long silence, Lord Kereg spoke again, and Kayli could hear the anger under his level voice.

"I want to know anything, anything at all, that could help us in the meeting tomorrow. All we know about these people is what your wife has told us, and—your pardon, High Lady—that may not be everything she knows."

"Lord Kereg," Randon said tiredly, "it's late, and Kayli

and I rode all day. I have no desire for an inquisition standing here in the dark.''

Lord Kereg muttered something angrily, excused himself, and strode away. Randon led Kayli to their tent, shaking his head in irritation.

''Well, it *was* a pleasant evening,'' Randon said ruefully. ''Do me a favor, Kayli. He and Lady Tarkas and Lord Disian won't be any happier tomorrow when I pull the reins on them. But let me be the one to do it; what they'll take from me they might not tolerate from you.''

Kayli and Randon rose early in the morning to dress for the meeting, then met Lord Kereg, Lady Tarkas, and Lord Disian. Kayli had to stifle her surprise—and amusement—when Randon announced without preamble that only he and Kayli would negotiate with High Lord Elaasar and High Lady Nerina. When all three would have protested, Randon raised a hand to silence them.

''I've learned a great deal more from Kayli about her family than you have,'' he said. ''Last night I sat in friendship with the High Lord and Lady of Bregond. I won't endanger that friendship now. You're welcome to attend with me, but you'll only be advising me and Kayli. And only when I—we—ask for that advice. As you say, it's a delicate situation.''

This time, to Kayli's dismay, almost every single guard in camp accompanied them across the border, flanking Lord Disian's wagons filled with trade goods. There was formality, too, in the Bregondish guards that met them in their best armor, swords polished to a fine sparkle.

There were, of course, the obligatory courtesies as High Lord Elaasar and High Lady Nerina were announced, together with Brother Santee, representing the Holy Orders of Bregond, Herdmaster Rakas, who spoke for the horse and *ikada* clans, and Wagonmistress Ishera, who coordinated the merchant caravans with the movement and seasonal needs of the clans. Kayli stifled a pang of disappointment when she saw Brother Santee; she had hoped that someone from her own Order might come. Then she realized to her chagrin that *she* might be the reason why they had not; when Kayli had sent no word for so long, the assumption by the Order would be that she wished to be left to her new life. Despite Brisi's permission to continue her studies, the Order had no obligation to track her like a mother might a wandering child.

Kayli's greatest surprise came, however, when Kairi joined them at the table and Elaasar and Nerina introduced her as their Heir to the throne of Bregond. The announcement at least explained Kairi's presence outside of her Order so soon after her ascension; for the first face-to-face negotiations between Bregond and Agrond, an Heir must of course be chosen and present.

Kayli quickly found that her father and Randon were indeed as alike in their way of thinking as she had said. Brother Santee, Rakas, and Ishera sat quietly, saying little except when the High Lord and Lady addressed them. Kayli, too, largely kept her peace, feeling she could say little about Agrond that Randon could not say better, and even less about Bregond than her father or mother might. Elaasar and Nerina ignored Randon's occasional mangling of Agrondish language or custom, and Randon omitted the courtly deviousness Kayli had seen so often—or, perhaps, she realized, he employed an even subtler form of manipulation in that very omission.

Randon's advisers relaxed slightly when he called on them to demonstrate the advantages of their offerings and to comment on Bregondish merchandise. Both sets of advisers gradually thawed as each grew enthusiastic over some new discovery. By the time the six were unabashedly chatting with each other, bargaining strategy, cultural differences, and their respective rulers forgotten, Kayli realized that they now had a perfect opportunity to adjourn the meeting for their hunt; the advisers would undoubtedly hammer out a trade agreement on their own.

At midday, Nerina called a halt to the proceedings.

"I'm certain we could continue all day," she said, smiling, "but our countries can't prosper if their rulers starve. Come, a light dinner, and then Kayli and Randon will ride with us to hunt, and tomorrow there will be time for more talk."

After supper, however, when Kayli would have returned with Randon to camp to change clothes, Kairi caught at her sleeve.

"Let me walk with you," she murmured. "We have had no opportunity to speak privately."

"Of course," Kayli said gladly. "Randon, would you object—"

"Not a bit," Randon said stoutly. "I'll walk ahead, and I'll change my clothes in my attendants' tent so you and your sister can talk."

When they were alone, however (except for the guards who followed at a discreet distance), Kairi remained silent, gazing at Kayli expectantly. Kairi at last took her hand.

"Tell me what troubles you," she said quietly. "I can feel the energies swirling unchecked around you like a windstorm. Tell me what has happened."

For a moment Kayli agonized over the dilemma. The Rite of Renewal was a secret of her Order, and Kairi was not entitled to hear it. At last, however, desperation won and Kayli told the whole story from the beginning. Kairi remained impassive throughout the tale, but when Kayli finished, she shook her head.

"You have woven a tangled web about yourself," she said slowly. "Have you spoken to your mentor?"

"No," Kayli admitted. "I feared her reprimand, but even more I feared learning that I had done some irreparable harm to myself or my child, or even to Randon."

"So far as I know," Kairi said carefully, "no one with the mage-gift was ever missed by testing, then later Awakened without training. No wonder he Awakened you so easily; in the same way that your magic affects him, his own Flame spark quickly set yours ablaze. Exposure to his uncontrolled magic may well have caused the problems in your own control. I am certain High Priestess Brisi would never permit you to be Awakened by this man if she had known."

"But it is too late for that," Kayli said anxiously. "Kairi, what can I do? Can you help me?"

Kairi shook her head.

"I have only just become priestess myself," she said regretfully. "But these matters are best addressed by your own Order. You must speak to your mentor. Perhaps she will come to you to help you, or perhaps a journey might be arranged for you to visit the Order, which would be safer from a magical standpoint. In the meantime I offer this advice: First, continue to drain his magical energies. I do not know whether in the long term such contact will help Randon or harm him, but the alternative seems more dangerous. Second, refrain from practicing your art until you regain your control. I need not tell you how dangerous fire magic unleashed could be.''

"I would call High Priestess Brisi this moment, but I left my speaking crystal in Tarkesh," Kayli said unhappily. "Could I use yours?"

"Brother Santee has the crystal," Kairi apologized. "As he represents the Orders here, he must contact them periodically. Tomorrow I will borrow it back for you."

True to his word, Randon had taken his clothes and left the tent to Kayli and her sister. Kayli gladly exchanged her finery for her riding clothes while Kairi unbraided her hair, combed it out, and braided it again comfortably for riding. Sensing Kayli's worry, and perhaps sharing it, Kairi kindly turned their conversation to more ordinary matters. She was eager to hear whatever Kayli would tell her of Agrond, and when Kayli recounted her swim in Randon's forest pond, Kairi laughed and hugged her sister.

"Yes, I have submerged myself in the water many times," she said. "And now it holds no fear for me. But to you it must be as terrifying as to me if I threw myself into the forge. You were very brave to do such a thing." She sighed. "I dream of submerging myself in this great southern sea, surrendering myself to its might, to feel the purest power of water in this world."

Kayli sobered, clutching her sister's hand.

"Perhaps too much surrender to the powers we serve is not a good thing," she said slowly.

Kairi sighed again.

"As you have learned. Well, you and I must content ourselves with dabbling our feet in the surf, so to speak." She shook her head. "Sister, your anxiety is as contagious as latewinter sneezes. Come, let us find your horse and your husband before they both give up and leave without you."

Randon was indeed waiting with the horses, his jaffs tied *properly*, and Maja and Carada were saddled, her bow and Randon's crossbow already strapped to the saddles.

When Kayli and Randon met Elaasar, Nerina, and Danine and saw that only four of the Bregondish guards were going to accompany them on the hunt, Randon sent back all but four of his own guards, and the thirteen of them rode out onto the plains together. For some time they sighted no large game, although Danine sighted and shot a good-sized *chakene;* the bird went into the young girl's game bag, and from time to time she reached back as she rode and patted the lump in the sack proudly.

Kayli was beginning to wonder disappointedly whether they would have to return to camp with nothing but Danine's bird when her father held up his hand, halting the group, and gestured at a large clump of brambles ahead. Randon nodded immediately, but Kayli had to look long and hard before she spotted the telltale white flash of a tusk boar's stubby tail among the thorns.

Nerina signaled to Danine to retire, and the disappointed girl rode back a short distance. Nerina, Elaasar, Kayli, and Randon moved their horses downwind, carefully positioned so they would not shoot across each other's path. The other guards fell back with Danine, except for three who rode around to the back to flush out the boar.

Kayli nocked her arrow, breathing deeply; she smelled the distinctive musk of the male tusk boar on the wind, and that struck a note of warning in her mind. If she could smell the boar from this distance, he was in rut and easily angered. She glanced over at Randon, but he was intent on the thicket.

Apparently her father signaled the guards while Kayli was not looking, for their charge from the back of the thicket was marked by shouts and the thunder of hoofbeats, followed by an outraged thrashing from the brambles. To Kayli's horror, not one, but *two* tusk boars, one male and one female, flushed from the thicket, squealing in anger.

Hunting strategy forgotten, Kayli loosed her arrow; to her dismay, it buried itself in the female's thick neck instead of the vulnerable spot under the ear. At the same time Randon's crossbow shaft struck solidly near Kayli's arrow, and Kayli was certain that surely one had penetrated the great neck vein, but the enraged sow never paused, only turning on its most recent tormentor, Randon, who was now reloading his crossbow.

Without thinking, Kayli urged Maja forward into the

sow's path. The mare responded as perfectly as Kayli could have hoped, drawing the sow's attention, then dancing nimbly sideways while Kayli snatched another arrow from her quiver. Dimly she heard the shouts of the guards behind her, the sound of hoofbeats, the squealing of the boar, but her concentration had narrowed to the sow and the tip of her arrow. She fired, but Maja's dancing caused her arrow to barely skim the sow's hide and thunk into the ground instead.

A scream from behind her—Kayli recognized her mother's voice, and true fear leaped up in her heart. This time, despite her tension, she let the sow change direction and charge, and when she loosed her third arrow, the point buried itself solidly in the sow's right eye, even as Randon's crossbow bolt hit the spot under the ear. Momentum carried the sow forward to the ground where she lay, twitching slightly.

Randon's horse flashed past, and Maja responded to Kayli's slight shift in seat, turning so swiftly that the arrow Kayli was drawing nearly fell from her hand. As her horse turned, Kayli saw what prompted Randon's haste—not Nerina, but her father was on the ground scrambling for his dropped bow, his horse belly-gored and dying as the boar set itself for another charge.

This time Captain Beran interposed his horse, trying to distract the boar's charge, but the boar found the man on the ground an easier target. Nerina loosed an arrow which would have pierced the heart but for the thick muscle of the boar's chest, and this time the beast turned, charging her instead.

Randon struggled only a moment longer to reload his crossbow, then flung it down with a curse and devoted himself to his riding. Carada dashed between the boar and Nerina's horse, and the boar turned again; then Kayli's heart stopped as Carada stumbled and nearly went down. In an amazing feat of horsemanship, Randon kept his saddle, but now the boar was at Carada's very heels.

Two guards' arrows thunked into the boar's flank and shoulder, but now the boar had spied Elaasar again, and this time it ignored the horse that darted across its path—

Danine!

When Kayli saw the horse turn too sharply and the slight figure tumble from the saddle, all rational thought fled her mind. She nocked her arrow and fired it, simultaneously focusing her power upon it, and the flaming arrow struck the ground directly in front of the enraged boar's nose, less than a dozen paces from her father.

Horses and arrows the boar might ignore, but fire, never. Now there was panic in the boar's squeal as it turned, presenting its face and side openly to the guards. Half a dozen arrows slammed into the animal, and one struck a vital spot, for the boar slowed, shivered slightly, and fell at last.

Finished. Kayli took a gasping breath and realized that she was shaking, her bow dropped from numb hands. She slid from the saddle, bolting for Danine, who was already standing, brushing dirt from her trousers.

"Are you hurt?" Kayli asked anxiously, running her hands down Danine's arms and legs to feel for broken bones.

Danine shook her head.

"No," she said, embarrassed. "But Father—"

"Your father is quite well," High Lord Elaasar said, joining them, "and quite angry."

He seized Danine by the shoulders.

"Never dare disobey me like that again," he thundered. "I would have had to defend you as well as myself, and the boar could have turned either way at the last moment. When I tell you to stay out of the way, you *stay,* do you understand me?"

Danine's eyes filled with tears, but she whispered, "Yes, Father."

"All right, then." Elaasar's voice shook slightly, and he pulled his daughter to him, holding her tightly. "You were brave," he muttered. "Foolish and disobedient, but brave."

He glanced past Kayli and nodded with satisfaction.

"I see you dealt with the sow," he said. "Good. We'll eat well tonight, though it's a poor trade for a fine horse." He shook his head, glanced back toward his dying mare, and waved the approaching guard away. "I'll see to her."

Kayli turned away, not wanting to watch as her father drove his long dagger into his mare's brain, ending her pain instantly. Randon slid from his saddle and put his arm around Kayli's shoulders, kissing her forehead.

"That was a good idea you had, that fire arrow," he said quietly. "Even if one of us had hit the boar with a killing blow, the sheer strength of his charge might've carried him on forward into your father."

"Aye, it was a masterful shot." Nerina threw one arm around Danine and one around Kayli. "Both my daughters are brave and resourceful—and headstrong." She laughed. "But look at these swine. They look like spinefurs instead of tusk boars. Who can claim the kills? The sow?"

"Randon," Kayli said at the same time that Randon said, "Kayli."

"Well, I lost my crossbow before I ever got a shot at the boar," Randon said good-naturedly. "Although it almost had a shot at *me*."

"And I never so much as touched it," Kayli admitted.

"Well, your arrow most likely kept my vitals in my belly, instead of hanging down around my boots," her father said wryly, wiping the blood from his hands on the grass. "And your husband tried hard to get himself killed in my place, so I'll cede the tusks to the two of you with my thanks. But how will we ever get our banquet home? We brought only the one sling carrier."

"I'll send two guards back for a wagon, High Lord," Captain Beran said. "We can't lose such a prize as the sow, and—begging pardon, High Lord, but we'd do as well to dress the two here, as your mare will draw scavengers anyway, and better here than at the camp."

"And my *chakene*," Danine put in. "Don't forget that."

"Aye, lady," Captain Beran said solemnly. "Best we don't forget it, as it was the cleanest kill made today."

While Kayli liked to hunt, she had never enjoyed cleaning her game, and she watched with Danine as her mother and the men gutted the carcasses, wrapping the tastiest organs in sacks and piling the offal beside the dead mare.

By the time the carcasses were cleaned, the wagon arrived with more guards and there were plenty of men to help shoulder the boar and the sow into the wagon bed. Danine's *chakene* was given a place of honor on the wagon seat, and Danine insisted on riding with it, Elaasar riding her gelding back to camp.

Apparently the guards who had ridden ahead for the wagon had sent word to Randon's cook, for the firepit had been widened and lengthened to accommodate both pigs, and a good bed of coal was lit. When the wagon arrived, it took nearly a dozen men to cut the meat into pieces, work the massive spits through the hunks of meat, and hoist them over the coals, but soon the appetizing smell of roasting boar filled the entire camp.

Lord Kereg walked up as Randon and Kayli were watching, joining them beside the firepit.

"Congratulations on the hunt, High Lord," he said, nodding at the meat roasting on the spits. "It seems successful beyond your expectations."

"Yes, well, I was nearly killed beyond my expectations," Randon said wryly. "Too much time sitting in a chair instead of a saddle." He grinned at Kayli. "We must do something about that when we return home. I'd forgotten the pleasure of eating my own kill."

"And I had forgotten how dangerous it could be," Kayli admitted. "And how much I enjoy that risk."

"Look here." Randon picked up a small bundle of cloth and unwrapped it, showing Kayli the cleaned tusks of the boar, so long and curved that they overlapped in a circle. "One for you, and one for me, so we don't forget again."

Elaasar, Nerina, and their daughters and advisers arrived shortly, and Randon ordered a cask of his best wine tapped for the occasion. This supper proved more jovial than dinner had been, no hostility or awkwardness left, and both sets of rulers amusedly ignored their advisers marveling over the fine Bregondish furs, the excellent *ikada*-milk cheese, Lord Disian's wagon wheels, or the plumpness of Agrondish turnips.

"You're awfully quiet," Randon murmured to Kayli after Lord Kereg had invited him to smell a Bregondish perfume for the fifth time. "I thought you'd be happy, this is going so well."

"Oh, I am happy," Kayli said with a sigh. "It is only hard, I suppose, to come back from our hunt and sit here with my family and talk of crops and pots and *ikada* hair."

Randon chuckled and reached under the edge of the table, squeezing Kayli's knee through her trousers.

"I could propose something a little more to your liking," he whispered warmly.

An answering heat welled up in Kayli's loins, and she laid her hand over Randon's.

"Do you want another adventure?" she whispered in his ear.

"Hmmm." Randon's hand slid higher on her leg. "What were you thinking?"

"Remember how clearly the stars shine over the plains," Kayli murmured. "Would you dare slip away tonight and risk all the dangers of the Bregondish plains—and a Bregondish lady?"

"Now, that's a challenge I could never resist," Randon said huskily. "But, I swear to the Bright Ones, if you say another word about it here at the table, I'll drug the wine so we can slip away all the sooner."

Kayli chuckled and returned her attention to the table, only to see Kairi glancing at her, a wicked amusement in her eyes. Kairi raised her eyebrows inquiringly and tilted her head slightly toward Kayli's tent; Kayli shook her head just as slightly and glanced out at the plains, then back at Kairi. Kairi's eyebrows jumped, and her hand flew up to cover her mouth; she coughed slightly, and Kayli knew that her well-disciplined sister was fighting down howls of laughter.

At the first opportunity, Kayli took Endra aside and told the midwife her plans. Endra delightedly entered into the conspiracy, only cautioning Kayli to stay near the camp.

It seemed an eternity before the two groups separated for the night, and even longer before most of the guards went to bed, leaving only the guards on night patrol. Kayli thought that Endra had forgotten her promise to help; at last the midwife emerged from her tent and walked up to the guard nearest Kayli's tent. Kayli could not make out what Endra was saying, but a moment later the guard followed the midwife out of sight.

Kayli nodded to Randon and slipped quietly out of her tent; he followed, clutching a blanket-wrapped bundle and dropping the tent flap behind them. They crept out of camp as silently as they could, and Randon followed Kayli into the grass. After they'd been walking for some time, however, he spoke.

"We're going awfully far, aren't we?" he asked.

"We must get well beyond the range of my father's guard

patrol as well," Kayli said, giggling. "And far enough that the glare from the fires will not spoil our view of the stars."

When she decided they'd gone far enough, Randon opened the bundled blanket and, to Kayli's surprise, drew out the wonderful cloaks that her father had given them.

"Randon," Kayli chided gently. "It is far too warm to need such coverings."

"I know," he said merrily. "But it's pleasant to lie on furs and make love, don't you think?"

He plopped down on the cloaks and pulled Kayli down beside him.

"So tell me," he murmured into her ear, "just what dangers I'm to face tonight."

Kayli gasped as his hand slid into the front of her tunic, and whatever answer she made, only the stars heard.

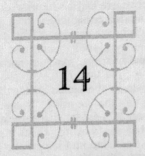

14

KAYLI WOKE ABRUPTLY AT SOME INNER PROMPT-
ing. For a moment she could not understand why she
was lying on the ground, wrapped in a blanket in Randon's arms with the great brilliant sky overhead; then she remembered and smiled. She stretched luxuriantly, enjoying the
smells of smoke and plains grass and sweet earth, the bright
stars above her—

Smoke?

Kayli jumped to her feet, eliciting a sleepy groan of protest
from Randon. Now she could hear a distant sort of roar, not
unlike that of approaching rain in Agrond, but as she saw the
red-gold line on the northwest horizon, she knew that it was
no rain approaching them. A part of Kayli's mind was shocked
to stillness—she knew how fast grass fires could travel.

"What?" Randon stood up leisurely beside her, stretching.
"What's the—" Then he saw it, and he, too, fell silent. "It's
between us and the camps, isn't it? Can we outrun it?" But
from the gentleness of his words, Kayli knew that he, too,
knew the impossibility of fleeing ahead of that hungry red line.

Randon grabbed Kayli's shoulders, turning her to face him.

"Can you survive that? Can you walk through that and live,
you and the baby? Tell me!"

Once again Kayli was shocked to silence as she realized

what he was asking. *Could* she walk unscathed through such an inferno? Possibly. Once she would have been certain. But even if she could, Randon could not. Must she, could she, choose between her death and his?

But there was another possibility.

"The wine," Kayli said rapidly. "Wet your kerchief with it. Tie it over your nose and mouth, and lie down on the ground. The smoke will rise. And do not dare distract me now."

"What are you doing?" Randon asked. "You can't—"

"Perhaps I can turn the fire aside," Kayli said. "Perhaps I can even extinguish it." Even as she spoke, she knew her words for a lie, but she took the ritual breaths of calming anyway, focusing her concentration on the fire, and opened the barriers she had erected between herself and her power, reaching to touch the fire.

Immediately Kayli reeled back, overwhelmed completely. Randon was beside her, not daring to touch her, saying something which she ignored. By the Flame, how could she ever hope to influence *that*? Why, she had lost her control to a simple forge fire. But this was the Flame unbound, dancing free across the plains and consuming all it touched, godlike in its magnificence, monstrous in its unseeing hunger, unbound—

Oh, how seductive the call of the roaring flames, much closer now, caressing her soul more exquisitely than Randon had caressed her body. She could surrender to that unimaginable embrace, let her mortal frame become ash and blow on the wind, but her soul would become one with that fire, burning more brightly with every moment—

No!

Kayli dragged herself free of her entrapment with a moan of disappointment. For a moment she wrestled futilely to damp the flames, to turn them, even perhaps to part them, but in vain. How could she rein in those flames when she longed so totally to abandon herself to them?

Kayli sobbed with despair. What was her magic if she could only make fire, not quench it? What good was—

"Yes!" she cried.

She could *make* fire.

Relief cleared her mind more completely than any discipline could. In utter clarity, Kayli extended her hands and let the fire leap forth.

Flame jumped to the grass and feasted voraciously, but this was Kayli's flame, and now it obeyed her. Tongues of fire darted to the right and the left, forming a line that pushed outward even as it spread to the sides. As it consumed the grass, the flames grew in size and speed, urged by Kayli's power. They crept forward, then rolled more quickly, until at last those bright tongues of fire raced rapidly to meet the red line, leaving a widening band of bare earth and blackened grass in their wake.

Through the corner of her eye, Kayli could see Randon tying the cloth across his mouth and nose as she had instructed him, gathering the bundle of the blanket, the cloaks, and their clothes together and packing it down tightly. Good—no stray spark would set *that* alight. Randon remained silent, and Kayli kept her attention focused tightly on her small backfire, pushing it outward and forward as quickly as she could. Her awareness spread outward with the flames until she felt herself stretched so thinly that her mind spun, reeling almost out of control. She knew immediately that her backfire would not be enough, that the larger fire would simply race around the edges of her smaller blaze—

A sudden boom of thunder directly overhead startled Kayli so that she almost lost the thread of her concentration. Then lightning reached down a glowing finger to stroke the plains, and she felt that tongue of fire whip upward through her bones and straight through to her soul. Somewhere beside her, a thousand leagues away, Randon screamed in agony, and then Kayli was flung aside, her link with her small backfire shattered as rain poured down upon them.

Kayli was too amazed and drained to do anything but sit there in the rain as the clean fresh water, mingling with her own sweat and tears, slowly washed the soot from her face. In the back of her mind she felt the great fire raging against the rain like a cornered beast fighting to stay alive, but its might was slowly sapped. At last, slowly, in small sizzling hisses that sounded like whistling gasps, it died.

"What happened?" Randon asked, loudly over the rain. He

ripped the wine-soaked cloth from his face. "I thought it rarely rained here. Did you do that?"

Not quite true; it rained more frequently, of course, near the border of Agrond. And there had been rain near the border not long before; Kairi had moved it into Agrond. And that meant that—

"Kairi must have done it," Kayli said, a cautious hope growing in her heart. "The sky was clear only a short time ago. Kairi must have brought the rain back from Agrond to stop the fire." She glanced at Randon; he was rubbing his temples again, his brow furrowed.

Kayli held out her hands.

"Send the fire back to me, as you did before," she said. This time there was a stronger sensation of power transferred from his fingertips to hers, and Kayli wondered uncomfortably whether Randon had absorbed more fire energy from the lightning, or whether the repetitive exposure to fire energy increased the amount he channeled into his own body, as was true with herself.

"Well, then, let's go," Randon said, hurriedly pulling his now wet clothes on over his wet skin. "Enough adventure for one night. I'll be glad to get out of the rain, even if it *did* save our lives."

They walked back over scorched and blackened earth, the ashes of plains grass and brambles. Rain and mud and ash formed a thick black paste that quickly coated their boots, and the plains earth, stripped of grass, became slick and treacherous. They slid and stumbled as they walked, each bearing the other up when they slipped, forced to keep their eyes on their footing; thus it was that they were almost upon the torn and scattered Bregondish tents before they saw them. Then Kayli saw the first of the bodies, and her elation and conscious thought deserted her in one raw scream of horrified denial.

Randon forgotten, grass fire forgotten, Kayli found herself on her knees in the mud, frantically turning bodies over, flinging aside scorched tent hides and broken poles, weeping with relief when she failed to recognize the bloody faces—

Until she turned over a charred and mutilated corpse and stared into her mother's unseeing eyes.

Kayli did not know how long she sat there, stunned and

numb, the world unreal around her, before Randon gently lifted her to her feet.

"Kayli?" When she did not answer, he shook her gently. "Kayli. I didn't find your father, or Kairi, or Danine. Maybe they got away. But—"

Kayli started to turn in the direction Randon had been searching, but he seized her shoulders again.

"No," he said. "Better not look, Kayli." He turned her away, but not before she had seen the two small bodies, smeared with soot and blood, flung heedlessly aside.

"My father," Kayli murmured numbly. "Kairi, Danine—"

"I said I didn't find them." Randon shook her gently again. "Kayli, listen to me. My camp is gone, too. I can't see any of the tents. But the bodies are hardly cool. It must've been raiders, and they can't be long gone. Maybe they're still searching for us. We've got to get out of here before they come back, but first I want to see if any of my people are alive."

Kayli moved as if in a dream, letting Randon lead her east to the Agrondish camp. There was little difference here, except the scorched remnants of the tents were gay-colored cloth instead of plain hide. Kayli was too numb and bemused even to react when Randon found Endra's body, her own dagger still thrust into her heart, and Anida and Devra similarly dead beside her. She reached dreamily for the midwife's hand, startled slightly from her fog when Randon pulled her abruptly to her feet.

"I hear horses!" he said, dragging Kayli across the scorched earth to the place where the grass began again. "Get down and stay down. Don't move." She lay where he pushed her on the ground. Something heavy fell over her, and when she smelled the odor of burned flesh, she realized with a dull horror that Randon had flung one of the corpses over her. But somehow even that knowledge could not move her, and she lay quietly where she was, the tall grass closing around her like a warm and comforting womb, the ground wonderfully solid and firm beneath her. She did not know where Randon had gone, nor did she care.

Hoofbeats now, louder and closer. A tiny, sharp thought of

Kairi made Kayli raise her head slightly, peering through the grass and the fringe of her hair. She could see little from her vantage point, but the brief glimpse of the gray horse that flashed past her hiding place and its high-backed saddle identified it as a Bregondish steed in Bregondish tack.

The recognition somehow shook Kayli slightly out of her fog of shock, and she would have risen, but before she could push the corpse off her, the sound of the shouting reached her ears. And the language was *not* Bregondish. Kayli froze where she was, stilling even her breath, until the sounds of hoofbeats and shouting faded away to the east. Then she waited even longer, her heart pounding, until she was certain she heard nothing more.

Kayli's stomach lurched as she heaved the bloody corpse off her, but she forced herself to stumble away from her hiding place before she bent to vomit. The mere act of purging her stomach helped, as if she purged herself at the same time of her fear and mind-numbing grief. More resolutely she stood and looked around for Randon, praying that the shouting she had heard did not mean that the raiders had found him. No—there he was, crawling out from under a pile of half-burned tent cloth. He ran to her, and for a moment they could do nothing but hold each other.

"Are you all right?" Randon asked breathlessly. "When I saw Bregondish horses, I almost thought—"

"We were meant to think that," Kayli said with sudden realization. "I, too, thought they were Bregondish—until I heard them speaking Sarkondish. Oh, Randon, what has happened here?"

"I don't know." He glanced around. "I didn't find the bodies of several of my guards, or Seba, and all the horses are gone. Maybe some of them got away. The raiders rode east, maybe to follow them."

"Then we must go west." Kayli took a deep breath. "But not until we have given the rites of death to our people."

"No." When Kayli turned to him in shock, Randon shook his head again firmly.

"Kayli, the only hope we have, our only advantage, is that the raiders likely think we're dead. They must have lit the grass fire to be sure. If we bury or burn the corpses, they'll suspect we survived, and they'll hunt us down—and they've got the speed of horses, while we're on foot. Our only chance is to leave this place as we found it and flee in the direction they're *not* looking for us—into Bregond.''

For a moment Kayli's mind utterly rebelled, refusing even to consider the idea of leaving her mother and sisters' bodies to rot under the sun without the rites of death. Then she breathed deeply, forcing her mind to silence.

''Yes,'' she said, forcing out the words. ''You are right, of course.''

''Just stay here and hide in the grass,'' Randon told her. ''I'm going to see if I can salvage anything, anything at all.''

When he returned, seemingly hours later, he carried a cloth-wrapped bundle.

''I found a little meat in the ashes of the firepit,'' he said, ''and some dried fruit in the wreckage of one of the tents. There's a dagger, too, that someone must've dropped, and another blanket that isn't in too terrible a shape. But there's not much water. And we'd best leave soon, before the raiders might take it into their minds to check the place one last time.''

Kayli's heart wrenched at the thought of leaving the dead as they lay, where scavengers would tear at their flesh and wind and dust scour their bones, but she said nothing. There was not one among her people who would not have bid her, if they could, to escape and survive at any cost. Calming herself, she chose two stout poles and a few tent stakes that could be used, with the blanket, to make a lean-to, and found a shorter section which had broken off sharply, useful as a digging stick, and followed Randon from the camp.

They walked west, back to the place where they had left the blanket, the cloaks, and what was left of the skin of wine. It was nearly dawn now, and the clouds were clearing, too.

''Well, what now?'' Randon asked slowly. ''We could circle south, I suppose, try to cross the border, but I don't want to risk crossing the path of those raiders, and they rode east.''

Kayli shook her head.

''If the raiders have any suspicion that we are alive, they will stay where they are, and search the border lands,'' she said. ''There is no one to stop them. Better we go west, instead, toward Olhavar. At least we will likely find a village soon, for the horse-clan trails run near the border.''

"West, then," Randon agreed. He was silent for a long time, staring out across the plains. At last he said, "You know, that wasn't any simple border raid. Those raiders had to either fight their way past our northern outposts or go a long way around them. And they were dressed like Bregonds.''

Kayli was silent, too, considering the implications of what she had seen. The raiders had indeed been dressed as Bregondish warriors, riding Bregondish horses—but they had spoken Sarkondish. No raiders, to the best of her knowledge, had ever tried to disguise themselves before. And some of Randon's guards, and possibly Seba, too, had escaped—been allowed to escape, most likely. They would return to Tarkesh and tell Terralt that the High Lord and Lady of Bregond, and Randon and Kayli, too, were dead, struck down by Bregondish warriors. Terralt would assume the throne of Agrond, permanently this time, and the treaty between Bregond and Agrond would be a quickly forgotten dream. That thought, more than any other, convinced Kayli that they should not try to return to Agrond immediately, not without troops to assure that Terralt would not prefer to finish what the raiders had started rather than surrender the throne he had wanted so long.

And who would benefit by such a series of events? Dissidents in Agrond and Bregond, of course. Sarkond, to a greater extent; the treaty was the greatest threat Sarkond had ever faced.

And Terralt, who would at one stroke gain the throne of Agrond, freedom from the treaty, the death of the half brother he disliked, and the sympathy and support of the Agrondish people, even those who had formerly favored Randon. Why, in the face of so bold and tragic an attack as to slaughter their High Lord and Lady, what citizen would not shift his loyalty to Randon's bereaved brother?

"I know what you're thinking," Randon said suddenly. "You're wrong. Terralt's simply not capable of this kind of treachery.''

Kayli said nothing. Terralt was capable of a good deal more than Randon believed, and she knew it.

When she made no response, Randon settled his burdens a little more comfortably and shrugged.

"Which way?" he said. "Where's the nearest village?"

Kayli sighed.

"I don't know," she said. "I spent the last years of my life in the Order. I don't know when I last saw a map of Bregond, and it is a changing place. Folk rarely settle as permanently here as in Agrond."

Randon stopped, turning to face her in astonishment.

"Well, then, where by the Bright Ones are we going?" he demanded.

Kayli crouched down, brushed a small patch of earth clear, and drew in it with her finger.

"The herds circle Bregond, from water hole to water hole," she said, drawing the trails in the dirt. "Our merchants follow the same roads. The clans will be in the north now, taking the herds to the cooler summer pastures, but we might be fortunate enough to meet a merchant caravan on the road. And the villages, such as they are, are spaced along the herd circuits as well. So our best chance to find people, shelter, and water is to follow those trails."

Randon glanced back longingly toward Agrond (Kayli wondered if her eyes had looked like that when she had ridden into Agrond, looking back at her home one last time), but nodded reluctantly. She wondered if he, too, doubted the welcome he would receive in Tarkesh if he returned now.

They walked westward, saying little, while the sun rose slowly overhead. As they walked away from Agrond, the shorter water-loving shrubs and grass tapered off, becoming the spiny brush, bramble thickets, and tall grass that Kayli remembered so well. Randon bravely pushed along beside her, but as the sharp grasses slashed at his tunic and then his skin, he cursed under his breath.

Kayli stopped, glancing up at the sun.

"We should stop," she said, "rest until dusk and then continue. When it is cooler, we can wear our cloaks, and they will protect us from the grass."

Randon nodded brief agreement, and they trampled down an area of the plains grass, laying their cloaks down there. The blanket and the stakes and poles they had brought formed a neat lean-to to provide some relief from the now hot sun, and they both crawled into the makeshift shelter.

"Bright Ones," Randon muttered, trying to settle himself on the hard ground. "I'm grateful to your father for these fur cloaks, but they're too damned hot to lie on in this weather and too damned thin for lying on hard ground."

"Take off your clothes and lie on them as well," Kayli suggested. She herself was not too uncomfortable; it had been months since she'd left the dry heat of Bregond, but she had already adjusted. Even with the baby growing in her belly, she would need little water.

Randon was another matter. Raised in the wetlands, without the benefits of Kayli's temple training, he would need a great deal of water and protection from the heat and the sunlight, and regular food and sleep as well. If only they had managed to find even one horse!

Randon fell into an uneasy doze, and Kayli slid silently out from under the shelter, staring out at the plains as she thought. It was a familiar pose; she'd stood this way hundreds of times before. As always, the sight of the sun on the gently waving grass cleared her mind, if not lightening her heart.

She fairly ached to sing to the spirits of her family to speed them on the spirit journey, to make her apologies for her shameful failure to accord their bodies proper respect. But for that Kayli would require a forge and hours of meditation. As much as her heart hung heavily in her for her neglect of her duty to her family's spirits, there was nothing she could do now but turn her thoughts to her own and Randon's survival.

The blanket and cloaks would make adequate shelter and protection from the plains grasses. There was little food, but they could find more; Kayli was not overly concerned on that account. But they had only one partly filled skin of water and a cup or two of wine. That liquid would last them two days, possibly three, but no more. And although Kayli had little knowledge of the geography of Bregond, she knew there were no usable water holes near the Agrondish border; the few that existed had long since been fouled or outright poisoned by the Sarkondish.

Kayli glanced back at Randon, glad to see that he now slept deeply. With luck and perseverance, they could walk most of the night. They would simply have to move as quickly as they could, and hope that they would meet someone on the road. In the meantime—

Once, sullen and resentful, Kayli had crouched on the plains outside the Order and compared the number of ribs in a blade of sedge grass with that of curling mousegrass. Now she crouched down again and focused her attention closely on the vegetation before her. As she almost unconsciously cataloged the plants she knew, she recited to herself the useful properties of each one—bee sedge, for curdling cheese; sourgrass, for tea; *ikada*'s vetch, valued for the salt that could be rendered from its ashes; barrelroot—

Barrelroot! Kayli hurriedly fetched the digging stick she had brought and used it to pry up chunks of the hard-packed soil. At last she unearthed the long, fleshy taproot and carefully worked it loose. By the time she heard Randon stirring in the shelter near sunset, she had located and dug up a dozen such roots.

"What are you doing?" he asked sleepily, crawling out of the shelter. "I thought you said we should sleep until dark."

"Water was more important." Kayli handed him one of the roots. "This can be peeled and eaten. It has some use as food, but its primary value is the quantity of water it stores. With these, we can make our free water last much longer."

Randon took the root, peeled it thoughtfully with his belt knife, and bit into it. He grimaced, but chewed and swallowed nevertheless.

"Tastes like soap," he complained. "Never mind, I've eaten worse. Congratulations, by the way. I didn't know that foraging was among your skills."

Kayli had to smile a little at the compliment.

"A knowledge of useful plants for food and the simplest medicine is one of the thirty-nine arts required of an accomplished Bregondish woman," she said, touching her braids. "Although medicinal plants are not my area of greatest knowledge, still I can find enough roots and young plants to at least supplement whatever game we can catch."

Randon smiled and shrugged eloquently, gesturing at the plains stretching all around them.

"What now?"

"Now we strike camp and walk while it is cool," Kayli said with a sigh.

Kayli would have taken part of the load, but Randon simply tied their belongings into two bundles and suspended them from the ends of the tent poles.

"I've had more sleep, and you're pregnant," he said firmly. "I'm relying on you to get me through this. I'm going to be in bad shape if you collapse and leave me to find the way. There isn't all that much to carry, anyway."

They chewed the barrelroot as they walked, and when that was finished, Kayli insisted that they might as well eat the roasted boar from the pack.

"It will soon spoil in the heat," she told Randon. "And especially here, where there is so little settlement, game is plentiful enough."

The half-moon rose obligingly to light their way, and despite the anxiety of their situation, Kayli could not keep from wondering once more at the beauty of her homeland. Moonlight silvered the waving grasses, and the wind made them whisper softly. The air cooled swiftly, and she and Randon were doubly grateful for the stout, warm fur cloaks.

"It looks like the sea," Randon said as they walked. "The grass makes waves. Even the sound is something like the waves coming in over the sandy beaches."

Kayli found that thought ironic, that arid Bregond should seem similar to the mythical sea which had so awed Kairi (Kairi! Did she dare hope Kairi was alive? Perhaps, for there was no other explanation for the rainstorm which had saved her life and Randon's. But best not think of that now—). But she supposed that to Randon, born and raised in the wetlands, Bregond must be as strange and incomprehensible to him as the sea was to her.

Near midnight they reached their first water hole, and although Kayli herself could not stifle a hopeful pang at the first sight of the small water-filled depression breaking the smooth rippling of the grass, Randon did not need her to tell him that they would not be filling their wine bottle with water here. The water was rank and scummed, and a few contorted animal skeletons on the banks announced plainly that this pool carried a death that might be certain, but not necessarily swift.

More encouraging was the trail that ran past the water hole. Although this pool was not used, and the herds would be detoured around the area to keep them from drinking the deadly waters, this trail would surely join the main road.

"How far is it to the next water hole?" Randon asked softly as they stood on the banks of the blighted pool. "Can we make it, with those roots you found?"

Kayli hesitated before answering.

"I do not know how far the next water hole is," she admitted. "But I do know that we have a decision to make. We could follow the trail north or south, and surely it will join the main road. Traveling on the trail will be easier than pushing our way through the grasses. North would be the best choice, as it would lead most directly to Olhavar, and we would be most likely to encounter folk on the road.

"But this trail may parallel the main road for some time," Kayli continued. "And by the time we rejoin it, we may have already passed the nearest water hole. Barrelroot will be more scarce along the road, because travelers use it."

Randon sighed resignedly.

"I suppose our best hope is west again, then, across country," he said. "Are you certain you won't get lost this way? It's not like there are many landmarks to go by."

Kayli stared at him blankly.

"The moon and the stars are the moon and the stars, in Bregond or Agrond," she said simply. "And here there are no clouds to obscure my view."

"I suppose navigation by the moon and stars is another of your thirty-nine arts." Randon chuckled. "I'd like to hear the whole list—"

"Hunting, trapping, riding, foraging, leathercraft—" Kayli began.

"—someday," Randon said quickly. "Right now I expect we'd better press on while we can."

By the time the first pink rays of the sun tinted the eastern horizon, Kayli was almost stumbling with weariness, and Randon, despite his rest, fared no better. They barely had strength to set up their lean-to before collapsing limply in its shade, and although Kayli thought briefly that it would be wise to set a watch, that thought barely flashed through her mind before she joined Randon in exhausted sleep.

She awakened in the late afternoon, aching and uncomfortably warm. Wearily she pushed herself up and crawled out of the lean-to to dig barrelroots for the night's travels. Kayli realized how soft she'd lived since she'd gone to Agrond; her muscles were stiff and aching, and even after a whole day's rest she felt tired. Unhappily she realized that there was nothing left to eat but a little dried fruit and a small piece of meat that was beginning to smell gamy. They would certainly have to stop earlier this time to forage and try to snare and smoke some small game, hopefully enough to last them for several days' travel.

Kayli took a certain guilty comfort in seeing that Randon, when he rose, moved as stiffly as she, but he made no complaint when she suggested that they eat their small store of food as they walked. They were both so sore and irritable that at first they walked in silence, but after some time Randon spoke.

"Kayli—you've said that we were heading for Olhavar," Randon said at last, very slowly. "But have you thought about why? Do you think your father will be—will have made it back there by now?"

"My father is dead." The words were out of Kayli's mouth before she admitted in her heart that they were true. Every time the thought had started to form in her mind, she had resolutely pushed it aside. She could hardly bear to remember her mother's torn and blackened body on the ground, and Melia, Kirsa—even now it seemed unreal, a terrible dream to vanish on waking.

But it did not vanish; like that same dream, the vision came back to haunt her again and again.

"My father is dead," Kayli repeated. "He would not have left my mother, nor Melia and Kirsa, to die. No. Either the Sarkondish killed him and bore his body away for"—her mind rebelled at the thought of what desecrations the Sarkondish might perform on her father's corpse—". . . for purposes of their own, or they captured him, and he is dead by his own hand."

Randon glanced at her rather warily.

"Are you so certain of that?" he asked. "Remember Seba and the others."

Kayli smiled sadly but said nothing. Children might be too frightened and confused to take their own lives as duty required, but High Lord Elaasar was well mindful of the advantages Sarkond could gain from his capture. No. Death was a small price to pay for the freedom and safety of his country, and a swift death at his own hand would doubtless spare him terrible torments later. In a way it was comforting to know that her father had died quickly and cleanly.

"What about the priest and your sister Kairi, and the other one, Danine?" Randon asked after another moment's thought.

"I dare to hope that Kairi lives," Kayli said cautiously, as if her words would break some mystical shell of safety around her sister. "The rainstorm that saved us could only have been her doing; Brother Santee was not a water-Dedicate. If Brother Santee lived, his first duty would be to save Kairi, as Heir. If Danine was with them, she, too, may be alive. And that is one reason why I travel toward Olhavar, for if Kairi lives, she will be bound for the castle to assume her duties there." She shook her head. "But first I would make a visit to my Order."

"Your Order?" Randon gave her a surprised glance. "Kayli, we hardly have time for visiting."

"My Order is the one place in Bregond where I can be sure of our safety and our welcome," Kayli said quietly. "Even if Kairi is—is not at the castle, even if every single citizen of Bregond rebelled against the alliance and would turn their hand against us, at the Order we would find sanctuary. When I have learned from High Priestess Brisi all that has happened in Bregond since I left, and perhaps what has transpired at the capital since the raiders attacked, then I will better know what we should do next. And if it would be—unwise—to return to Olhavar, the High Priestess can Gate us back to Agrond."

"There's sense in what you say," Randon admitted. "All right, then, I'll trust to your judgment."

The mere thought of returning to the Order, however briefly, awoke a pang of longing in Kayli's breast. There she would find the dearest friends she had ever known, people she could trust without hesitation. There would be help for her, Brisi's sage counsel to help her regain her lost confidence in her magic, and help for Randon's sensitivity, too, surely. And at the temple she could properly mourn her family and send their spirits on with her prayers.

Those thoughts lightened Kayli's feet, and as her muscles gradually warmed to the long hours of walking, her heart lightened somewhat, too.

Shortly after midnight they emerged from the grass onto a true road, or a least a well-worn and heavily rutted track. Moreover, tracks and fresh droppings indicated that a caravan had passed in the not-too-distant past, a caravan which Kayli and Randon might reach if they kept their pace throughout the night.

"But what if we do catch up with the caravan?" Randon asked practically. "What kind of a welcome can I expect here?"

"A very poor one," Kayli admitted. "But I will think of some story by that time. And I dare not tell my identity, either, and we have nothing to trade for assistance except the cloaks. But I can think of no alternative."

"Now I'm sorry I made such a fuss about your speaking crystal," Randon said abashedly. "You said I might one day find it useful, and the Bright Ones blight me if I don't wish we had it now."

Kayli laughed, then paused, thinking.

"There may be another way," she said hesitantly. "But we must first build a fire."

"More magic?" Randon asked her, hope lighting his eyes.

"Of a sort." Kayli was somewhat dismayed at his eagerness, for she had far less faith in her skill than he. "There are rituals by which one fire-Dedicate may communicate with another through fire, but I had not progressed to those rituals. What I can do is perhaps—improvise. But you must promise to go far away while I try," she added quickly. "I cannot concentrate and protect you from my magical energies at the same time."

"Then let's try it," Randon said, nodding quickly. "After all, we have nothing to lose."

Kayli wanted to retort that she had a very great deal to lose, indeed, but she remained silent. Randon helped her to clear the ground and dig a firepit, hacking at the hard earth with her digging stick while she walked up and down the road gathering dried horse droppings to burn. When the fire was readied, Kayli knelt beside the pit and began a calming ritual to clear her mind for the effort to come.

She had hardly seen, much less studied, any of the fire communication rituals, although they were nearer her level of skill than the Rite of Renewal and far less dangerous. Still, what need had she had for those methods when she had the speaking crystal? So now she had not the slightest knowledge of the format of the proper rituals.

Just as an Initiate could dispense with the elaborate purifications and meditations of a novice's first firewalk, priests and priestesses learned in time to work their magic without detailed rituals, using their magic almost instinctively within the framework of their carefully honed control. Kayli understood the principles of magical communication, and she certainly understood the Flame; she only hoped her control was sufficient to find the meeting of the two.

By dint of careful concentration, she was able to light their small fire without scattering sparks, and that small success bolstered her confidence. Kayli gazed deeply into the flames, focusing her thoughts upon Brisi, just as she had done when she had used the speaking crystal. She built an image of the High Priestess's face in her mind, feature by feature, picturing it among the dancing flames, and when the image was complete, she sent her message through it in a single stream of tightly focused thought.

For a moment it seemed as though Kayli was shouting into a great empty void, with no knowledge if any could hear her; then her thoughts found that special twist, as if a bolt slipped smoothly into place. Brisi's countenance within the fire grew clearer, and slowly other images began to form about it, until Kayli recognized the High Priestess's own chambers.

"Kayli!" Brisi's expression flickered from amazement to relief. "Child, you have no idea how great is my joy to learn that you live! Only hours ago word reached us from an Order near the edge of the country that the High Lord's party had been killed to the last! Where are you, and how do you fare?"

"My husband and I are unharmed," Kayli said, fighting to speak and still retain control of her makeshift spell. "But we have little food and water and have no knowledge of our location, only that we are two days' walk from the border on one of the roads. Can you send help to us?''

"Send help? Oh, my student, I can do far better than that," Brisi said quickly. "I will cast a fire Gate and bring you here immediately."

"No, no, you must not do that," Kayli said quickly. "My husband Randon is—is sensitive to fire magic, but untrained. I do not know how passing through a fire Gate might affect him."

"I shall attend to that," Brisi said firmly. "It will take me some time to make preparations. Stay where you are, and in the meantime you must prepare a firepit large enough for the Gate. Any fuel will suffice, even grass, for we will sustain the fire from our side. Prepare, and wait." Brisi's image vanished abruptly from the fire.

"Well, what's next, then?" Randon asked, when Kayli had called him back to the fire and explained what had transpired.

"We wait"—Kayli sighed, picking up the digging stick—"and dig."

It was midmorning by the time they finished enlarging the firepit. When they finished, Randon suggested that Kayli rest while he kept watch; she demurred, however, insisting that she needed to keep a fire burning in the firepit and monitor it for whatever magic Brisi might bring there, and besides, she wanted Randon as far away from such magic as he would consent to go.

The sun reached its zenith when the fire in the firepit began to grow. Kayli stopped placing new fuel on the fire; these flames, she knew, drew their life from a different source. Within moments the small blaze had grown to the size of a large wagon, and the flames had taken on a silver hue, and Kayli knew that Brisi's fire Gate was complete even before the High Priestess herself stepped forth from it, her dust-pale robes and the stray ends of her white-streaked braids fluttering as if the inferno around her were a mere summer breeze.

"Kayli, my child," Brisi exclaimed, taking Kayli's hands and smiling with such warmth that for a moment Kayli was dizzy with relief. "There is no greater joy than I feel at this moment, seeing you standing safe before me, unless it will be the delight of bringing you home once more to the Order." She turned and smiled rather more formally at Randon. "And this is your Agrondish lord for whom you have dared so much."

Randon bowed with a dignity that belied his torn and smudged clothing and sunburned face.

"It's my honor to meet the mentor of whom Kayli has spoken with such affection," he said. "And for your assistance, I know that you're as wise and kind as Kayli portrayed you."

"Well! Your words are as handsome as your face, young lord," Brisi said with some amusement. "But for now I would put courtly chatter aside and see you safely within the walls of the Order before one of our folk slits your handsome throat. And for your protection, I have brought you this." She drew a vial from her pocket and handed it to Randon. "A potent sleeping draught. It should prevent you from being affected by the energies of the Gate. Drink, and when you sleep, Kayli and I will bear you across. Now, if you please. The Gate will not remain open for long."

Randon uncorked the vial and sniffed the contents, his eyes flickering to Kayli. She nodded, and after another moment of hesitation, he tipped the vial up and swallowed the contents. A moment later he swayed on his feet, and Kayli hurried to ease him to the ground when he would have fallen.

Brisi joined her at Randon's side, taking one of his arms while Kayli took the other.

"Quickly, now, child," the High Priestess said. "This Gate was hastily cast; I would not like it to collapse while we are yet within it."

Kayli steadied Randon against her side, took a calming breath, and with Brisi, stepped through the Gate.

Kayli had never passed through a Gate before—there had been no necessity, when her family home lay less than a day's ride from the Order—but whatever she might have expected, it was not the instantaneous and seamless transition from the dry plains to the great firepit of the Order's inner temple. Kayli stumbled from hard-packed dirt to coals to the flagstones of the floor without even feeling the heat of the fire, then eased Randon down to the stone floor, nearly collapsing with him, as much from relief as from a great and soul-deep weariness.

In the greatest possible sense, she was home; this temple's residents had been her family as surely as her parents and her sisters, and now they were all she had left.

"When there is time, you must tell me all that has passed," Brisi said, steadying Kayli when she swayed on her feet. "But for now I see you are exhausted. Come, I have a room prepared for you, and the novices will attend to your lord. He will sleep for some time—and from the look of you both, that is all to the good."

The hallway outside the inner temple was fairly lined with priests, priestesses, and novices, and while they kept their faces carefully impassive, the welcome Kayli could see in their eyes was the best homecoming she could have imagined.

Kayli had expected to be taken to her old novice cell, but to her surprise the High Priestess opened the door to a vacant room farther within the temple, where the priests and priestesses lived. Brisi smiled slightly at her surprise.

"You are an Initiate, child," Brisi reminded her. "And an honored guest besides. And when your lord awakens, you must have room for him, too."

That was true, and Kayli was simply too tired and drained to argue in any event. When her mentor had left her alone, she barely managed to pull off her boots before she collapsed on the pallet and slept deeply, with the relaxed abandon that only a homecoming could bring.

15

KAYLI WOKE TO A GENTLE KNOCKING AT HER door. Gone were her novice days when she rose from her bed at morning serene and refreshed; now she groaned, stretched her aching muscles, and croaked, "Come."

Second Circle Priestess Vayavara opened the door only wide enough to look in.

"High Priestess Brisi wishes to break her fast in your company," she said coldly. "Prepare yourself quickly."

"What of Randon?" Kayli asked, but it was too late; the priestess had already closed the door again.

Kayli's room might dwarf her spartan novice quarters, but the same copper pitcher of cold water sat in the same copper washbasin, a small pot of rendered-fat soap beside it. Kayli made the quickest toilet she could; her tumbled braids, stray tendrils of hair fluffing around them, would have to wait until she had the time to comb out her hair, preferably wash it, and braid it again.

A clean buff priestess's robe hung on a peg on the wall. Kayli fingered the robe uneasily; it seemed presumptuous to wear the robe when she had never formally undergone Initiation, much less ascended to the rank of priestess. But the robe was clearly placed there for her use, and the only alternative was her grass-torn and travel-stained riding clothes. Reluctantly she donned the robe and made her way to the High Priestess's quarters, knocking timidly at the door.

"Come." Brisi's room was exactly as Kayli remembered it, but she was hard put to keep her expression calm and impassive when she saw the High Priestess herself. Brisi had aged visibly since Kayli had seen her the night before, her cheeks gaunt, her eyes hollow, but with a sort of frenetic fire burning deep within them.

"Come, sit beside me and eat," Brisi said, and Kayli was somewhat reassured to hear the same calm, gentle strength that her mentor's voice had always conveyed. She quietly seated herself in the empty chair across from Brisi, waiting for the High Priestess to break bread before she reached for a cake.

"I thought Randon would be here," Kayli said at last.

"Your husband still sleeps." Brisi smiled and poured hot *cai* into Kayli's cup. "The potion I gave him was quite strong, and he appeared to need the rest. From what I hear of events in Agrond, he has been sorely tried in the last months. Be assured that he rests in comfort and safety, but I do welcome the chance to speak to you alone. Do you regret that opportunity?"

"No," Kayli admitted. In truth she wondered how she would have dared speak of her doubts in Randon's presence.

"But this," Kayli said, touching the robe. "I am not entitled to this honor."

Brisi waved a hand dismissively.

"As you could have no Awakening here within the temple, there could be no formal Initiation performed here," the High Priestess said. "But you are Awakened, and you have continued your studies as an Initiate. And any of my novices capable of performing the Rite of Renewal successfully—or nearly so—is a priestess in fact if not by formal ritual."

This time Kayli was shaken to her core.

"How did you know?" she whispered. "How did you know that I had performed the Rite of Renewal? And that—that I had not—"

Brisi smiled a little sadly and reached across the small table to pat Kayli's hand.

"You were my student for more than a decade," the High Priestess said gently. "I know that student well. When I bade you not attempt the ritual, I saw in your eyes that you would disobey. When you never called me again and I had no word of your death, I knew you had succeeded. And when I first saw you and felt the Flame burning wild through you, I knew that your success was less than perfect."

The High Priestess extended her hands, gazing into Kayli's eyes. Kayli hesitated, but after so many years trust was ingrained; she took her mentor's hands. Immediately a shock ran through her fingers and up into her arms, setting her body alight so powerfully that Kayli cried out involuntarily and snatched her hands away. Brisi nodded slowly.

"You will be overjoyed to know there is no great harm done," the High Priestess said kindly, gesturing at Kayli's cup. Kayli quickly swallowed the hot, bitter liquid, and Brisi refilled her cup. "Because you had no previous exposure to the greater fire magics, you were unprepared for the intensity of it, and you opened yourself more to the Flame than was advisable for one so inexperienced."

"That much I know," Kayli said slowly. "But still I cannot understand—"

Brisi held up her hand, silencing Kayli.

"You know the cycle of magic," she said. "The gifted are sensitized to magic to which they have an affinity, and attract such energies to themselves. In time they learn to use this energy properly, focus it outward, but if by chance they manage to manipulate those energies before they learn control, it is in a random way, dangerous to themselves and those around them.

"In absorbing the potent energies of elemental Flame," Brisi continued, "you sensitized yourself to fire in all its forms. And just as your awareness of those energies increased, so, too, you increasingly draw them to yourself, and increasingly send them outward. What you felt when you touched me was your awareness of my own fire energies and your instinctive attempt to draw them into yourself. Have you felt that sensation otherwise since the Rite of Renewal?"

Kayli felt the blood rush to her cheeks.

"When I first returned from the Rite of Renewal," she said. "When I first touched Randon—"

Brisi nodded sagely.

"Of course, I speculated that he might have some trace of the mage-gift. If he has any affinity to the Flame at all—"

"He does," Kayli interrupted, remembering how her small fire had danced in his hand, however briefly.

"—such exposure may have sensitized him, in turn, to *your* magic," Brisi finished. "He is, of course, completely unprotected, and just as you unconsciously draw on his fire energies, so he unconsciously draws on yours. If he does not manifest those energies, at least he will not become a danger, for if he has not managed it before now, he likely will. But you are another matter."

Brisi leaned forward.

"A fire in the forge, however hot it burns, is a useful tool," she said. "The tiniest spark flung uncontrolled into the grass is a danger beyond estimation. And you, my student, are more than a spark. You are an inferno."

"But what am I to do?" Kayli whispered. Brisi's words had confirmed her worst fears.

"The fire must be safely chained once more within the forge," Brisi said gently. "You must return to us, of course, and relearn the control to safely harness your magic. You are a danger to yourself and to everyone around you, and even to the child I can sense that you carry."

"But I cannot return here," Kayli said, trying to force the desperation from her voice. "I have responsibilities as the High Lady of Agrond." And Randon. She remembered the way he had gazed into her eyes when he had drunk Brisi's potion. In that moment Kayli had felt a great truth, that at last a bridge, however tenuous, had spanned the chasm between them. She could not leave him. And her father would never—

Kayli's heart gave a great wrench.

No. Her father could never give or refuse permission again.

"Clear your mind." Waiting only briefly for Kayli to obey, Brisi laid a shallow iron bowl filled with oil in the center of the table; almost immediately it flared alight. As soon as the flames leaped up, a picture formed among them.

Terralt, sitting on the throne of Agrond—and wearing the surcoat of Randon's house.

"Word has reached Terralt that you and your lord were

slain by Bregondish warriors," the High Priestess said. "Immediately he claimed the throne of Agrond, and no one could say him nay. Now he summons together Agrond's army to march against Bregond, to avenge the death of its High Lord and Lady, and willingly they gather to do his bidding. For it is now believed that the marriage arranged by High Lord Elaasar was only a ploy to lull Agrond and coax its High Lord to the border where he could be assassinated, leaving Agrond vulnerable to invasion."

"But my father himself was killed," Kayli protested.

"Did you see his body?" Brisi countered. "Those who fled to tell the tale, some of your lord's guards, and a young girl of Bregondish birth—"

"Seba," Kayli whispered.

"—knew only that the Agrondish camp was attacked by Bregondish warriors. Terralt was prepared for such news. He was ready to take such steps as he has taken."

Brisi was silent then, and in that silence dread settled into Kayli's heart.

"It was he who caused the raid," she said. "He allied with Sarkond to see Randon killed so he could take the throne with no blood on his own hands, and win the sympathy of Randon's supporters. He told the raiders where they could ride to avoid the troops at the border. And he had them disguise themselves as Bregondish warriors to give him excuse to break the alliance and invade Bregond."

"I cannot see his thoughts," Brisi said, dissolving the flame picture. "Only events which have already transpired."

"What of my father?" Kayli asked. "What of my sisters Kairi and Danine?"

"Your father is dead." Brisi said the words flatly. "You knew that before you asked. The fate of your sisters is hidden behind the smoke." She gazed steadily at Kayli. "You must mourn your family, child, and let them go."

"Yes." Kayli sighed. "But the throne of Bregond—Kairi was Heir—"

"You have three sisters who still live," Brisi said sternly. "One of them will assume that burden. If a raging grass fire rules the land, there is soon no land to rule."

"But what of Randon?" Kayli asked, ashamed that she had almost forgotten her husband.

Brisi smiled reassuringly.

"So you have formed some attachment for this man, only a few months after an arranged marriage which you would have refused if you could?" she said gently. "There speaks the generous heart I knew. But you know that if he returns to his home, he will certainly be killed. Nor can he stay here, exposed to our magic. But we can Gate him to another country where he can live safely, or perhaps he will choose to make his home in Bregond, where in time perhaps you can be together again."

Brisi gazed probingly into Kayli's eyes.

"But you may find that your path of service to the Flame and to Bregond lies within this temple."

Longing shook Kayli to her core. To spend her life in the temple, to become a part of that great work, to wield the Flame as a tool for the good of her country, her people—

Resolutely she pushed her mind away from that thought. The first precept even in the temple was duty.

"I cannot do as you ask," she said. "I am blood-bound to my husband, and I carry his child. My place and my duty is with them." But perhaps at least she could spend some time in the Order, regaining her discipline and control. Surely Randon could not deny her that much.

Brisi smiled.

"You have a great deal to consider," she said. "Go and meditate on what I have told you, and we will speak again soon."

Vayavara was waiting outside the door for Kayli, an unreadable expression on her face; without a word, she turned and led her down the hall. To Kayli's surprise, they did not return to Kayli's rooms, but turned to another section of the inner temple quarters. Vayavara paused outside one of the doors.

"I would have words with you," she said, rather coldly. "My quarters are warded. Will you come in?"

Kayli was surprised, but intrigued. Vayavara had been polite to her during her stay at the temple, but had made no effort to be friendly. At last she nodded and followed the priestess through the door. There was a brief, unpleasant disorientation when she stepped through the wards, but the effects passed quickly.

Vayavara's quarters were as large as the room Kayli occupied now, but to Kayli's surprise, the priestess had kept her rooms even more barren than Kayli's simple novice cell. Vayavara's pallet on the floor was empty of padding, and there was no blanket. There was no other furniture, either, not even a table for the books stacked neatly by one wall or the copper pitcher and bowl in a corner. There were two plain woven mats on the floor; Vayavara sat on one, motioning Kayli to the other.

"You have listened to Brisi's words," Vayavara said without preamble. "Do you believe all that she told you?"

Kayli paused before answering. Was this some sort of test? Vayavara's eyes were unreadable.

"Are you saying I should disbelieve what my mentor has told me?" she asked carefully.

"I am saying that you should listen both to what she tells you, and what she does not," Vayavara said flatly.

"And what has High Priestess Brisi not said?" Kayli asked.

"Ask yourself that." Vayavara smiled slowly. "Ask yourself also why your husband sleeps on, and in what state."

Kayli was on her feet before she realized she had bolted up from the mat.

"What do you mean?" she demanded. "Are you telling me that Randon is in danger? Explain yourself!"

Vayavara rolled to her feet in one fluid motion, and although her expression remained calm, her eyes flashed fire.

"You have earned no right to speak to me in that way," the priestess said coldly. "Nor to make demands of me. Wearing the robe of a priestess does not make you my equal in this temple."

Kayli took a deep breath, forcing herself to a semblance of calmness that she did not feel.

"Pardon my discourtesy," she said. "There is no excuse for my lack of respect."

Vayavara stood silently for a moment, eyeing Kayli critically. Then she turned and walked to the door.

"Follow me," she said without looking back.

Kayli wanted to seize Vayavara's shoulders and shake her until the priestess explained her hints, but she did not doubt that Vayavara could blink away any threat that she could possibly pose. The priestess would tell her exactly what she wished to tell and not one word more, and if Kayli wanted even that, she had best not provoke Vayavara.

Vayavara led her deeper into the temple; rounding a corner, Kayli found herself following the priestess down a staircase she had never seen before. The stone stairs descended to a surprising depth; at last they ended in a long stone hall with doors on both sides. Vayavara produced a key from her pocket and unlocked the nearest door, motioning to Kayli to look inside.

The room was small and almost barren. Randon lay on a plain cot, innocent of cushions or blankets, in the center of the room, with a single lit torch at each corner of the cot. Drawn on the floor around the cot was a circle of runes which glowed with a faint but steady flame. To Kayli's dismay, he wore the same torn and dirty clothes he had come in, and his face and hands were still smudged with dirt as well, his hair tangled. He lay so still that for an agonizing moment, Kayli wondered whether he actually breathed; then a single slow inhalation lifted his chest, and what seemed an eternity later, a long exhalation lowered it.

The whole sight so amazed and horrified Kayli that she would have charged into the room immediately; when she stepped forward, however, Vayavara raised one arm to bar her way.

"I do not understand," Kayli said desperately. "High Priestess Brisi told me Randon would be tended."

"He has been attended to, there is no denying it," Vayavara said with a touch of irony. "And, as Brisi said, he sleeps. Indeed, he will continue to sleep until he is awakened—or until he is beyond all waking."

This time Kayli could hardly swallow her fear and rage.

"Tell me what you wish to say," she said slowly. "Play no games with your hints and implications. I am in no position to match myself against you, as well you know."

Vayavara gazed narrowly at Kayli, then nodded slowly.

"Come back to my room," she said. "Within the wards we may speak freely."

"But Randon," Kayli protested.

"He will stay where he is, as he is," Vayavara said indifferently. "At this moment he is in no danger."

Reluctantly Kayli followed the priestess, but she carefully noted the route back to the small cell. This time she sat with less hesitation when Vayavara took her own place on the mat.

"High Priestess Brisi knew of your marriage to the Agrondish lord before any message ever reached her," Vayavara told her. "Did you never question why?"

"She said that the temples listened to rumors of important events," Kayli said slowly. "Or perhaps she foresaw it."

"You know nothing," Vayavara said contemptuously. "It was Brisi herself who suggested the marriage to High Lord Elaasar. Do you believe that the Orders are merely a training ground for young mages? Not so. Warriors are the arrows of Bregond, but we are the hand that pulls the bow. The High Lord is the mouth of Bregond, but we are the will that speaks through that mouth. Are you truly naive enough to believe otherwise?"

Kayli said nothing, too stunned to make any argument.

"Always the Orders have been a silent power," Vayavara told her. "We healed the sick, brought the rain, stopped the great grass fires, and more—but most of all, we assured our people of their safety, a sheathed sword to be drawn in time of need. The Sarkondish raids were a reminder that we would always be needed. But now, with this scheme to ally Bregond with Agrond, that sword seemed soon to be broken."

"Why do you speak of Sarkond?" Kayli asked, forcing out the words from a mouth gone suddenly dry.

"Do not be a child," Vayavara said impatiently. "Ask yourself this: What would become of the Orders if Agrond and Bregond became one?"

It took all of Kayli's self-discipline even to consider the question when her heart still gazed into that small room at the sleeping form of her husband. But Vayavara's words roused her curiosity. What would happen, indeed? With no further threat from Agrond, with Agrond's troops allied with theirs to repel Sarkondish raiders, perhaps make a decisive strike against Sarkond itself, the great battle magics of the Orders would become useless. As the borders opened and trade increased—well, what matter if the rain did not come, when grain could be purchased in abundance from Agrond? Who needed the earth magics to guide the herds to good grazing when lush pasturage lay just across the border?

And there were so few mages in Agrond, the magical strain must run thin in their blood. When Bregonds and Agronds intermarried, as surely they would, there would be fewer mages born. And each year the Orders would grow smaller and fewer.

But what if the High Lords of both countries made such an alliance, threatening the power of the Orders? How could the Orders protect themselves without at the same time showing the sword that had, until then, remained sheathed?

Kayli felt the blood drain from her face.

"Are you telling me," she said hoarsely, "that the Orders allied with Sarkond from the beginning? Caused the raids, the killing, the enslavement?"

" 'Caused' is too strong a word," Vayavara said calmly. " 'Encouraged' would be a better choice. But when your father thought to ally with Agrond, encouragement was no longer enough. Terendal had a bastard son groomed to take his place. This son disapproved of the alliance, but his ambition outgrew his disapproval. If his word to carry on his father's plans was required to secure his position, he would give it—and unfortunately he would keep it. But Terendal had a younger son, unmarried, less favored. If this son was chosen as Heir, the people would reject him, especially if he took a Bregondish wife. And when he was removed from power, the elder brother would take the throne, and all would be as it was before."

"But why take such a chance?" Kayli asked warily. "There was no certainty that Randon would be deposed."

Vayavara gave her a pitying glance.

"There was never any risk," she said. "Lord Randon could not be confirmed as High Lord unless his wife bore an heir. And a novice who trusted her mentor would never guess that the 'fertility potion' she drank would in fact prevent conception."

"You must be wrong," Kayli said, clenching her hands

hard to stop their shaking. "Why would High Priestess Brisi give me the very spell to negate such a potion?"

"She gave you the grimoires to study," Vayavara corrected, "to keep you loyal to her, and because she had plans for you to take her place in the temple. No, you would be assumed barren and set aside as Randon's wife. Terralt would use that opportunity to have Randon removed from power, and Brisi's goals would be accomplished with no open intervention.

"Unfortunately you and your lord did not oblige her," Vayavara continued. "You were gaining in popularity, both of you. It seemed possible that you might remain on the throne long enough to suspect that your failure to conceive was, in fact, no failure of yours. So additional measures were taken."

A shock ran through Kayli's body.

"You cannot mean for me to believe that my High Priestess had me poisoned," she whispered. "After what you have said, how can I believe she wished me dead?"

Vayavara laughed coldly.

"How innocent you are. I have told you that Brisi took no risks. When she can manipulate you into taking your own poisoner into your household, it is simple to arrange for that poisoner to know—and administer—the remedy. One simple move accomplished much. *Arrabia* is a Sarkondish poison, so suspicion would naturally fall upon that country or its agents. And it is a slow poison. By the time it took effect, your lord's closet supporters would seem the most likely suspects, causing a schism between him and them. The slowness of the *arrabia* would allow time for the cure to be given. And, of course, one effect of *arrabia* poisoning is lasting barrenness."

Kayli gasped as if struck. How could she not have seen it? That a Bregondish slave child should escape her master and stumble into Kayli's very path, that she should be familiar with the temples and their rituals, all the better to secure a position close to Kayli—it should have been obvious. But Seba was the very picture of an innocent victim.

And how ironic that of the maids Kayli had loved so dearly, only Seba had survived to escape the raid that—

—the raid that—

"No," Kayli whispered. "Oh, by the Flame, no."

"You begin to see," Vayavara said grimly. "You and your

lord had been confirmed rulers of Agrond. You had conceived his child. Even Terralt's supporters were warming to you. There remained only one way to avert the alliance.''

Kayli covered her eyes with her hands as if by doing so she could hide from her sight the horror of the truth. It would be simple. A short message to Sarkond would suffice. Raiders frequently captured Bregondish clothing, weapons, and horses. And raiders dressed in Bregondish garb could travel through Bregond without detection, easily eluding border patrols to complete their deadly task.

But how could Brisi be certain that Kayli would be spared? Had the High Priestess consented to sacrifice her at last? Kayli groaned and shook her head. Again, there was no risk. Brisi could fire-scry, know exactly what transpired. Kayli and Randon had assumed that the grass fire was set by the Sarkondish to finish any survivors, but why should the Sarkondish set a fire to burn into Bregond when they thought their quarry had fled into Agrond? No. Fire was Brisi's element, and if she could start it, she could stop it. That fire would ensure that no raiders would pursue the pupil she wished left alive.

''But why?'' Kayli whispered. ''Why is it so important that I live?''

In response, Vayavara only shrugged.

''You were Brisi's pupil and malleable to her will. One day she would see you placed on the throne of Bregond, where you would serve the interests of the Order. Even your child, after you conceived, served her purpose, for a child conceived by so powerful a ritual would surely be touched by the Flame, and would come to this Order to study—would come under Brisi's influence, just as you did.''

Kayli was numb now, incapable of even surprise at Vayavara's words. Two thoughts circled endlessly in her mind. *I should have known. I should have known.* And: *My father. My mother. My sisters.*

Then another thought pushed its way to the surface, almost unwelcome: *Randon.*

''Why have you told me this?'' Kayli asked slowly. ''What do you want from me?''

''I offer you two things, besides the information I have already given,'' Vayavara told her. "I will wake your lord, and I will set the two of you free of this place.''

"A Gate?'' Kayli asked.

Vayavara shook her head.

"Such powerful fire magic as a Gate I could not conceal from Brisi. I can give you horses, money, food. There will be other aid when you have left these walls.''

"And in return?'' Kayli pressed.

"You know the answer to that.'' Vayavara's eyes bored into Kayli's. "If it lies within your power, set me in Brisi's place. My skill is second only to hers in this Order.''

"Why?'' Kayli asked softly. "Why betray your High Priestess, why help me? And do not tell me it is loyalty to your country, for I do not think even you believe that.''

Vayavara's eyes narrowed.

"I was second only to Brisi,'' she said coldly. "But it was you she chose to succeed her, and that only because she could manipulate you as she could not manipulate me. You were the daughter of the High Lord, who in her scheme would one day claim great power, while I was but an *ikada* herder's child. You were to be given as a gift what I had earned many times over. Brisi is the betrayer, not me, or do you not agree?''

Kayli took a deep breath, but somehow she could not bring herself to recite, even in her mind, one of the calming rituals Brisi had taught her.

"Very well,'' she said at last. "If I find your words true, I will grant your request if I can. But answer one last question.''

"What question?'' The eagerness, almost greed, in Vayavara's eyes troubled Kayli deeply.

"The other Orders,'' Kayli said softly. "Were they together with Brisi in this?'' *Please*, she thought. *Not Endra. Not Kairi. Oh, bright Flame, spare me that at least.*

Vayavara shook her head.

"Of that I know nothing,'' she said. "Messages were sent and received, but I was not privy to them. That High Lord Terendal sickened and died so conveniently, that Brisi's agent in Agrond had so great a skill in poisons, that carries the flavor of one of the healing Orders. I believe other Orders share Brisi's goals, but she could have accomplished all with no aid. If any acted with her, I do not know it.''

The answer did not reassure Kayli, but she nodded.

"Thank you," she said. "When can you wake Randon?"

"Tonight, when the others sleep," Vayavara told her. "In the meantime go to the third meditation chamber. Tell any who ask that you will mourn your family. No one will interrupt you. Tonight I will meet you there."

The meditation chamber was just as she remembered it, a simple bare room with a woven mat and an oil lamp. Kayli knelt on the mat and lit the lamp, gazing into the small flame. How could she focus her thoughts when a thousand questions whirled in her head like a dust storm? How could she compose herself when her world had been burned to ash around her?

How could any of Vayavara's words be true? And yet there was no lie in the priestess's eyes. Every fiber of Kayli's soul wanted to deny what she had heard, yet Randon's magical sleep and his neglected state proved that Brisi had lied to her.

And what motivation did Vayavara have to lie? For if what she had said was false, Kayli had no further place in the Order, and in the natural course of time Vayavara would succeed Brisi as High Priestess anyway. She would have no need of Kayli's assistance—unless what she had said was true.

"Father, Mother, forgive me," Kayli whispered. They had sent her to Agrond to end centuries of hostility between their countries; instead, through her self-focused naïveté, she had allowed herself to become the spark that might set both countries aflame. How she had shamed her parents!

And yet when Kayli closed her eyes it was Kairi's face she saw. Was Kairi alive? And if Kairi had been a part of Brisi's plot, the Kairi that Kayli had loved so dearly, Kayli thought sickly that she would rather her sister were dead. Was this pain in her heart what Randon felt when he wondered whether Terralt had been the one to betray him?

Resolutely Kayli focused on the flame of the lamp. One by one, she visualized her concerns and let the image of the flame burn each to ash as she had been taught; then she summoned the vision of a sweet fresh breeze blowing in from the plains to waft the ashes away, leaving her mind clear and calm.

For the first time in months Kayli felt peace. There was little enough she could do at this point, but one step she *could* take—she could bring her own power back under her control.

If she could do that much, then she and Randon would have that tool—or weapon—at their disposal.

She focused on the lamp flame. She could feel it at the back of her mind, a small pleasurable tickling sensation. Carefully Kayli sent that small flame deeper inside her, letting her own spark of the Flame pull it inward. She followed the small flame deep within until she felt light ahead of her—and a scent of burning grass. The small flame darted into the greater light as if shot from a bow, and it seemed to Kayli that the bright light grew stronger as the smaller flame was absorbed.

It took Kayli a few moments for her "eyes" to adjust, even in a visualization; however, when the brilliance no longer dazzled her, she could see before her a huge fire burning white-hot, smaller flames flickering out to the sides and sparks spraying outward to light smaller fires nearby. Although the sight was alarming, Kayli was reassured. Yes, the visualization was a good one, solid and true.

Brick by brick, Kayli imagined a stone floor around the fire; immediately the small side fires died and the smell of burning grass vanished. Next she built up the wall of the forge, pressing inward on the flame and forcing it into a smaller and smaller space until the fire was confined to a good-sized firepit. Again and again the flames tried to escape their confinement, sending out tendrils of white fire and spraying sparks outward, but each time Kayli patiently confined it. Last, she filled her forge with the details that made it real to her—coal and bellows, pokers and shovels and barrels of water, tongs and hammer and brooms, until the solidity of the stones under her "feet" was as real as the memory of her forge in Agrond. As long as she periodically tended this visualization, her power would remain her servant.

Kayli emerged slowly from her meditative trance to the sound of a quiet scratching at the door. She stood slowly, stretching her muscles and groaning as her numb feet came painfully awake, and hobbled to the door, opening it just wide enough to see Vayavara standing outside.

"Follow me," the priestess said quietly. "All has been prepared."

To Kayli's amazement, the temple was dark and still and the halls were empty; it had been some time since she spent so many hours in meditation. But at least she had not spent the whole time worrying and pacing the small chamber.

Vayavara led her unerringly through the corridors despite the darkness, and Kayli wistfully recalled a time when the temple—at least the sections to which she had had access—had been as familiar to her. She followed Vayavara down the stairs they had descended before, and once again the priestess unlocked and opened the door to the room where Randon slept.

Randon lay exactly as he had before. This time Kayli stood back while Vayavara stepped into the doorway, raising her hands. The priestess recited no ritual—at the priestess's level of skill, Kayli would have been surprised if she had required any formal ritual at all—and abruptly the light of the runes winked out, although the torches burned as before. Vayavara traced a last symbol in the air with her fingertip, then stepped briskly into the room, motioning for Kayli to follow her.

Kayli knelt at Randon's side, folding his cold, still hand between her own. Her heart ached to see him so pale and motionless, the rise and fall of his chest so shallow and slow. She could barely feel his heartbeat in his wrist.

Vayavara laid her hand briefly over Randon's eyes, then removed it. Kayli was overjoyed to see him stir then, and his breathing grew deeper and more frequent, but he still did not wake. Kayli glanced worriedly at Vayavara.

"His spark has been banked for many hours," the priestess said impatiently. "You can fan it alight better than I."

Kayli stifled a flash of impatience of her own—how was she supposed to know how to deal with such magic?—but she bent to press her lips to Randon, putting all the desire she could into her kiss, at the same time flexing her new control to allow a tongue of her own Flame to flicker through her to him. Immediately a shudder went through Randon's body, and when she sat back on her heels, his eyes opened. Kayli sighed with a double relief; she had wondered whether Vayavara actually expected her to couple with Randon then and there.

Randon's eyes slowly focused on her face.

"Kayli?" he murmured groggily. "I can't—don't—what's hap—"

"Not now, Randon," Kayli said hurriedly, easing her arm

under his shoulders to help him sit up. "We are in danger, great danger. Can you walk?"

"Danger?" He shook his head and rubbed his eyes. "I can walk. I think. If it's not far." He glanced around blearily. "But isn't this—"

"Not now," Kayli insisted. "Come, let us be away from here quickly."

In the end, however, Vayavara had to loop Randon's free arm over her shoulder and help him stumble down the hall. Kayli remained silent, but she worried when Vayavara led them deeper into the cellars, not back up the way they had come. At last, however, Vayavara pressed a spot on the stone wall and a section of the stone swung silently aside, revealing a dark, narrow passage leading steeply upward.

"Here I leave you," she said, lifting Randon's arm from her shoulder. "This passage ends in the stable. Your horses are saddled and packed. I suggest," Vayavara added wryly, "that you proceed with haste."

"Thank you." Kayli bowed her head slightly in lieu of a proper bow acknowledging the priestess's rank. "I will consider all you have said, and when I know the truth of what you have told me, I will keep my word to you as best I can."

Vayavara inclined her head slightly, but said nothing. A moment later she had vanished back into the dark corridor.

Randon pulled his arm from around Kayli's neck, although his hand still clutched her shoulder and Kayli could feel him swaying slightly on his feet.

"I think I can walk now," he said. "But what's happened? We're still at the temple, aren't we? What's wrong?"

"Please, not now," Kayli said, leading him into the narrow passageway. How she could explain what she had learned, she did not know, nor what she could say if Randon disagreed with her conclusions. If she once began to doubt herself, she would never manage the courage to leave, so she must do it now before she thought about it too much.

"All right, then." Randon's voice was still so weary that it wrenched at Kayli's heart, and she realized guiltily that he had had neither food nor water since before the Gate, and she did not know if he had even truly rested in his magical sleep.

The passage ended in a wooden door; Kayli pushed on it

until it slid smoothly aside, and to her surprise they emerged inside one of the stalls. Kayli helped Randon past the drowsing horse, and once they were out of the stall, she found two horses saddled and ready. She was grateful to see that Vayavara had chosen the swiftest horses in the stable, but wondered whether that really mattered; if Brisi wanted to track or pursue them, she had means far swifter and more sure than horses.

Saddlebags already hung at the horses' sides, but Kayli took the time to inspect the contents before she helped Randon to mount. The warm cloaks her father had given her had been brushed and packed, and there was food and water, but nothing else—no tent, no sword or bow. Olhavar was, of course, only a short ride from the Order, but Kayli wondered uneasily whether they would require weapons before reaching their goal. Unfortunately there were no weapons kept at the Order except—

Except—

Kayli made certain that Randon sat steadily on his horse, then hurried to the back of the stable, feeling on the shelf for the bundle of oiled leather containing her hunting bow and arrows. There! she fastened the bundle to her saddle, carefully not wondering whether she could bring herself to fire those arrows at any Bregondish warriors who might see her and, not knowing who she was, attack what must surely appear to be spies from Agrond.

"All right," Randon said tiredly. "Let's go if we're going. But I wish you'd tell me where we're going, and why."

"As to where, there is only one place," Kayli said as they rode out of the stable. "The palace—my father's palace in Olhavar. And as to why, I will tell you as we ride."

Randon remained silent as she talked, asking no question. Kayli told him all that Vayavara had said, omitting only the priestess's speculation about High Lord Terendal's death. Vayavara's other accusations could be proved or disproved with time; any hint that High Lord Terendal had been murdered could likely never be proven now and would only anger Randon needlessly. When Kayli finished, Randon rode without speaking, apparently considering her words.

"This priestess, this Vayavara," Randon said slowly at last. "Do you believe her?"

Kayli shook her head.

"I know not what to believe," she said just as slowly. "But I dare not discount her words completely. The state in which I found you was proof in itself."

"This priestess could have arranged that, if her ambitions are as great as you say," Randon said after a moment's thought. "Why didn't you confront the High Priestess with these questions? You said she'd been your teacher for years."

A pang shot through Kayli's heart.

"For myself, I might have taken that risk," Kayli said quietly. "Even if what Vayavara said of High Priestess Brisi was true, I would be of no use to her unwilling, and I cannot believe she would ever do me harm. But you—"

"If it was true," Randon said slowly, "she might have used me to control you. Or she might have killed me—or simply let me die sleeping down there—to at least be certain the alliance fell apart."

"Oh, to the darkness with the alliance," Kayli exploded. "It is not worth the price we have paid for it already, much less the demands it makes of us now and in the future." She ruthlessly swallowed back a few bitter tears.

Randon nudged his horse forward so that he could reach out and touch Kayli's hand.

"This is the second time you've given up your Order for me," he said gently, "and this time it was by your own choice. I don't know that I've done anything to earn that kind of loyalty from you, but I swear by the Bright Ones, if we survive this, somehow I'll find a way to make you glad you chose as you did."

Kayli said nothing. There was nothing, in fact, to say. Months ago she had taken her leave of the Order; tonight she had simply made that separation irrevocable. There was no doubt in her mind that some part of her would grieve over that choice forever, just as there was no doubt that no other decision was possible. Her marriage vows and the baby growing in her belly bound her more securely than the pledges she had once made to the Order. And remembering Randon's eyes on hers as he had drunk Brisi's potion, the same potion that might have meant his death, Kayli knew that she could never regret her choice. She twisted the temple ring on her finger;

at last she quietly removed it, tucking it into her pocket.

"Kayli?" Randon pulled his horse to a stop; Kayli reined in beside him. "What's that?"

Starlight sparkled on a shining surface, and Kayli squinted at it puzzledly. Was it metal, polished brightly?

"By the Bright Ones," Randon said softly. "A pond, here?"

Kayli stared at the shining surface, then glanced around in confusion. The grass was dry and brittle as always in the summertime; the earth was hard and cracked. But there was no denying that the starlight reflected off of water. It rippled slightly in the night breeze.

Kayli slid from the saddle and walked slowly toward the strange sight. It was no illusion; now that she stepped closer, she could smell the moisture in the air. Unbelievingly she fell to her knees; her fingers plunged into coolness.

"How could this be here?" Randon murmured, kneeling beside her. "I could swear there hasn't been a drop of rain fall here in—" He reached behind him, broke off a dry stalk of grass. "Well, in a long time."

Suddenly the cool water pulled away from Kayli's fingers. She could do nothing but kneel where she was and watch as the water impossibly drew itself up into a rippling, shimmering ball. She heard Randon's gasp, but quietly, as if from a great distance; at that moment she could only stare at the unbelievable sight before her. The shimmering ball flexed and stretched, flattening and drawing itself out until it once more formed a shining disk, but this time hanging in the air before them like a great shimmering mirror.

"What is it?" Randon asked softly, reaching his hand out but not quite touching the water's surface.

"A Gate," Kayli said just as quietly. "A water Gate." And her heart sang, even as she shivered with dread, for she knew with absolute certainty who had cast it.

Kayli glanced at Randon; he gazed back just as soberly. Then he smiled.

"I'll get the bags and unsaddle the horses," he said. "We'll have to leave them."

Kayli laughed a little shakily.

"We have hardly ridden half a league," she said. "They

will soon find their way back to the Order. Thank you, Randon.''

Randon said nothing, only gave Kayli a weary grin, slung the saddlebags over his shoulder, and held out his hand. She forced a smile in return, clasped his hand firmly, took a deep breath to still her own shaking, and, with Randon, stepped forward.

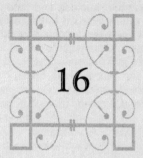

16

"**O**PEN YOUR EYES," A FAMILIAR VOICE SAID with a little chuckle. "Or would you stand there all night with that terrible grimace on your face?"

Kayli squeezed Randon's hand tightly a moment longer, then opened her eyes. There was no disorientation; as when she had stepped into the temple, she had an immediate sense of place. She stood in the cellar of the palace, only a step from the edge of the palace well, which, contrary to custom, was lidless. Kayli hurriedly stepped back, then yelped in startlement. The stones of the floor were wet and slick, although to her surprise, her skin and clothes were dry.

"I trust you will pardon the surroundings," Kairi said wryly, stepping forward to take Kayli's arm to steady her. "This meeting required secrecy, and there are few places outside my Order where I could muster enough water for a Gate."

"But the pool," Kayli said hesitantly. "How did you manage that?"

Kairi shrugged.

"There is always water deep within the earth," she said. "The trouble is finding it, and bringing it to the surface. That, of course, is why priests and priestesses of the water Orders are so needed throughout Bregond. To bring the water forth alone from such a depth was more difficult than—'' Kairi shook her head. "But I am near to boasting. Come, I have ordered all the servants to their rooms. You need food and drink and"—she glanced at Randon—"washing."

"But how did you find us?" Kayli pressed, even as she followed her sister from the room. "It was you, was it not, who brought the rain that stopped the grass fire and saved us?"

Kairi glanced at Kayli and raised her eyebrows slightly.

"You give me too much credit, sister," she said gently. "For a time I believed you dead. Yes, I brought the rain back across the border from Agrond so that a great grass fire would not sweep through Bregond—and to gain water enough for a Gate to bring myself and Danine home."

"Then Danine is safe?" Kayli asked eagerly.

Kairi nodded.

"She sleeps in her room," she said. "Brother Santee also escaped with us, but he has returned to his Order. I told no one what I would do tonight."

"But then if you thought we were dead," Randon said before Kayli could speak, "Why did you go to so much effort to have that water Gate ready, and right on the path we were traveling?"

Kairi gave them both a patient glance.

"I was called through my speaking stone," she said, "by a priestess of Kayli's Order. When she told me you were leaving the Order tonight, and why, I knew you would come here, and that was the most direct road to Olhavar. When Kayli approached my Gate, I felt her presence. We are, after all, sisters."

To Kayli's consternation, Kairi led them to another cellar room instead of up the stairs. The room had been hastily cleared, and a small table held a cold supper, a lamp, a steaming pot of *cai,* and a pitcher of water.

"There are few hours left before dawn," Kairi said, "but there is time to refresh yourselves before you must go."

Kayli was still, the tart she had lifted frozen halfway to her mouth.

"Go?" she said quietly. "Go where? What do you mean, Kairi?"

"Back to Agrond, of course," Kairi said calmly, meeting

Kayli's eyes squarely. "I cannot have you here, sister."

Very slowly, Kayli laid the tart back down; beside her, she could feel Randon touch the hilt of his dagger. Under the edge of the table, she laid her hand over his.

"Oh, Kairi," she said softly, "please tell me you are not—"

"Involved in the games of the High Priestess of your Order?" Kairi said grimly. "Your priestess told me all."

"Forgive my rudeness," Randon interrupted, "but at this point, I don't think Kayli's suspicions should be held against her. We've got the safety of two countries to consider."

"And so have I." Kairi shook her head. "Kayli, I cannot cast a truth spell. Can you?"

Kayli shook her head numbly.

"Then believe me or not when I tell you that, while I—and my Order—do not agree with the alliance between Agrond and Bregond," Kairi said deliberately, "our disagreement does not extend to treason and fomenting a war. And now, Kayli, I must ask the same question of you."

"Me?" Shock momentarily robbed Kayli of all emotion. "Kairi, how could you believe that *I* might be involved?"

"You stand to gain greatly by Brisi's plan," Kairi said levelly. "You would be rid of a marriage you never desired. You would gain leadership of your Order, an ambition I know you treasured. And you would gain the throne of Bregond as well. I, however, have no such rewards to anticipate, and in any wise, our father had already declared me Heir when he was killed."

"But the High Lord and Lady could have changed their minds if they learned you didn't agree with the alliance," Randon said. "If you thought they might choose someone else later, it might suit your plans very well to have them killed."

Kairi whirled suddenly, grasping Kayli's wrist.

"Fire meets water, sister," Kairi whispered. "But we are not evenly met, one to quench the other. Feel my power and know it."

And Kayli could indeed feel that power, pulsing below Kairi's skin. Water was not an ephemeral element like the Flame; Kairi's magic was swift rushing but strong and steady, cool and deep and enveloping, and Kayli wrenched her arm free desperately before she could drown in all that magic.

"You see?" Kairi said quietly. "You are young in your magic and unskilled. You could not match me and you know it. If all was as your lord said, it would suit me best that you and he die, and your heir with you. If so, you would never have stepped through that Gate alive. Nor would I send you back to Agrond to reclaim what is yours."

"Why *are* you so eager?" Randon interjected. "Surely Terralt's force can't march against Bregond so soon."

"Terralt's force will never march against Bregond," Kairi said grimly. "Look." She snatched the pitcher from the table and poured the water out onto the floor before them. The surface of the water shimmered, then cleared, and Kayli cried out involuntarily at what she saw there—Sarkondish warriors, hundreds, perhaps thousands of them, raising their swords in the cold predawn light.

"Your High Priestess never planned this, yet she should have foreseen it," Kairi said. "The High Lord and Lady of Bregond lie dead, and to the belief of the assassins, so also do the High Lord and Lady of Agrond, burned in the grass fire. In their thoughts, both countries are without leadership, ripe for the taking. Even now Sarkond prepares its forces to cross the border north of Polonwila, where their great army will divide. And I cannot hope to have our military at the border in time." She gazed levelly at Randon and Kayli. "You can. But only if Terralt's troops march north toward Sarkond instead of west toward us. Do you understand now?"

"Wait a moment," Randon interrupted. "*I* don't understand. How could they think we're dead? Surely Stevann must have scried out what happened to us."

"Either he attempted to learn your fate while you were at the Order," Kairi said patiently, "where the wards would not reveal your presence, or he has allied with your enemies. In either event, he did not reveal your survival."

"I want to believe you," Kayli said softly to Kairi. "But if what you say is true, why the secrecy in bringing us here? Your best defense against Brisi's plan is to show us, your greatest proof, to all."

Kairi shook her head.

"Kayli, now more than ever, our people must not lose their

faith in the Orders," she said softly. "They have lost their High Lord and Lady. If the Orders fall under suspicion, how can they accept a priestess as their ruler? And there is yet another reason."

"What reason?" Kayli asked.

"You have no place here." Kairi's voice was gentle, but her expression remained unyielding. "You are part of Agrond now, and at this moment Agrond is our enemy, although soon it may be our ally. Dissidents would see you and your lord killed, or held hostage against Terralt. At the best you would only undermine my efforts and confuse those who must now obey me without question. As long as you are here you will be used—by High Priestess Brisi, or by others. So you must go, sister, and I pray that when we meet again, it will be in peace."

Kayli turned away from the table, too sick at heart to eat or drink. Kairi was right, of course, but it was a truth that hurt worse than the firebrands Kayli had tried and failed to hold in her temple training. She had thought she had nothing left to lose, but she had lost Kairi, too, for now they could never again be sisters as they had before; now they were rulers of countries on the brink of war, and that knowledge stood between them far more completely than the leagues of land from Olhavar to Tarkesh ever had.

"Yes," Kayli said quietly. "I understand. But I made a promise, Kairi, that Brisi would be removed from power and Vayavara set in her place. I ask that you, as High Lady of Bregond, honor that promise. Vayavara is ambitious, but I do not believe that her ambitions reach beyond the temple."

Kairi nodded with a formality that wrenched at Kayli's heart.

"I will do as you say," she said. "And in return I ask this: that you say nothing further of any plot by the Orders. This matter is mine to deal with, and deal with it I shall, but as long as Bregond needs the Orders, they must not fall."

"Very well," Kayli said, although the promise troubled her deeply.

She turned to Randon.

"We must hurry, then, back to Tarkesh while Terralt is still gathering his troops," she said. "But riding back would take many days, and there may still be Sarkondish raiders near the border.'' She glanced at Kairi. ''Can you create another Gate?''

Kairi nodded.

''It is difficult to create another Gate so soon after the first,'' she said, ''but necessity requires it. Unless you can create your own Gate?'' she added hopefully.

Kayli laughed a little bitterly.

''I have had little time to study my magic,'' she said, at the same time rather ashamed of herself. There would have been opportunity, had she not run from her own power like the rankest novice. ''The creation of a Gate is beyond my present skill. And I know of no fire in Agrond large enough for the far end of our Gate, in any event, while Agrond suffers no lack of water for yours. Perhaps you could use the castle well, as you did here.''

''That's no good,'' Randon said quickly. ''Here, she could uncover the well. The well in our castle's certainly covered, and I have no way to tell anybody to open it.''

Kayli thought of being trapped in the darkness in the well, trying to stay afloat—until the time came that she would slide under the surface, and the water would fill her mouth and nose and—she shivered violently. It had been hard enough to step through the water Gate the first time.

''I know a place,'' Randon said suddenly. He touched Kayli's arm. ''The pool in the forest, remember? From there we can walk along the north side of the Coridowyn; that area's never patrolled. Then we can swim across near the castle. I know a way we can get inside undetected.''

Kayli would have protested—the notion of Gating into that deep pool, *then* swimming a river, was almost unbearable—but Kairi nodded briskly as if that settled the matter.

''Very well, then,'' she said, gesturing at the puddle of water on the floor. ''Gaze into that water and picture the place where you wish the Gate to emerge. See it in your mind, and in the water, that I may see it with you.''

Randon obediently turned to the puddle, staring into the water. Kayli saw nothing, but apparently Randon's efforts were successful, for Kairi nodded again.

"A good choice," she said. "Come, we will fetch your belongings and I will begin."

No more, Kayli thought desperately. *Please, no more.* It seemed an eternity since she had slept, and she was so tired. But one look at Randon's dark-ringed eyes and pale cheeks and she was heartily ashamed of herself. If she was tired, he must be near collapse. And yet he went on, undaunted. Kayli swallowed her complaint and followed Kairi back to the well. Randon slung the saddlebags over his shoulder and leaned against the wall to watch.

"My energies are waning," Kairi warned Kayli. "When I open the Gate, I cannot keep it long. So we must make our good-byes now."

Kayli hesitated, gazing into Kairi's eyes and seeing a deep sadness that mirrored her own. Kayli swallowed a sob and embraced her sister quickly. She would have given much to see Danine one last time, but—she stepped back to join Randon, and her eyes were dry.

"Proceed," she said quietly. "We are ready."

Kairi gave her a small, understanding smile and nodded, raising her hands and beginning a chant. Kayli could feel the same cool, smooth power she had sensed when Kairi had grasped her wrist, but now this power was gathering in the room, as flowing water might gather in a basin, swelling, pulsing, as deep and regular as the Flame was fierce and consuming and fleeting. The water in the well swelled with that same power, swirling up from its pit not in a ball as Kayli had seen before, but in a twisting spiral, flowing upward and outward until it formed a shimmering disk such as Kayli had seen before.

"Now," Kairi said breathlessly. "Go."

Randon grasped Kayli's hand, pulling her quickly forward. Kayli gave her sister one last look—*Will I ever see her again? Will she or I ever wish it so?*—and stepped through the Gate.

No smooth, effortless transition this time. Kayli emerged from air into churning water, and her scream of surprise became a breathless gurgle. Randon's hand was gone, and although she flailed desperately about, she could grasp nothing. Water flooded her mouth and nose, and she felt a sort of cold fire burn its way down into her chest, choking her, drowning her—

Something jerked the back of her tunic hard, and Kayli was dragged up through swirling foam. The world began to fade—

Then there was fresh cool air on her face, and she coughed out water, her lungs screaming protest as she desperately gasped in air. She felt blessedly solid earth under her, and she coughed and coughed again, spewing forth what felt like gallons of liquid. At last she opened her eyes and saw moonlight, and leaves, and Randon's wonderful face.

"Just lie there a moment," he said kindly. "You'll be all right in a bit." He wiped her mouth with his wet sleeve.

"The—the pool?" Kayli asked hoarsely.

Randon chuckled.

"Your sister isn't as good as she thinks she is," he said wryly. "We came out of the Gate right under the waterfall. You're lucky I found you at all with the currents there. Come on. If you sit up, you'll breathe easier."

Randon would have allowed her time to rest, but Kayli staggered to her feet as soon as she could. She thought to herself that the sooner she got away from all that water, the better.

When they emerged from the woods, the sky to the east was paling, and Randon hurried her across the open fields down to the river.

"There," he said relievedly, pointing, and Kayli saw the castle wall through in the dim light. "There it is."

"Where can we cross?" she asked calmly, although she wanted to weep. The Coridowyn seemed a league across to her untrained eyes. *At least,* she thought with a sort of desperate amusement, *we did not have to swim the Dezarin.*

Randon scratched his head.

"The current here is pretty strong," he said hesitantly. "I think we'd better just get into the water here and let the river carry us downstream to the castle." He glanced around, pointing to a fallen tree that lay mostly in the water. "There. We'll use that log and just float across. Trust me, it's much easier than swimming. Lucky the floods left so much deadfall."

Kayli hoped desperately that he was right; it took almost all her strength to help him push the log from the sand bar it had caught on, and she could only cling desperately to the trunk of the tree while Randon pushed it out deeper. She could not stifle a yelp of dismay, however, when the log came wholly free, floating down the river at an alarming rate.

"It's all right," Randon said, panting as he gripped the tree trunk beside her. "Just look at the other shore and kick your feet. Don't worry; the log will hold you up."

Kayli tried to obey, but when she saw the bank of the river fading behind her, she merely closed her eyes tightly and kicked, and kicked, and kicked.

I am back in the pond, she thought desperately. *Just a little farther, and I will be at the other bank. Just a little farther—*

The log jolted under her, and Randon gave a grunt of satisfaction.

"There," he said. "Let go, and hurry, before the current carries you off with the log."

That thought was enough to make Kayli open her eyes, hurriedly seize Randon's shoulder, and slog out of the water as quickly as her shaky legs would carry her. She stumbled in the mud and fell, wanting to kiss the ground as she crawled forward as fast as she could. Laughing, Randon helped her up.

"All right, all right," he said, pulling her into his arms. "No more swimming for a while."

"No more swimming ever," Kayli panted. "Never, ever, *ever,* do you understand?"

"All right," Randon murmured into her hair. "No more swimming *ever.* Come on. Let's go home."

Strangely, with river water dripping from her hair and the castle wall before her, Kayli felt indeed a sense of homecoming.

Well, best that it is so, she thought tiredly. *For good or ill, this is all the home I will ever know again.* She grasped Randon's arm a little more tightly, and when he squeezed her hand reassuringly, she thought, *It will be enough.*

To Kayli's surprise, there were no guards patrolling the castle wall. When she remarked on the lack, Randon shrugged.

"I doubt if there's any civil unrest at the moment," he said wryly. "You and I were the controversy. With us gone, Terralt's reassigned them somewhere. Never mind, it works in our favor tonight. I don't want anyone seeing us until I'm sure they're loyal to me. Come on, I'll show you the family secret.''

They worked their way around the wall, Randon alternately squinting at the stones in spots and glancing worriedly up at the lightening sky.

''I haven't used this entrance in ages,'' he muttered. ''I used to use it to sneak out when I should have been studying.'' He grinned at Kayli. ''I used to meet—ah—friends outside the wall.''

''Lady friends,'' Kayli corrected, grinning back.

''Lady friends,'' he admitted. ''Ah! Here it is.'' A small section of the wall swung inward, and Randon urged Kayli into a dusty tunnel even smaller than the passageway in the temple. Kayli found a piece of dry wood and set it alight for a makeshift torch, stooping almost double to follow Randon inside. The small passage emerged in one of the cellar storerooms.

''Well, here we are,'' Randon said, sighing with satisfaction. ''Bright Ones, what I wouldn't give to fall into bed and sleep for a week. Never mind, we'll find Terralt and settle all this, and with any luck we can manage a few hours of sleep before my advisers descend on us like a swarm of bees.''

Randon reached the door and tried it; frowning, he tried it again.

''Locked!'' he said impatiently. ''Locked outside. But why? We never kept valuables in here.''

''Is there another way out?'' Kayli suggested. ''Another secret passage, perhaps?''

Randon shook his head.

''Only back the way we came and around the wall to the front,'' he said. ''And I don't want to do that unless we have to. Have you ever picked a lock?''

''Like a thief?'' Kayli said indignantly. ''Certainly not!''

''Neither have I, but it's that or break the door down, and I know we can't do that,'' Randon said resignedly. ''This door is two thick layers of wood with iron in between, to cover the family's escape if we needed to use the tunnel. Well, let's give the lock a try.''

With Kayli holding the torch, Randon tried the tip of his

knife blade first, and when that proved too large, took one of the pins from her bedraggled knot of hair and tried that; after patient effort, however, he admitted defeat.

"Well, there's nothing for it," he said. "We'll have to go back around. Unless you can burn through the door," he said with sudden hope.

Kayli shook her head.

"Not without great danger," she said gently. "To burn through such thick aged wood, with iron between, would mean a fire so great that you might lose a castle so that we could walk through a door."

"All right, then." Randon sighed. "We'll just go—"

The sudden scrape of a key in the door lock interrupted him. Kayli froze, her gaze meeting his. There was no time to seek a hiding place among the casks and crates, but she grasped the hilt of her *thari* firmly in one hand, the torch in the other, and she and Randon flattened themselves against the wall on either side of the door.

The door opened slowly inward, and the thick wood blocked Kayli's view even as it concealed her; she held her breath and listened for Randon's attack. To her amazement, however, after the first bootstep, she heard a low, bitter chuckle and a familiar voice.

"Well, brother," Terralt said, closing the door behind him and holding up a lamp, "I wish I could say I was wholly surprised. But with the way my luck turns, it could have been nobody but you anyway. No, no!" He held up his hand as Randon stepped toward the door. "Stay where you are. I have half a dozen guards outside, all outland mercenaries with no loyalty but to the coins I'm paying them, who will gladly rush in on my word and tie the two of you if necessary." He turned to Kayli and bowed. "My lady. Somehow it seems that every third or fourth time I see you, you're in a draggled and exhausted state. Still, I'm delighted to see you both alive."

"Terralt, there's no time for these games," Randon said impatiently. "Now let us out of here, or we'll go back out the tunnel and—"

"And run into the rest of my mercenaries at the exit," Terralt said calmly. "I've had a guard on watch outside this door ever since I got word you'd been killed, and as soon as he heard noise in this room, he put the other guards in place and sent for me. I knew it could only be you, Randon. But you're not getting out of here until I figure out exactly what it is you've done—and what I'm going to do about it.''

"Listen to me," Randon said impatiently. "There's an army heading for the border—"

"Oh, I know that," Terralt said carelessly. "But when they try to cross the border, they'll find we're soon ready for them. I've been sending troops west ever since you left. We've got eight garrisons now on the border, just waiting for the first attack, and there's a steady flow of soldiers moving west, too, to join those garrisons. I think we can deal with any advance force Bregond could have mustered by this time."

"You fool," Randon exploded. "It's not *Bregond* that's attacking! How, without a High Lord and Lady to gather the troops?"

Terralt raised an eyebrow, but only said mildly, "The guards that searched the camps didn't find the High Lord's body. Nor yours, of course. But you'd have me believe it's Sarkond that's poised at our borders? How, then, do you explain Bregondish warriors attacking your camp?"

"They were not," Kayli said, stepping forward. "Bregondish warriors would not have slain their High Lord and Lady, no matter how they disagreed with their rulers' policies, nor would they have slaughtered the royal family down to the merest child, when killing the enemy rulers would have sufficed to assure their goals. Nor would any Bregondish warrior have believed that a simple grass fire could kill an Initiate of the Order of Inner Flame—nor, in fact, would *Bregondish* warriors set fire to the very land across which they must ride! But Sarkondish warriors riding Bregondish horses and dressed in Bregondish clothing might well do such things."

Terralt's eyes narrowed thoughtfully, but he said, "I can see how such a ploy might fool Randon's guards, but what about a girl born in Bregond? She swore the raiders were Bregonds."

Kayli closed her eyes briefly. The thought was still a sharp pain in her heart.

"Seba was no slave," she said quietly. "She was a spy sent to stop the alliance between our countries in whatever manner she could. The heads of the guilds did not poison me at dinner; I was poisoned before dinner, with the *arrabia* in the wine Seba brought me.''

"But she's the one who brought you the antidote," Terralt said slowly.

Kayli nodded.

"I cannot tell you who was behind that poisoning," Kayli told him reluctantly, "but they wanted the alliance dissolved to preserve their power, and they wished me returned to Bregond, not dead. *Arrabia* is a slow poison, and it has the added advantage of leaving its victims barren for some time afterward." She shrugged. "Have Seba questioned under truth spell and she will confirm what I tell you."

"I can't do that." Terralt shrugged. "She vanished almost as soon as she'd told me her story and the guards had confirmed it. Ridden back to Bregond, I thought. Besides, I can't have a truth spell cast at all. When word came that you were dead, and I took the seat of Agrond, Stevann gave up his post at the castle and left. Said he couldn't in good conscience serve under me."

Terralt was silent for a long moment. At last he shook his head.

"I can see you've put a lot of thought into this story," he said. "And when I have time, I'll listen to the rest and try to sort out what might actually be true. But for now, whether it was all or part of Bregond responsible for the attack at the border doesn't really matter."

He turned to Randon.

"I'd be lying to you if I said I was glad to see you, little brother," he said wryly. "At the same time, while we both know I'm the one who more than earned the throne of Agrond, we also both know that gaining it by assassinating you isn't to my taste. And it wouldn't do much for my popularity, either. So I'm willing to give you a choice.

"In two days my advance force is marching into Bregond," Terralt said. "By the time they engage Bregondish troops, the second wave of soldiers should have arrived. When the Bregondish army has fallen, I'll have it told about that my troops found the two of you, captured but alive, and brought you safely back home. You'll have your throne back, little brother, and two countries to rule from it."

"You know I can't agree to that," Randon said, his face flushing darkly. "I signed that alliance with High Lord Elaasar, and I know he's done nothing to break his word."

"Then you have another choice," Terralt said, turning the wick of his lamp up slightly so he could see Randon more clearly. "You leave Agrond and take another name. I don't care where you go as long as you swear you'll never return. With you dead, at least as far as the people are concerned, I marry Kayli. There's nothing I couldn't do with a wife like that at my side. In return, I'll pull back my army or send it against Sarkond, whatever she wants. It'll be years before Bregond chooses a leader and works its way back up to being a threat again anyway." He grinned at Randon. "Well, little brother? What do you say? You'll keep your word, protect your precious alliance, and you'll lose the onerous responsibility of ruling Agrond, all in one blow."

To Kayli's consternation, Randon actually looked as if he was considering Terralt's offer. Of course, she realized, Terralt had no idea that Kairi had survived, or that she had already taken the throne of Bregond and begun to gather an army of her own. Randon was only buying time while he thought.

"There is a third choice," Kayli said coolly. "We kill you and your mercenaries and walk up those stairs to reclaim our thrones."

Terralt grinned.

"By the time either of you draws a dagger, I could have six guards in here," he said. "And I don't see any other weapons."

Kayli held out one hand; fire leaped into life in her palm.

"My weapons are seen only when I wish it," she said. "Before you open your mouth to call your guards, I could burn you to ash. By the time your guards drew their swords, their ashes would join yours. Believe that this is true, for it would grieve me greatly to prove it."

Terralt's slightly mocking grin never faltered.

"You expect me to believe you'd stand there and kill me when I haven't so much as drawn a dagger?" he taunted.

"I expect you to believe that I will never again be bartered like a horse or a wagonload of grain," Kayli said icily. "You have no power to release Randon from the oath he swore as High Lord of Agrond, or me from my marriage vows, and before we break those oaths, yes, I would take your life. It would be the first human life I have ever taken, and it would weigh heavily on my soul, but by the Flame I swear I will do it if I must."

"Then it appears we have a stalemate," Terralt said, not moving. "If none of us will yield, then at least one of us is going to die here."

"It need not be so," Kayli said levelly. "Give me a chance to prove what Randon and I have told you, and you will quickly see that it is not Bregond who is your enemy. I ask— no, I beg that you will give me this opportunity before kinfolk spill each other's blood. You lose nothing by doing so."

Terralt stood there silently for a long moment, so long that Kayli was certain he would refuse, but at last he nodded slowly.

"All right," he said. "Just how do you plan to prove what you say?"

"I will need my forge, and my grimoires as well," Kayli told him. "And then you can see with your own eyes."

"Kayli," Randon began hesitantly. "You promised—"

"I promised to say nothing," Kayli said gently. "I did not promise to show nothing. And when Terralt sees the truth, I believe he will use that knowledge properly." *At least I pray so,* she thought. She was playing a game of trust with Terralt more dangerous than any Randon had dared, for while she knew at least that Terralt would never take any action which would harm Agrond, she had no such assurance where Bregond was concerned.

"All right," Terralt said at last. "You've piqued my curiosity, if nothing else. But my guards will be right outside the door of the forge." He grinned. "And I believe I'll leave Randon with them, just to be certain."

Randon flashed Kayli a worried glance, and Kayli nodded reassuringly.

"All right," Randon said. "I'll stay with your guards. You'll be in more danger than I will, anyway, Terralt."

Terralt was not lying; there were, indeed, six guards outside the door, and they fell in silently behind Randon, Terralt, and Kayli. Terralt stopped at the door of the forge.

"We're going in," he told the guards. "My brother will wait out here with you."

Kayli took a deep breath as she stepped into the cool familiarity of the forge, but she felt no reassurance. A firescrying was powerful magic the like of which she had never yet attempted, and she was so tired, so drained.

Terralt closed the door behind him, then shrugged.

"Well?" he challenged. "Are you going to show me something, or merely roast me to cinders?"

"Be patient, Terralt," Kayli said wearily. "Please. You would not wish me to rush, believe me."

Her long hours of meditation at least had been of some benefit; when she focused on the torches, one after the other, and the firepit, each obediently flared alight, neatly and without excessive energy.

Kayli paged quickly through the grimoire, making no attempt to keep Terralt from looking over her shoulder (she doubted he could read the ornate Bregondish anyway) as she studied the ritual. It was a simple enough procedure; in the normal course of her study she would have mastered it soon. But it required great concentration, and Kayli wondered if her weary body and her wearier mind were capable of that kind of focus. At last she closed the book and turned to Terralt.

"Before we begin," she said quietly, "I must show you something. Something you should have known long ago." She extended her hands. "Give me your hands."

Gazing steadily at Kayli, Terralt held out his hands palm up. As Kayli took his hands, she felt that same surge flow up her arms, and she saw Terralt jump slightly. Kayli nodded.

"Watch," she said quietly, "but do not move." She brought his hands together to form a bowl shape, cupping her own hands outside of his.

The small flame jumped into life in Terralt's palms, and if not for Kayli's grasp of his hands, he would have jerked away. He breathed in sharply, then stood quietly as the small flame grew to fill the cup of his fingers. Kayli sustained the little fire for a few moments, then released her own energies, taking her hands away. The small flame burned on a little longer between Terralt's fingers, then slowly died.

"Randon was not the only one who carried the gift of magic," Kayli said softly. "That was what you felt when we touched, the waking of your own magic as it recognized mine. I am sorry it is too late to train your gift, but still you should know, lest you mistake the touch of magic for—" She hesitated. "For something else."

"I see." Terralt stood silently, staring down into his empty hands. "I see." He looked back up at Kayli. "And is that the proof you wanted to show me?"

"No." Kayli knelt beside the firepit. "I wanted you to know that you have at least a touch of the gift, because when I cast my fire-scrying, I will relinquish my vision to you."

"Vision?" Terralt squatted beside her.

"I will create and sustain the spell as long as I can," Kayli said, praying that the fire-scrying ritual could be used as she said, "but you will choose the vision. Concentrate on what you wish to know, past or present, but I am not yet powerful enough to reach into the future." She turned to Terralt. "I am trusting you with my power, that you will know I conjure no illusion to deceive you. To see the proof of our words, you need only look for it."

Turning back to the firepit, Kayli began her chant, wishing fleetingly that she could simply *do* it as Kairi had done. At least releasing the tension from her body was no effort; she was, in fact, perilously near the end of her strength. But she had dealt with hunger, thirst, and exhaustion before, and now she was grateful for the rigors of her training, the fasting, the nights when sleep was not allowed, the endless meditations.

An image began to form in the flames, and Kayli closed her eyes; if she watched, she might inadvertently direct the vision. She heard a murmur of amazement from Terralt next to her, but ignored it as best she could, sharpening her focus on the firepit not in front of her, but within her, feeding the flames steadily, building them high, yet keeping them tightly confined. The fire within and without filled her body with a restless heat, but Kayli ignored it. She did not know what Terralt saw, but from time to time she heard startled exclamations, and once the sound of Terralt's knuckles cracking as he clenched his fists hard.

Kayli sustained the vision as long as she could, but when she felt the last of her strength fade, she released it. Better to lose the spell than for it to go awry.

When she opened her eyes, Terralt had turned his back to the firepit; Kayli could see his shoulders shaking slightly. Wearily Kayli pushed herself to her feet and laid her hand on his shoulder; her energy was at such a low ebb that she felt only the slightest tingle pass between them.

"I don't know why," Terralt said dully. "I don't know why I had to watch her die again." He forced his voice to steadiness. "I suppose to remind myself that once there was something, someone, that was really mine."

"There are four such people upstairs in the nursery," Kayli said softly. "And it is their safety, their future, you must think of now."

Terralt stood where he was, shaking his head slowly. Suddenly he strode to the door, jerking it open; he dragged Randon back into the room by one arm, closing the door after him.

"All right," Terralt said, gazing steadily into Randon's eyes. "I'll make you one last offer. Take it or leave it."

"What's that?" Randon asked warily.

Terralt sighed; then he gave Randon his old mocking grin.

"The two of you go upstairs and take your thrones," he said, chuckling wearily. "And I lead the army. North."

Randon raised one eyebrow.

"Are you sure?" he said slowly.

"I'm sure." Terralt glanced at Kayli. "Very sure. I think this lady's too much for me after all. Keep her and welcome."

"All right," Randon said, clasping Terralt's hand. "I can live with that."

17

"**A**RE YOU SURE THIS IS GOING TO WORK?**"**
Randon asked for the tenth time.

For the tenth time Kayli said patiently, "I cannot know, Randon, until I try. And I cannot try until you let me concentrate."

"I thought you said it was too late for Terralt and me to learn magic," Randon said, and Kayli bit back an impatient retort.

"It *is* too late," she said slowly, "and Terralt will *not* use magic. It is only a variation of the fire-scrying spell, something like the speaking crystal you have seen. But Terralt cannot use a speaking crystal, nor can he fire-scry, and so I will be the one contacting him. It will not be difficult; I am well acquainted with the feel of his energies—"

Randon made an undefinable sound, and Kayli glanced over to see him grinning ruefully.

"Sorry," he said. "I know what you mean. Go on, and I'll be quiet. We need to know what's happening at the border."

Kayli sighed and began the painstaking task of building her scrying field one more time. She had practiced this spell variation a number of times with Randon over the past days, but she was far more comfortable with him—and, of course, he was not separated from her by leagues and leagues. She'd had little time to work with his brother, and there was Terralt's distrust of magic to overcome. Still, she reminded herself, Terralt's magical energies were far stronger than Randon's, and his ability to concentrate was better.

It was futile, she had decided, to attempt to visualize a path across Agrond to Terralt; first, she was unfamiliar with Agrond and could not easily picture it, and second, neither she nor Randon knew exactly where Terralt was now. According to the messages he had sent by messenger bird, he ranged over a large territory, directing smaller forces within the main army.

So Kayli did not attempt to visualize the path to Terralt. Instead she pictured herself in a dark room, looking all around her for the glow of a particular fire. Sparks flickered here and there all around her—those were mages, she realized, or citizens with traces of the gift—but none of them bore any resemblance to Terralt's rather hard, driving energies. She enlarged the radius of her search, stretched her awareness thinner and farther. At the very limit of her range she felt a pang of recognition, and she focused her attention on that particular spark.

There you are, Terralt thought, and Kayli cringed at the intimacy of that touch. *I admit I doubted this would work.*

"Can you maintain this focus?" Kayli asked.

I'll try. It makes my head hurt. Kayli got the distinct impression of a chuckle. *Well, Randon and I are used to these headaches. Here, I'll show you what's happening.*

Then there was nothing.

"Terralt?"

What? Can't you see?

"No." Kayli sighed with disappointment. "I have not enough contact to see through your eyes."

"What's happening?" Randon asked worriedly. Kayli raised a hand to silence him.

All right, then. I've got six companies of foot soldiers at the front, and crossbowmen behind the tree line. They've stopped sending their horse archers out since we dug spiked pits all across the front. But my soldiers can't advance a step either. They're just too good with those bows. They've got supplies arriving, too, it looks like, at intervals. Not much magic so far, but my troops are spread very thin, and we're taking heavy casualties. Ask Randon whether I shouldn't pull my western companies back.

Kayli relayed the message slowly, to make sure she repeated it correctly, and Randon shook his head.

"No. They're testing his line, looking for a weak spot," he said. "If we let any of them get around from the west, they'll attack from the rear."

I heard that, Terralt thought. *But I can't hold the men spread so thin for much longer. There's no cover to the west, and they don't want to be there, defending Bregondish territory. When can I have more troops here?*

"Not for another three days," Randon said in reply to Kayli's question. "They're moving as quickly as they can."

Can't Stevann just Gate them here, like he did me? Terralt thought, and Kayli could hear a note of desperation in his thoughts. *I tell you, we can't hold this much longer. If it weren't for the cover of the trees, they'd have beaten through before now. Even our crossbows can't get the range on those damned longbows, and they've got three men to our one. If we can't—wait. There's a message from the field.*

For a moment the contact wavered; then it vanished entirely. Kayli groped desperately for the lost thread, and at last she felt Terralt's energies again. This time it was much more difficult to reach him, and she could feel the strength draining from her like water from a punctured waterskin.

They've sighted another force approaching from the west, Terralt thought, and now his thoughts were leaden with despair. *They're all mounted and advancing fast. I can see them now. There's thousands of them. I don't think we can even pull back fast enough to—*

"Wait!" Kayli said, her heart pounding. "Are their spear tips leaf-shaped or oval?"

They're still almost a mile away, Terralt thought irritably. *I can't see their spear tips.*

"A banner, then," Kayli pressed. "Are they carrying a banner?"

A moment's pause, then: *Yes. But I can't make it out.*

"Do not fire on them!" Kayli said quickly. "You must tell your men not to fire! Sarkonds carry no banner. Those are Bregondish troops, your allies!"

I think you're right. Terralt's thoughts took on an excited tone. *Yes, they're turning north, taking up positions along our western edge. Give me a moment—I'm going to give orders for our troops to fall back toward the east, get out of their way.*

"Wait!" Kayli said, but it was too late; the contact was gone again as abruptly as before. She sagged forward against the stones of the forge, nearly exhausted.

"What happened?" Randon said insistently, laying his hand on her shoulder. "Is something wrong?"

"I—I lost the contact between us," Kayli panted. The room was starting to swim around her. "It is—difficult to maintain. A great company of Bregondish troops arrived to join with him. He broke away from me to give orders."

"Can you reach him again?" Randon pressed. "I need to know what's happening."

Kayli lay where she was on the hard stones of the forge floor, panting. She could feel the heat of the fire on the top of her head, the tips of her fingers, and that heat was a tiny but sweet pulse of energy flowing down through her body.

"The fire," Kayli whispered. "I need the fire."

"You need to be closer to the fire?" Randon stood, slid his hands under her arms, and pulled her closer to the edge of the firepit.

"No." Kayli sighed. "I need to be *in* the fire." She forced herself upright, her fingers fumbling with the ties of her robe. At last she gave up and simply hauled it over her head.

"In the—" Randon knelt beside her. "Kayli, are you sure? You're so tired. And you're pregnant."

Tired as she was, Kayli had to chuckle at Randon's words.

"After I tried to stop a grass fire by myself," she said gently, "and after being Gated twice in as many days, now you are concerned about the effect of magic on our child? Do not fear. Stevann says our child's life spark is strong and bright. But mine, I fear, wants fuel."

Pushing her robe aside, Kayli slid the last few feet to the edge of the firepit. As soon as her hand passed the edge and touched the glowing coals, a shock of pure power shot up her arm and into her body, as bracing as a drink of the coldest water at the height of summer heat. Then she rolled over onto the hot bed of coals, and the Flame surged up from the firepit and into her soul.

Kayli dimly heard Randon's cry of fear, but that no longer mattered. Her weariness washed away like a speck of dust in the river she had swum with Randon, and with it her own fear, her confusion. Flame filled her and buoyed her up more lightly than the water of the pond, sent power racing through her veins.

And yet it was different than the Rite of Renewal. This was no unsure fumbling, no tentative opening to a new lover that quickly became abandonment. This was the welcoming home of an old and well-loved friend, a friend who nevertheless would neither ask nor presume too much. No, the Flame was no longer an outsider to be feared. It was part of Kayli, just as she was a part of the Flame, and in that instant she felt the both of them becoming together a part of something even larger, a great and powerful Order that took in both countries, the world, the universe.

More power flooded into Kayli than she would have ever thought possible, but this time no fear rose with it. She could contain the magic, wield it as a part of her, for indeed that was exactly what it was, as she could feel it a part of the new life growing inside of her (a son, Kayli realized almost irrelevantly; Randon would be pleased to know that). She reached out almost effortlessly for that spark she recognized as Terralt, touched it, and without stopping to wonder how she did so, swept closer to that spark.

There you are, Terralt thought to her relievedly. *I thought you'd gone off to the privy or something.* He paused. *What are you doing? It's like you're standing here next to me.*

For Kayli the feeling was similar. Suddenly she looked through his eyes, gazing down from the wooden tower the troops had constructed, watching as three armies came together in a hot fusion of flesh and blood and metal and hatred.

How fiercely Kairi's warriors fight, Kayli thought admiringly (*And once I would have called them "my people."*) *Such anger—and yet, behind that anger, such love for this hard land they defend. Randon's soldiers will never fight like that, for Agrond will never demand such love.*

What in the world are you talking about? Terralt demanded.

Nothing. Nothing. The Sarkondish troops were slowly being forced backward now, Kayli was glad to see, but she was surprised that Terralt did not share her gratitude. *What troubles you?*

So, what have we gained if we beat them back? Terralt thought. *They'll only attack in sneaky raids like before. We need to crush their army completely, and it's not happening. Even with both countries fighting together, it's not happening.*

Then we will make it happen, Kayli told him. *And for one moment I will give you a taste of magic.* Instinctively protecting Terralt (How? Did she know? Did it matter?) Kayli poured her power through him and out, striking there where the Sarkondish soldiers clustered the most thickly. Light flared and fire sprang up, great hungry flames, and the Sarkondish warriors scattered with no thought of defense, running heedlessly onto Agrondish swords or into the fire of Agrondish crossbows. Another touch of Kayli's power and Sarkondish ranks parted to admit a horde of Bregondish riders, firing their bows and howling with joy as they flung themselves into combat.

Then thunder crashed across the sky and lightning caressed the ground behind the Sarkondish line, and Kayli pulled back her power, momentarily startled.

Are you doing that? Terralt thought, as startled as Kayli.

Not I, but I believe my sister has seen the merit in my notion, Kayli thought. Reluctantly, she drew back from Terralt. *I think I will leave this battle to you and to her, now that matters are well in—*

Abrupt cessation, as if the contact between Kayli and Randon—and her contact with the Flame, as well—had been cut off with the chop of a hatchet. Kayli plunged from light into darkness, screaming in shock as she fell.

Cool stone under her body; warm arms holding her very tightly. Gone was her weariness; gone, too, was her ecstatic power, that wonderful sense of *completeness* within a greater order of things. Kayli allowed herself a small sigh of regret before she opened her eyes.

She still lay on the floor of the forge, but now she was far from the firepit. It was Randon, of course, who held her, but Kayli was horrified to see that his clothes were mostly charred, and the skin of his arms, legs, and face were reddened and even blistered in places. But his arms held her strongly, and the expression in his eyes warmed her soul as even the Flame could not.

"What happened?" she said softly, touching his blackened tunic. Charred bits of cloth flaked away under her fingers.

"For a moment it seemed like—like you were on fire," Randon admitted. "So I—well, I pulled you out."

"You pulled—" Kayli bolted upright, glancing over his shoulder at the firepit. A trail where the coals had been pushed aside, as if someone had been dragged, led from the very center of the firepit. *"You went in after me?"*

Randon's eyes widened slightly at her words, and he glanced back at the firepit, too, then down at his clothing. He grinned then, but the grin trembled slightly.

"I suppose I did," he said unsteadily. "I never actually thought about it, I just saw you burning and—"

Kayli laughed, embracing him carefully so as not to hurt him.

"I congratulate you, my husband," she said. "For you have just made your first firewalk, and with great success, I would say, considering that you had neither training nor preparation."

"My first? My last, you mean," Randon said firmly, glancing at the firepit again and shivering. "If there's no more swimming for you, by the Bright Ones, there'll be no more firepits for me, understand?"

"Indeed." Kayli stood and helped him gently to his feet, picking up her own robe. "At least I did not require the services of a healer after my swim.

"The battle was still proceeding when you pulled me from it, but I believe the Sarkondish warriors will be thoroughly routed," she told him as she pulled her robe on over her sooty skin. "And I do not doubt that for many years to come, when Sarkondish warriors talk over their ale of the war with Agrond and Bregond, there will be fear in their voices."

Randon nodded, taking Kayli's hand.

"We'll never forget, either," he said. "And after us, our child—"

"Our son," she said, smiling at Randon.

Randon raised an eyebrow doubtfully, but smiled back.

"All right, then. Our *son* will take up that vigil. But in the meantime—"

"In the meantime?" Kayli asked as Randon opened the forge door.

"In the meantime my advisers are waiting," he said ruefully. "There'll be a tax increase to pay for the war, titles and land grants to be given to the heroes, pacifying speeches to be made about the alliance, trade schedules to be drawn up with Bregondish merchants, perhaps the building of a proper road or two between the two countries, policies to be made about travel across the borders, and let's not forget the slaves and—"

Holding Randon's hand, Kayli sighed, smiled, and walked out of the forge.

And into the fire.

NICK O'DONOHOE

T◆H◆E
HEALING OF
CROSSROADS

Veterinarian BJ Vaughn spends her days traveling throughout different realms, both real and imagined. She finds that outside of Crossroads, the creatures of myth and magic are falling ill—and the land she loves is now in danger from the evil that has followed her home...

___ 0-441-00391-5/$5.99

UNDER
T◆H◆E
HEALING
SIGN

As the creatures of Crossroads battle among themselves, a sinister outsider breeds mistrust and mayhem, BJ wonders if wisdom will be enough to defeat the powers of ill will—and brute force...

___ 0-441-00180-7/$4.99

T◆H◆E
MAGIC AND THE
HEALING

BJ has been chosen as part of a special group that will venture not only to the frontiers of science, but beyond it...To Crossroads, a world where the creatures of the imagination live and breathe—and hurt. BJ will discover the joy of healing— and the wonder of magic...

0-441-00053-3/$4.99